ENDEMIC

ROBERT CHAZZ CHUTE

ENDEMIC

Please direct media and rights inquiries to Holly at expartepress@gmail.com.

ISBN (hardcover) 978-1-927607-76-3

ISBN (paperback) 978-1-927607-74-9

ISBN (Ebook) 978-1-927607-75-6

PRAISE FOR ROBERT'S WORK

Chute sucks you in from word one and pulls you down his post-apocalyptic rabbit hole! You will sleep with the lights on, covers pulled over your head, and dust off the old teddy bear for comfort. Chazz ranks among the top tier of our generation's storytellers. ~ Alex Kimmell, Author of *The Key to Everything*

Robert Chazz Chute is such a skilled spinner of tales that the reader is more than willing to suspend any possible disbelief to go along for the ride. ~ David Pandolfe, author of *Jump When Ready*

It's not very often one finds a writer with such a dark side that has such a great sense of humor. ~ Glenn Roberts, Amazon reviewer

The author has a definite talent with words and ideas. ~ Love to Read!, Amazon reviewer

His words lift and dance off the page, bringing the story to life. ~ Kindle Customer, Amazon reviewer

The world-building is horrifically well done with twists and turns and deceit around every corner. ~ Wanda, Amazon reviewer

RCC blends characters' beliefs & worries concerning society's failures, plus vivid action scenes skillfully. ~ RMerkl, Amazon Reviewer

Nothing but sheer exhaustion could tear my eyes from the captivating dance of words choreographed by Robert Chazz Chute. ~ Halph Staph, Amazon reviewer

Wonderful action constantly holds your interest. ~ Sharon Finn, Amazon reviewer

The complexity and attention to detail throughout absolutely blow me away. ~ Kindle customer, Amazon Reviewer

Very few authors impress me with their actual writing style, it's usually always about the story. But this author paints such beautiful vivid pictures with words that I found myself not only enjoying the story but enjoying the way the words created images in my mind. I know that sounds corny, but it is true. ~ B.H., Amazon reviewer

Chute gives us a story worthy of Stephen King. A read both thoughtful and fun. ~ Linda Beer Johnson, Amazon reviewer

The author does an excellent job building the characters and getting you invested and involved. ~ Michele L. Hebert, Amazon reviewer

I just can't say in words what a powerful author this is! ~ Delinda L. Calkins, Amazon reviewer

Robert Chazz Chute writes so skillfully as to make the supernatural seem perfectly logical - and terrifying! There are twists, turns, and surprises galore. You will be glad you bought this book - until you lose sleep because you can't put it down. ~ johligo, Amazon reviewer

When I want to read apocalyptic books or zombie stories, those books have to also be extremely well written and something that I could recommend with zeal and confidence to everyone I know. Robert Chazz Chute's books are exactly that. ~ Mazie Lane, Amazon reviewer

He makes the stuff that is obviously fiction, believable. ~ W. Nickels, Amazon reviewer

I am a lover of paranormal, dystopian novels and depth of story as well as intelligence in writing style, and Robert has it all. Humor, wit, depth, intelligence, and an awesome way with words/writing. ~ Amazon Customer, Amazon reviewer

FOR ANYONE WHO HAS EVER BEEN PUSHED AROUND.
AGAINST THOSE WHO DO THE PUSHING.

INTRODUCTION

"In our play we reveal what kind
of people we are."
~ Publius Ovidius Naso

Most of *Endemic* was written in 2020. As I write this, the plague still rages. Night is falling and I'm racing sunset, trying to finish this introduction before darkness falls, and the mosquitoes come out for blood. Today was a warm sunny day, but that's just at first glance. The virus still stalks us.

I live in a hot spot, trapped in a seemingly endless revolution of stay-at-home orders, lockdowns, gray zones, red zones, and emergency brakes.

The title and the terror I write here are not some opportunistic marketing ploy. (I don't believe that sort of thing sells books anyway.) I've been penning variations of the end of the world for over a decade. Be it robots, nukes, zombies, aliens, or plagues, this niche of suspense thriller is my wheelhouse.

Endemic feels a little different, though. World events made writing this novel more real. In earlier iterations, despite all the fictional action and carnage, I was more optimistic. COVID-19 lowered my estimation of the human race, and our ability to respond to threats. If we can't adequately defend ourselves against a clear and present danger, anything slightly muddy and more challenging like the climate crisis seems beyond our ken.

So why read on? What have I got for you if it's only a scarier arc from where you've already been? What's left? Love, I guess. Despite my darkest impulses, I have to leave readers with a little hope. It won't be what you expect, but the reward is waiting for you at the end of the journey.

Hold on to that knowledge as you turn these pages. Brace yourself because Ovid Fairweather is about to go through some things. We all are.

~ RCC
   May, 2021
   Other London

EPISODE ONE

"In the middle of the journey of our life I found myself within a dark wood where the straight way was lost."

~ Dante, *Inferno*

~

"Nobody realizes that some people expend tremendous energy merely to be normal."

~ Albert Camus

1

SHADOW

As daylight ticked down and July's shadows grew long, the city's streets lay nearly deserted and almost dead. I picked up my pace and tried to ignore the girl following me. Half my age, she would have caught up were she not half-starved, limping, and crazed. Mumbling something incomprehensible, my pursuer was relentless.

Sometimes, when the heat lingered and grew mean, it seemed as if all of New York had emptied. But we, the survivors, still lurked, furtive as foraging rats amid the ruins and debris, wary as skittish rabbits too far from the safety of the warren. I wondered, *Is this a Monday afternoon?* It certainly felt like a blue-gray Monday, full of hot gunmetal dread, far from any cooling respite. In the desert of discontent, there is no oasis. All that remained was the grim resolve to keep moving.

Remember how it felt when, from another room, you heard a plate shatter in the kitchen? There's that second or two of shocked silence? In that pregnant pause, you wondered if you should ask if anyone's hurt or haul yourself off the couch to get the broom. Would there be blood or relief? A catastrophic heart attack or mere clumsiness? That's the kind of nervous silence that descended upon the city and refused to leave.

Rising too late to the alarm, the nation failed to become immune to the disease's churn. Though vaccinated against the first iterations of the virus, various strains mutated too quickly for us to protect ourselves. The variant storms had claimed many victims and murdered most. Some survivors, Thirders, were left with cognitive impairments like that of my pursuer.

The Zeta-3 variant often scrambled Broca's area, the brain's speech center. My pursuer's ruin was a slow, cruel erasure. Imagine termites in your brain, chewing away at your ability to communicate and digesting the foundations of who you once were. This unfortunate woman might once have become a teacher, a research scientist, or a firefighter. She could have fulfilled any number of roles before the variant storm zeroed in. Many had died of earlier viral iterations, but Z-3, also known as the Third Kentucky Variant or TKV, was brutal. When the disease process stalled, some Thirders babbled. Others went mute.

My father — typically inaccurate and casually cruel — grinned as he pronounced Thirder as "turder." TKV casualties had been objects of pity once. However, since they neither died nor healed, disaster fatigue had set in. As food supplies dwindled, people were often unkind to these wandering beggars.

Since What Was, people had become more superstitious, too. They searched for omens, alert for deception, and gloomy to the nth. And no wonder. Central Park — now Central Memorial Park — was commonly called Hell's Basement because that's where the bodies were buried. Manhattan was Hell's Office. We referred to Brooklyn as Over the Rainbow Bridge. Queens' nickname became Hell's Dying Room, and the Bronx was Hell Central (because of the riot fires). Staten Island was still Staten Island.

That odd voice in my head that spoke like a tough British man chimed in: *Hey! Morbidity and comorbidities are everywhere, love. No need to pile on by being morbid.*

"I gotta be me," I replied. "And I still don't know why you're

British. I'm a middle-aged woman from Maine whose farthest travels have been to Canada when I was a child. For God's sake, what are you and why are you?"

He didn't reply. We were often short of reliable answers. Like the truth of the pandemic, disaster relief was also promised but never arrived. Nevertheless, some still held their breath, waiting. I don't know what they expected. Change, I suppose. Isn't that what everyone is waiting for? *Was* always waiting for?

Despite the great numbers who had fallen — no one knew how many — most of the survivors remained in the city. Border restrictions were strictly enforced and punishments were harsh. Armed militias backed the travel bans. Slipping past them was risky business, and the price of their bribes was high.

Though the Big Apple had rotted, there were still mouths to feed, and I had a business to run. Survival is my business. Every new day offered a narrow toehold to the future. Each step felt tentative, as if I were climbing a steep cliff, the ledges greased and slick. Each hand-hold was too small and not to be trusted.

My pursuer was gaining. "Hey!" she called. "Humannahell ... humanmahelp ... *whoooo! Yoo-hoo? L-lady?*"

A filthy curtain rustled high above the street. The weight of the gaze from spying eyes fell upon us. New Yorkers used to live in small boxes and work in cubicle farms. Our domiciles were now either fortresses, crannies, or crypts. I was one of the lucky few who owned a secret farm.

The girl called after me again, "Watchu? Watchu?" She mumbled on. I couldn't decipher the rest.

Preferring to conserve energy, I resisted the urge to sprint. They were easily distracted, but running encouraged them to give chase. I tried not to think of those cursed by TKV at all. Some, especially Taxmen, called them mean names like dim bulbs, whistle heads, or brain-dead. It wasn't true. Thirders were often sensitive and emotional. You could sense something of what they once were behind their eyes. Sometimes they spoke gibberish, but many spoke in full sentences that didn't necessarily connect.

Conversation by approximation, the British voice added.

"*Sh!* Not now!" I whispered back. "You're distracting me."

I scanned the street, looking for a way to evade her but also hoping the girl wasn't inviting more unwanted attention. Taxmen hated anyone who possessed nothing of value to steal or extort. They'd get nothing from the girl, but I had much more to lose.

Downfall, demise, destruction.

I shushed the voice in my head, though that only worked haphazardly.

I quickened my pace again — almost a run now — but so did she. Though that poor soul was wounded, it was I who felt hunted. Every door was barred, and every ground-floor window boarded. I serpentined among abandoned hulks of long-dead vehicles.

Some cars had been left in the middle of the street when their fuel ran out. Others, the burnt wrecks, had been used as barricades during the riots. Blockages and clots wound through the heart of the city that went on for miles and miles, choking the life from it.

As I cut down a side street, I wondered how my pursuer had survived this long. What did she eat? Where did she sleep? How did people like her keep going under these conditions? Someone fed her, surely. I knew because I had one of my own to feed.

Rats, maybe. That's the only plentiful food supply.

I shuddered with revulsion at that. The voice in my head was like me in that we both meant well, but often fell short of the mark.

My pack slowed me. It was heavy with supplies and made my shoulders sore and my back ache. I carried too much, but everything on me was essential. I needed to be able to bug out and abandon everything if things went awry. My blue tote bag held the only food I would eat that day: a sweet potato and a couple of green tomatoes.

I slipped in and out of her sight as I made my way south. She kept coming, close enough for me to hear her ragged breaths and slurred muttering. When I deciphered her muddled speech, I found she was fixated, stuck on repeat: "What you got in the pretty blue bag? Huh? Whatcha got for me? For me? For me! Huh? L-lady?"

I clutched my tote tighter to my side. My empty canteen bounced on my hip. It had been more than two years since What Was fell to pieces, perhaps never to be reassembled. I was tired.

Call him, then. Be Daddy's little girl and retreat to safety. Physical safety anyway.

"That would be too easy." I could try my luck breaking borders, or my father could simply pay the necessary bribes and not feel the pinch in the least. My Alamo was in Maine.

But you know what happened at the Alamo, Ovid.

We still had one viable and very expensive cell network. Somewhere, high up, satellites spun in orbit, cold machinery oblivious to our earthly problems. Not all cell towers still functioned and communications from Poeticule Bay were sometimes spotty and sounded crinkly and crackly, as if Maine were on the Moon. My father insisted I could be home within a couple of days. All I had to say was yes.

When Lloyd Fairweather said "Come home," he meant "surrender."

2

PRESSED

Remember driving in a trance? How you'd work on automatic and then snap out of it, hoping the traffic lights had been green in the last few intersections you'd sailed through? Even with a Thirder on my trail, my mind wandered, as if my consciousness drifted off to the left. Triggered by stress, that's how it often began. I found myself on the phone with Dad again.

Lloyd Fairweather — *father, fatter, farter* — was still alive, well, and well-to-do on his farm in Poeticule Bay. The area had been touched relatively lightly by plague, and there was no blight in all of Poeticule County. He paid for my phone, but only so he could remind me to make the decision to come home to him.

"New York? It's a wasteland. What's there for you, Ovid?"

It's not so much what's here, I thought. *It's who's not.*

"The city is broken," he continued. "More people means more trouble. You're unprotected, but 'round here, the virus has pretty much washed through. Cases are low. But you? There? You make no sense."

"Dad — "

"As if that weren't enough piss in the gas tank, the blight is so bad out west, they say the fruited plain is no longer fruited. Come up to God's country. Back by the bay, you'll be safe."

It couldn't be God's country. Dad was there. I preferred my hell to his heaven.

"If your mother were alive — "

Mother, smother, monster.

"She'd tell you the same. Maybe you'd listen to her better. I'm alone here."

"You aren't alone, Dad."

"I miss your cooking. You might not possess an iota of sense, but at least you were a decent cook!"

"You have people to boss around, and I don't want to be one of them. You know how I feel about collars and choke chains. If you want to put a leash on somebody, you need a dog."

"I've done nothing but help you — "

"Sorry, gotta go."

It had been a week since he'd last called. He would call again soon. Looking at the phone made me almost as anxious as getting chased down the street.

Welcome back.

Race walking, I felt as if I'd been underwater too long. I needed fresh, cool air, but the number one rule of the apocalypse was this: Comfort is always sacrificed before safety. That's one reason I was still alive.

Turning another sharp corner, I slipped down an alley. The girl kept up her crazed shouting as if she could still see me. Haunting echoes bounced off bare walls. Slowly, her voice faded. Panting, I hugged my bag to my chest and waited for her to wander farther on.

No more fox and hounds, I thought. But I was wrong.

"Hey." The gravelly voice came from the shadows at the far end of the alley. I still had my reading glasses, but the prescription on my regular glasses was so outdated I didn't even bother with them. Squinting, I could make out the silhouette of a large man.

"Said *hey*," he said.

A complete stranger had not spoken to me in weeks. I slipped the paper bag out of my tote. The bag was always on top, within easy reach. It concealed my sharpest pruning shears, the ones with the tips honed to a razor's edge.

I took a deep breath and let it out slowly.

Attempting to sound cheery (and failing), I recited, "The worst of the infected are wandering about — "

"So don't pout, cover your snout, watch, weave, and don't get caught out," he finished the macabre rhyme for me.

Between the day's heat and exertion, sweat had soaked through my clothes. I pulled my hood back to get some relief, but the stale air on my bare nape felt like a hot breath.

"Gettin' dark soon," the man mused. "It'll be curfew and the Taxmen will be pullin' and having their giggles. You should get on home. I could walk you."

The curfew had once been by governmental decree. Now it was just common sense to avoid being out after dark. Since there was no wood to knock, I bit my tongue for luck. "Sorry, is this your patch? I'll be on my way in a min. Just letting her" — I waved vaguely toward the street — "you know."

The man took a few steps closer. No PPE. That was always a red flag. I fidgeted with the straps to my mask and goggles to make sure they were ratcheted tight.

"You okay, lady?"

Turning my body slightly so he couldn't see, I lowered the shears, still in its paper bag, down by my right thigh. From thrillers I'd edited, I knew that he shouldn't see my weapon until after I'd used it.

"You look familiar," the man said.

"Not possible." My face was hidden. "It's the mask," I said. "They all look alike. Remember early on? When people had all kinds of fancy masks? I wore a tartan one for a while."

"No, seriously," he insisted. "Couldn't forget *that* head of hair and your voice."

I cursed myself for drawing back my hood.

"I *do* know you, but only sorta. See, I remember the tartan mask, too. Like blue plaid, right?"

Though I'd said next to nothing, I'd already given too much away. He had to be lying. If I'd said I'd worn a mask with a sunrise on it, he'd be telling me he recognized that, too. "You think you know me? That's a really old pickup line." I tried to make it sound like a friendly joke, but not too friendly.

"Your voice, I know it."

I never liked my voice. Curse it and curse me.

"Name's Roger. Used to work in your building, down in the cafe. Pilkington Press, right? You never said much to me, but I remember y'all came down mid-morning and mid-afternoon with one or two of your friends."

Friends? Not friends. Co-workers. Sometimes they called me Mouse when they thought I was listening to music on my head-phones. That was when they were kind. I heard them joking about me by the photocopier, too. They called me "that twitchy bitch" because I never knew what to do with my hands when people spoke to me. Eventually, I solved that problem by sewing pockets in all my dresses.

Roger stepped closer, and I squinted harder. I didn't recognize him, but he wasn't wrong about my former workplace.

With a sudden venom that made me tremble, he raised his voice. "Not gonna lie, I got impulse control issues. You better come across with the truth!"

"Yes! Pilkington Press. Yes, you're right.."

"Soy milk. Two shots of hazelnut? Am I right?"

"How could you remember that after all this time?"

"Hasn't been that long, only feels long. We didn't know it at the time, but those were the good ole days, huh? Lots of bad times now. Lots of bad times to come before somebody sorts things out."

Roger really did know me from What Was, back when I edited books for a living, and the virus was still incubating somewhere on the other side of the planet.

I did not have many friends in New York. Preferring the company of books to people limited my social life. Books didn't judge. Besides, I liked the person I was when I worked in publishing. In my small way, I liked to think I made the world a better place, or at least helped to give readers a happy distraction from all that was wrong.

In that moment of nostalgia, I softened and let my guard down. "Nice to meet you again, Roger."

My mistake.

3

THINGS FALL APART

Though Roger couldn't see my face, I'd been taught to smile no matter how I felt. The reflex to keep the peace ran deep. I gave an exaggerated nod to let him know I was agreeable. In a weak echo meant to appease, I whispered, "You are right. Lots of bad times now."

"Never said much to me, you, but I had the idea you were high up in the company. You were the tall one of the group, always on your phone with all that hair hanging in your face. Shame, really. Nice long, thick hair, you got there. As I recall, your nose is on the big side but your hair is pretty-pretty."

I wasn't high up in the company, but always looking busy and staring at my phone gave me something to do when other people were around. For as long as I could remember, looking people in the eye made me feel naked. People's open gazes were too sharp, pricking my skin like tiny hot needles.

"What happened to your company?" Roger asked.

"Same as with everything else. We hung in as long as we could. Things fall apart. The center cannot hold."

Quoting Yeats, Ovid? He wrote "The Second Coming" in 1919, and his vision only took about 100 years to take hold.

"Got a name?" Roger's question sounded like a demand.

My mind drifted off to the left again. My therapist called the phenomenon "time traveling." I called it a flashback.

Don't go anywhere! The danger is right in front of you! Don't —

Pilkington Press. Our firm had prestige, but fell short of the top tier. For every profitable spy thriller, romance, or cookbook I edited, the owners insisted on pushing three "important literary works" that rarely broke out of the snobby cocktail circuit. A few of those high-minded books were considered for national book awards. Most were returned and remaindered in bulk, reduced to pulp. Relegated to trawling the slush pile and copy editing in the genre department, I never got to work on the prestige manuscripts.

On rare occasions, I passed our company president in the hallways. He made a show of struggling to remember my name. The owners' domain was a floor above me, that faraway land where the carpets were deep and soft, and each executive had their own private bathroom.

Five women worked in the offices along the west wall of glass on the twelfth floor overlooking the park: two senior editors, an accountant, an office manager/publicist, and me, the proofreader and junior copy editor. I freelanced from home, too, always struggling to make ends meet, trying to prove to Dad I could read and think for a living in one of the most expensive cities in the world.

Other employees and interns came and went, but we five staff were the beating heart of our little company. I was always putting the right words in the right order and never seeming to do much better than get by. I was at the last desk, next to the big photocopiers. It was too loud, and the nearby kitchenette smelled of burnt coffee. No one cleaned up after themselves, but since my desk was closest, I took on that job, too.

Early on, the office manager Angelica invited me to join the editorial staff on coffee breaks downstairs.

And Roger was watching.

"It's not just coffee. It's team-building and coordinating synergy,"

Angelica said. Perhaps, by including me, she was just being polite. I suspect it was pity.

When I was eight, Mom once told a neighbor, "Our girl's no social butterfly. She's more of a Death's Head Moth."

The visiting neighbor, Dorothy Engel, glanced my way uncomfortably and gave a kind smile. "Ovid is very bright. I'm sure what you mean to say is that your daughter is a good listener."

"Nope! Look again. Ovid couldn't buy a friend, so she talks to herself all day. She's a Death's Head Moth!"

It might not have been so bad if she'd sounded like a desperate mother seeking help. Instead, Mom sounded absolutely gleeful over my shortcomings. She'd called me that before, so, of course, I'd looked it up.

"Actually, Mom, there's no such thing as a Death's Head Moth. It's a Death's Head *Hawk*moth."

The lure of pedantry which would serve my clients so well as a book editor was not appreciated in childhood. Taking a long drag of her cigarette, my mother rolled her eyes and flicked ash in my face. "Nobody likes a know-it-all!" She looked to our neighbor with a look that declared no one had suffered as she had. "See? Told you!"

If Dorothy had asked me to come live with her and get away from my parents, I would have abandoned my childhood home in a heartbeat. With nothing but my library card and the clothes on my back, I would have escaped to a home where Pop-Tarts, coconut cookies, and sugary cereals were ready in the cupboard. Caramels were always in the candy dish. Dorothy wouldn't have been like Mom, who hid bags of potato chips until they were long out of date, stale, and tasted like salted paper.

The voice in my head observed: *Food is always better in other people's houses, but perhaps that's true for everyone.*

I must concede that Mom wasn't wrong about my friendlessness. At Pilkington Press, I took stabs and had spasms of friendly overtures. Sometimes I'd share anecdotes about odd writing I'd come across in manuscripts from the slush pile. The biggest laugh I ever got was from a writer who described a lover's penis as "the silk and steel of him." I never topped that for entertaining my co-workers, and it wasn't even my idea, just something amusing I'd parroted.

Much of the last year of my life in publishing had been devoted to editing a thick manuscript called *Grow Anything, Anytime, Anywhere* by Nora Jean Stone. If not for that gardening book, I wouldn't have survived the apocalypse.

Roger cleared his throat.

Unfriendly reminder, Ovid! The danger is in front of you!

He must have said something I missed. A military thriller I'd once proofread advised the main character to "maintain situational awareness." I wasn't heeding that good advice. "Pardon?"

"I asked your name. I asked where you live so I can walk you home."

"I'll be fine."

His tone softened, trying too hard to sound casual. "What happened to those women you worked with? Do you keep in touch? They were cute. Where are they now? Y'all stick together? Survivors tend to stick together."

Four of my coworkers had fallen dead within two weeks of each other. I was the fifth in that line of desks, still breathing and wondering why I'd been spared. I'm a little OCD. Maybe my survival was as simple as washing my hands more often, more thoroughly, for longer, and with hotter water. I did clean that kitchenette sink assiduously.

The voice in my head nudged. *Paranoia ain't all bad. You need more of it now.*

4

SHEER TERROR

Dizzy, I leaned against the wall. I wanted to shrug off my heavy pack and let the concrete cool my sweaty back. When I glanced up, Roger had stepped even closer, just outside of arm's reach.

"What's wrong with you?" he asked.

"So many things. Sorry, I'm very tired. Long day."

"We all got the same twenty-four hours, but when you got nothing to do, it stretches out. Where do you go? What do you do?"

"I keep busy."

"Some places uptown, you'd think everything was almost fine. Long as you don't look too close, normal is still here somewhere. The city's still here. It's just…"

"Diluted?"

"Diluted. Yeah, that's good. Diluted. You know what else? Those uptown people? I got a little work from them."

At the market, I'd heard of wealthy people who did not leave New York before the state borders closed. Details were too sketchy for the whispers to be believed.

"It's a small group of trust fund kids, gathering resources, trying to get the old order back. You say things fall apart. They say put 'em back together."

"How?"

"Same as they always did, takin' care of them and theirs at the expense of you and yours. I got asked to help 'em out. That's how I take care of me. To get by, everybody's got to be a little selfish, right?"

His tone of accusation crept in again. "Do you think you're a selfish person, Pilkington?"

"I take care of myself."

"How do you do that?" He pointed at my tote and my backpack. "Trading, right? Growing? I've seen you around."

I said nothing.

"Do you think things can go back to normal?"

"No."

"Why?"

"The reasons are ... multifactorial."

He mimicked me. "*Multifactorial*. Friggin' multifactorial, huh? I see how it is. You got height and long legs, so that's nice. On the other hand, you got no boobs, and you sound like a politician."

A politician? There were few worse insults. "I should go."

"The people I work for, they'd be interested in knowing how someone like you is still running around."

"Someone like me?"

"Female, older, mousy, and — what really stands out — you're alone. You hardly ever see a woman on the street alone. I know some hard dudes won't even poke their noses outside without somebody to watch their back."

I could hear the smirk in his voice.

Smirk, smug, smash, smite!

"What's in the bag, Pilkington?"

"So ... you're a Taxman," I said.

"No, the people I work for are bigger than the Taxmen. I'm a headhunter, keeping an eye out for talent. I think you've got skills and resources they can use. That's my mission."

The city's vultures always wanted food. They needed something to eat or steal so they could trade for sustenance. I couldn't afford to allow anyone to steal my labor or resources.

"I've got nothing for you, Roger. I have to go now."

"No one is really waiting for you, are they, Pilkington Press girl?"

As I turned to run, he leaped at me, grabbed me by the hair, and yanked me back.

"Where do you get all that friggin' food you trade?"

Struggling, I almost went down, but he held me up by the hair as he reached for my tote. Sitting on my left hip, the bag's long strap was across my right shoulder. In attempting to pull it away from me, he spun me into him. I used the momentum he'd given me. The tips of my pruning shears broke through the bottom of the paper bag as I thrust up into the thick meat of his triceps, just short of his armpit.

I dug in and dragged the sharp tips of the blades toward me. Roger gasped, let go, clutched his wound, stumbled back. He cursed me rather imaginatively. Having never stabbed anyone, I neither leaped in to finish the job nor did I run away. I just stood there, frozen and mute.

I wanted to say something defiant and cool. In the men's adventure novels we'd published, a clever hit man made jokes and laconic observations in terrifying moments. I could have said, "Wrap it quick, and you won't bleed out tonight. Keep it clean, and maybe you won't die slowly of sepsis. Maybe ... probably."

But I wasn't a clever hit man. I was a book editor in the apocalypse. Trembling, I watched as my former barista ran away. The shears, dripping with thick blood, shook in my cold, trembling hands. "God, I miss my therapist."

Do you think you killed him? My inner voice sounded more curious than alarmed. I liked that about the voice in my head.

I pictured my dead therapist, Dr. Anna Rosa. From her deep, worn leather chair, sipping chamomile tea, she asked. "How do you feel about what you did?"

"Mom and Dad used to inform me what emotions I was *supposed* to feel — "

"We've been over that. They aren't here. I'm asking you, Ovid."

"Do you think all wounds heal, Doctor? I know that's your paradigm, but I'm not certain that's an accurate reflection of reality. I mean, is closure a real thing? People talk about it, but I think I'd need a lobotomy — "

"So you doubt the value of our sessions?"

"I mean no offense, Doctor, but I'm no kid. I just have to wonder at this late date if closure is a myth. Lots of things don't hold true on examination, like elite bodybuilders who don't use steroids or suffer dysmorphia. Or cauliflower that's supposed to taste like mashed potatoes but sure as heck doesn't."

Dr. Rosa tapped her pen on her pad. "A couple of debatable points there, but I'll concede you got me on the cauliflower thing. Let's put a pin in that and get back on track. I asked what *you* feel. Try to stay present in this moment and avoid falling back into daughter mode. I'll ask again — "

"Roger was not scared of me. He saw me as bookish, like a mouse wearing glasses. I'm an urban farmer now, but on whatever scale used to measure a person's capacity to intimidate, editor to farmer is a pretty lateral move. No surprise there. I mean, caught in a dark alley by a mugger, I quoted Yeats! *Yeats!* Quoting Bukowski would have sounded more butch."

Dr. Rosa quirked an eyebrow at me. "Was that a joke?"

"It wasn't supposed to be. Was it funny?"

She sighed. "Okay, moving on, upon reflection, what would you have rather said to your attacker?"

"My name is not Pilkington Press girl. I am Ovid Fairweather. I don't push, but I do push back."

That should have sounded cool, but I merely whispered it, empty bravado at best.

Dr. Rosa told me, "If it's true about his employers, he was hunting you."

"That frightens me."

"So? What are you going to do about that?"

"I'll have to become something ... else. That's okay. I never liked me much anyway."

"How do you plan to become something else?"

"I'll make it work ... you know, hero's journey and all that. My imagination has kept me alive this long. In fact, pretending is all I've ever done. I'm pretending to have this conversation with you right now!"

5

THE OUTSIDER

I had to get back to my apartment complex. Darkness brought more dangers so I raced against sundown. I ran, first at a sprint, then at a steady pace. My heavy backpack jostled, and the straps pulled at my sore shoulders.

Working a sedentary job, I'd been as soft as any office worker. When Pilkington Press went away, my new job — *occupation, concentration, preoccupation* — became getting fit and finding new ways to survive. From the beginning of the pandemic, I knew the coming horrors would test me. Determined not to become another statistic, I'd prepared, exercising hard since the very first lockdown.

Spite kept me from admitting failure and returning home to Poeticule Bay. Fear motivated me to work on my cardio, do planks, push-ups, sit-ups, and practice Ashtanga yoga at the end of each day. Battling insomnia, some nights I worked out until exhaustion forced me to collapse.

Every morning, I checked my weight and forced myself to look at my naked body in a full-length mirror. Physically, I was much stronger than before. Still, no matter how hard I trained, I couldn't manage to build a six-pack or a thigh gap. I didn't seem to have the genetics that would allow me to look like one of those models made of lacquer sprayed over twists and skeins of wire.

Maybe not enough protein, I thought. *It'll have to do.*

Despite my physical improvements, I still felt like the kid who disappointed her high school gym teacher. I couldn't climb the rope or do pull-ups, so to Coach Jimmy McKenzie, I'd wasted his time. Only track stars had been worthy of his attention.

The school librarian, Mrs. Garilyn, recognized me as one of her nerd brigade: the contingent of misfit kids destined to leave Poeticule Bay and never look back with longing. Glad to give me fuel to launch, she always greeted me warmly. Her library became my second home, safer than living with my parents.

One apocalypse, several viral iterations, and a plethora of lethal variants had occurred since leaving Maine. I was lean and strong, but I couldn't say I felt differently on the inside.

Still Daddy's little girl!

"Shut up," I muttered as my apartment building loomed in the distance.

Dr. Rosa had not prepared me for the fallout from sticking Roger. The adrenaline dump had me sweating and panting by the time I arrived at the door to my complex. In books and movies, heroic protagonists rarely seemed to dwell on the violence they perpetrated. To those fictional beings, such violence was a curious misadventure, shrugged off, and soon forgotten. I'd never forget Roger's sharp intake of breath or the sound of tearing fabric and ripped flesh. Even the patter of blood falling to the pavement sounded louder than was possible.

Louder and somehow accusatory. What are you becoming, Ovid? And was Poeticule Bay really so bad?

The ID scanner was broken. Fortunately, Old Heather waited at her station by the door. There used to be a Young Heather, but the Lambda-2 variant had taken her breath away. To avoid the reminder of mortality, I just called the old lady Heather.

Lurching up from her rocking chair, Heather gave me a friendly wave. I'd never seen her step outside for fresh air. Instead, she sat and read books, mostly romances and histories about the First Civil War. I often contributed to her to-be-read pile, which Heather referred to as her little library. The old woman acted as the complex's self-appointed door monitor. Not many tenants remained, but she knew everyone who lived in the three connected buildings. She was a sweet gatekeeper, but a double-barreled sawed-off shotgun sat atop her little library, always within easy reach.

Heather never wore a mask nor had she ever been tested for a variant. Resolute in showing her naked face, she once told me, "I got other things to think about. Wish I was immune to arthritis and bunions. At my age, every morning is an unkind surprise. Just lucky to be alive, I guess."

Or unlucky, I thought.

"In my opinion, I'm immune," she'd told me. "Immune or ready to go should the virus change its damn mind. If I was supposed to get TKV, it sure is taking its sweet time. I slept in the same bed as my husband. He died. Had two grown children and they got taken, too. Through it all, I was their sole caregiver."

Above her head, like a brilliant yellow halo, I saw: *sole, soul, solo.*

No one else saw that sad trio of glowing words. As long as I *knew* no one else could see that, I wasn't crazy. Mentally, I might not have been entirely seaworthy, but given the dire circumstances, I thought it fair to grade myself on a curve.

Heather didn't know my real name, so she just called me Honey and always met me with a smile. One of my crops was cannabis. I liked lovers of books, so I gave Heather a discount on her glaucoma medicine.

As I passed under the sprayers in the entryway, they wheezed with useless puffs of air. The mechanism's decontamination tanks had long gone dry, but the nozzles still cycled upon each entry. Without any sterilizing mist, it was like getting breathed on by a robot with emphysema.

The old woman gave me a wink. "You bring back anything for me from the outside world?"

"Your favorite." Her preferred variety was Jamaican Haze, a sativa-heavy cross between the Jamaican strain and Amnesia Haze.

"Jamaican me crazy!" She made the same joke every time, and she always offered a tiny jar of jam in trade.

I slipped a joint onto the arm of her rocking chair and, despite her gnarled hands, she managed to palm it like a pro. In return, she left me a tiny jam jar. She seemed to have access to an endless supply.

One day, perhaps bragging a little, Heather revealed that she used to work at one of the big hotels. She also let slip that she still had a friend who worked at the Four Seasons in Manhattan. That's where the jam came from.

I warned her never to tell me or anyone else where she got the goods she traded. "If someone can go straight to your friend, they'll cut you out. Then where will you be? You might even put your friend in danger."

"Oh," she said. "I hadn't thought of that. I'm sure I can trust you —"

"Trust no one. It'll keep you safe. You start letting people in, you open yourself up to all kinds of problems."

Heather looked worried about me. "Letting people in? You mean living?"

"I'm not talking about living, just not dying,"

"Doesn't sound too ambitious," she said.

"Sounds safer."

6

BLOOD?

When I'd told her to keep her supplier a secret, Heather patted me on the shoulder. "I trust *you*, darlin'."

I recoiled and instantly regretted it. Hers was the first kind human touch I'd experienced in a long time. Since that day, Heather followed protocol. Nothing was passed hand-to-hand, and she knew to sterilize the jam jars.

Watching me panting as I recovered from my run, she nodded to the side pocket into which she placed that night's jam jar. "Peach this time. Sorry, no raspberries this year, even for the rich folks. I'm not sure they're growing raspberries anymore. You got any in your magic bag, Honey?"

I didn't have the heart to tell her none of her jams contained real fruit anyway. I loved the taste of real raspberry jam, but there was no way I could sacrifice that amount of real estate on my little farm. A raspberry crop would take up too much space and deliver too low a yield. "Peach is fine, thanks."

Each Christmas, I fantasized that I would grow Heather some Calluna, the plant that was her namesake. However, heather requires rich acidic organic soil and needs a lot of sunlight. I wanted to do something special for the old lady, but I could not sacrifice the resources or space for a plant I could not trade, smoke, or eat.

I wasn't the only grower around, of course. One of the side effects of the pandemic was the quarantine garden phenomenon. We all came to realize that we'd favored form over function, aesthetics over food. Homeowners associations had defied nature for years by insisting on certain varieties of grass in their suburban neighborhoods. Kentucky bluegrass had been native to Europe and the Middle East. Bermuda grass had been a staple in Atlanta because it was drought resistant. That was all a waste. We needed food, not genetically altered grass.

We never faced one disaster at a time. Disease was bad enough, but double-trouble came with the Blight, the crop killer. Makeshift greenhouses were safer. Outdoor industrial farming was more vulnerable. A plant's leaves would look fine one day, then they would yellow the next. Within days, crops withered on the vine.

Growing anything was difficult. To lose an entire crop meant starvation. If I had to choose between a cure for the virus and a solution to the Blight, I wasn't sure which was more important. Supplies of canned food would not last forever, so our food banks were ticking down to useless. Blight hit the South and West hardest. Though we were relatively fortunate in the Northeast, many still went hungry despite our best efforts. Not everyone was an able farmer. Heirloom seeds were a rarity. Many novice farmers, so enthusiastic in the spring, were disappointed with their harvests by fall.

For people like me, profit was found in the margins and in the failings of others. Broccoli was nutritious and could provide a high yield, but the plant was too finicky. Garlic was easy to grow, but no one would survive on garlic alone. My focus was to succeed where others failed.

The virus killed countless millions, countless because the people who did the counting were dead. However, the new leading cause of death was starvation. I guessed the second leading cause was suicide, either because of loneliness, boredom, or the collapse into pointlessness. Too many people wanted to wish the pandemic away. They tired of being patient, and that's not what patience is.

When I edited books, I echoed the motto of one of our authors: "I'm in the brain tickle business!" As an urban farmer and trader, my job was still to alleviate boredom. My crops saved people from a mono-diet. When you couldn't face yet another night of thin cabbage soup, I was the one to find at the market. I helped keep the survivors going another day, whether it be cannabis or chives to go with potatoes.

When my inventory became thin, I broke into houses to scour for leftovers from the medicine cabinets and nightstands of the dead. The only products almost as popular as food were drugs. Somewhere, a few surviving chemists were cooking meth, painkillers, and hallucinogens. Since What Was ended, New York's rat population had exploded. Creating new rat poisons out of hogweed had become a booming business.

I still hoarded my prescriptions in my backpack. Though they were weaker than they used to be, I still craved the yellow ones that calmed my nerves. I didn't touch my stash of cannabis since it tended to make me more introspective. That way led to tears. The last thing I needed was to dwell on the past more than I already did. I have a theory that if we live to old age, we accept death with grace and gratitude. The end feels easier when you take into account that you won't have to pore over the same old mistakes repeatedly and forever.

In the fourth grade, you pronounced Arkansas with a non-silent s on the end, and the teacher laughed at you. The whole class laughed at you. You were short and fat then. The mean girls said your new name was Flounder, and you agreed to it.

"You okay, Honey? You're trembling," Heather said.

You stabbed Roger, but you didn't kill him. Another mistake.

"Uh ... r-rough day."

"What's wrong?"

"The future."

"What about it?"

"There's not enough of it. I need more time. I still haven't finished Asimov's *Foundation* trilogy."

Too many regrets stacking up, Ovid? Too many failures and apologies? Not enough vengeance, maybe?

Heather's smile faded as she peered closer. Her eyes widened as she glanced down at my dirty black coveralls. "Is that blood on your shoes?"

7

THE LADY BECOMES MACBETH

The bother with blood is that it is easy to spot, sticky, and hard to get out of fabric.

Hard to get out of your mind, too.

I tried to reassure Heather that I was not wounded, then I realized I was. Somehow, I'd cut the heel of my left palm, probably as I pulled the pruning shears out of the meat of Roger's arm. I'd been so full of adrenaline, I hadn't even noticed. It wasn't a deep gash and would not require stitches. Still, looking at it seemed to awaken the nerves. It stung.

"Sit down and I'll clean that up for you," Heather said. "Were you out there looking for trouble?"

"I never look for it. Trouble comes looking for me."

A metallic click on the glass by the entryway reached us. I whirled around expecting to find Roger or perhaps more goons sent by his employers. Instead, Virgil Sine stood outside, maskless and waiting to be buzzed in. A huge man with a machine gun strapped on his back loomed behind Virgil.

Before I could stop her, Heather called, "Virgil! Barry! This woman needs help!"

Heather used her cane to press the button to release the lock to the entryway. Virgil stepped through and waited for the sprayers to cycle uselessly so the inner door would unlock. As the door buzzed to signal its release, I dared a glance at his handsome face. His skin seemed poreless, not quite real.

Healthy, hale, halo.

I knew his name from my circles at the food banks and the market. Everyone seemed to know Virgil, AKA the Unicorn. Neither suffering the virus nor a carrier, his was a rare status. Free to pass checkpoints anywhere he pleased, seven days a week, Virgil drove a truck to deliver leftovers and scavenged extras to the food banks.

Manhattan was a fortress. Greenwich Village and Cobble Hill had no-go zones, blocks of gentrified mansions, and complexes that served as retreats for the more fortunate. Farther out, the borders to the Hamptons and Princeton were guarded by high walls, killer drones, and a small army of mercenaries. Virgil could go wherever he liked.

Where luxury still lived, I was told strongholds even had restaurants. The rich threw us their crumbs and called it charity. We called it guillotine insurance. Their scraps weren't enough, but keeping the survivors low on calories was a feature, not a bug. Subsistence levels of nutrition kept everyone on edge, but we lacked the energy to storm their castles.

Virgil had been among the Unicorns studied at Johns Hopkins and at the CDC. His immune system possessed some odd quirk that was not fully understood. Apparently, his good fortune couldn't be replicated, either. Perhaps one percent of the population was so blessed. Poked and prodded and experimented upon, he was released from the labs with little actionable data. He could have gone anywhere. Instead, he returned to New York to serve his community. Whenever he appeared, several of the women and a couple of the men got quiet and stared, as if he were a supermodel lottery winner.

"What's the trouble, little grandmother?" Virgil asked.

"This woman's bleeding. Wounded, I should say."

I stared at the floor. "It's fine. Most of the red stuff isn't mine."

"Pardon me? What'd you say?"

I couldn't look at Heather, but the distress in her tone was evident.

"Th-there was ... an a-a-altercation, that's all."

"What happened exactly?" Virgil asked. His voice was deep, his accent musical.

I kept my gaze on the floor. "I was attacked."

"I am sorry to hear that, my queen. You hurting?"

"Just a little."

"The person who attacked you, they hurting?"

"Yes."

"Killed?"

"No."

"If they're still around, you should tell Barry about it."

Barry turned out to be the man who had arrived alongside Virgil. He was a fiftyish giant, maybe six foot seven with long platinum hair tied in braids. "Who came after you? Do you know where he is now?"

"He ran off," I said. "I cut him pretty deep, but it was just his arm. He'll probably be fine."

From my proofreading and fact-checking days at Pilkington, I knew the difference between cutting and stabbing someone. A cut did not necessarily convey the intent to kill. In some states, stabbing used to carry harsher punishment. I did not stab Roger. I cut him. Had I directed my pruning shears a little northeast, I could have dug into arteries and inflicted mortal wounds.

Unseamed him from nave to th'chops, and fixed his head upon our battlements, Shakespeare said of Macbeth. *You know, Ovid, if you were a better person, you'd be more upset.*

There was another line from *Macbeth* I adored: His brandish'd steel smoked with bloody execution. I'd been OCD Lady Macbeth for most of my life, scrubbing my hands raw and muttering, "Out, damned spot." But Macbeth was the more interesting character. He was the one who "carved out his own passage" with a sword.

I went from trembling to shaking. I'd come close to murdering Roger and I'd *wanted* to.

Heather and Virgil were sympathetic as they bandaged my

wound. By his eyes, I knew Barry was smiling behind his mask, kind and reassuring.

They see you as a victim, Ovid.

Though I hated that they saw me that way, I loved the trio for their kindness and easy grace. New York had always come up a little short in that department. The city was much worse with so many dead and the remaining so hungry.

8

COMPANION

Virgil stepped close and whispered, "You're good. No one will hurt you now. You're safe." He touched my shoulder to steady me. Usually, I would recoil at close contact. Human touch was repellent, a source of fear. However, Virgil was a Unicorn, incapable of carrying the virus. I wanted to throw my arms around him, cling to him like a life preserver in stormy waters.

He guided me back down into Heather's rocker, patting my uninjured arm gently.

Barry remained at a distance. The big man knelt on the floor and asked my name.

I shook my head.

"I call her Honey," Heather said, "because she's sweet."

"Very well. Do you want to tell us anything more, Honey?" Virgil asked. "Did the man touch you … inappropriately?"

"A girl — one of the Thirders — was following me and wouldn't leave me alone. I slipped down an alley to lose her, and the guy was there. We sort of knew each other from before."

Barry raised his huge head. "Oh? Tell me about that."

"He knew a place I used to work."

"Big city," Barry observed. "Running into him in an alley was no coincidence. That guy was following you and waiting for an opportunity."

A chance meeting with someone from What Was? Yes, unlikely. The thought hadn't occurred to me until Barry gave that fact voice. I'd been too upset to think clearly. I cursed myself for my naivete. Fuzzy thinking was one of the many things that got people killed. There's less room for human error at the end of the world. It's too easy to fall off the edge.

"What toll did the troll demand?" Heather asked.

"He grabbed me and tried to rob me."

"I recognize you from the food banks," Virgil said. "You're a grower, I think, yes?"

I nodded. There was no sense denying it. My wares made me a target.

"He may know you where you live," Barry said. "Unfortunately, this might not be over."

"I've never had a stalker." Trying to control my breathing, I took a deep breath and let out a long sigh. "I don't think this one will settle for an autograph."

Heather let out a little chuckle. I hadn't meant to make a joke. Most of my jokes were something I discovered I'd done after the fact. When people laughed, sometimes I'd think, *Oh, that was funny.* Mostly, I assumed they were laughing at me.

"You ever see the guy around here?" Barry asked.

"No."

"Get a name?"

"Roger. I don't know his last name."

"Give us a description," Heather said brightly. "You know I won't let him in."

"And the Watch will keep an eye out," Barry said.

"Barry's with the militia," Virgil explained.

Barry's sheer size was reassuring. Virgil stood like a statue of a sentinel. Heather was the mother I wish I'd had. I'd been alone a long time. It was far out of character for me, but I wanted to hug them all. I settled for thanking them all profusely.

"Barry can spread the word," Heather said.

"I prefer to be called a Hand of the Watch," Barry said.

Heather rolled her eyes and waved him off. "Whatever, Gigantor."

I began to describe Roger. Then I began to blubber. It wasn't the threat that I suffered or the violence that I'd done that made me weep. These three didn't even know my real name, but they showed me such compassion that I was touched. Compassion was not something I was used to. Worse, I didn't think I deserved it because I didn't feel bad for stabbing Roger. I wished I had gutted him like a fish.

When I was a child, my mother forced me to play tennis. I didn't want to. I hated how the heat of the sun baked the pavement and seeped up through the soles of my sneakers. I hated that it was a tennis *court*. Courts are a place we are judged, and my mother's rulings were harsh.

"Ovid, you're a poor sport. You move with the grace of a giraffe on roller skates, and your strokes are weak because you lack follow-through. You're afraid of the ball. Seems like you're afraid of everything." My mother's judgments were not delivered on the car ride home. Her humiliation rituals took place out in the open, in front of everyone, where they could do the most damage.

She softened every bone in your spine, sewing each vertebra with doubt. It's a wonder you can stand up straight at all.

"I would have killed Roger," I muttered, "but my backhand lacks follow-through."

Heather, Barry, and Virgil glanced at each other but said nothing. I had a habit of creating awkward silences. I had no idea how to avoid them.

"I shouldn't have gone down that alley. I shouldn't have been so afraid to deal with that Thirder. She was no real threat — "

Virgil gripped my arm gently. "Look at me."

I glanced up and away, hit and run.

"No, really look me in the eye, please."

I forced myself to do as he asked.

"Please believe me when I say this was not your fault, Honey. This is all on this man, okay? Do you believe me?"

"I believe you believe it."

"No, no, Miss," Barry insisted. "Plenty of bad guys out there. Don't blame yourself for the sins of another. That's too many sins to carry. Too heavy."

Heather nodded along as she bandaged my wound with a scrap of cloth, tying it at my wrist and forearm.

"Have any of you ever heard of a large group of Taxmen, organized and working together?" I asked.

Heather and Virgil shook their heads, but Barry nodded. "There are rumors of a group, nomads maybe. They call themselves the Memory Keepers."

Heather grinned. "Memory Keepers? You mean, like a diary?"

Virgil's bright eyes narrowed. "I thought they were a myth. Taxmen have always been small-time thieves living off others."

"I hear things sometimes, through the Watch," Barry said. "Word is, the Memory Keepers raided container ships and FEMA supply depots, really cleaned up. If the rumors are to be believed, they're a small army trying to become a big army."

"Scammers and hoarders always have grand ambitions," Virgil argued. "Mostly, they come to nothing."

"I haven't run across them personally," Barry admitted. "I heard they started out in Albany early on, when order collapsed. Raided warehouses and worked protection schemes so traders and regular folks would pay them tribute."

The Unicorn's brows furrowed. "But you don't really know who they are? We shouldn't worry this lady too much about uncorroborated rumors. Look around. Nobody's much organized anymore."

Barry shrugged. "I admit, could be the Memory Keepers are a conspiracy theory cooked up among predators to scare prey into thinking there's bigger forces at work. Is that what Roger told you, Miss? That he worked for the Memory Keepers?"

"He didn't mention that name," I admitted. "He only said the people he worked for were recruiting, looking for folks like me."

Barry nodded as if he'd heard that same tired story a thousand times. "Anyone with stuff to take or skills to use."

I shifted uneasily in my chair and made a show of examining Heather's handiwork in first aid.

"The creep must have been bluffing," Virgil assured me. "I've been through the five boroughs, and I can tell you, everybody's just barely hanging on. Your stalker caught you out in the open alone and wanted to make you think he wasn't acting alone. Don't worry about him. You cut him in a way that I expect would be very discouraging. I doubt you'll ever see this Roger person again."

"In times of chaos, everybody wants to think there's a bigger plan," Heather offered. "In all my years, I've not seen any such thing yet. There's a term for what we are: godforsaken."

Barry's words haunted me. *That guy was following you, waiting for an opportunity.* How else could he have recognized me under all my protective gear?

Worse, did Roger already know the location of my grow-ops? I depended on my little crops to survive. It was possible my office building garden had been compromised. I wanted to rush to check immediately, but night had fallen and darkness meant more vulnerability. I would have to wait until dawn before I could venture out again.

Your pulse is pounding in your ears, and you're still breathing too fast. Slow down to calm down, Ovid.

Many members of the Watch were ex-military or former NYPD, but the militia did not possess the resources of the city's disbanded police force. Our new centurions, volunteers all, tried to keep the peace. However, as with police everywhere, crime prevention was the hard part. Even before the pandemic, police would only have appeared after the fact to find me murdered. The Watch could do no better. Survival was a responsibility that fell to me alone.

Memory Keepers or no Memory Keepers, allowing Roger to escape had been an unforced error. I'd been a farmer and a trader. To keep on living, I would have to become a hunter.

Knowing and doing are separate skill sets. Can you do what it takes to keep on living?

Unlikely. Follow-through was never my strong suit. Retreating into books was my zenith, interacting with people my bête noire, dealing with conflict my nadir, and doubt my forte.

It's just you against the world, Ovid. But then, that was always the case until I came along. You're always alone. At least you're never lonely.

9

THE BEST DAYS

After thanking Heather, Virgil, and Barry profusely, I made my way up to my apartment through the stairwells. No one used the elevators anymore. Even if they had still worked, the prospect of sharing a cramped space and breathing the same air as a stranger gave any thinking person shivers.

As I stepped onto the top floor, cloying heat and stale air settled on me like a heavy wool blanket. Though eager to get to my apartment, I took the time to stop, look, and listen to make sure I was not followed. Muffled laughter and the shrill weeping of young children reached me from behind a closed door.

An omen. Again, I bit my tongue for luck and hurried down the dark corridor. Sore from my long run and slowed under the weight of exhaustion and dark foreboding, the wisps of laughter and cries trailed after me like persistent ghosts.

I knew none of my neighbors. What few of us who remained in the complex kept to ourselves. The threat of the virus precluded friendly overtures. No one wanted to deal with an appeal for free food or an offer of expensive drugs.

I rarely saw children anymore. It wasn't just that many little ones had died or were locked away for their own safety. Given the pandemic's vicissitudes, few would-be parents had the desire, energy, or resources to make new people. We'd begun to run out of hope long before we fell short of batteries, food, and answers.

Dirt shed by hundreds of feet had so penetrated the old green carpet that it was gritty. It seemed every surface had absorbed decades of vague musty odors: unfamiliar cooking smells, spices, and sweat.

Is that burnt cabbage, or the odor of claustrophobic despair, Ovid?

When I moved to New York, this was only supposed to be my first apartment, a stepping stone to something better. I'd met the people who owned Pilkington Press on several occasions: media events, posh Christmas parties, and book launches for the more famous authors in our stable. The company's senior partners lived in brownstones on the Upper East Side. The rest of us lived in poverty and squalor. That was the case long before the unending pandemic struck, of course. Publishing had always been a sucker's game.

Foundering, frustration, failure.

I often resented my bosses' wealth, but in the end, there was no need for envy. They lost their business, and their cushy quarters with views of Central Park. Pilkington's three senior partners had only seemed wealthy. As with many in What Was, most of their worth was mired in debt. They were not wealthy enough to escape to one of the strongholds of the elite. One died of the virus early on. Though she did not appear to recognize me, I saw another at a food bank one day. Perhaps she was embarrassed, pretending not to see me, denying that the virus had brought her down to my level. The third was rumored to have fled to Canada before the borders closed.

Our farm off Poeticule Bay lay close to the Canadian border. On clear nights, my father claimed he sometimes heard the buzz and rat-a-tat-tat of killer drones at their grim work, firing at the unauthorized and unwelcome attempting to cross. Canadian, British, and French armed forces formed an alliance. Working together, the northern patrols stomped out unwanted refugees. As our former friends worked together to repel us, the British Prime Minister, in a wry remark laden with schadenfreude, dubbed their cruelty by an ironic code name: Operation Destiny Manifested. In fairness to our former allies, we abandoned them first. The United States stood alone, and so it fell alone.

The southern border was no more permeable. The desert was a daunting obstacle, but anyone daring to trek south was met by all the combined might of the armies of South America. When the pandemic struck hammerblow after hammerblow, we thought we were safe at first. Vaccines were quickly developed and delivered. But then the variant storms hit us again and again. It was not ammunition that devastated the greatest military force in world history. We'd been fighting the wrong war and fighting with each other. Variants took down our economy and culled a huge number of our populace. At the end of this brutal equation, the Age of Viruses even subtracted who we thought we were.

The President's recorded message, broadcast from a secret location, never changed. Everyone suspected he was already dead. We'd soon tired of being told, "Every surviving citizen must come together under one flag in the spirit of empathy and healing."

As if we are still children who would believe anything anymore. His tone-deaf decree reminded me of my mother who, when I was little and scared to go to school, would hit me to *stop* me from crying. "Get your scrawny butt to school and love it," she ordered. "These are the best days of your life!"

Then and now, I worried that was true.

Despite appeals to patriotism and promises of a cure, we were alone. After the riots, we didn't leave it to the authorities to drop us into mass graves. Volunteers did the burying and when they got sick, the next group to volunteer took charge of the mass cremations.

Unlocking the four deadbolts on my apartment door, I'd finally made it to my sanctuary. Before entering, I checked one last time to make sure no one was loitering or peeking to see which door I unlocked. The corridor stood empty, a fetid maw.

Alone. The way you like it.

"Not entirely true. Zeta-3 or not, I like Carl."

I'd made several modifications to my place. The door looked the same as any other from the outside, but I'd added a layer of steel and reinforced the hinges. Carl helped me with that project back when he was still himself, operating at full speed and mental capacity. Editing a spy novel, one of the things I learned was a door is only as solid as the wall and frame it is placed in. Carl set me up well. We didn't know we were in a race against his infection then.

My biggest secret was the hole in the floor. The super had cut off the water to my place, 12C, so I'd come up with a workaround down to 11C.

Resisting the urge to tear off my mask and goggles, I cleansed my hands with sanitizer before touching my gear. Then I rushed to my little balcony to sit down out of sight. Grateful to be free of my goggles, I yanked off the mask. Free of three layers of filters, I took in deep gulps, drinking in the fresh air as if it were cold water.

My hair was wet and stuck to my forehead. Aching and needing to be free, I pulled off more of my clothes until I was naked. As darkness gathered around me like a shroud, I pressed my bare back against the rough concrete, allowing my overheated body to cool.

If your father could see you now, he'd tell you to come home.

"Poeticule Bay was never my home, only a point of origin."

My father described me as a terminal introvert. "You should be closer with family. If not for family, you'll always be alone."

"Friends are the family we choose," I'd told him. "If the only choice is family, sometimes loneliness is preferable."

He didn't get that I was insulting him. Dad's not big on subtlety.

"Maybe you'll surprise everyone and make new friends in New York. You just have to find your tribe." Dad didn't mean it though. He laughed as he said it.

10

THREE NAMES

I used to know one neighbor here, but too briefly: the guy from 11C. Dave Champion had held a middle management position at a health insurance company. Directly below me, he complained about the noise my treadmill made.

At our first meeting, Dave was angry. "It sounds like you're banging a drum over my head every night," he said.

"I read as I run," I said. "Sorry, it's an old wooden manual job, no electricity."

"But you're pounding away for hours!"

I apologized profusely and made sure only to use the machine when he was out of his apartment. Then the flirtation began — all his, never mine. It began with a gift basket of chocolates delivered to Pilkington Press. He'd scrawled a sweet note with several spelling errors apologizing for coming across "like a dick."

I would not have been averse to honing the social skills my therapist insisted I was capable of. However, Dave started coughing. Then I found an envelope taped to my door. I recognized his scrawl and the same spelling errors. The hospital was swamped with patients, but he was going to try to see a doctor he knew at Mount Sinai West.

Dave left a key and asked that I water his plants. He wrote, "Next time I see you, I want to kiss you on the balcony."

I sanitized his apartment and watered his plants. Dave Champion never came back.

Later, when Pilkington closed and I failed to get my last check, the rental dispute blossomed. Deaf to reason, the landlord shut off my water. I had nothing more to give. However, the courts were a distant memory for petty civil disputes such as these.

Dave was paid up far ahead of time, so I began hauling buckets of water up to my apartment from 11C. When all seemed lost, my goals became more ambitious. Supply chains were sure to weaken, and I needed to grow food. I turned to the only friend I had, the security guard at work.

"Before I got into the doorman's union, I was a half-assed carpenter, but this is more about destruction than construction," Carl told me. "If you want the full ass, I can't help you. I know how to operate a level and a saw but I never managed to make anything look pretty. I can help you with your project. Just spare me some of your crops down the road."

True to his word, Carl didn't manage any carpentry that looked finished, but it was good enough to help us survive the fall of civilization.

He broke through my floor and rigged a garden hose and hand pump. My apartment and Dead Dave's became one as 11C and 12C were connected by a rope ladder. That's how my first garden, and my survival strategy, began.

It's possible I'm an asymptomatic carrier. I still wonder if I killed David Champion. I hope not. I don't want to know. Certainty could be devastating.

Many people who didn't deserve to suffer had perished. There were still quite a few who *should* be dead but whatever was in charge — Fate, God, or Chaos — had spared them.

Fate, God, or Chaos? Maybe that's three names for the same thing.

Sitting there, naked with my back against the wall, I thought again of Roger. I couldn't help it. My attacker was still out there.

Maybe the Memory Keepers were real. How long had he been tracking me? Did they know where my grow-op was? Did they know where I live?

What are you going to do about it besides be afraid, Ovid?

Popping open the blister pack, I dry swallowed a cortisol blocker. The formulation was supposed to help me sleep through the night, though the ashwagandha component often led me to fitful sleep, just below consciousness. The pills tended to help me sleep longer, but they also put vivid movies in my head.

Massaging my scalp, I dug through thick hair to scratch and pull, impatient for my pulse to slow. Dr. Rosa had taught me a breathing exercise to slow my racing thoughts, but the effort seemed to pay fewer benefits to someone fresh from a mugging.

Instead, I performed a relaxation exercise of my design. An author who was a neurobiologist had written that it was possible anyone could forget their own name if it was never repeated. To keep memories fresh, they had to be repeated. Fearful of dementia, I reminded myself of trivial details from What Was.

Who was that old actor Mom loved so much? Elliot Gould.

What was the name of that long-dead action star from Dad's favorite movie, the one where he played a downed pilot? Powers Boothe.

What was I worth to Mom and Dad? Less than a nickel. I was just a book editor turned farmer.

Check that! You're a terrified book editor turned farmer. You're not the girl with the dragon tattoo.

My combat skills would not make Batman envious. However, I'd spent my life reading about protagonists who had defied the law, raised revolutions, and rebelled against expectations. Some had been anti-heroes, but they were all laudable. Why did we so prize rebels in fiction, but condemn them in real life?

I lifted my wounded hand to inspect the job Heather had done dressing the wound. It still stung a little, but it wasn't worth wasting a painkiller. Pulling the bloody shears from my bag, I inspected the blades in the dim light. The moment I plunged the shears into Roger came back to me. I'd acted decisively and with force. That was new and it felt good.

Be honest. It felt great!

When I looked in the mirror again, I hoped to see someone different staring back at me. Perhaps, some*thing* different and lethal.

"Editors delete and farmers prune, all to make things better. Roger needs deleting or pruning."

You can't be Fate. Becoming God is too far to stretch. You could be Chaos, though.

A small smile tugged at the corners of my lips as my chin dropped to my chest.

11

THE UNRELIABLE NARRATOR

Winter's afternoon sunlight, powerless, cold, and clean, slanted through Dr. Rosa's office window. I sat stiffly in a chair opposite her counseling throne. She waited for me to speak, but I didn't fall for the pregnant pause trick. Instead, I fidgeted under her gaze. My therapist sighed and gave up. "As a person who says she has challenges conforming to expected norms of — "

"*Weird*. The word for me is weird."

"You complained your parents called you that."

"I'm trying to take it back, normalize it."

"Is it possible to normalize a term that's a catch-all for abnormal?"

I considered this for a moment. "Reject the premise. Nobody's normal. Society only has averages, a default. Normal is a collective hallucination meant to keep us functional, buying stuff, and paying rent. I mean, look around. Doesn't everything seem crazy to you?"

"Perhaps I'm more optimistic."

"I admire people whose delusions get them further ahead in life. Gregarious people who think the best of others and somehow love the world are amazing."

"You admire the sentiment, but feel you can't 'love the world,' as you put it?"

"I'm from Maine, where cynicism is a synonym for smart. I don't think that's wrong. I like the idea of the happy hallucination, but if we could read each other's minds, we'd all be at each other's throats."

"So everyone's bad?"

Gotcha question. She thinks she has you. Disabuse her of her comforting notions. She wants to give you therapy, but let's go for the win!

"There's more nuance to good and bad than we're told," I said. "Ever been attracted to a client, Doctor? Or despise them or judge them harshly? One errant thought to a mind reader and *boom! Poof! Disaster! Weeping!* Gnashing of teeth and rending of garments! No labels on soup cans and bookshelves totally out of alphabetical order. Chaos."

"I see."

Does she, though? Or did you just undercut her entire worldview and professional life?

Dr. Rosa consulted her notes. "Your IQ scores suggest superior intelligence. You only scored lower on the mathematical elements."

"I'm just an educated fool, but you can't do much career-wise when you're arithmophobic. Without a calculator to figure the tip, my palms get clammy. One time I forgot my phone and had to figure the tip in my head. Hyperventilating in public is embarrassing. I just put all my money on the table and hurried away, never to return to that Appleby's."

"When did you first notice this anxiety around math?"

"For a while, I thought I'd like to be a vet because I liked animals. Then, in sixth grade, my mother and a teacher stood on either side of me to berate me for not liking math. They said if I wanted to be a vet, I'd have to love it so I wouldn't kill a cat with too much sedative. Oh, and it's not only generalized math anxiety. I'm also numerophobic, particularly three and thirteen." I bit the tip of my tongue hard four times to appease whichever god was in charge of number-based smiting.

Dr. Rosa made an effort to keep me on track. "How did you respond to this information from your mother and the teacher?"

You said berate. She said information. Typical neutral language, not making value judgments. You'd like her more if she made it clear she's on your side.

"I didn't like animals enough, though I'm still very fond of big dogs. If I didn't live in the city, I'd get a Great Dane. Almost forgot. Add coulrophobia to my endless list of personal deficits, blunders, and afflictions."

Dr. Rosa made a note in my file. "Fear of clowns. Got it. Let's circle back to that, shall we?"

We didn't.

"I'm a delightful smorgasbord of neuroses, aren't I? Are there many patients like me?"

Dr. Rosa cleared her throat. "It's not a competition, and I don't discuss other patients. However, it's not uncommon to have more than one challenge to address. For instance, many people are unaware you can have depression and anxiety at the same time. It's quite common. Anyway, I can assure you that you're not alone in facing more than one obstacle."

The British voice in my head told me: *So, your judge/therapist will not rule or even admit there's a patient ranking system in the psychologically burdened Olympics? I bet you win, Ovid!*

She scanned my intake questionnaire again. "You've written that you worry about the voice in your head."

"I talk to myself a lot, yes." I pointed at my skull. "It's dark in there."

"Do you remember when you started having conversations with yourself?"

"Third grade, in early April."

"Surprisingly specific."

"My parents sent me to a private Christian school in Orono. In Bible study, the teacher spoke of heaven as a cathedral 'resplendent with light incandescent' wherein we'd sing hymns in praise of God forever."

"And?"

"Uh ... well ... I went home that day to look up the word resplendent. Kind of heavy for most kids in third grade, but I knew I loved the word incandescent. It tasted bright in my mouth, and I said so, out loud. Everyone laughed at me, including the teacher. Was it funny? It wasn't funny to me."

"You kept your thoughts to yourself after that?"

"I looked it up. The way I see and feel things mostly doesn't impair my function, so you can't call it pathological, right? It's often comforting. The voice, it's like this invisible friend keeping an eye on me."

"Let me ask you, what would your life be like without that voice?"

"Besides lonely? I don't know. Like trying to eat soup with a fork, I guess. Compared to people I work with, I feel like I put in eight times the effort for little reward."

"Okay, it sounds like this voice shares your load. It might be something akin to a self-soothing behavior, as when someone who is grieving touches their own face. I can assure you that, of all your concerns, I worry about that voice in your head least."

"My parents said talking to myself meant I had money in the bank. Then they laughed because I'm broke."

"Everyone talks to themselves, Ovid. Children do so the most, sometimes with imaginary friends. Later, they learn to speak silently to themselves. Many adults continue the habit. There's a theory in neuroscience that we are not really one self. We are numerous subselves."

"Subselves? What do you mean?"

"Most people act differently depending on numerous factors. That could include who you're speaking to, where you are, your mental state. As long as it's not a competition, and you remain in the driver's seat, the voice in your head wouldn't be a priority for me unless it's a priority for you."

"So you're saying ...?"

"Let's not worry about it unless it gets in the way of living your life, okay?" Dr. Rosa gave me a reassuring smile, or perhaps that was her professional subself masking her impatience with me.

"Good. It's never a real problem except when I let him speak."

"Him?"

"The voice in my head. I let him out to dress down my sixth-grade teacher once. I told her that she and our other teacher should coordinate because they were giving us too much homework. It was all busy work anyway. I struggled with math and four hours of homework a night seriously cut into my reading time. My next report card said I was truculent and averse to doing the work. I don't like the word *truculent*. It tastes like rust and makes me think of an old broken-down tractor left to rot at the edge of a field."

"What happened after you let the voice speak for you?"

"My parents got pretty upset about it. Even though Mom admitted the workload was a little heavy, she still insisted I should read less and get outside to play more. I think she wanted me out of the house. The voice in my head suggested she should go outside and play because that's where the skin cancer was waiting."

"You shared that suggestion?"

"I did."

"And how did she react?"

"He spoke up, but I was the one who got the wooden spoon. I remember running for the sun porch. As I ran from her, I looked over my shoulder, and Mom was right behind me, smiling because I was headed for a dead-end. She enjoyed using that wooden spoon. Wooden spoon sounds less scary than getting beaten with a stick, doesn't it?"

"Let's clarify about now. In the present, as long as you don't let this voice speak for you, you don't see it as interfering with your quality of life?"

"When his voice comes through, it's usually to defend me. Sometimes he makes observations, but I don't know if I can trust him. I mean, I can't even trust myself to get things right. In my inner dialogue — shouldn't it be inner monologue? I guess for me, it's a dialogue."

"What about your inner dialogue?"

"I swear a lot. Silently, but, I mean, a *lot*! Do normal people do that, too?"

She smiled. "I can't quote any statistical research but I think so. I wouldn't be concerned about it, except its strength and frequency might be a symptom of the anger you carry."

"Anger? Me? Nah."

"The anger you carry and dwell upon."

I looked out her window. "I'll have to look up how often people swear when no one can hear them. I'll Google — "

"You're deflecting."

"Sorry. I do want to give the right answer — "

"Our process here is not about telling me what I want to hear."

I shrugged and said nothing, hoping she would move on.

Instead, Dr. Rosa pushed. "Sometimes I don't think you're being entirely truthful with me, Ovid."

"Ah, the unreliable narrator problem? I think I'm as truthful as I can be."

"Mostly, you've spoken about your concerns about interacting with your workmates. Do you feel you can be honest with them?"

Workmates, cellmates, primates, but never intimates!

"That feels risky," I admitted. "What makes you think I'm a liar?"

"Let me rephrase. I wonder if you're honest with yourself. You've told me several times that you have difficulty reading people's reactions in a social or work setting. However, you've demonstrated to me several times that you can be quite insightful."

"Why would I deceive myself about that?"

"Because you don't like what you see. I'm wondering if you're retreating as a defense mechanism instead of engaging with difficulties."

Her inflection went up at the end as if there was a question mark punctuating that sentence. However, Dr. Rosa trod that territory where psychology and diplomacy meet. It was really a statement aimed at provoking a reaction.

She got one. I began to sweat. "Why would anyone 'engage with challenges' if they had a workaround?" I asked.

"Because dealing with challenges — "

"Isn't worth it ... sorry for interrupting. Challenge is a weasel word meaning problem or difficulty. Really, is it worth it? Not every problem is worth solving, surely. For instance, has anyone who used the phrase 'Let's clear the air' actually done so? For me, it's just more insomnia fuel. And you know what's worse? The victims always get the burden of the bad memories. The offenders gaslight us, claim their rudeness wasn't so bad, that they weren't wrong or mean. After the fact, they'll even claim they don't remember how shitty they were."

"You claim not to harbor anger, but you sound angry now."

"Is that bad?"

"Please, Ovid, stop acting like this is a test. You don't pass or fail with me. Just open up and tell me one true thing."

Always the overachiever, I gave her three.

EPISODE TWO

"Man is the only creature who refuses to be what he is."

~ Albert Camus

∾

"Accepting oneself does not preclude an attempt to become better."

~ Flannery O'Connor

12

THREE TRUE THINGS

"When I was nine, my mother sent me into town to buy sneakers. Shopping alone for the first time felt like a big girl thing to do. None of that thing where my mother pushed her thumb down, feeling for my big toe, and ordering me to pace back and forth."

Dr. Rosa smiled. "I remember that, too."

"Mom insisted I wear white shoes so my newfound autonomy was mixed with the frisson of a tiny rebellion. I came back with blue sneakers, Nike high tops. When I gave her the receipt and her change, the drama started. 'You got the wrong change! He cheated you! Tomorrow morning, you're marching right back there to get the right change!' Then my father, who never missed jumping on Mom's bandwagon, joined in to berate me until big, fat, baby tears streamed down my face. 'Either you were too lazy to count the change, or you can't do simple math. Which is it?'"

"That must have been difficult," Dr. Rosa said.

"Finally, I asked them how much they were owed. You know how much the change was off by, Dr. Rosa? One nickel!"

And darkness fell upon the land. Young Ovid learned an awful lesson that day, but not the lesson her parents intended.

Stunned, Dr. Rosa stared back at me, searching for words. I plunged on, "I stopped crying and snarled at them. 'You made me cry over a nickel? A *nickel?*' My parents looked at each other, and in retrospect, I sensed an unspoken communique between them that acknowledged, 'Well, would you look at that? We're pieces of shit.' Still, I received no apology."

"Ovid, I'm so sorry they — "

"True story number two. A couple of years later, I'm minding my own business when Dad comes rushing in holding a book in his hand. It was *The Handgun Bible,* and it had a sticker on it for $17.99."

"You were reading a book about handguns?"

"A catalog of exotic handguns. I've always had eclectic tastes. I read E. M. Forster, too, but *A Room with a View* was a bit too prissy to fuel my revenge fantasies — "

The doctor's eyes widened. "Revenge fantasies?"

"Don't worry, we'll get there. Anyhoo, Dad is mad. He's the prosecutor and, once again, I'm the accused. 'You paid $17.99 of my hardearned money for *this*? You don't know the value of a dollar!'"

"Terrible."

"Thank you, Doctor, but wait, it's a little better this time. I'm a couple of years older, and, remember, they've taught me who they are. He eventually winds down and runs out of reasons I'm a disappointment doomed to failure. That's when I hit him with, 'Are you done?' He nods and I let the hammer fall. 'It is a library book.'"

Dr. Rosa grinned. "What did he say to that?"

"Nothing. Again, no apology. What I remember best is that he looked disappointed, like it was less about the money and more about putting me in my place. Righteousness. We all crave it, don't we? It's not enough to be right. Others must be wrong."

"Ovid — "

"Third true thing! On a hot day in June in junior high, I'm next in line for the water fountain. This hockey jock, Chris Haig, cuts in front of me. He's big and tall and entitled, a loudmouth who never had two good words for me. I pinch his shoulder muscle where it joins his thick neck and tell him it's my turn. He only pauses long enough to tell me it doesn't hurt and keeps on drinking as long as he likes. He's the kind of asshole who puts his whole mouth over the spigot of a public drinking fountain, and ... it's like I'm not there...."

That rising feeling in your chest is a bad thing, but it feels good, too. Tell her. Tell the doctor. No point to therapy unless you're honest.

"Ovid?" Dr. Rosa pulled me back from blanking out. "Stay with me."

"To Chris Haig, I am worth less than a nickel."

I am nothing to him. Even my weird name tells my story. Ovid is an anagram for void.

"What happened next, Ovid?"

"Um, he was bent over, his mouth on the stainless steel spigot and ... *so vulnerable*. I had this sudden violent urge, stronger than I'd ever felt. I wanted ... no, I *needed* to grab his hair and bring all my weight down on the back of his head until the fountain's basin was full of teeth. I had to see blood from his empty gums washing out to sea. I couldn't stop until I was pulled off him, until he curled up on the floor crying and begging for mercy with a new lisp and newfound respect."

"Oh, my! What was the fallout from that, er, event?"

"I'm sorry. You misunderstand. The incident at the water fountain is the worst of my three true stories, not because it happened, but because it didn't. I let him cut in line and drink until he was done. He walked away, teeth intact. I guess I'm just like my father. I crave righteousness, too."

"At the beginning of the session, it seemed you were denying some feelings. Now it seems you harbor a lot of anger, after all. Do you feel that now? Am I reflecting back what you're giving?"

"Anger? *Hmph.* Rage, more like. Hot and burning, reflexive and ever ready. All the more tragic, isn't it? Because it's *impotent* rage. Years later, neither of my parents claimed they could remember the incidents of the blue Nike sneakers or the library book. I'm sure Chris forgot me and the water fountain a minute after he sinned against me. He walked away whistling. That's the hell of it, isn't it? Offenders minimize or forget their sins. They gaslight us and blame us and never feel the weight of one small regret. Instead of getting justice, we put the burden of forgiveness on the victims. No restitution paid, no contrition needed. They walk away light, and the memories and shame I carry for the rest of my life are heavy. That kind of pain doesn't fade or get lighter with time, not for me anyway. In my mind, I can still see my mother's fury, my father's disappointment, and Chris Haig's smug face."

"And you think about these incidents often? I notice you tell these stories in the present tense as if you're watching — "

"It's not like it happened decades ago or yesterday. For me, it's happening again, right now, as I tell it. It'll come again, and soon, out of the blue. These memories will keep me up tonight. Everything I should have said or should have done comes back for a visit with equal frequency and intensity. I suspect regret is nature's way of making it easier to die."

"Oh? How so?"

"You get enough of this stuff piled high enough, maybe you get to the end, and it's a relief. Unless you've got the conscience of a serial killer or the memory of a goldfish, you're stuck with all these memories you don't want anymore. Brain death would be one sure therapy-free way to let go, wouldn't it?"

"Ovid, do you ever think about hurting yourself?"

Ha! You're too much of a coward for that. On the other hand, harming others ....

"No," I said.

Dr. Rosa was intelligent, sensitive, and experienced. She knew I needed a few beats of silent acknowledgment before she prodded me. I reached for the tissue box and wiped my tears, but my well of sorrows did not run dry. Telling my truth only replenished the well.

Finally, the doctor leaned forward and gave me what I am sure was her most earnest and empathetic look. "Ovid, why is it so important what other people think of you?"

Ooh, you don't want to answer that!

"Because of the Jersey question," I blurted.

"Pardon me?"

"The Jersey question. It's a cliche, an old joke. I don't see the humor in it, but the Jersey question is, 'You think you're better than me?' My whole life, I've been trying to prove I am better and failing. Where's my parade?"

My father's voice pops in my head again: *You're nothing. Not even worth a nickel.*

"Be the bigger person and forgive and forget, they say. But, Dr. Rosa, there is a fourth true thing ... a secret thing I've never dared tell anyone."

"Therapy only works where there's trust. You know you can share with me."

The British man in my head gave me permission to reveal myself, *The floodgates are open, Ovid. Tell her.*

"I want to be the kind of person who could knock every fucking tooth out of Chris Haig's stupid head and walk away whistling."

I did not admit that the tough guy was the monster I wished I could become. He let me speak, but I did not dare let him out.

13

THE BEAUTY OF THE #2 PENCIL

Naked and shivering, I awoke. Darkness had descended upon the city. I'd only dozed for forty minutes or so, but for a moment, I wasn't sure where I was. My respite did not last long. When I closed my eyes, I saw Roger coming at me again, how it felt when he grabbed a fistful of hair and yanked me backward.

Stiff and aching, I got to my feet and pulled the blackout curtains closed. I was tired physically, but nervous energy demands to be burnt. I paced the apartment in small circles.

One task at a time. Give yourself one productive thing to do, Ovid.

There were many things to attend to. The fish needed feeding, and the tomatoes required water. According to Nora Jean Stone, author of *Grow Anything, Anytime, Anywhere,* "Tomatoes like a lot of water, but like many plants, they don't like to get their feet wet, so do not overwater." Nora Jean never got a royalty check from Pilkington Press. I was still performing a line edit on the manuscript when we went into our final lockdown and everything fell apart. I left Pilkington with her book, my office supplies, one cactus, and a small pot of lavender I'd kept on my desk.

Nora Jean enthused that lavender was "calming and classy, even in a hectic work environment." I wouldn't say she was wrong about the plant's calming effects. I would observe that lavendula, a genus of forty-seven species in the mint family, was insufficient solace for my jangled nerves and jumbled needs.

Frantic, I checked the apartment door. I'd shot the deadlocks, but I had to touch each one to be sure, then touch them again. Four checks, four touches, four bites of the tongue — all good numbers. Three is an unlucky number unless employed in humor. In that case, the rule of three applies. No one knows why the rule of three works, but it does. With the gods of obsessive-compulsive disorder satisfied, I was less likely to be cursed with cancer, ALS, or the plague. My OCD had improved since moving away from Maine, but under stress the old habits came back with a vengeance.

As a teen, I'd studied a plethora of pathologies in *Merck's Manual of Diagnosis and Therapy,* so I had plenty of nightmare fuel. Too late, my mother took the book from me and forbade the librarian to lend it to me again.

"But doesn't your daughter want to be a doctor?" the librarian asked innocently.

"What she wants is to drive me crazy by driving herself crazy," my mother replied. "Don't feed the snakes in her brain, okay?"

I'd never heard anyone raise their voice in a library before that day. My cheeks burned with embarrassment. I never went back to that branch. Forbidden to read nonfiction because it set my terrors on fire, I began visiting another library. Mom thought she'd won. Then I discovered the horrors offered up by Stephen King and Tananarive Due.

Horror stories didn't terrify me the same way the *Merck Manual* did. I didn't have to bite my tongue to keep cancer at bay or bats out of my hair. Instead, little rituals calmed me. I made notes on words I wanted to remember. Instead of dog-earing a page, I used ribbons as bookmarks. When I finished a hardcover, I used it to press flowers between the pages as a kind of thank you.

At Pilkington Press, I was the proofreader who always had a dozen sharpened pencils on my desk: six #2 pencils, two blue pencils, four red. The highlighters, two blue, two yellow, two red, were always lined up perfectly and within easy reach. I'd often been mocked for these quirks, especially since most of the editorial work did not require editing a paper manuscript.

"The work is all done digitally now," the office manager told me.

"I prefer to make editorial notations on paper the old-fashioned way first. I catch more than I would editing on screen alone."

"Dated methods slow our processes." Angelica had the bright eyes and plastic smile of someone taking glee in catching me out.

I knew that look well. "You don't think I'm aware that we edit digitally? You don't think I'm dumb, do you?"

"No, no, Ovid, but ... really, it's just that it's ... silly."

I took a beat to look her up and down. The only thing about her I admired and respected was her power pantsuit. She would always be a manager, never a friend. "Angelica, if I had an office with a door, you wouldn't have to see how silly I am. I'll work faster and with fewer errors doing it my way. That will *save* time. Am I really bothering anyone with how I organize my workspace? Unless ... oh, did you come over here to make me feel stupid and small? That's what small people do, you know."

"I don't — "

"I've heard what you and the others said about me. It wasn't nice. Calling me a 'twitchy bitch' is not kind. It doesn't promote your favorite word. *Synergy*. It doesn't promote synergy, Angelica."

After that, she probably just called you a bitch.

An unfamiliar calm settled over me. I looked her directly in the eyes for the first and last time and wronged her with the right words in the right order. "I could kill you with kindness, Angelica, but I don't suppose that would work. I'd have to use something sharper." My gaze did not waver as I sharpened a #2 pencil.

She shrank away and did not bother me again.

Was that a glimpse of your true face, Ovid? Or were you channeling your parents for a moment there?

Had I known Angelica was a couple of weeks away from succumbing to the virus, I would have been more patient. Of course, if she knew she was about to drown in her fluids, maybe she would have been more forgiving of my work habits.

In the apocalypse, my obsessions were often useful. Checking and rechecking locks, for instance, was a solid survival strategy. Even if the scrubbers in the building's entryway had still worked, I wouldn't have trusted them. What may have been considered pathological in What Was became merely cautious.

But it seemed I hadn't been sufficiently vigilant. Roger had touched me, grabbed me, pulled me by the hair, and ....

My mind went blank again.

Dr. Rosa called these spells dissociation. "Are you aware of any feelings around that state?"

"State? You're asking if I associate anything with my dissociation?"

"I'm asking about your state of consciousness before each episode. Perhaps you're avoiding something from your history. Stress can trigger a dissociative event, maybe a painful memory — "

"It's like meditation, Dr. Rosa."

"How so?"

"I'm only aware of it as I come out of it. Seems like a nice place to live, as quiet as floating in space. Sometimes, that's my fondest wish. Imagine the tranquility, free to do nothing but stare into the stars and bask in the beauty of the universe."

"Your fondest wish is to float in a cold void?"

"Nobody judges a rock in space. Even a meteor that crashes to Earth and wipes out the planet wouldn't be judged. We don't blame Nature with a capital N, but people spend way too much of their time passing judgments on nature with a small n. It's not my fault I am the way I am. I'm not straight or gay, normal or abnormal. I am Ovid Fairweather."

14

MIRROR, MIRROR

My mind was no longer quiet or remote this time. I still felt Roger's hand gripping my hair. His attack returned with such clarity that my molars hurt from clenching my jaw. I rushed to the bathroom and threw up in a bucket. I hadn't eaten much that day, so there wasn't much to give but spit and a few dry heaves. Exhausted, sweaty, and panting, I resisted the urge to sink to the floor.

"The floor is where the bugs and germs wait for you," my mother would say.

I steadied myself against the wall and flicked on my electric lantern to come face to face with my reflection in the bathroom mirror.

"Be pleasant," my mother had instructed. "And if you can't be pleasant, fake it."

"If I could fake it — "

"Nobody likes a whiner, Ovid. We don't want to hear your problems. Let a smile be your umbrella."

"I always carry an umbrella. A real one."

"I know, dear. It's not appropriate to take to the pool party."

"I don't want to go to the pool party."

"Doesn't matter. It's your friend's birthday party."

"Sarah isn't my friend. She's just in my class. That's not friendship. That's proximity."

"Your classmate, then, and you're invited so — "

"I heard you talking to Sarah's mom on the phone. You made them invite me."

My mother slipped my hand into hers and gripped my fingertips so hard they went white. "To make friends, you have to be a friend."

"Sarah and her friends are mean to me."

"Because you don't fit in. To fit in, you have to practice." She slipped her hand down to my wrist, and her grip tightened again, grinding the bones there.

Trying to teach me to fit in, Mom thought she was saving me. Instead, I learned I could not confide in her and to trust no one.

My teeth ached and my jaw would not relax.

Dr. Rosa's lessons were more helpful. A common pattern with PTSD is that the body tends to deal with stress well in the moment. That's one of the legacies of our animal DNA. We run from danger. When trapped, we fight. It's only later, when we eke out some temporary refuge from horror, that the weight falls upon us. Panic floods in. Headaches and tears arrive just when we've eluded the rabid bear.

I'd come to fear those few moments of feeling safe. Always vigilant and alone, I felt more vulnerable just when I should have been able to let down my guard. My stress headaches came on like a hot band tightening across my forehead, as if my head were in a vise.

Where's a happy dissociative episode when you need one?

I wanted to feel as cold, quiet, and remote as the moon again. No sweet retreat arrived to rescue me. My eyes got wet. Teardrops fell.

The blurred shape of my mother stood over me again, assuring me she was trying to help me.

"Then why does it hurt?" I asked.

"Change hurts, particularly the things we need to change most about ourselves."

Early in the pandemic, when masks became mandatory, I might have been the happiest person in New York. I wore a KN95 plus a fabric mask with a filter to prevent the spread of the virus. It was another kind of protection, too. I was more relaxed in crowds.

Your face has always been a mask, Ovid.

Studying my reflection, I said, " You were never enough."

Roger had found me by some means I could not guess.

"Mom was right. Nobody likes a whiner. Unless you want to be a victim, you're going to have to become someone else. Who are you going to be now?"

I brushed my hair every night, one hundred strokes. Counting it out had been a calming ritual. I pressed the hairbrush into my scalp to feel each slow stroke. Dave Champion said he liked my hair, but so had Roger. Then my attacker used it against me.

My father told me my memory was too good. "How much of the bad stuff are you gonna hold on to? Bitterness never did anybody any good. Try being sweet."

"Bad memories are like laughter," I said. "They are involuntary. What you call holding a grudge, I call learning. With every word, people teach you what they think of you. For instance, you decide how much respect to give me based on how much money I don't make."

"No, I don't!"

Replied, denied, lied.

How many horrible memories was I determined to hold on to? It was a good question. How long would take for the intensity of Roger's attack to fade? How many days would I have to wait before I didn't think of it every day? How many night's sleep would I lose?

It's not all bad. Roger is stabbed and Mom's dead.

"How did he find me? And am I prepared to do what I have to do when he comes at me again?"

I reached into the drawer to my right. Though the light was dim, I didn't have to look. I am organized. I know where everything is, including my sharp scissors. They always sat between the brush and straight razor.

Scissors first then the straight razor. When I was done, I would have no need for the brush.

The voice in my head often sounded like a British tough guy. He helped get me through some difficult times. Dr. Rosa hadn't seemed concerned, and I did assert that talking to myself wasn't pathological.

That night, the voice in my head was my own. However, the sentiment that emerged from the cloak of the ether didn't sound like something I would say. Staring at myself, half-shorn, my hair falling to the floor like snow, I gave voice to the words to test if they sounded natural.

"Who are you? How many people are you? Do you like what you see? What are you? I'm not so sure anymore. When I stabbed that man, was that really me or was it you?"

I heard myself say, "We shape the world, and the world returns the favor. This world is twisting you up."

The pale, naked ghost shivering in the mirror suddenly seemed unfamiliar.

15

AN ANGEL AMONG US

After a few hours of fitful sleep, I arrived in the lobby to find Virgil sitting in Heather's rocker. He looked up and smiled. It was strange to see a smile on a friendly face. The people who refused to wear masks never had kind smiles. I suppose Virgil's Unicorn status allowed him to be the exception. "Feeling better today, Honey?"

Because of Heather, he still thought my name was Honey. "Is Heather okay?"

"Sure, sure, just having some breakfast. I told the old lady I'd watch the door until she's ready. Late start today, gotta drive uptown later."

"What's it like being you?"

"How do you mean?"

"Having the freedom to go through gates, dealing with the guards and all that? I haven't gone anywhere since the checkpoints."

"With so many dead, it's easier than it used to be. People recognize each other now. Most guards know me on sight, and after a while, you figure out who to avoid. They leave me alone. Sometimes, somebody gets a little cranky."

"Cranky how?"

"Y'know, messin' with you, searching the truck again and again."

"If they know you're helping out the food banks, why do they bother you at all?"

He stiffened and turned back toward the door. "It's rare, but sometimes it's an angry guy flexing, showing his power like any Taxman. Other times, they're just hungry and have a family to feed and want first pick. It works out because they never dare to take too much. Nobody wants to see another Torches and Pitchforks Month.

"There is another kind of person I run into who's not so cool about it. They're jealous of my status." He pulled back his sleeve to show me the bracelet on his wrist that signified that he could not be a carrier. "The CDC gave me the green dot."

"It sounds so carefree," I said.

"Free, not carefree. I'd thought I'd never get out of that damn lab. They got every bodily fluid and asked everything from how much I sleep to what I ate as a child. The CDC squeezed all the juice and information out of me they could before they finally let me go. They taught me what it feels like to be a prisoner. Some of the researchers resented me, as if knowing I wouldn't die from the virus was taking something from them."

Through the iterations of the virus, Virgil watched us suffer and die, a show he could watch with detachment. He had suffered personal losses and grieved, but he wasn't a target. I envied his ease, the attitude that nothing bad could happen to him. I didn't understand that feeling at all. I'd never had it, but I wanted to learn.

Careful, Ovid. He walks among us like an angel among sinners, in our world, but not of it. Virgil thinks he's suffered, but he's oblivious to the depth of our pain.

I understood their jealousy. While Virgil was fed three meals a day and undergoing testing in Atlanta, backhoes dug up Central Park for mass graves. In the beginning, the city kept records of everyone dumped into those deep troughs, and each corpse was given the fragile dignity of a shroud. By the end of the last wave, the bodies were simply bulldozed into fire pits. Sweet smoke hung over the city for months. Only after the dead became charred jumbles were they covered in slaked lime and dirt.

The mistakes made at the beginning of the pandemic rattled on, echoing across every state as the virus kept mutating. Through isolation and following the lead of the rest of the world, the cull did not hit everyone equally. Puerto Rico, Alaska, the US Virgin Islands, and Hawaii were spared the worst of it. As for the continental United States, the government covered over their mistakes with transparent lies and six feet of dirt. The slaked lime was never proven to accomplish anything. We called such empty gestures "virus control theater," the mere appearance of doing more while adding nothing.

"Honey? You okay?" It was Virgil, out of the rocking chair and standing next to me, gazing into my blank eyes.

"Huh?" I looked away.

"You spaced out for a minute there."

Dereliction, devolution, dissociation.

"Probably a concussion from yesterday."

"Really?"

"No, but I'm still reeling from my encounter with senseless violence."

"No such thing," Virgil said.

"Pardon me?"

"You heard me. Stabbing, shooting, throwin' hands, there's always an origin story. Deserved or undeserved, there's always a reason. Maybe there's a goal to be attained. Could be offense, could be defense, or strategic —"

"Maybe it's a flaw in the psyche, a holdover from when we were not much more than monkeys," I said. "Since last night, I've been wondering if we all have it in us."

"It?"

"The will to hurt, maim, and kill."

"Given the right motivation, sure," Virgil replied.

"I hope you're wrong —"

"But you're worried I'm right." He gave me a broad smile. "Point is, there's a foundation to everything, even what happened to you. When we ignore the reasons for what is done, we fail to fix anything."

"I have never heard that take before."

"Now you have. What do you think?"

Suddenly uncomfortable, I scanned the street and said nothing.

He shrugged. "I could be wrong. I'm used to being on the outside looking in."

Just like you, Ovid.

"It must have been odd to come back to New York to walk among us mere mortals," I said.

"When I got back, most of my friends and all my family were gone. I was down in Atlanta for months, and it took me another three to get back. Home wasn't home anymore, like waking up in a strange place and not knowing where you are — "

"But never coming out of that dizzy feeling."

He bobbed his head. "You got it."

"People like to be understood," Mom instructed. "Even if you don't understand them, make them feel as if you do. Nod a lot. Smile more. Get along. That's the main way to get by in this world."

"Lying?" I asked.

"Living," she said.

"You sure you're okay?" His frown was of the concerned variety, not the mean kind. I was almost sure.

"I will be. I didn't get a lot of sleep last night."

"You cut your hair real short, huh?"

"Down to the nub, yes." I ran a gloved hand over my bare head. Neither Roger nor anyone like him could grab it again. "Do I look like a Marine?"

"Stylish, but badass, too. *Très chic.* Don't take this the wrong way, but you look much better without the bangs. It shows off your eyes. I've never met anyone with two different colored eyes before. It's cool."

For that brief few moments, I'd slipped into the past, Virgil must have gazed into my eyes. I pulled up my goggles.

"The condition is called heterochromia iridium," I said. "Dad always said I was 'fulla shit' on my left, so that explains my brown eye. Mom told me I was 'a quart low' so my right is green. Kids used to call me a witch because of my eyes."

"Is that why you hardly ever look at anyone directly?"

I adjusted my goggles and pulled up my hood. "That's not why."

Distant laughter from the street reached us. "My bus is here. They call themselves the mourning group, mourning spelled with a *u*, I imagine."

"Clever."

"Not really. Labels do more than name things. Groups who feel the need to create a name for themselves often do little good for the whole. Walking with a bunch of other women is safer but — "

"You're thinking of this Memory Keeper business," Virgil said.

"Demonyms, cognomens, and group appellations are exclusionary: group members are on the inside of the clique, screw the rest."

He smiled. "That's a lot of fancy words for 'I was always picked last in gym.'"

"Yeah, I'm a nerd."

"What did you do before?"

I shrugged. "I was in the brain tickle business."

"You intrigue me, Honey."

I was stabbed with the sudden urge to tell him my real name.

Don't!

Instead, I rushed to the exit. Walking down the middle of the street, the women passed by the front of the building. I'd never once seen their faces. They'd worn face coverings and burkas long before the pandemic. Still, I trusted they were harmless and traveled with them to the market most mornings. I traveled alone when my destination was home or to my grow-op.

Roger said he often saw you alone. If he followed you in the afternoons, he and the Memory Keepers might have an idea where you're coming from. Are your crops still where you left them, Ovid?

I had to find out fast. My survival depended on my farm.

16

THE MOST DANGEROUS GAME

I fell into step beside Adilah. She wore a bright blue hijab. Despite my virus filters, I sometimes caught the faint scent of saffron. I loved that smell. For allowing me to travel with her group, I gave her a good deal on mushrooms. We kept six feet apart and rarely faced each other. I liked the camaraderie of common purpose devoid of other social pressures. Over time I'd managed to get to know enough of the group that they became good trading partners.

"So?" Adilah began as she always did. "How goes it, Girl from Maine?"

To them, Girl from Maine was my name. They'd decided upon that alias when they heard me pronounce the word supper as *suppah*. My New England accent popped out occasionally when I wasn't paying attention.

I pulled back my hood to show her the haircut I'd given myself.

"Oh, my! What did you do?"

"It started with a trim, and I got carried away."

Roger almost carried you away. People used to say karma will take care of people like him. Karma's too slow! Punch him in the throat now!

"You look like a soldier," Adilah said.

"Oh."

"But it looks good," she hurried to assure me.

She was lying. Perhaps sensing my unease, Adilah moved on from my new hairstyle quickly. "Those mushrooms you gave me last week weren't very good."

"Best you'll find."

"Who do you get them from?"

"Sources."

"The next time you see this person, tell him they weren't very good."

I hated criticism, particularly for something I took pride in and thought I was good at. "What was wrong with them?"

"I don't know, just not very good."

"Mushrooms are easy to grow, but they aren't high in nutritional content so you're kind of lucky I have any at all— "

"Excuses!"

I stopped abruptly and scanned the street behind us, taking a moment to gather my thoughts instead of reacting to her immediately. Dr. Rosa taught me the French proverb, "Curl your tongue seven times in your mouth before speaking." I took a few deep breaths, too.

There was nothing wrong with my mushrooms, but I could think of no way to say so without sounding defensive or rude. Adilah was looking for sympathy to get a better deal on our next trade. It was her pattern. Annoying, but it was easier to keep an old customer than to find a new one.

"Maybe it was how you prepared them," I suggested gently. "These things aren't easy."

"I know how to cook, Girl from Maine."

"I'll make you a deal on your next purchase. What have you got to trade today?"

She nodded toward the huge canvas bag on her back. "I found a lovely quilt. I expect to get a lot for it at the market. I'll see what I can trade for it and then come find you. I am hoping for onions."

"I can get you purple onions and a ripe butternut squash."

"What am I going to do with butternut squash?"

"Soup. It lasts longer."

"It will last too long and spoil. My children are sick of soup."

"Then you have spoiled them."

She burst out laughing. "You bet I spoil them!" The others in the group tittered and nodded in agreement. "I lost three of five to the pestilence. For the two that are left, I do everything and give everything. I try to make their lives less cruel at any cost, but it is complicated."

We walked on in silence. Despite the long shadows and the early hour, this summer day was to be another hot one. I kept quiet and listened to the women's banter. I doubted that Adilah's quilt would get her the goods in trade she imagined. With so many dead, such luxuries as a pretty quilt were both commonplace and superfluous. Empty homes and apartments throughout the city had been raided of their luxuries long ago. Even the most impoverished citizens of New York now owned fine quilts, carpets, and kitchenware.

People wanted useful hand tools, construction materials, jewelry for easy trading, weapons, and something nutritious and tasty to put on their plates. People needed things that provided safety. Food filled bellies. Solar panels fed batteries. Ammunition nourished both weapons and confidence.

I slowed my pace. As soon as Adilah noticed I was falling behind, she slowed, too, just enough so we were out of earshot of the others. "Do you know who I would ask about a good price on a gun?"

"First your beautiful hair and now this. What's happened?"

I glanced around and gestured vaguely at the ruined city. That should have been a sufficient explanation. I didn't want the group to know about Roger. If they thought someone was stalking me, they might band around me, but it was more likely they'd abandon me to protect themselves. My mother was right. I should have learned how to make friends.

"I don't know anyone who owns a gun, at least not one they'd part with for any price."

"Then ask them again."

"Girl from Maine, the hunting in the city is slim pickings unless you love the taste of rats."

"I need a weapon with stopping power for bigger game."

"The kind that roam around on two legs? If I could get my hands on such a weapon, I'd have one myself. People are very unwilling to part with their guns unless you have a king's ransom lying around. "

"Ironic, isn't it? We've got more guns per capita than anywhere else in the world, and I can't afford one."

When it was rumored the borders would close and supply lines would be compromised, my first thought was where to get more seeds. I should have gone out and purchased an AK-47 while credit cards were still a thing.

17

ONE IS THE HAPPIEST NUMBER

"I've asked around already for myself," Adilah said. "Frankly, I've only heard of someone trading one weapon for a better weapon or more ammunition, not for food."

"I've only got food to trade," I said.

She eyed my bare head for a long moment. I pulled my hood up again. "Just ask around again, please."

"There is no point. If I can't get a pistol and a box of bullets for myself, I certainly can't get one for you."

"But you know more people than I do, and I know you, so just ask. Asking should be free."

"Me asking for you will not be free."

"Fine."

"Somebody is bothering you?"

"At the moment, just you, Adilah."

"You going to use the gun on me?"

"I have no plans for that, no."

"If I can get you one, you will have to let me borrow it first. I know someone who doesn't have enough holes in them." She laughed and I joined her to make sure she knew we were still ... well, not friends, exactly, but friendly. My laugh sounded forced, but it was the best I could do.

The empty street echoed to the sound of our feet. I used to get up early to go to work at Pilkington Press, eager to get there before the others so I could get more proofing done without interruptions. I could have read all the manuscripts at home, but my bosses assumed anyone who would do that was looking for a way to shirk work.

The company's executives often used that phrase to cajole, guilt, and scare us into toiling longer hours. The easy rhyme seemed to give the implicit message more power. "Don't shirk work! Are you shirking or working?" Then they'd go off for three-hour lunches at fancy restaurants.

Mom called New York "the early bird, busy bee city." This place used to be chock-full of people eager to escape their stuffy little apartments and get to work in hopes of earning enough to afford a bigger apartment. Our priorities had changed, and so had the city. People didn't jog for exercise anymore. They ran to avoid people, to evade the Thirders, and to limit exposure.

Tramping through the empty street, I remembered a word I'd cut out of a post-apocalyptic novel: *kenopsia*. It referred to the eerie quiet of a once-busy place now abandoned. I loved learning unfamiliar words, but Pilkington's policy was to "dumb it down." The acquiring editor insisted I delete kenopsia. The rewrite went something like: Tamara felt the emptiness of the place. It reminded her of how much she missed cheeseburgers and line dancing.

After another few blocks, closer to the market, more people appeared, traveling in thin groups. New York's sidewalks used to look like blood cells zipping along, intent on their work. At first glance, it looked like chaos, but every individual had somewhere to be. Since the plague, people often traveled as families, cliques, gangs, or clans. There was safety in numbers, but for someone like me, groups offered a different kind of threat.

Like Dad said, "Ovid, you're a pigeon who never found her flock."

After the second wave, most people had hooked up with a group. Loners, introverts, and misfits didn't tend to do well in the apocalypse, but I couldn't trust anyone with my secret except Carl. I depended on my main grow-op for trading.

Starting up again elsewhere could range from tricky to dangerous, if not impossible. I'd managed to construct my big grow-op with a lot of help from Carl. My father had grudgingly supplied seeds and soil before the state borders closed. It was an act of generosity he often said he regretted. Dad wanted me back in Poeticule Bay, and Carl had become a Thirder. I was alone.

You'd think you'd get used to it by now, wouldn't you?

Mom was sure the solution to my awkwardness was team sports. "You've got to learn socialization. You're always squirreled away in your room with your nose in a book. Look at you, standing there with your bare face hanging out! I've got news you can use! The Fairweathers are not scared little squirrels. You want a choice? Baseball, soccer, or field hockey."

She was looking for coconuts at the drugstore with that ploy, wasn't she?

"Choose two of three. That's the choice you get," Mom said. "Time we stopped coddling you."

"You coddled me? When was that? I must have blinked."

Eventually, Dad talked her out of bullying me into participating in high school sports. "Ovid's an indoor cat. She would not fare well in the wild."

I got my way through emotional manipulation. If Mom had her way, I swore I'd take his deer rifle and walk into the woods behind the house. "I won't leave a mess. I know you and Mom worked hard on putting up all the wallpaper yourselves."

I didn't mean it, but it got me out of the snake pit of competitive team sports.

Theoretically, I could attempt to join a group for protection. But what would a group want from me? What tax might they demand? What hazing ritual might I have to endure to be welcome in a new tribe?

Experts used to worry that social media isolated us from each other. That wasn't a bad thing for everyone. I was much more outgoing when I could tweet and post on Facebook. As a remote and digital presence, I appeared relaxed. No one on the internet had suspected I was an introvert pretending to be an extrovert. Being social was easy from behind a keyboard. Never really knowing me, my Facebook friends never suspected I was a mess.

My firewall comforted me as I posted recipes for vegan casseroles and videos of cute dogs doing something funny. Memes of cats looking resentful of their owners were popular. I shared it all to a group of friendly strangers I would never meet. I could still access what was left of the internet, but it had become far too expensive to use for anything frivolous. Dad paid black market cyber-coyotes so he could badger me to return home. I carried the phone, but he always initiated the calls. Because he paid the bill, I could not refuse to answer.

But I missed the support and frivolity of the Internet Age. If I complained about a bad day, strangers used to send hearts and words of love and support. "We're here for you!" I accepted that most people were basically decent when life was easier, and our assumptions about who we were went unchallenged.

That attitude soured when my friends from the cybersphere began to get sick and die in the Age of Viruses. I used to share inspirational memes of stentorian speeches from clever congresspeople who spoke of rising to the occasion. Later, I became certain we'd failed when they stopped telling us how many citizens were dying each day. Despite the bodies piling up, some still sought comfort in denial. Eventually, even the most stubborn came to believe the pandemic was not a fiction. For some, the clincher only came when they dragged an infected loved one to a hospital only to find it empty but for the corpses.

Hope can keep people going for a while, but I'd learned to distrust the impulse. False hope and empty promises are too cruel. Optimistic expectations and glorious aspirations had become too dangerous. In the end, all I ever wanted was the same thing I wanted in high school: to be left alone. Humans were too dangerous and complicated, especially under the gargantuan weight of the pandemic's stressors.

But you are human, Ovid.

"Not like them," I muttered.

"What?" Adilah asked. "Speak up!"

"Nothing," I said. "Bug in my ear."

18

THE FIRST DISCIPLE

The group was only a few blocks from the market. I had to turn off to check on my farm. Not knowing if my grow-op was secure was driving me foolish. "Adilah? I have to go pick up something. Can you save me some table space next to yours, please?"

"You know our spots are first-come, first-served, Girl from Maine."

"You've done it before."

"For a price, not a favor. I'll be looking to get a good trade on my quilt," she said.

"I can't promise that."

"Then come get a table like the rest of us."

"What do you really want?" At the market, whenever the price asked was too high, that was the proper question. I'd often heard Adilah ask the same of a hard bargainer.

"My husband says he needs something. He sits on the couch all day waiting for me to come home to do more work."

"Are you asking for sedatives again? I already traded all I could get my hands on and couldn't find more."

"How about Adderall?"

"You may as well ask the moon for the quilt."

"You had it before, you can get it again."

"I'm more a grower, less a scavenger."

"You want me to find you a gun? Start scavenging again."

I preferred my new identity as a grower, someone who brought life into the world. Scavengers were takers, stealing from the dead, breaking into plague houses, clawing through debris for resources that continued to dwindle and might never return.

"Are we bargaining or are we not?" Adilah demanded.

At her outburst, several of the women in the group looked back, their eyes wide. My cheeks burned with embarrassment. Adilah must have noticed the looks she got from the group. Her voice softened, and she spoke in a whisper I could barely hear. "You always hold back something for a rainy day and, for me, it's a downpour. I must appease my husband. Four pills, please."

"One pill."

"Three."

"Two."

"Done."

The trade was always going to arrive at the number two, and we both knew it. Why the charade? Why did one thing always have to mean another?

I dug into my fanny pack and produced two little pills the color of rust. Adilah eyed the medication suspiciously. "These aren't like the other ones you gave me."

"It's Mydayis, not Adderall. Basically the same."

"Basically the same is not the same. Give me another."

"That wasn't the deal."

She shook her head. "Adderall was the deal."

"Mydayis is just another name for the same thing. It's made from amphetamine salts. Stop making a fuss before someone decides to take these from you."

At that, she slipped the pills up her sleeve into a concealed pocket. "A deal is a deal. I will hold the table for you."

Adilah. A deal. A-deal-lah.

"You drive a hard bargain. Make sure to tell your husband not to take them both at once. Spread them out so the effect lasts longer. It's powerful prescription medication."

"Very well." Adilah never said thank you at the conclusion of a trade. Very well was Adilah's shorthand for, our trade is concluded. It was like how in Instant Messenger, no one ever typed goodbye. Instead, they clicked the thumbs-up sign to signify, "We're done talking now." Adilah once told me, "If a trade is equitable — you got what you wanted, and I got what I wanted — why should I be the one to thank you? It is weakness. There's no room for weakness now."

She was right, there was no room for weakness. That's why I lied. The little rust-colored pills were not the stimulant she'd sought. They were caffeine pills, of which I had many to spare. Maybe it was the placebo effect, but this ruse had worked before.

With a table at the market secured, I headed for my secret farm, my grow-op in the offices that once housed Pilkington Press. I took a circuitous route, doubling back several times, always scanning the street for watchful eyes. I never approached the building the same way two days in a row. Sometimes I wore different clothes or faked a limp. It would not do to become a fixture in the neighborhood. To the casual observer, I no doubt appeared to wander without purpose, perhaps even another hungry and homeless Thirder.

Many survivors opted to take over the houses of the elite dead. For instance, two families had taken over the residence of the senior partner at Pilkington. The brownstones opposite Central Memorial Park looked nice, but they were less secure. More to the point, the idea of taking over the house of a dead family gave me the shivers. I'd rummaged through the houses of the dead many times. Plague victims in family photos seemed to glare at me with cold accusing eyes.

Dr. Rosa once asked me if I believed in ghosts.

"Of course not," I said. "Why would you ask that?"

"Because when you speak of Maine, you seem haunted. You live in the city, but your mind often wanders back there."

"When I go into the past, all I see are the things I should have said but didn't."

"What about the present and your future?" my therapist asked.

"The past angers me, the present is sad, and the future is frightening."

And here we are in the scary future. You're still reviewing conversations with your dead therapist, cataloging your regrets.

"Shut up," I said.

Abandoned businesses, boarded up and as dead as their owners, appeared on my route. Most of the office buildings had been abandoned. Built for commerce and not convenient for habitation, office towers were simply too tall to be comfortable and useful for most survivors.

Racing the rising sun, I hurried down trash-filled streets until I was satisfied I had not been followed. I slipped past a dead water fountain and between two buildings until I arrived at a narrow loading dock. The big door was closed and locked, as usual. I saw no evidence of a break-in or that my home away from home had been disturbed.

I did not write "Do Not Enter" on any of the doors. For some, an explicit warning was an invitation. People hate being told what to do. Instead, I'd spray-painted a big official-looking X in Day-Glo orange on every door to the building to warn of the viral danger lurking inside. People tended to avoid piles of rotting corpses. The orange X was a warning the FDNY used, back when there was a fire department.

I wore the key to a side door around my neck. I checked left and right before sliding the key into the lock. As soon as I opened the door, a shaft of early morning light cast a shadow that was not my own. The figure scurried away from the light. This was no ordinary Thirder who roamed the streets and followed survivors hoping for scraps. Carl was *my* Thirder.

I slammed the door behind me and shot the deadbolt home. The air was stale. I pulled the bandanna up from my neck and over my mask to serve as a redundant barrier.

"Carl?" I called gently. "It's Ovid! It's okay!"

He appeared in the cast of light from the lobby windows.

Sweating heavily, Carl was naked from the waist up. The gray pants of his old uniform were soiled.

"It's just me."

He retreated back into the shadows and peered out at me from around a corner so I could only see a sliver of his silhouette. Carl had been one of the building's security guards. He'd had a quirky sense of humor which allowed him to find me amusing. Every day I arrived at work earlier than the other staff, but he was always at the guard desk, ready to unlock the front door.

Ours was the kind of friendship born of ritual. "How are you today?" I'd say.

"Same as usual: all day, every day — terrible!"

Few office workers besides me spoke to him. I knew what that was like, so I went out of my way to be friendly. One day I asked him about his surname. Anderle. The next morning, I stopped just long enough to tell him that his last name was derived from Andreas, Christ's first disciple.

"I don't remember any apostle named Andreas," he said.

"The older brother of Simon Peter," I explained. "In Christian traditions, he was called Andrew, probably to make white people feel more comfortable. Some people still think Jesus was white."

"You religious?" Carl asked.

"Not if I can help it. God's so high up, he looks down on us. You know how some insects can be shiny and even kind of beautiful at a distance? If gods are as great as we're told, we don't compare well."

"I don't understand."

"Ants look fine on the sidewalk, but if you look at an ant's face under a microscope, it's a horror. Check it out and you won't sleep at night. If God is so powerful he sees us for what we are, no wonder he treats us so badly."

"You're not much for small talk are you?" Carl asked.

"Where I grew up, people gas on about the weather and nothing else. My idea of small talk is asking strangers if they believe in an afterlife, and if so, should damnation be eternal or temporary?"

"You must be fun at parties."

"I am not," I said earnestly.

Carl laughed and bobbed his head. "Oh, I know!"

"Do you think I'm a little quirky or all the way crazy?"

"You're fine," he replied.

"Thank you. Lying at the right time is a courtesy I appreciate."

When Carl's namesake was crucified, he requested that he be put up on the cross diagonally. He didn't think he was worthy of dying the same way Christ had. Somehow, that fit Carl, too. He didn't die as others had. Stuck in the twilight between humanity and death, the disease had turned him into a faint echo of his former self.

Since the virus got to his brain, Carl wasn't much for conversation anymore. I had to double up on chatter for both of us.

19

INVASION

The worst part of losing my friend was that we saw it coming. His Zeta-3 infection began with a low-grade fever and cough that went on for weeks. Just when we thought the disease had run its course, he got worse. Fearful of infecting his family, I helped him set up a bunk in a back office at work.

"If it gets really bad, but not so bad that I die, you know what to do," Carl told me.

I stared back, mystified.

"C'mon! You've seen zombie movies."

"I certainly have not!"

Carl made a slicing motion across his throat.

I didn't think it would come to that. By then, we were so far into the pandemic, by the law of averages it seemed the worst had to be behind us. With fewer people left alive, the infection rate came down. The virus didn't move around on its own. The bug traveled with people. Most survivors tended to be careful. Still, the virus didn't play fair. It was patient. It stalked us and showed no signs of disappearing because each time we neared herd immunity, a new variant evolved.

One day, Carl's fever spiked and did not come down. His temperature had gone up before, but eased after a day or so. His words became jumbled. His sense of humor evaporated. He got quieter and quieter. A suspicious, wild-eyed look replaced his characteristic unflappable calm.

I considered smothering him in his sleep, but what if he woke up and began to struggle? I could have poisoned him, but I worried it would cause him pain. Despite his downward spiral, I couldn't bring myself to do as he'd asked.

When I was away, I locked him on the first floor of the building and fed him from my gardens. He'd cut the hole in my floor to access the apartment beneath mine. He'd worked in construction and knew where to steal the right tools for the job. I owed him.

After he cut a hole in my apartment floor, Carl helped me set up the farm high above us, too. I shuddered at the idea of trying to set up another location on my own now that he was so impaired. He could still weed and water plants under supervision, but I couldn't trust him with power tools anymore.

When confronted with all the evils of the apocalypse, it is easy to imagine oneself as the protagonist of the story. We see ourselves at the center of the world, each and every one a hero or heroine. It's more complicated than that. In awful moments of clarity, I would admit to the sin of utilitarianism. I justified the expense of food by telling myself that intruders were less likely to enter the building if they heard a Thirder banging around the lobby day and night.

Holding my arms wide to show I was harmless, I called his name again. "It's still me. I look a little different because I cut my hair."

Carl stepped into the light, his eyes narrowed. "Ovid?"

"Yes, Carl."

"Apples."

"I don't have any apples."

"Thomas Jefferson ... Hamlet ... Hamilton, parsnips," he said.

I paused to scan the tower's lobby. The coffee shop where Roger worked was abandoned. When he left, he hadn't bothered to draw the steel gate down to seal it off. For one irrational moment, I expected Roger to rise from behind the counter, laughing. That moment passed, but the anxiety remained.

"You want to come with me to the rooftop garden?" I asked Carl. "How about a tomato? They were green, but I should be able to find a couple that are reddening up by now. Or we could check out how the root vegetables are doing."

Before Carl could reply, someone pounded on the glass by the front door. Carl ran off down a hallway. Caught in the open, I froze. Cheryl Anderle, Carl's wife, pounded on the glass. Two men stood behind her. They looked angry.

I could stab one attacker with pruning shears, but taking on two would be foolish. I'd already been seen, so there was no hiding. I had to try the ploy I hated most: giving up.

"Open up!" Cheryl shouted.

A hot trickle of sweat slid down my spine. The men had matching six-guns on their hips as if they were cowboys. With their shaven heads and prominent blue veins throbbing at their temples, the pair might have been twins, except one was much taller than the other. They were so thin, their clothes hung from their frames. These were obviously Taxmen, but their haggard and drawn look made me think of starving wolves.

I unlocked the door. The lock had not been touched in a long time so the bolt turned stiffly. "Yes?"

"Have you *still* got my husband in there?" Cheryl demanded.

"Good morning," I said. "That's how conversations usually start, right?"

Before either of us could say more, the Taxmen pushed past me. "Mrs. Anderle tells us you have a garden here. Where is it?"

"Uh, sorry, who are you?"

The taller one put his face an inch from my nose even though he wasn't wearing a mask. "I'm the guy asking. Where's the grocery store?"

"Grocery store? There used to be a Whole Foods — "

He slapped me across the face with an open hand.

Carl roared out of the gloom, racing to defend me. Placing himself between me and the Taxman who hit me, Carl grabbed the man's arm. The shorter Taxman leapt forward, drew his pistol, and smashed my defender over the head with the butt of his six-gun.

Cheryl screamed as Carl fell to the floor clutching his head.

"You tryin' 'ta die, deadhead?" the short one asked with a sneer.

"The lady wants to see her husband, and she says you've got food here," the taller Taxman told me. "Don't mess with us or" — he raised his hand — "I'll give you a fresh one."

"You'll find what you're looking for upstairs," I said. "One flight up, take a left."

I hoped they'd try to take the elevator and fall down the empty shaft to their deaths. The elevator cars were both stuck in the bottom of the tower at the second level of the parking garage. That was too much to hope for. They made a beeline for the stairs.

Still holding his wounded head, Carl got to his feet and raced down a hallway toward the rear of the building.

Cheryl shouted his name, but her husband paid her no heed. Then she turned to the men she'd brought to defile my secret sanctuary. "What about my husband?"

"We got you in," the shorter man called over his shoulder. "Never promised more than that."

Rubbing my cheek, I turned to her. "What did you hope to achieve here?"

I could only see her eyes over her mask. They were like ice. "When Carl started to get sick, he told me he'd hole up here so I wouldn't get it. That's fine, but when he went away, he wasn't bringing food back, either. It's been months."

"If you wanted food, you should have come to me."

"I don't have anything to trade."

"Everyone has something someone else needs. We all need something." I turned my back on her and trailed after the Taxmen.

Cheryl followed on my heels, cursing me with each step. I gestured vaguely down the hallway. "You'll probably find him in the back office on the right."

"What do you do with him here?"

"Cheryl, you know what he is. It would be better if you remember him as he was. Nobody comes back from becoming a Thirder. You may feel the urge, but keep your distance and don't hug him or anything, not unless you want the virus eating into your brain, too."

Her high heels thumped down the hall. No one wore high heels anymore. She had dressed up for her husband. Many Thirders I'd encountered seemed barely aware of their surroundings. They tended to obsess over minutiae, and their connection to reality often seemed tangential. I was angry with Cheryl, but I felt pity, too.

I found the Taxmen in the second-floor conference room. They pulled out bags they'd brought with them and filled them with cucumbers picked straight from the vine. Carl had helped me set up a system of twine to allow the plants to climb. The strategy used the space more efficiently and increased our yield. As spindly as the plants were, it was impressive how they adapted to curl around the twine to support the weight of their fruit.

"Please leave me some," I said. "At least don't take more than you can eat."

The one who'd hit me straightened and glared at me. "I thought there'd be more."

"That's a lot of cucumbers."

"Not enough calories, but maybe we can trade them. Got anything besides cucumbers?"

I gestured around the room. "There's some marigolds and devil's helmet in the corner if you'd like some flowers to beautify your home. If you want more vegetables, I guess you could do what I do and trade for the rest. Or do what you do and find someone else to steal from."

"Mouths to feed," he muttered.

The shorter one cast a dismissive glance at the marigolds and went back to filling his bag. "How much can we get for this?"

"Not enough," his partner replied. "I told you, we have to find a serious operation, maybe some butcher who still has a line on where to get meat."

"That still a real thing, you think?" I asked.

"I've heard rumors of an abattoir in Jersey," the tall one ventured.

"Cows, pigs, or people?" I asked. They did not reply.

With their bags full, they headed for the door. I said, "Thank you for shopping, gentlemen."

I should have kept my mouth shut. The tall one turned and ripped my mask from my face. I covered my mouth and nose with my sleeve as I stumbled backward.

"Why don't you have more?" he demanded.

"Logistics. I'm growing vegetables in an office building. Plants need water. You try hauling enough rainwater up more than one flight of stairs day after day. Not to mention all the soil I had to get up here."

"Too bad." He loomed over me.

"Please don't hurt me," I said. "Haven't you done enough? I'll never recover from your looting."

"It's not looting. It's survival." The man whirled and headed for the door.

"I'll starve," I said.

"Better you than us. That's the way of the world. Always was."

This must never happen again. Make sure they get what's coming to them.

That note of defiance sounded much louder, braver, and certain in my head. I didn't dare say it aloud.

20

SPITE

I followed the Taxmen at a safe distance and locked the front door behind them.

Cheryl had never come to see her husband before. Emerging from the rear corridor, Carl's wife appeared dazed. She stood in the center of the dim lobby, high-heeled shoes in her hand, mascara streaming down her cheeks. "When he got sick, Carl told me not to come," she began. "He told me, 'If I don't come back, it's because I can't.' I figured that meant dead, not ... that. He didn't even look at me!"

That was true. He'd leapt to my defense and had not spared her a glance.

"Carl is a Thirder now," I said. "I take everything personally, but I would advise you not to do that. He's ill."

"I thought I wanted to see him. I was wrong."

After a long silence, I said, "They took all my cucumbers."

She pushed past me, and to make a grand exit, tried to whip the door open. However, I'd locked it, and she struggled with the dead-bolt. Cheryl's curses began as whispers, but the volume and anger in her voice climbed until she was screaming incoherently. It was awkward, but she was in the way and wore no mask. I let her yank on the door handles until she gave up. Panting and flushed, she finally gestured for me to help.

I waved her away. She'd already turned the key but had neglected to pull back the bolts at the top and bottom of the door frame. I popped the bolts and held the door wide, turning my head to avoid breathing her air as she hurried past.

With the door secured again, I went off in search of Carl. I found him on his narrow bunk in the back office. He lay there sweating, clutching a filthy pillow to his bare chest.

"Met your wife. She seems ... nice."

He raised his head to look at me. With tears in his eyes, he said. "Cheryl...goodbye. Bad bye. Parsnips?"

"You want some breakfast?"

Despite his communication deficits, Carl managed a lopsided grin. Despite my social deficits, I understood.

Dad had a golden retriever on our farm named Tippy. He'd ask the dog if he wanted to go to the beach. His pet would bound up and wag his tail, eager to get going. I wanted a dog, but Tippy was always my father's pet, never mine. Sadness and embarrassment struck me when Carl got excited as I offered him food.

As long as Carl kept his distance and I kept my mask on, I did not fear my sick friend. It was healthy survivors like the Taxmen who had me lying awake at night plotting clever vengeance.

Carl climbed the stairs. I trailed behind him, much like my father following that old dog to the beach. I was so grateful to Carl, I might have helped his wife. However, she'd proven herself untrustworthy. Raising plants taught me that Nature is unforgiving, intolerant of mistakes. If my squash leaves succumbed to bacterial wilt, I had to pull them out, and I couldn't even safely compost the waste.

But people can be composted, Ovid.

I wanted to compost the Taxmen, starting with the one who didn't hit me. In my fantasy, I'd gut him slowly, giving the pain time to take over without letting him escape too easily into death. That way, the one who had assaulted me would have more time to ponder his fate.

You've read a lot of slush pile thrillers.

The top floor of the building had not been leased by Pilkington Press. When I first told Carl my plans for the top floor and the roof garden, I mused, "This firm could be a farm. We'll turn this cubicle farm into a quarantine garden." Those offices, now part of my grow-op, had once been used by a company that made its profits by collecting debts. We thought our lives would be easier without the debt collectors, but without credit, every good thing came harder and with plenty of sweat.

Carl had all the keys and the skills I needed. The freight elevator still worked when we put in the rooftop garden. We hauled up all the soil and construction materials we needed. Rain barrels on the roof collected water to irrigate the soil. Using gravity, it was a much simpler system than the garden hose arrangement back at my apartment. Once we got the rooftop garden going, it was Carl who suggested we put the cucumber patch on the second floor.

"But it has no east-west exposure."

Carl had insisted. "It's not a *garden* garden. It's a *decoy* garden."

Nora Jean Stone had not covered the topic of decoy gardens in her otherwise excellent manuscript.

"If the supply chains bust," Carl told me, "this square footage will be more valuable than any bank vault. Give anybody who'd rob you something to steal that you won't mind losing." I didn't mind losing the cucumbers. They were too low in caloric density and nutritional value.

Glancing around my domain, I took in the hydroponic towers of tomato plants and the beds of crops I'd created from seed potatoes from my father's farm. Root and cruciferous vegetables were the priority. I'd lost a crop of broccoli, but the sweet potatoes, cabbages, and cauliflower were doing fine.

My father had sent me three solar panels to power the lights and a freezer. "I don't want you to starve to death before you come to your senses." Dad was convinced I'd return home as soon as the border restrictions relaxed. He'd even offered to send a sailboat to pick me up, but I assured him that had been tried. Ships arriving in the harbor were either sunk or pirated. There were plenty of boats at the bottom of New York's harbor.

Fear made me weak. I sometimes toyed with the idea of escaping New York and heading back to Maine. On Dad's farm, I'd have more security, but I couldn't say it was truly safe. Dad would still be there, waiting to torment me for my shortcomings, eager to criticize my inability to fit in, ready to gloat. After Mom died, he took on the burden of castigating me twice over for good measure, making up for her sudden silence. Apropos of nothing, he'd muse, "You sure are odd. If not for me, how would you make it in this world?" Dad constantly complained about my awkwardness, but his social skills were on par with that of a brain surgeon working with a chainsaw.

As I stewed in silence, his coda to each harsh blast would be, "Just statin' a fact." Or "I'm just trying to help."

That was probably true, which made his criticism all the more acidic. Returning to Maine would be an admission of failure. It wasn't a sense of mission, a stubborn quest for survival, or courage that got me up each day to tend to my gardens, trade with other survivors, and deal with the constant threats of Taxmen and getting sick. Dad would say he'd told me so. That's what really kept me in New York. I couldn't allow him to win.

Sometimes, spite is enough, at least for a while.

21

THAT FAIRWEATHER GIRL

Carl followed me around as I tended the garden in an old conference room. The tomato plants needed pruning. If I allowed the new shoots to have their way, the leaves would get too big, deliver less energy to the fruit, and provide a disappointing yield. I used the same shears that I'd used on Roger. Simply holding the tool I'd used as a weapon, it was as if I was back in that alley. I felt Roger yanking me by the hair toward him. My stomach turned.

Closing my eyes, I sensed the resistance of the shears tearing through cloth and into flesh. I heard his startled gasp of pain again. The more I visualized pruning my attacker from the human race, the better I felt.

As Carl watched through rheumy eyes, I found myself distracted from my tasks. With the Taxmen having made off with my sacrifice crop, I would have to take more aggressive measures. Deception had worked once. Until I could develop another decoy garden, I was more vulnerable than before. I couldn't set traps on the ground floor. As Thirders went, Carl was fairly lucid. However, if I somehow got hold of a bear trap or fashioned a reasonable facsimile, it wouldn't take my old friend long to blunder into it and hurt or kill himself.

"I'm going to have to invest in more locks and get myself a weapon, maybe two or three," I told Carl. "I was attacked last night. I'm worried a guy named Roger or his employers might be hunting me. I'm going to have to do something drastic about that, aren't I? Want to know the crazy part? My mugger used to work down in the coffee shop! Can you believe that? Millions of New Yorkers dead and the three of us still alive."

Alive, yes, but not all three of us were well. Carl gazed at the ceiling as if all the answers we needed hung above his head. Sometimes, his quiet moods were more disturbing than when he blurted bits of word salad.

"There are too many variables in life, aren't there, Carl?"

He grunted. Was that agreement or his usual bewilderment? I chose to think it was the sound of sympathy.

"I'm not the same person I used to be. Identity is fluid. Just yesterday, I had long hair and wasn't thinking about killing anyone. I haven't changed enough, though. Dad still expects me to be the little girl in his photo albums. A better, more cooperative version of me exists in his mind. There was a girl down the road who died early on. She was the ideal daughter, bound for great things .... "

My friend's brow furrowed. "Ovid? Sugar and spice?"

"Not necessarily very nice. Did I mention I'm thinking of killing someone? Someone bad. Sorry, I still refuse to kill you."

Carl's gaze became so laser-focused that I had to look away. I turned my attention to piling dirt into higher mounds around the potato plants to encourage the growth of more spuds.

"Identity, consciousness...sexuality," I muttered. "Nothing's simple. Consciousness is barely understood. People say sexuality is on a continuum, but really, it's a labyrinth. People are so hard to understand, they scare me."

Scar you.

This time, when Carl grunted, I sensed irritation. Or maybe he was just hungry. He got to his feet and paced back and forth the way animals tread back and forth behind the bars of cages. "Thank you, Ovid, but I'm worried about the worms and the plants."

Sometimes, if I talked too much, he became more hostile, perhaps frustrated at not understanding me. Maybe he understood plenty, but could not communicate effectively.

That was the scariest thing about Thirders like Carl. Their behavior often hinted at a residual intelligence. Perhaps my friend, who had saved me from starvation and poverty, was still with me, trapped in a body that garbled his mental commands. It was as if his brain still worked, but the lines of communication between his mind and his tongue were irrevocably broken. If so, he was trapped in horror.

I'd seen something similar before the world went all the way into the handbasket. Jane was a local girl from Poeticule Bay. Her mother had early-onset Alzheimer's. The community held fundraisers to help the family with the medical costs. When Jane's mother appeared at an event to express her gratitude, she announced, "I'm still with it, don't y'know? I recognize what's going on. Someday I won't. Part of me is looking forward to the day when I don't know what's happening. That will be a great relief."

She never received that small grace. One day she began to cough. Soon her ragged breaths became shallower and shallower.

On a visit home, early in the pandemic and long before the state borders slammed shut, I ran into my old classmate at the Bargain Barn. With little preamble, Jane told me, "The plague got Mom before her brain rotted."

As her mother's flame guttered and went out, Jane couldn't be with her mother. As the ventilator hissed in the background, a nurse held a phone to the patient's ear. Jane told her over and over, "Thank you, Mom. We're going to be okay. We're all going to be okay. You can let go, and we'll see you again someday."

I wondered if Jane believed that as I muttered something about how sweet her farewell words were.

Jane became angry, as if I was responsible for her mother's death. "They call it decompensating. Do you know what that means? Suffocating. Mom slowly suffocated."

Dry drowning, I thought. *Drowning on dry land.* That's what the rest of us called that terrible death.

"Some people tell me her death was a blessing," Jane seethed. "It spared her a decline into early dementia and drawn-out death. Since she was going to die anyway, people talk as if her death doesn't matter as much, but she was still my mom."

"Some people are idiots," I said, trying to soothe her.

Jane would not be placated. "If not for the plague, we would have had more good days. She still had some good days ahead of her. I want those days back!"

Despite my attempts at correct sympathetic overtures, Jane stalked away mad. It was as if I had placed a pillow over her mother's face and killed her myself. Jane stayed in Poeticule Bay in the same house her parents lived in. Every house, particularly those with carpets that absorb aromas, has a unique smell. I imagine Jane was quite content to open her door and get a whiff of that same aroma each time. Perhaps staying at home reminded her of the best of her childhood. I envied her contentment.

"That Jane girl," my father said, "I like her. Took care of her mother, never a harsh word. Could use a dozen of her around here."

I'd been one of those kids who couldn't wait to leave their hometown for the big city. I made the mistake of showing my eagerness to get away too early. No doubt, my dreams of moving to New York were annoying to those who were stuck in Poeticule Bay. To those who loved small-town life, I was an even greater irritation.

In a small town, everyone is under a magnifying glass. Every mistake, real or imagined, is broadcast through the neighborhood grapevine. Everyone knew how I, "That Fairweather girl with the odd Roman name," was messed up.

I didn't actually do anything wrong, but I said a few things that no one in my high school let me forget.

They thought you were like me, the British tough guy said. *Dangerous.*

I was only defending myself.

Roger and the Memory Keepers will be looking for you. You're going to have to become what you pretended you were. You've got your soldier haircut, but are you ready to get really tough?

"No."

EPISODE THREE

"She could never be a saint, but she thought she could be a martyr if they killed her quick."

~ Flannery O'Connor

⁓

"I intend to speak of forms changed into new entities."

~ Publius Ovidius Naso

22

OF GODS AND WORMS

Brain surgeons really had to know what they were doing. Were the rest of us, mere mortals, faking our way through life? Did anyone really know what they were doing? I pretended to be another person for the first eighteen years of my life, but I didn't do it well. Trying to fit in with the people of Poeticule Bay was like acting in a play where everyone else in the cast but me had read the script.

On the day I graduated high school, Dad asked, "What can you do in New York you can't do here?"

"I'll go find out." All I wanted to do was read books, but I wasn't sure how to make a living at it yet.

Dad, the Plan Man, didn't appreciate my improvisations. "University is a pretty penny. What are you going to do with an English degree? We both know you aren't going to teach. You came home from school bawlin' every time you had to stand up in front of the class. You were always bawlin', never could stand and deliver. Not like your old man in court. I'm surprised you're even thinking about New York. Bravery is not exactly your thing, is it? I'm not saying this to be mean, mind. I don't want to see you hurt."

Unless you're doing the hurting, I thought.

Nothing I could say would have been good enough for him, so I said nothing. He would only help pay for my education if he approved of my choice. He'd threatened me that way several times. I call it blackmail. He called it helping. I told him I was studying agricultural management, but I got an honors degree in English. The irony of how things worked out was not lost on me. Training as a professional grammarian wasn't serving me as well as Ag Management would have. I'd die before admitting that to my father.

Freshly graduated, I launched a desperate job hunt, peppering publishing houses with my resume. One month in, I came home for a brief weekend visit. Cornering me in the barn, Dad was already impatient, hounding me to give up and come home to stay. "By the time I was your age, I'd already had a house, a cottage, a boat, and two cars. What are you doing with your life? Things are good here. Why do you have to muddle things? Is this what I paid for?"

I wanted to tell him I owed him, but I was not owned. Instead, I tried to be nice. "Dad, we've talked about this. Stop trying to manipulate me. I've told you I'll pay you back — "

"How you gonna do that without a job?"

"I'm working on that, and I'm working on myself, trying to be my best self — "

"Just be a person, Ovid!"

"I *am* a person."

"Are you?"

"I think what you mean to say is I'm unlike anyone else you know. I am not responsible for your limited experience with people like me."

He laughed at me. "You've got DOG! Delusions of grandeur!" He elucidated his disappointment in me with the stentorian tone of a condescending king. "In my generation, somebody like you might join a punk band until they realized they weren't British and not nearly tough enough to go it alone. But you? The only friends you've got are in books."

"Fiction is my escape. Sometimes there's even a happily ever after. I want to feel that — "

My mother proved no ally. "You're a girl who thinks she's too good for us. You always have your head in the clouds and your nose in a book. You aren't better than us. Someday, reality is going to come a-knockin', and you're gonna have to deal with it, just like the rest of us."

"Why would you want that for yourself or anyone you cared about?" I asked.

My answer came in a slap. She left a red welt on my cheek that did not fade until the next day. "Too fragile by half, whining and crying about every little thing!"

When Mom died, I did not grieve. I wept because I did not miss her and thought I should.

The British tough guy informed me: *If you have to make up your grief, it's just performative. She wanted you to face reality? Face this, your father is no champ, and your mum was dead dodgy.*

The sound of water spilled on the floor brought me back to the present. Carl was pouring water from one canister to another. I went to him to steady his hand. Boiled water tastes flat, but I'd read somewhere that pouring the water back and forth got the oxygen back in it, thus improving the taste.

"You know, Carl, Cheryl loves you. It was nice that she came to see you. She still cares. It wasn't about her looking for food. Her tears were real, I'm sure. Nobody cried for me like that. I've never cried for anyone else like that, either. Do you think that makes me a bad person?"

Carl said nothing, so naturally, I took his silence for a yes.

As my father would say, "Just statin' a fact. Can't you take it?"

Given time and distance, I came to some conclusions about people on my enemies list. The virus killed so many, yet, by my count, the disease missed a few who also deserved deletion. I imagined myself as an editor again, this time taking my tormentors out as easily as slashing with a red pen. I pictured the Taxmen dead and composting in the rooftop garden. And Roger, of course. The more I thought about every slight, every regret, embarrassment, and petty affront, I wished my father were deleted, too.

I pulled a small Styrofoam box from my bag and introduced fresh worms to the garden soil. I'd dug them up the previous day. Some were for the garden. The rest would serve as protein for my next stew.

Did divine beings look down on us the way humans see worms, serving some function, but unworthy of love?

"Carl? If there is a God, do you think it judges and punishes us forever? Infinite torture for finite crimes doesn't seem fair, does it? Some would have us believe that even having nasty thoughts is a sin. God shouldn't judge humans so harshly. I am weak, so I understand human weakness. God should leave the judging and punishment up to me."

Carl wandered away to look out the window. "Fair-weather friend." He did not look my way again until I handed him a tomato. He grunted his thanks, but went back to staring out the window. Searching for his wife on the streets below, perhaps? If he was still that aware, I didn't want to contemplate the depths of his sadness.

"You know what I like about you, Carl? You don't pretend to have all the answers. You have just as many answers as anyone else. You are a good listener. You're the epitome of satisdiction. It's the $10 word for, 'Enough said.'"

23

ANGELS WITH DIRTY FACES

Some habits of living were still automatic with Carl. He remembered how to use the composting toilet I set up for him. He could put on pants, socks, and shoes. Shirt buttons frequently defeated him. Perhaps that's why he seemed to prefer to go shirtless. I made a mental note to find more T-shirts.

Drawing on the skills I learned caring for my dying mother, I gave Carl a quick sponge bath. He was cooperative and remained silent, which is more than I could say for Mom. He was grateful. She was resentful of appearing weak. I handed him a fresh pair of pants and left him a basket of food by his bed before locking him in.

As I wound my way back toward the market, I went over the things I could have said to the thief who hit me. Several ideas from the manuscripts I'd proofread came to mind. "Do that again and I'll eat your little black heart" sounded threatening, though the tone was vaguely dated. "You hit like a little bitch" was okay to my ears, but also sexist. I settled on "Try that again. See what happens."

Cheryl had tipped them off and used them to get in. I would have let her into my sanctuary had she asked. I shouldn't have been surprised at her hostility and distrust. People experienced road rage because operating a vehicle is dangerous. Driving ramped up excitation in the amygdala, putting drivers in a combative state even if they were only going out for ice cream. Most people didn't drive anymore, but road rage was the perfect parallel to living with the virus. Amid the plague, permanent hypervigilance and acute anxiety were part of the price paid for survival.

The sound of gunfire reached me, then angry shouts. Somewhere, perhaps one block over, a large engine roared. It was coming my way.

There were no alleys to duck into, but across the street an old bakery stood empty. Its front door was closed and probably locked, but the front window had been shattered. I ran to it. One jagged piece of glass still stood at the bottom of the frame, like a sharp tooth ready to impale me.

The engine roared again, closer. I smashed the tooth inward with a gloved hand and climbed through. There had been a window display, but someone more nimble than me had slipped past the glass and shoved the shelving aside. The bowels of the shop were dark, but I detected no movement or alarm at my intrusion. Crouching, I listened for the approaching vehicle.

It was a large truck, two-and-a-half tons. Had the streets been clear, the occupants might have caught me out in the open. However, they had to weave around abandoned vehicles. Where the street was open for a short stretch, the driver gunned the engine, trying to get up to speed quickly before coming to the next obstruction. When their path became too narrow, they slowed to push rusting hulks aside.

As they passed, I lay on the floor. I couldn't see the woman in the shotgun seat, but I could hear her shouts as she leaned out the window. "Attention, bitches! There's a new sheriff in town! If you trade at the market in Hell's Kitchen, get yourself over there for more developments! Traffic on the twos and weather at the bottom of the hour!"

As if to punctuate her announcements, she fired a pistol into the air. At least, I hoped she shot into the air. She sounded drunk. What shocked me more was that someone would be so bold as to waste rounds of ammunition. Did she have a huge arsenal, or did she have an armorer skilled in making bullets?

After the truck passed, I dared to raise my head to sneak a look. A column of men and women trudged behind the truck. They were all connected by slender yellow nylon ropes. Bound at the wrists and by their necks, several armed guards flanked them. The prisoners looked thin, dirty, and dejected, their chins on their chests.

I should have flattened. Instead, I peered at them in shock. I'd seen a lot of bad things, from deadly riots and piles of burning corpses to bodies left to rot in the street. But taking a large group of prisoners this way? Another norm shattered. I hadn't been sure at first. I decided each captive had to be a high-functioning Thirder.

The voice in my head whispered: *Given time, sociopaths can normalize any behavior, rationalize any loss, forgive themselves any sin.*

The youngest in the column was a girl of no more than nine or ten with tousled hair and a dirty face. Her frame was almost skeletal. Tattered clothes hung off her like drapes. I wondered if her clothes were borrowed or if she'd once been fat. For a moment, our eyes locked. She seemed familiar. We stared at each other, and everything else faded away. Even the sound of the big truck's engine disappeared. The child and I stood in our own dimension, apart and safe from the rest.

Careful, Ovid. Maintain situational awareness.

I ducked back down. When I put my hands over my face to shut out the world, I could still see the girl's pleading eyes.

Once the last of the column had passed, I left my hiding place and followed at a discreet distance as they made their way toward the market. The woman in the truck was still screaming out of the truck window and occasionally firing shots.

In my heart, hatred competed for dominance with fear and despair. Since the pandemic began, my only focus had been day-to-day survival. However, more than a tiny virus was killing us. Selfishness is a disease and lack of empathy a killer. I had no plans yet, but I knew I needed to rescue the girl. Until that moment, I had been determined to save only myself and Carl. Seeing the starving girl with the dirty face, I didn't *want* to save her. I *needed* to save her.

24

MESSAGE RECEIVED?

I followed the column, careful to stay out of sight of the guards or their captives. The woman in the truck's passenger seat wasted more rounds firing into the air. Occasionally, she shouted. Between the distance and the sound of the engine, I couldn't make out all her words, but her tone was exuberant. I did catch snatches here and there. "New world order!" was repeated often. So was "Kneel or squeal!"

When I edited novels, I sometimes had to pull authors back from making their villains over-the-top. I insisted that motivations had to run deep. The woman screaming drunkenly and firing random shots was a selfish person, empty of feeling for others. It didn't go any deeper than that. Since the cycle of plagues began, I'd seen enough such behavior that I didn't need more convincing. Screw the banality of evil. Evil is often cartoonish.

As they slowly made their way toward the market, other Thirders began to follow the procession. Within a few blocks, their numbers grew. They were focused on the drunken noisemaker, so I slipped in with the loose parade of the Zeta-3 infected, just another face in the horde. As I fell into step behind a disheveled woman in a ragged nurse's uniform, I became her shadow and she, my camouflage.

"Can't do more" was her mantra. With every stride, this poor woman's brain was a record player whose needle was stuck in a groove. "Can't do more. How much is enough? What do you want? Can't do more. Can't. Just can't. Got nothing left to give. Can't."

When the truck's engine roared, the Zeta-3 infected became more agitated, moaning, and twitchy. I sympathized with their pain. Too much stimulation, particularly too much noise, overloaded my circuits with what Dr. Rosa called neural stress. Walking among the Thirders so easily, my newfound invisibility was comforting. All I had to do was hang toward the back, move with the herd, keep my head down, and stay silent. I'd been less comfortable sitting in classrooms in high school.

The woman we followed had a driver, a weapon, and enough means to fuel a behemoth of a truck. She had acquired all that power in the middle of the apocalypse. Functional and insane are not mutually exclusive states. My mother had been well off, functional, but fairly crazy, too.

"Crazy is an impolite word," she once told me. "Don't use that word."

"How about crazed? Would you consider yourself crazed?"

"Glass houses, Ovid, glass houses."

Mental illness ran in my family on my mother's side. My maternal grandfather Jake Curry and my Aunt Leona were dangerous people. Grandfather killed people in war. He regretted having to stop after he was dishonorably discharged. In civilian life, he threatened people often. He would go into grisly detail about what he had done and all the terrible things he wanted to do in the future. He terrified people, but one day he made the mistake of threatening a judge. That got him arrested. Jake Curry died of the virus in a county jail while awaiting sentencing.

My father said, "Old Jake got the death penalty for something that probably would have got him six months or less. Jake being Jake, though, who cares? Finally, some peace around here!"

As for my aunt, she burned down two houses and an apartment building, the last with her in it. That's all I know of Aunt Leona. After her first arson, no one spoke of her. It was as if my mother's sister were erased, easy as wiping a blackboard. I suspected my mother had the same cursed gene. Perhaps in a mean act of projection, Mom had, at various times, called me variations of mentally impaired. On various occasions, she called me disturbed, deranged, and demented. (And those were just the mean names that started with *d*.)

"At least I try to quiet my impairments," I told her. "I wish you would."

That got me a slap across the face — fast, sharp, and stinging. Each time she struck me, Mom would ask, "Message received?"

I wish I'd counted the number of times she hit me. I lost track once I hit puberty's awkward and lanky era — a stage I never felt I exited. Though her assaults were indelible, she seemed to forget her acts of violence almost instantly. I've often found that with mean people. My mother did not forgive others' trespasses nor did she dwell on her own. Other people were nothing to her, so what did she care about whom she offended?

The frequency and amplitude of her attacks increased through my adolescence. I noticed she got more vicious once she detected my hormones were at work. She mocked my acne and began to refer to me as "formerly cute."

As tough as my parents had been to live with, I hadn't always lived in a constant state of high alert. I missed those relatively easy times when I could retreat to my room and into books and forget how miserable I was — even forget where I was — for hours at a time. Doing without iced cherry Kool-Aid and hot roast beef at Thanksgiving was a loss. However, of all the luxuries the virus had taken away, it was the freedom from fear that I missed most.

Thinking of the captured girl, of the Taxmen, and, of course, Roger, I felt a familiar ache over my heart and in my gut. When my jaw ratcheted this tight and defiant, all I wanted was vengeance. I wanted to get hold of a machine gun and mow down my oppressors. I wanted to wipe any opposition from the face of the Earth. Cataclysmic sins seemed the only way to right the balance of good and evil. Evil had reigned for far too long.

Was my fascination with violence an inherited trait? Perhaps stress had awakened a cursed gene. Maybe my violent fantasies were a product of epigenetics: the theory that ancestral trauma is passed down from previous generations. Before the Fall, in some rejected manuscript, I'd read that descendants of abused indigenous peoples and Holocaust victims carried anxiety and depression attributable to their forebears' horrible experiences.

The virus made danger normal. Besides the nuances of urban gardening, the virus taught me that people can get used to just about anything. If we were awake, we were probably afraid or angry. Perhaps genetic flaws and inherited tendencies were not necessary to feel the seduction of violence.

Always wary, I suspected that even if we someday beat the variant storms, my hypervigilance would remain as long as I breathed. Unrelenting fear and chronic rage were also diseases, and they had become endemic.

25

THE HAND THAT HOLDS THE SPOON

The crash and shriek of metal on metal echoed down the canyon of the city street and agitated the Thirders further. Those who were able ran toward the truck. The rest scrambled and stumbled forward as if the noise were a whip. I was too far back to see, but I guessed the truck had come to a halt at an obstruction. Gears ground. The truck's engine roared as they attempted to push and smash their way past some barrier.

The nurse ahead of me put her palms over her ears. "Too much. Too much! Too much! I can't. I can't! W-won't!" Wound up, she broke into a shambling run, leaving me behind.

The Thirders trailing the column must have numbered more than thirty. Their babbling got louder, as if to try to shout down and block out the truck's engine noise.

One young woman cried out, "Where's my baby? Have you seen my baby?"

A man wearing a long T-shirt, but nothing else, was more loquacious than most of the Zeta-3 infected. He demanded, "Where's the soup kitchen? Is there soup in the kitchen or can they make something else? I want stew. When I was little, we ate rabbit. You got rabbit stew?"

In the controlled environment of the office tower, Carl was usually calm. Sometimes his utterances seemed on target, or, if tangential, at least adjacent to reason. Most Thirders I'd encountered on the streets, if they could speak at all, wanted questions answered.

"Which way? To the Memorial? Which way?"

"Is Mom back from work yet?"

"Is it over?"

"Can I sit a minute? Please? Can I just sit a minute, please?"

"Where's home? I...lost. I'm lost. Are *you* lost?"

"It'll be okay, right? It's going to be okay, right?"

As I slipped to the side of the street and hid behind some steps, the Thirders called out these questions and more. When we're upset, we all have more questions than answers.

Peeking down the street, I watched as the column's guards whirled and trained their guns on the infected. The prisoners trailing behind the truck shouted in fear and threw themselves down or were pushed to the ground.

The followers received one answer to all their questions: gunfire.

I ducked back down, squeezed my eyes tight, and pressed my palms over my ears to form a seal.

Now would be a good time to dissociate, Ovid. Your circuits are overloading. Block everything out!

Many blamed the infected for their plight. "If they weren't weak in some way," or "If they'd been more careful." The shaming went on and on. People who focused on pointing fingers instead of finding solutions exhausted me.

The dead are silent and have the good grace to be buried out of sight. Addled and helpless, the walking wounded had become a nagging reminder of our failure to combat the variant storms. Many survivors called Thirders by mean names. If we'd called them patients instead, perhaps we would have treated them differently. But maybe not. Long before the plague, we turned away from those we'd failed. We looked the other way when a homeless person asked for help. We put Time's victims in nursing homes and pretended that wouldn't happen to any of us.

I think we failed the infected because we don't like to lose. They said the infected should have quarantined even when they were forced to work. We blamed the infected for their comorbidities instead of acknowledging that the variants infected human beings, not willing targets. Many pretended they were safe, as if they could separate the Zeta-3s' fate from their own by sheer force of will. It is always easier to blame someone for their circumstances than it is to help them. Not better. Just easier.

When bad thoughts occurred to me, and I couldn't knock wood right away, I bit my tongue. Intellectually, I knew it was a silly superstitious act to ward off dark forces. However, it was soothing. When I saw Thirders, I always bit my tongue, as an unspoken "there but for the grace of God" sort of thing.

Gunshots. Screams. Agony. More gunshots.

The noise brought me out of my reverie, and I didn't go away long enough. A few feet away, machine gun rounds chunked the wall above my head. It was all I could do to stop myself from screaming along with the slaughtered Thirders.

Go back to Maine, Ovid. Now!

And suddenly, I wasn't a woman cowering behind cement steps. Hot tears tracked down my cheeks. I was young ... I don't know. Maybe five? Six? Looking up at my mother as she cursed me out because I'd made a mess in the kitchen.

Glancing down, a mixing bowl sat between my legs. There was porridge, a pitcher of spilled water, a spotted banana, and two emptied boxes, one of corn starch, the other of baking powder.

"I'm making dinner for when Daddy comes home."

My mother pulled me up by the hair. She hit my bottom with a wooden spoon several times. It stung badly and I cried out. I would have run, but she gripped my hair with her fist. When I put my hand in the way, trying to protect my bum, she struck my palm. That was even more painful.

If I hadn't twisted away, leaving her with a hank of my hair in her hand, I don't know when she would have stopped. I crawled under a kitchen chair, clinging to it like a shield as she stood over me, trembling with rage.

"They say kids need mothering, but you are not normal, Ovid."

Mother, smother, monster.

I stopped crying when she said that. The pain in my bottom had ebbed just enough that rage replaced my fear.

"Don't grit your teeth at me, girl!"

"I'm gritting my teeth so I don't say something you won't like!"

She knelt down and shook the wooden spoon in my face. "Yeah? What is it you want to say? Let's hear it."

I said nothing.

"I didn't think so," she said.

"Ask me again when I'm bigger."

She dragged me out from under that kitchen chair and used the wooden spoon some more. The pain was sharp, but every time she hit me, she made the memory more indelible and strengthened my resolve.

I will get through this, I told myself. *One day, I'm going to be the one holding the spoon.*

26

AWAKENING

I came out of that ... what was it? A memory? A nightmare? A fugue? A vision born of time travel? Whatever it was, when I broke from my trance, the prisoners wept as the guards laughed.

The woman in the truck congratulated the guards through her bullhorn. "Good on ya! No more pestilence! No more waste! No more smooth brains than are useful! This is how we get back to normal, people! We get back to normal with normal people! And we only use what's trainable! No mercy for the brain dead! Get the prisoners up and moving so they don't hang themselves in the ropes! Leave the rest for the birds!"

Of all the iterations of the virus, the Zeta-3 mutation carried the most terror for me. Near the end of What Was, a comedian joked that the collective IQ in America dove precipitously, but "with congressmen and senators, it's hard to tell any difference." Despite the silly jokes and cruel comparisons to *The Walking Dead*, brain erasure was my greatest fear. I was already marginalized. When victims are dehumanized, it's easier to be cruel and dismiss them as acceptable losses.

Sitting with my knees tight to my chest, my head buried in my arms, I thought of old stories, manuscripts I'd edited, and movies I'd seen. Each of those heroic stories began with one person standing up, ready to push back harder than they had been pushed.

The British tough guy suddenly did not sound so tough. *Dream of vengeance all you like, you are a lone middle-aged woman. Say nothing, do nothing.*

"Be nothing and nowhere," I said. "The only way to be safe among predators is to not exist." If I'd had better camouflage, Roger would never have picked up on my trail.

The voice in my head wasn't wrong. My fear told me to hide, but anger got me moving. I got to my hands and knees to check the street. Surveying the dead, this had been no battle. It was a senseless slaughter of sick people who could not defend themselves. *The Naked and the Dead* was a good title. Norman Mailer's debut novel had in part depicted his WWII wartime experiences. He would never have imagined the same horrors visiting New York.

Up the street, the truck broke through another obstruction, and the column moved on. I checked the straps on my mask to make sure they were tight before rising from cover. The dead lay at my feet, bloody and twisted. The bullets had riddled their bodies, but every single one had a head wound for good measure. Someone had stood over each Thirder and looked their victim in the face, probably acting out some grisly fantasy about being the heroes of their own story, cleansing the Earth. They'd left the Thirders to the sun, the birds, and the rats.

The gunmen kept their prisoners alive, but they'd showed no mercy for those who'd trailed the column. If they'd just been quiet, they wouldn't have attracted such a crowd of Z-3s. Perhaps asserting dominance through cruelty was the point.

Give anyone power over others and they'll abuse it, Ovid. That's hard science.

Behind me, a scrabbling sound. I whirled to find two men, dirty and disheveled, coming up behind me. Their long beards were twisted tangles of black and gray. Barefoot and hunched, they looked much alike, but with forty years between them. Father and son, perhaps?

My muscles tensed as I prepared to run. However, the pair hurried past, sparing me a glance. So focused were they on the dead it was as if I were not present, a ghost walking amongst cadavers. The men rushed to the corpse of an old woman. The older man knelt, cradling her lifeless body in his stick-thin arms. The younger man sat cross-legged and began rocking forward and back in grief. They wept.

I'd edited a book about Chi Kung once. In meditation, when the meditator rocked forward and back like that, the author called it "knocking on the door of enlightenment" or sometimes "knocking on Buddha's door." But this was no meditative practice or peaceful ritual. The old man's face was creased with dirt and pain.

Agony, torment, distress, sorrow, heartbreak, I thought. There are so many words for pain because, although we are programmed to adore babies and puppies, suffering is fundamental to humanity.

The younger man muttered the same phrase over and over, as if in prayer. His words were in a language I did not understand. They might have been gibberish, but no witness could miss the depth of the man's anguish as he rocked forward and back, his shadow kissing the dead woman's face with each bow.

It took me a moment to realize that the pair of mourners were Thirders, too. Perhaps it was fright, not intelligence, that had made them flee the gunfire that killed their loved one. In those touched a little lighter by the virus, scraps of their old lives remained. Often this resulted in parody. I'd once passed a disheveled woman in the garment district holding a brick as if it were a phone, still posing for selfies. In theory, it should have been funny, but seeing it in person I found it frightening and sad. Some of the infected seemed to have no more brains than a smart German shepherd.

The grieving men let out a long, keening wail. They might not know their own names anymore, but they understood the depth of loss.

I thought of Carl peeking out from his brain fog to say something cogent. For instance, he would often note, "The garden needs more weeding," and, "The worms need the soil, and we need the worms."

Sporadic gunfire and shouts rose again in the distance. The words were muffled, but by their tone, I guessed the killers were still congratulating themselves and each other.

Sickened, I whispered to the two mourners, "I'm sorry. Those who did this call you animals, but they aren't even people anymore. They're monsters."

The mourners reached for each other, embracing in grief, suffering together, perhaps sharing the weight of their loss. The Thirders lacked IQ, but they possessed a quality of which Dr. Rosa assessed I was "a quart low." They had Emotional Intelligence.

"You're a sensitive person, Ovid," Dr. Rosa told me. "But that doesn't always come across as you interact with others. I've caught glimpses that suggest to me you are blocking your empathic abilities to protect yourself. You're scared to be vulnerable."

"And why not? Normies are a mystery," I'd told her. "Besides fear of starvation, what gets people out of bed in the morning? Why does anyone act the way they do? They're so unpredictable. Why do people say one thing and do another?"

"Because they're human. So are you, by the way."

Humans, with all their intelligence and organizational ability, had murdered sick, helpless people in front of me. I wasn't keen on being part of the species anymore. Given all the Thirders suffered, I did not envy them their gift of EQ, either.

I'd often doubted Dr. Rosa's assertions that great change was possible through talk therapy. Though I'd pictured my transformation as a slow evolution, circumstances had changed. Having fantasized about brutal revenge on bullies since childhood, I edged closer to my vision. My taste for vengeance grew with each step. Teeth gritted, I picked my way through the fallen to follow the marauders. It was safer to hide, but rage easily erases good judgment.

The voice in my head warned, *There is no justice.*

"People concede defeat to what they think they can't get or don't deserve," I told myself. "Maybe there is no justice. Still, we shouldn't give up on the idea. Not even now — *especially* not now."

27

CRUEL INTENTIONS

T he truck stopped at the edge of the market square. What had once been a block of townhouses, razed during the eviction protests early in the pandemic, had become our market. Amid the rubble and the ruins, survivors came together to trade goods and services. The place held the comfortable familiarity of an outdoor flea market. The marauders announced their arrival with gunfire, turning the scene into bedlam.

I ran forward, sprinting on a diagonal to emerge a block down from the marauder's truck. When I peered around a corner, a dozen gunmen stood in the beds of eight pickup trucks. I'd never seen so many Taxmen working together. They each wore a brightly painted mask. *Clown masks!* A nightmare beyond my imaginings unfolded.

Shuddering, I pulled back behind the corner of a building to catch my breath and waited for my heart to stop racing. Dr. Rosa once explained to me that my fear of clowns probably did not originate from some childhood trauma at a birthday party. That made sense since I'd never had a birthday party.

"A mask, especially if it is immobile, represents death," she told me. "Even clown makeup disguises the features and trips the fear centers in your brain because you're wary of what the clown's actual intentions are. They may have a painted smile, but you can't read them, so your thoughts turn to distrust and worries of evil intentions."

Wielding automatic weapons, the clowns fired across the square. In this case, my phobia was justified. Bodies lay on the ground before them. After a few minutes, the gunfire became sporadic. When I dared to peek around the corner again, several kiosks and tables were alight. The clowns seemed to be done firing, but I guessed they stayed to make sure no one put out the fires they'd started.

Wild-eyed, I turned to escape the way I'd come. At that moment, another pickup roared up and slid to a halt, blocking my way. I cut to my right and headed for the old post office building at the edge of the square.

From editing military thrillers, I understood the difference between cover and concealment. Cover connoted something thick, bulky, and resistant to gunfire. Concealment, in the context of trying to avoid getting shot, meant a hiding place, somewhere it wouldn't occur to a gunman to lay down fire. A concrete barrier might provide cover, but a stone building gave me concealment. Running there was the best available choice.

I had traded at the market many times in the shadow of that building. The windows on the first and second floors were boarded up. I'd had no idea anyone had made a home there. Weathered and rotting plywood remained over the main entrance, but what looked like an obstruction was really a makeshift door. The board hung by a single rusty spike and slid aside easily.

I entered the gloom and searched for an exit. That was a lesson from spy novels: To survive, keep moving. However, there was no other way out. The barred windows were too high. The rusty metal doors at the rear of the building were locked tight.

As I searched for a key to the worn padlock to the loading dock door, I heard someone breathing behind me. Whirling, I raised my pruning shears, ready to strike. A wide-eyed girl with blue eyes and bright red hair blinked at me innocently. No more than ten or eleven, she put a finger to her lips. "Momma says to tell you to be quiet. We can all hear you banging around down here."

In my panic, I'd forgotten one of the keys to survival in the thriller genre: Don't be the idiot who makes so much noise you draw the enemy to your position.

"Momma said you need to shut your filthy mouth."

"I wasn't aware I said anything."

"You yelled a lot of swears."

"Sorry."

The child beckoned me to follow. Reluctantly, I abandoned the search for an exit. Together, we hurried up a staircase to what had once been administrative offices. It was apparent several families lived there, perhaps benefiting from their close proximity to trade and commerce. There were few comforts. They'd hauled in dirty mattresses and cast them about on the bare tile floor. What had once been a large meeting room had been converted into a playroom for children. Books lined the shelves. Toys for a wide range of ages were scattered across the floor. One corner held a chessboard, a jigsaw puzzle, and a plastic sheet with large dots of various colors.

Twister, I thought. *That game was called Twister.* I vaguely remembered its existence, but I trembled at the thought of playing in the middle of a pandemic. Getting that close to others would make my skin crawl.

"This way," the girl hissed. "Hurry up!"

As more shots echoed across the square, I ducked under several hanging blankets. The improvised walls provided the squatters a little privacy from each other.

Someone outside yelled through a bullhorn. The distorted voice bounced and echoed through the market's collapsed buildings and broken walls. I assumed it was the same crazed woman from the big truck, but the sound was so muffled, I couldn't be sure.

At last, I burst past a greasy pink blanket and found myself by the front wall that faced the square. Four armed men, two exhausted-looking women, and nine hollow-eyed children stared at me. None of them wore masks. Instinctively, I took a step backward.

Two of the men holding shotguns gave me the once-over. Apparently, they decided I bore no threat and went back to peering out of peepholes in the plywood over the windows. Despite my mask's filter, a stench permeated the room. The post office must not have had running water. Bathing was a luxury here.

"I recognize you from the market," one of the women whispered. "You're the lone grower. You cut your hair, or somebody did that to you? Were they tryin' to scalp you?"

"She was alone, Mama," the red-haired girl told a thin, haggard woman whose hair was more gray than blonde. She looked too old to have a daughter so young. Too much sun is hard on fair-haired people, and pandemic living is hard enough.

The woman hugged her daughter. "Good job. I'm proud. Now watch the little ones and keep them quiet, please."

The girl bobbed her head and went straight to the youngest of the brood. She took an infant from a teenage boy. The baby was swaddled tightly in a gray blanket that had once been white. The girl cooed at the baby briefly and began to rock it back and forth in a way that reminded me of the mourners I'd just left. All the children remained quiet. I wondered if their discipline developed out of long practice or was taught using repeated beatings.

Ignoring the six-foot rule, the mother of the red-haired girl stepped so close she could have whispered in my ear. I turned my head and held my breath. She spoke at full volume like an angry teacher, urgently pronouncing each word as if she were lingering on each syllable. "We heard you as soon as you banged through the front door. You can't do that!"

"Sorry. I didn't know anyone was here."

"That was the idea. I'm Margaret. I've seen you trading at the market. I usually trade medical supplies." She tossed her head toward one of the men surveilling the square. "That tall ginger fella is my husband Tom. Until recently, his specialty was fixing people up with plumbing and making water filters. Looks like that's all over now."

"What's happened?"

"Didn't you see them roll up on us? They set fire to a bunch of kiosks. Didn't even issue any ultimatums first. They're here to make an example, marking territory."

"They'll be taxing us heavy later," Tom added absently.

"They shot a few resistors before speechifying. I won't bore you with the details," Margaret said. "Suffice to say, we can still trade, but they get first pick now."

"Do you know a woman named Adilah? She's a friend who's here most days. She and her group are in burkas — "

Margaret shook her head. "Don't know no names. We stick to ourselves."

"I've had run-ins with three Taxmen since last night," I said. "I've never seen such a large group so organized. Usually, they fight over resources, robbing each other as much as they come after us."

"Get with the times," Margaret said. "These arsonists and killers don't call themselves Taxmen. They said they're — "

"Memory Keepers?" I guessed. "Someone told me they were supposed to be a myth."

"That myth just killed a bunch of our friends," Tom muttered. "At least they died fast. Unless we get out from under the new system, I think the rest of us will die slow. Should make tracks out of the city. With these assholes in charge, we're done."

28

MEET THE NEW BOSS

"First they set fire to tables and kiosks," Margaret said. "Then they shot anyone who dared to object."

"What is the new system?" I asked.

"They take what they want," Tom replied. "We get the crumbs."

A fresh tear tracked slowly down Margaret's dirty cheek. She turned away and moved to her husband. "We can't keep living like this. We have to leave."

Tom shook his head. "But how's that going to end? We run off to another borough or try to get out of the city altogether? What then? We'll be too far away from the few people we know. People trade us stuff, we trade to others who know us. The logistics won't work, honey. It'd be like starting over from nothin'."

"We'll make new contacts or find something new, get new skills or — "

One of the men piped up irritably. "I don't know if you guys heard, but since way back when the lockdown cycles started, the Learning Annex is closed."

"We may as well be Thirders," Tom said. "Better off with a smooth brain, wandering around hardly knowing where we are."

Fresh staccato bursts of automatic fire rattled across the square. I dropped and clamped my hands over my ears. Closer to the floor, I felt safer. The children stayed quiet, but as new rounds of gunfire *rat-a-tat-tatted*, several of the kids followed my lead and put their hands over their ears, too. They squeezed their eyes tight to shut out the world.

I did the same thing when my parents fought. Comparing my small traumas to theirs seemed silly now. These children would never get to speak to a therapist. They'd have to suck it up and keep quiet. Survival leaves no spare time and demands so much energy, even complaining about being tired is a waste. Comparing my history to their future, I felt ashamed.

The men kept to their posts, peering through their peepholes. "They're not shooting any new people, I don't think," Tom muttered. "I think they're just shooting into the air."

"You aren't sure?" one of the men asked.

"It's not exactly like I have a full field of view here, Daniel. I'm tryin' to spot killers through a knothole. If you want a full murder, weather, and traffic report, why don't you go downstairs and poke your head out? If you don't get your head blown off, you could romp back up here, and we could get more fully elucidated on how screwed we are."

A couple of the children whimpered. Margaret shot her husband a censorious glance.

"Sorry, everybody," Tom muttered. "It's just the pants-crappin' terror talkin'."

Eschewing social distancing out of necessity, I leaned close to Margaret's ear. "These men have guns. Did they get any of the Memory Keepers or — "

"The marauders got machine guns. We've got shotguns and a couple of hunting rifles," Margaret told me. "The guns are to make the kids feel better. If we actually have to use them, it's over. There's a lot more of them than there are of us. We need an army — "

"*Sh*," Tom ordered. "They're talking again"

The Memory Keepers used some kind of public address system. "Attention, skids! This is your wake-up call and your only reminder!

All traders are subject to search and seizure. You *will* provide a full accounting of your wares. We'll leave you enough to live on, but the flow is always to the Memory Keepers first. All our questions are to be answered honestly and without hesitation. This is still the land of opportunity! Pursuit of happiness guaranteed, right? That's what we're doing! We're chasing glee."

My gaze drifted from face to face around the room. The children were frightened. I expected that. It was the look on the faces of the adults that bothered me more. No one put up a brave front. No one looked defiant. They were beaten.

"The age of haggling is over!" the disembodied voice continued. "We demand. You give. We let you live. Hold out on us and punishment will not just fall on you alone. Retribution will fall on those you trade with, your loved ones, your friends, and anyone you are found with. We are not messing around. I'd ask if you understand, but I don't care. The dead here today didn't understand. They tried to resist. Ask them how that worked out."

After a long silence, Tom told us the Memory Keepers were still in the square. "I think they're conferring."

The group I'd walked with early that morning were down there somewhere. If I hadn't gone off to check on my gardens and been delayed by Cheryl and the Taxmen, I would have been in the square.

"How many did they kill?" I asked Margaret.

"We took the children up here as soon as we saw them roar up in their trucks. You could tell right away they were amped up and looking for trouble. When I looked back, I saw the first Molotov cocktails thrown. No warning. The fire was the warning, I guess. Most everyone ran. From what little I saw, it looked like they were shooting randomly. Just marking their territory is all. They didn't have to do all that. We were already terrified."

Horrors, hatred, havoc. Establishing dominance and terms, I thought. *Shoot more now, waste fewer bullets later.*

"I don't know what happened after that." Margaret's voice cracked as she added, "No time to do a body count. Just running and hiding. We're the little bunnies. They're the hunters."

The voice of the Memory Keeper in the square reached us again. "We will be back tomorrow, ready to accept your tributes. Be here by noon. We've been watching all of you for weeks. We already know who you are and where you live, so don't even think about not showing up. If we have to come to you, you will not like what happens next."

"I don't like bullies," I said.

Margaret shot me an accusatory look. "Yeah? What are you gonna do about it? What can any of us do about it?"

"Something."

"What?"

"I don't know yet, but when it happens, I'm sure it will have to be precipitous and lethal."

The British tough guy whispered: *You've been scared all your life, Ovid, but you're getting braver.*

29

BAD

Long blasts from car horns sounded across the square. Tom, still at the window, broke into a grin.

"What is it?" Margaret demanded.

"The playing field just evened up. The militia has arrived! I'm going down there."

"No, you're not!" his wife insisted. "Stay here! If anything happens to you — "

Tom was already headed for the exit. "There's a bunch of them, and it looks like some of the Memory Keepers have already left. There's only one truck down there and after all their bragging, threats, and ballyhooing, I want to look them in the face when the Watch shows them what's what."

Margaret caught his sleeve. "Don't go. Please."

"They'll need a witness to help sort this out. Stay with the children, Margaret. It'll be fine."

She stood in his way. "Let the Watch intervene first. They've got the real firepower."

I stalked toward the exit.

Tom called after me, "Where are you going, stranger?"

Casting a glance at his children, I muttered, "I've got less to lose."

It wasn't bravery or self-sacrifice that spurred me on. Anger propelled me out the door and down to the front steps of the building. I paused behind a pillar to survey the market. To my left, two militia trucks stood at the edge of the burning square. To my right, the last of the Memory Keepers' raiders stood by the truck I'd followed. In front of me, I glimpsed perhaps a dozen men and women of the Watch advancing toward the raiders, weapons up and ready.

The woman with the bullhorn bellowed into the device as if she didn't trust it to amplify her voice. "C'mon! C'mon, get some!"

I spotted Barry Cupper. Virgil's friend was hard to miss. Tall and commanding, dressed head to toe in black Kevlar, and carrying an assault rifle, he didn't look at all like the soft-spoken, gentle giant I'd met the night Roger attacked me. He led the way, stalking through the smoke.

The woman with the bullhorn seemed undeterred. I soon found out why. Two squads of the Watch emerged from the smoke blanketing the market. Barry was perhaps twenty-five yards from the Memory Keepers' truck when they pulled down the canvas to reveal a heavy machine gun.

Barry fired one shot in the air. It was as if the whole city stopped to listen as the shot rang and echoed. "Hold on!" he yelled. "Let's talk about this!"

The woman took a seat behind the gun but held on to her bullhorn. "You want to talk?"

Barry's voice boomed, "Diplomacy is war by other means! Let's try that first! No more people have to die today! Get out from behind that gun and we'll talk!"

She did as he asked and waved him forward.

The rest of the militia followed Barry, wary and ready, but not ready enough. The woman raised her hands to show they were empty but for the bullhorn. However, the bullhorn was the weapon. "We are the Memory Keepers, independent, strong, defiant, and in charge! You sheep will feed us! Let's eat!"

As signals go, it was pretty corny. To the snipers the Memory Keepers had left lying in wait, it was sufficient. The trap was sprung, and their attack was so expertly timed that as they fired on the Watch, it sounded like one loud shot echoing across the square. Most of the militiamen fell dead at once. The rest scattered, heading back for the cover of smoke. Barry was among those spared by the first fusillade.

From my position, I counted eight dead militiamen. The woman with the bullhorn took a moment to gloat, cackling. It was an evil, grinding sound.

From the bed of the truck, a new figure rose to take a seat behind the heavy machine gun. I caught only a glimpse, but at the sight of him, naked from the waist up, my knees went weak, and my bowels turned watery. Skinny and bald, the young man's bare torso was painted white. His was a painted face, that of an evil clown. He opened fire, spraying those in retreat, firing into the smoke in short, fast, careless bursts.

His aim was erratic. A burst of rounds tore into the old post office, chunking out bits of stone and wood. As I threw myself down and crawled behind a pillar, children screamed above me. I hoped Tom, Margaret, and the others could still count themselves among the survivors, but I didn't dare check. Sure the clown's fire or a sniper's scope would find me next, I couldn't move. If I could have dug a tunnel straight down, I would have.

Hoping to see Barry emerge through the smoke at the militia's trucks, I scanned the battlefield. Those who had stayed behind, either to guard their stall or help put out the fires, scattered left and right, unsure which way escape might lie.

With my back to the stone pillar, I slid up to a standing position, craning my neck, trying to spot Barry. Instead, I saw a familiar figure through the smoke. My jaw dropped as I spotted the sling on his right arm.

Roger!

My assailant from the night before carried two backpacks, one slung over his left shoulder. The other hung in his left hand. He tossed the first behind the wheel of a militia truck. Roger tossed the second into the back of the other vehicle and ran.

Roger, bomber!

I didn't think about the snipers. Sprinting into the open, I didn't even consider the chance of getting cut down by the clown's machine gun.

People trying to escape the mayhem fled the sound of the heavy gun. Many were headed toward the trucks. Pandemonium swallowed my words so no one heard me shouting, "Stay back! Get away from there!" My heavy backpack bounced on its aluminum frame, and the belt at my waist yanked and pulled at my torso with every step.

I knew from books I'd edited that to defy snipers, one should run in a zig-zag pattern, doing the unexpected. However, a straight line is the shortest distance between two points, and I was out of my mind. I ran in a straight line, screaming, warning everyone as much as my breath would allow.

I lost sight of Roger in the smoke and couldn't see Barry at all.

Don't be late! Don't be late! You hate being late!

Then ... *detonation.* Both trucks exploded in blindingly bright white bursts. Twin concussions shuddered over my pounding heart. I was still far enough away that all I felt from the explosion was terror and a hot blast of air that pushed me back. It was as if a giant hand had given me an angry shove. My ears rang, but I did not fall.

Screams of anguish reached me. Stunned, I froze before twin towers of smoke roiling above fierce flames. Survivors of the initial attack must have thought the Watch's vehicles were their salvation.

"And now they're dead," I whispered.

I should have unclipped the belt and let my heavy pack slide from my shoulders, but I'd had tunnel vision. I'd thought only of the distance between me and the innocent lives I hoped to save. That miscalculation had slowed and probably saved me, but it didn't do the bombing victims any good.

Burning and blackened bodies lay around the trucks. The heavy machine gun ceased, but the market was not quiet. Fires crackled. Many cried out, some for help, some in pain and grief. Somewhere, someone begged for water. Something in the wreckage, perhaps a cache of ammunition, exploded anew.

Numb and in shock, I became a statue, rooted to the ground as if stuck in deep cement.

The British guy asked, *What now, Ovid?*

"Disappointment. That's all I've got. Disappointment in everything and everyone."

The honey fungus is the largest single organism on Earth. It looks like a bunch of mushrooms, but it's all one. Once upon a time, I'd believed that people were like that, appearing to be separate, but at our roots, mostly the same. Shared experience should have united us against our common enemy. Empathizing and resonating with others was the reason fiction worked. In relating to others, we held up mirrors to ourselves. The phenomenon did not translate to nonfictional challenges. Instead, when the pandemic struck, we broke into tribal factions, pandered to crazed outliers, and decreed facts were subjective. Relying on patriotism failed to support public health measures. Community became an empty word.

Fresh bursts of gunfire erupted from the other end of the square. The Memory Keepers were not done.

You're out in the open! Head for the smoke!

I found my legs could work again. With no conscious thought, I zig-zagged among the tables and stalls, searching for a hiding place. Coughing and choking on thick smoke, I was soon staggering, almost blind.

That's how I found Barry Cupper. I almost tripped over him. Covered in blood, he was so ripped up I had to look away. His armor had not been enough to save him from the heavy machine gun's rounds.

The woman with the bullhorn was still cackling and crowing over her victory. In my mind's eye, I saw the clown's bright red smile as he searched for a target.

Rage is too small a word for the enormity of what I felt. "Roger, you're on my list. I will find you ... you and every damned Memory Keeper. When I'm done, there will be nothing left of any of you but bad memories. Haunt me if you like. What you've done will keep me up at night. What I will do to you will cure my insomnia, and I'll sleep with a smile on my face."

When rage is impotent, it builds upon itself. As frustration's pressure builds, an equal and opposite reaction is the only law left. Another explosion of violence was imminent.

30

WORSE

Nauseous, I doubled over as a bullet whizzed past my head. If I hadn't been bent and retching at that moment, the sniper's round would have ripped through my neck, probably decapitating me. Instead, it took a chunk out of the frame of the stall beside me.

Tumbling to the ground and rolling, I hoped it might appear I'd been hit. I crawled into the nearest stall, hugged my knees to my chest, and bowed my head, trying to make myself so small the world would leave me alone. It didn't work when I was a little kid, and it didn't work then, either. The Memory Keepers' triumphant shouts went on and on, and they were sweeping the market to ensure their victory over the Watch was. complete. Scrambling, I hurried to conceal myself within the next stall, a cramped space consisting of four tables and a flimsy tin roof. Hand tools surrounded me.

Barry Cupper's right eye stared at me, curious and somehow dreaming all at once. His left eye wasn't where he'd last left it. Thanks to the evil clown, that eyeball was closer to his chin.

"Sorry, Barry. You deserved better. We all do."

I was trapped, both by the Memory Keepers and Barry's dead

stare. Then Barry gave me a last bit of parting advice. His mouth didn't move, but I heard his voice in my head: *Fade, Ovid. Fade to black.*

There was nothing with which to cover myself so I grabbed a rusty ball-peen hammer and curled up in a ball in a corner beneath the display table and hoped to become invisible.

"Invisible? Like in high school?" Dr. Rosa asked. "Tell me more about that."

I wasn't hiding from the Memory Keepers in a burning market anymore. I sat on the ugly, yet comfortable, paisley couch in my therapist's office.

"When bad things happen, fading away and being somewhere else is my superpower, Doctor."

"Given all you've told me about your past, do you think it might be more helpful to try to stay in the moment and not 'fade,' as you put it? You know, deal with the here and now?"

That was the most blatant directive Dr. Rosa had ever given. Upon our first meeting, she pointed to the box of facial tissues that sat within easy reach. "I never hand anyone the box," the doctor noted. "The subtle social cue I want to avoid is telling you to shut up. This is a safe space to talk and get out whatever you need to, okay? Be it tears or words, let them flow."

Safe space. Sedate pace.

"I suppose if you're going to dissociate, it's a compliment coming back to fond memories of your time in my office," Dr. Rosa told me. "People with guns aren't hunting you in a burning market. You're on my paisley couch, comfortable and relaxed. If you concentrate, I bet you can smell the caramel whip I put on top of my espresso."

I did smell caramel. My shoulders loosened and the tension in my jaw eased. I was unusually relaxed in her presence. Though she rarely offered advice and let me supply my own answers, telling me what to do would have been the easier course. After all, she seemed to have her life together and I didn't. When I called her on her passive therapeutic style, she smiled and told me, "All good psychotherapists are a little passive-aggressive that way. If you do the work and come to your own conclusions, you'll value those discoveries. If I tell you how to fix your life in a handy ten-item to-do list, you won't really do those things, and I'll be out of a well-paying job."

I laughed, but in a rueful way.

Dr. Rosa sat back, crossed her legs, and tapped her pen on her pad. "As we concluded our last session, you said that this time you wanted to talk about a difficult phone call with your father."

"Yes. It was the spring my mother first got sick. Dad had the farm by then, but he let other people run the day-to-day operations. At that time, his work took him away a lot. He used to be a circuit judge. He'd worked as a lawyer for a long time, but once he became a judge, he felt entitled to more respect than before, deserved or not. His word was law, and he was always on the job, always judging. The Fairweather family! Where criticism is love and hate is humor!"

"Where were you at this time?"

"That spring? Away at chess camp. Another kid from Poeticule Bay told me my mom had been taken by ambulance to a hospital in Bangor. Dad didn't tell me. I had to hear it from a neighbor kid who'd heard it from his uncle."

"And when you called home, what was that exchange like?"

"Mom had gone for some tests, but she was back home by the time I called. Dad answered, not her. Right away, I knew he'd been drinking. I asked to speak to her."

Dr. Rosa looked confused. "Did you get along better with your mother at this time?"

"No, but I was trying to be a good daughter. Calling her and acting concerned seemed like the right thing to do."

Dr. Rosa nodded for me to continue.

"I didn't get to speak to Mom. Dad was ... well, he was verbally abusive, more so than usual. He said several hurtful things, personal things. He called me a control freak and said he was smarter than me ... much smarter."

"How did you deal with that outburst?"

"I didn't, really. I got quiet, didn't say much except that I was hoping to check on Mom. He failed to acknowledge that, didn't even tell me how she was. It was mean and uncalled for, undoubtedly fueled by his drinking."

"How did you resolve this conflict with your father?"

It was my turn to look confused. "Resolve? Nothing's ever resolved. I remember the breaths of his pauses as he berated me."

"So you carry grudges."

"In a bucket around my neck, yeah."

"And years later, you still resent your father?"

I scooted forward, eager to share. "I heard this joke, once. I forget where, but it gave me an idea. Sometimes I stay up nights, replaying the scene in my head, refining it. I'm not good at telling jokes, but ... maybe I shouldn't — "

"Please, try."

"Okay, okay, so I'm sitting at the back of a church, and it's my dad's funeral. The minister is at the front, and he says, 'Here lies a good man, a loving father, a respected man, a man well-loved in his community, someone we will miss greatly.' Then I stand up and yell, 'Holy cow! How many people are getting buried today? And where's my dad?'"

"That's funny."

I hate it when people say "that's funny" but they don't laugh.

31

WORST

I sat back. "Well, as I said, I don't tell jokes very well."

"You must harbor a lot of anger toward your father," Dr. Rosa said.

"Not just him, though. I have a hard time ... "

"A hard time ... what?"

"Sharing the planet with mean people. I don't like bullies."

"I've often found patients who harbor anger don't feel power in their lives."

I suppressed the urge to roll my eyes. "Between paying rent and our addiction to eating, who's left that feels any power? In *this* economy?"

"I'm not necessarily talking about the power to buy what you want. Your father has money and resources, though, right?"

"And I don't."

"Do you feel he still has power over you?"

"Doesn't he?"

"I'm talking about self-determination, the feeling that you're making choices in how you handle stress, that you possess the locus of control within you."

I looked out her office window. Car horns honked and a fire

engine passed, its siren wailing. I did not speak again until the Doppler effect faded, and a tear had rolled all the way down to my chin. "Locus of control ... yeah, I don't know what that would feel like, Doctor."

"Let's focus on your father for now. Did anything change after that phone call where he was particularly mean to you?"

"I didn't call him again after that. He has to call me, and I keep it short so it doesn't devolve, y'know? I just get so mad sometimes ..."

"Did he ever try to bridge that gap? Apologize?"

"It would never occur to him. I'm sure he forgot about it a moment later. That's how mean people operate. They either play down their sins or deny they've transgressed."

"Interesting that you say sins rather than mistakes."

"Trying the wrong key in a lock is a mistake," I said. "Talking to me the way he did? That's a sin."

"Ovid? Do you see retribution as something biblical? Sanctioned somehow?"

"Offenders who show no contrition or make zero restitution deserve no quarter."

"That sounds ominous. Remind me to never get on your bad side."

"It might sound scary, but I wouldn't hurt a puppy. Couldn't. That's why that mean phone call wasn't satisfying on my end. After I hung up, I thought of all the things I should have told him. My best retorts come too late, and often later at night to keep me from sleeping."

"What did you want to tell your father that day?"

I took a deep breath and let it out slowly, waiting for my pulse to slow. "That he was right about one thing. I *am* a control freak. I am the way I am because everything is so chaotic! He's wrong about my intelligence, though. He felt the need to tell me he's smarter because he doubts himself. Accusations are often admissions. I wanted to tell Dad that his lecture on my shortcomings sounded like the projections of an insecure little man. Ironic, given his profession as a judge.

Every mean word drooling from his drunken piehole called into question his character and judgment."

"But you never shared those retorts with him in all the time since?"

"Not exactly. I mean, fixing broken people is your job, not mine."

"Can you clarify what 'not exactly' means?"

"I was doing a freelance book doctoring gig for a crime fiction author. I told her my anecdote about the conversation with my father. She had a villain who needed fleshing out and used the scene in a thriller. It helped the narrative and justified the villain's grisly end. Action should always flow from character, and she needed to explain where the main character's violent tendencies came from."

"I see. Grisly end, eh? How did the bad guy die?"

"Meat cleaver, then set on fire." I grinned.

Clever, cleaver, cleaved.

"Oh." Dr. Rosa wrote something on her pad.

I hastened to add, "People don't usually change much. Even if Dad apologized, I'd never believe he meant it."

"If people don't change, why are you here, Ovid?"

"Um ... I guess there's been some kind of misunderstanding. I don't really expect to change, but I'm trying to be less self-conscious about how and who I am. Mostly, I need to manage my stress. Insomnia plagues me because I obsess over every one of my mistakes and every insult or slight directed my way. I still fantasize about wreaking gory vengeance on critics who never liked anything and weaponized their sadness via mean book reviews. As if trying and failing to entertain someone was an unforgivable sin. I picture using a glowing hot branding iron that reads: *Not everything is for everybody.*"

"Does that strike you as a healthy coping response?"

I shrugged.

"You shrug a lot," the doctor observed. "That's a sign of helplessness, ignorance, or surrender. That's a story you tell yourself, but I don't believe it. Please engage. Do you think your retreat into revenge fantasies is a healthy coping mechanism?"

"Makes me giggle when I fall down in dark places." I cleared my throat and added in my best audiobook narrator's voice, "Insert audible shrug here, she said helplessly in ignorant surrender."

Dr. Rosa did not laugh or even smile. "You do joke occasionally, but it's usually an effort at deflection."

"The funeral joke is honest. Not a deflection. In fact, it's illustrative."

"This habit you have ... the voice in your head narrating your life, distancing yourself — "

"You asked me what I hoped to gain from therapy. My expectations are low and realistic, I think. The inside of my head has never seen sunlight, but it's not all about branding irons and getting even. I do replay that phone call with my father in my head a lot. That and the funeral joke. I'm not good at dealing with people, and I would prefer the company of dogs. I'm trying to find a way to live with that knowledge and still make a living. If forced to work retail, my story would be a rampage ending in a bloody murder-suicide so I'm working with what I've got here. I gotta be me."

"You doubt you can adapt and overcome your history? Your distancing techniques?"

"Sounds like you're demanding deep fundamental change? How often does that happen? It's like trying to win an argument with somebody. Never really happens, people just walk away mad. Humans are much more interested in winning than being and doing right. *That's* fundamental."

"Sometimes you talk about the human race as if you're not running alongside us, not one of us."

"Maybe," I admitted. "I don't understand them, and I've never felt welcome in the club."

Dr. Rosa put her notepad aside and leaned forward.

That must be her concerned face, I thought.

"Did the author you worked with suggest the meat cleaver, or did that come from you, Ovid?"

Someone — a man — shouted outside Dr. Rosa's door.

"Ovid? Are you still with me?"

The man cackled, far too pleased with himself.

Memory Keeper.

The rusty ball peen hammer appeared beside me on the paisley couch. It didn't look like it belonged there. I picked it up so it wouldn't soil the fabric.

"What number is your anxiety on a scale of one to ten, Ovid?"

"Twelve."

"And your pain on a scale of one to ten?"

"Ten, all in my head. It's like my skull is a pressure cooker."

Dr. Rosa tapped her notepad to keep my attention. "If you picture your health on a line between one and ten, where is it? Zero is you, full of bullet holes. Ten is total health, and all your many enemies are dead."

"I don't know!"

"Sure you do. First number that pops in your mind is right. What does your instinct tell you?"

Worth less than a nickel.

"Four."

"Okay, now put an arrow on that number. Which direction are you pointing, getting better or getting worse?"

The Memory Keeper was not articulating words, just whooping vowel sounds of victory. And coming closer.

"Stay with me, Ovid," Dr. Rosa warned. "That man is outside your safe space. It's safer — "

"Yeah." I hefted the hammer. "But from the sound of it, he's got something I need. He sounds very happy and satisfied, doesn't he? I need that. I need to go *get* that."

"Ovid, I am advising you to stay still. Stay here and be silent — "

"I know what's behind that door, Doctor. The hero's journey is waiting. I'm the protagonist. That means I have to do things, right?"

"I understand that's part of your filter, your coping mechanism, how you deal with stress, but what if this is a bad idea? You couldn't even talk back to your father. What if doing nothing keeps you from getting hurt? The technical term is masterly inactivity. Sometimes it is better to do nothing."

"That's not what protagonists do, Dr. Rosa. I know how to fix my numbers and direction." The hammer felt good in my hand. I liked the weight of it.

"Ovid, everybody thinks they are the star of their movie. You said yourself that action flows from character. You've never been truly brutal."

"I guess I might have to act the part."

"But what if your role is just an extra in someone else's movie?"

"Then I'll rewrite the script."

EPISODE FOUR

"There is no greater sorrow than to recall our times of joy in wretchedness."

~ Dante, *Inferno*

❦

"It is not necessary to change. Survival is not mandatory."

~ W. Edwards Deming

32

DOWN AND UP

D r. Rosa stood in my way, and I pushed her aside. Throwing open the door, I found a big, burly man with his back to me. The Memory Keeper stood over Barry's shattered corpse, hands in the air in triumph as if he'd won some kind of hideous championship. I could only spare the bullet-ridden militiaman one glance before tears stung my eyes. My memory would never let go of what Barry had been reduced to: bloody, limp, and ruined. In death, his image was indelible. My inability to forget any bad thing was my greatest weakness.

But it could be your superpower, Ovid. Use that energy.

There was more to the horror. The Memory Keeper held a yellow nylon rope in his left hand. At the other end of the leash was the starving girl I'd seen trailing behind the Memory Keepers' truck — the girl I'd promised myself I would save. The pitiful Thirder stared up at her captor, shivering in the cold winter of his shadow. That's when I realized where I had seen her before. She lived in alleys at the edges of the market, wordlessly begging for food, always yearning, never content. Her eyes, huge, wet, and pleading, made my heart stumble in its race.

She caught sight of me as I emerged from my hiding place. Her look spoke one clear message: Help.

The big man was giggling, a high, sharp trill empty of tenderness. I recognized the sound of soullessness when I heard it. The torments I'd endured were far less substantial than this poor girl's experience. Everyone's torments are unique, but the bully's laughter hit similar notes: derision, humiliation, superiority.

Laughter. That was his mistake.

The Memory Keeper must have heard me step into his blind spot. Or perhaps he turned to follow his slave's gaze.

Time dilated as I raised the ball peen hammer. No longer in my body, I watched the murder unfold as if I stood outside myself, a mere observer. All my life I'd been trapped in the confusion, self-loathing, and intensity of first-person present tense. As the next few moments crawled by, I found I'd suddenly emerged in the third person singular. I wasn't me. I was she, new and free.

In slow motion, the Memory Keeper managed a half turn. His smile began to fade.

Resonance, I thought. *Do you recognize the monster in me? She's been hiding for so long, waiting for this moment. I knew she would be tested. I didn't know you would be my test.*

Later, when doubt slithered back into my brain, I told myself that it wasn't me holding the hammer. It must have been that voice in my head coming out and taking over. The lies we tell ourselves are the most comforting.

The rusted tool had become a weapon. I swung the hammer down. His arrogant, mocking laughter died.

And up.

And down.

He went down hard.

I raised the bloody hammer again.

And down.

And up.

And down.

A pause ... then one more squishy smash for luck. Head wounds gush the most blood. I didn't expect gray matter on the ground and bone fragments on my clothes.

I sometimes comfort myself with the lie that I was only acting on instinct, anything to place the blame and locus of control elsewhere. But I was not someone else. That was me covered in gore. It was me in every stretched-out second.

At the time, taking action felt good and right. I had become one of the heroic killers I'd read about in so many thrillers and seen in so many movies. In fiction, the rule is the hero can do anything as long as the person they're killing is worse.

By birth, we are all connected. In attempting to own another, the Memory Keeper had unplugged from that network.

I'm going to have to own my actions, I thought, *but no one owns me. No one will own her. He broke the rules so the rules don't protect him anymore. People like him always thought people like me would lie down and take it.*

Heroes can act like villains and never feel a moment of doubt, regret, or trauma. At least, that's true of fictional heroes. Dazed, I stood over the hollowed skull I'd created. Gunfire sounded, but muffled and far away.

Dr. Rosa's voice came to me on the warm breath of a breeze. "Stay with me, Ovid! I tried to stop you, but you're committed now. If you remain here, standing over one of their soldiers, you'll die. Maybe you're thinking that's an escape, but it will hurt first. A lot. If you decide to be a character in one of those pulpy action adventures you love, you get to live. Choose! Choose now! What would one of your stupid fictional heroes do? For a change, embrace change."

"I was a nail. I am a hammer."

In this new script, I decided what was wrong or right. No conflicting thoughts zipped through my head. A life without doubt is rich and blessed. Stupid and amoral, but blessed. Only a few seconds could have passed, but the gap in time felt closer to a month than a minute. I'd arrived at a new understanding. Righteous indignation and precipitate action wasn't even half bad. It is incredibly freeing to feel no shame. There was fear of getting caught by the Memory Keepers, but I could find no sin or mistake.

The hammer had stuck in the burly man's skull somehow. With some effort, I yanked it free. Though it had seemed as light as air a moment before, it now felt impossibly heavy. The bloody hammer was useless against guns so I dropped it.

"Run!" I told the girl.

I sprinted back toward the burning trucks, away from the Memory Keepers and sniper fire. The Thirder followed, tight to my heels. I'd never run so fast nor been so sure a target was painted between my shoulder blades.

I shouldn't be ashamed, I thought, *but I could have stopped after one blow. Maybe the slaver could have survived one blow —*

The British guy stepped in. *No, never mind all that weak shite.*

Whatever I was supposed to feel, I could not find regret within myself. I escaped and survived. I had killed, yes, but I had not murdered. Words matter and there is a difference. Through brutal catharsis, I'd finally found the locus of control Dr. Rosa had long encouraged me to discover.

People who didn't understand might say, "I could never, I would never." But weren't they just fooling themselves? However, even those who believed in the right of self-defense might not forgive me if they knew how much I enjoyed my act of violence. Both sides would raise their voices in horrified condemnation if they knew my secret: I found my ball peen hammer experience therapeutic.

The British tough guy in my head was quiet, as if he were listening. For a change, the voice waited for me to speak.

"Stay strong, protect the weak," I said.

33

DON'T LAUGH

When I was in high school, some of my classmates called me the Ghost. I rarely spoke. My preferred haunt was the school library. I prayed teachers would not call upon me. I never volunteered an answer, and my lowest marks were for my lack of classroom participation. When a student in a nearby seat was called upon, I'd think to myself, *The bombs are falling close.*

Once, following a debate in history class, one of the popular girls came over and detailed my every fault. "Your voice shook and we could barely hear you. You stammered and your knees were knocking. It was really quite pathetic."

"I know," I replied. "*I was there.* These things shouldn't be mandatory. Public speaking isn't for people like me."

After that, a mean trio would follow me through the halls between classes, standing too close for comfort and taking every opportunity to mock me. The popular kids referred to them as the 3 Cs: Christine Cayhill, Joyce Cantley, and Trish Credditch. To me, they were Tormentors #1, #2, and #3. Three is my unluckiest number, so when they appeared as a group, I knocked on wood or bit my tongue before speaking to them.

"Ovid shouldn't *have* to go to class," they whined. "It's not for people like *her*." Or, "Ovid doesn't shower. Bathing isn't for people like *her*."

I put up with their harassment for weeks. Finally, I whirled on my bullies. "Why don't you leave me alone? I'm nothing! I don't matter to you, so why don't you go back to ignoring me?"

"We're just teasing," Tormentor #1 said.

"I don't like to be teased."

"What's the matter? Can't take it?"

"Why should I have to?"

Tormentor #2 smirked. "Ovid, you're *so* defensive."

"Because you're offensive."

Tormentor #3 rolled her eyes. "Don't be so sensitive. Jesus, you are such a baby!"

The trio laughed. That was their mistake. I'd just read *In Cold Blood* by Truman Capote and from that book, inspiration struck. Two bad men killed the Clutter family, undeterred in part because their victims' farm was isolated. No close neighbors made their crimes easier. We all bused to school from Poeticule County so, like me, the mean girls lived on isolated farms.

"You know what's sensitive?" I asked them. "The nerve endings in your hands. Your eyeballs are sensitive, too."

The Tormentors fell silent.

"I think about that a lot," I said. "Since you won't leave me alone, I think about *you* a lot."

"You're threatening us?" Tormentor #2 asked.

"Are you too stupid to hear it? Do I need to be clearer? No matter what you do to me at school, you have to sleep sometime. Keep it up. Keep coming after me. One night, say about three a.m. when you come out of deepest sleep, you might wake up with me standing over you. You'll already be tied up. Then we'll see what happens next. I can't wait to find out," I said cheerily.

"So you're not just weird now? You're crazy?" Tormentor #1 asked.

"I wouldn't sleep deep if I were you. Who knows what might happen?"

The trio was happy bullying others. I'd never seen their eyes wet.

For the first time, I saw them as scared little girls pretending to be sophisticated women. They tore their gaze from mine and looked to each other, suddenly unsure of themselves.

"She's bluffing, but let's get her expelled," Tormentor #1 said.

"Screw that, let's call the cops," Tormentor #2 replied.

Speaking to them as if they were dim children, I explained, "Police don't prevent crime. They show up after it's all over. But go ahead. Call them. What do you think will happen? Maybe they'll give me a stern talking to, even after I insist you're all mean liars. Maybe I'll get suspended and grounded, but I know something you don't. I know where my dad keeps the gas for our tractor. Poeticule Bay only has one fire department, girls. Almost sounds like an SAT question, doesn't it? How many fire engines from how many counties can get out in time for three house fires burning out in the country in one night?"

I told myself I was bluffing to get them to leave me alone. It's true, I never would have made good on my threats. However, it's also true that, in *that* particular moment in the hallway of Poeticule Bay High, I *did* mean it. Every word.

They left me alone after that. Everyone did. I was shunned, but that's what I wanted: a return to ghost status. They gossiped about me, of course. I heard their worried whispers in the hallways as I passed the lockers. No one wanted to be my lab partner, but I didn't mind that, either. In any group project, I'd always done the bulk of the work anyway.

A guidance counselor took me aside to tell me she'd heard rumors that concerned her. I told her not to worry. School suddenly got better after I set boundaries. Besides avoiding mixed metaphors and knowing how to use the word *comprise* properly, setting boundaries was the most useful lesson I learned in high school.

Upon graduation, I swore I'd never return to Poeticule Bay. Leaving on the train, I felt lighter and lighter with each mile put behind me. Those women were long dead from the first variant storm. Somewhere along the way, while I tried to make my way in the big city, I'd forgotten that crucial lesson from Tormentors #1, #2, and #3: boundary setting.

Staring out at the Memory Keepers' carnage, I remembered how bullies operate. They choose easy targets. As I ran my hands over my newly shorn scalp and felt the stubble at the nape of my neck, I felt more connected to the ghost who had turned on her tormentors. I'd been an easy target for too long. To survive the Memory Keepers, passivity would not do.

All things considered, I'd shown restraint in high school. It took a global pandemic and colossal loss for me to take murderous action. Someone will judge me harshly for what I did, but I don't think they should. There is only so much a human being should have to take before they strike back.

It had not been twenty-four hours since Roger attacked me. I'd witnessed enslavement and mass murder. Worst of all, an evil clown with extreme firepower was on their side. People can get used to the constant drone of danger and the dirge of steady loss, but there is a limit to anyone's patience. The Memory Keepers had come into my life fast and hard, like a jolt of shock therapy. I had to do more to push back, to do something to haunt their dreams the way I haunted my high school bullies. But what? Bashing in the head of one of their soldiers wouldn't do the job.

Hiding in an alley beyond the market, I could still hear the woman with the bullhorn. Her parting words made me tremble. "We're looking for a woman who attacked a Memory Keeper last night. Anyone who knows Ovid Fairweather, tell us where she is! There's a reward and we want her alive! For now, anyway."

Evidently, Roger was alive, and he must have remembered my strange name.

34

ADILAH'S QUILT

A couple of blocks away from the market, I had to slow down to catch my breath. The girl I'd freed followed me, the yellow rope still around her neck. The street was busy with people fleeing the burning market, but all were too deep in the darkness of pain and panic. No one paid me any attention. I beckoned to the girl, and she approached cautiously, like a dog that has been beaten, but is also starving.

"You saw me do what I did, but I won't hurt you."

She nodded and came closer. When I reached for the rope, she cowered.

"Easy, easy." I moved slower and she tolerated that approach. "That man isn't going to hurt you or anyone else ever again."

The girl allowed me to loosen the knot and slip the loop up over her head. I tossed it into the gutter and made a shooing gesture. "You're free."

She did not move.

"Go! Run! They could be coming for us!"

Resolute, the girl was undeterred.

Digging into my bag's side pocket, I pulled out sanitizer and cleansed my hands. I'd brushed the nape of her bare neck as I pulled the rope off her. The accidental skin-to-skin contact shot me with a frisson of the jitters. Briskly, I rubbed my hands together. As the girl watched and waited just a few feet away, the breeze shifted and she straightened. She crept closer to smell my hands.

"That's close enough," I warned. "And yes, that smell is piña colada. It's a mix of pineapple and coconut. I used to drink those cocktails a lot in college. It's another one of life's little beauties that's not coming back, not in New York anyway. It reminds me of a vacation I took in Orlando years ago. Whenever I catch that scent, I think of suntan lotion and tattoos. That's one thing I thought there'd be more of in the apocalypse. In all the apocalypse movies, everybody had a lot of crazy tattoos. Since we're all covered up to avoid contact, body art is a low priority."

The mute girl's steady gaze did not yield any meaning. Maybe she understood my nervous babbling and, on the inside, was screaming. Or maybe she was just as thick in the head as many assumed all Thirders were.

"Sorry, I've fantasized about killing lots of people. First time, no longer a virgin. I hear it gets easier, but I hope not. I've always hated casual cruelty. If we have to be mean, it should be a formal affair: gowns, tuxes, self-defense, a kickass soundtrack, and a truly deserving piece of crap on the receiving end."

Her eyes were wet.

"Sorry, again. You're traumatized, I'm traumatized. Let's jump in a time machine and go back to a simpler time, like before birth." I laughed nervously. She did not.

"My God, I'm hysterical, aren't I? Like the mental breakdown kind, not the fun, fun, funny kind."

She stared.

"Okay. Good talk. Go away now. The Memory Keepers are looking for me. It's not safe to be around me. If they were pissed over what I did to Roger ... well ...."

The girl remained so I dug into my pack again and pulled out a stale protein bar. I broke it in half and chewed one, enjoying the taste of peanut butter. Gently, I tossed the other half behind her, and she dashed after it. I left her to it and hurried away.

I did not get far. Ahead, four women in burkas appeared. They carried a body, and I had no doubt it was Adilah. The beautiful quilt she'd intended to sell that morning had become her shroud. The women from my morning commute had become her pall-bearers.

I ran up and blurted, "What happened?"

Nura's yellow burka was covered in blood. Weeping in grief and anger, she whirled on me. Her voice trembling, she demanded, "What do you think happened? And where were you, Girl from Maine? Why weren't you there?"

I wasn't about to touch my face to rub my eyes, so I just let the tears come until they clouded my vision. Adilah had been a hard bargainer, but underneath her tough exterior, she was a kind soul. It was she who allowed me to join the walking group to the market in the first place. She rarely spoke of her home and family, but she worked hard to provide for them.

Trying to make sense of a world where there was little to be had, Nura searched for someone to blame and settled on me. I wondered if any of them suspected it was me the Memory Keepers were hunting.

"Where were you?" Nura repeated. The others carefully placed Adilah's corpse on the ground and turned to stare at me with accusing eyes.

"What's going on here? I had to run an errand and get some supplies. A couple of Taxmen robbed me, and I got stuck behind one of the marauders' trucks on the way to the market. By the time I got there, hell was boiling over."

Elham, the youngest of the group, pointed at me. "She's got blood on her. How'd that happen? That's a lot of blood."

"It's not mine."

"Who then?" Nura demanded.

I didn't want to say I'd killed a Memory Keeper. "One of the victims," I said. "A member of the militia I knew went down."

"Fat lot of good the Watch did," Elham said bitterly. "They took forever to show up, and then they walked right into an ambush."

"Don't say that. The one I knew was a nice man."

"We don't need nice men," Nura said. "We need killers more brutal than the threat we face. How are we to survive these Memory Keepers with their hands in everything?"

"And they know everything," Elham said. "They know who we are. They knew Adilah by name. They knew all of us. The only person we don't know by name is you, Girl from Maine."

"Spies don't give their real names," Nura said. "The Memory Keepers must have been watching us and collecting information for weeks, maybe months."

My gaze fell on the bloody quilt. "Please tell me what happened to Adilah."

"She tried to argue with a gun," Elham said.

"Who murdered my friend?"

"The little white woman," Nura replied.

"The red-haired one with the bullhorn is a maniac," Elham added. "She's obviously one of the leaders. Do you know her name, Girl from Maine?"

I shook my head.

"Then you and she have that in common, *hm?*"

"Where are you taking Adilah's body?"

"To my house," Elham said. "I have a backyard. We can burn the body there. I am not very religious, but Adilah was. My partner knows the words you say over a body."

"I'm sick to death of words," Nura complained. "I want weapons and I want to fight. It's the only way to survive. We're barely holding on as it is."

"Please don't," I said. "The Memory Keepers have a lot of weapons, superior weapons. They must have raided an armory."

"Laying down for them so easily, I see how it is. So you admit you're a collaborator, Girl from Maine?"

The oldest woman of the group, Thana, looked five to ten years younger than me. Her veil hung to her chest, and her hair was in disarray. However, her presence was commanding. She stepped around Adilah's corpse and pushed to the front. "Enough! The Watch had weapons and look what happened. Our friend is dead, and she's not the only one. Leave Girl from Maine alone. Look at her. Does she strike you as spy material? She's always prattling on about books — "

"The ones who don't look or act like collaborators make the best spies," Nura said.

A lump formed in my throat. I'd walked with these women to the market and to food banks countless times, but none of them could really be called friends. And why should they trust me? I had a secret garden, and I didn't trust them to tell them my secrets, not even my real name. "Adilah has a family waiting for her to come home tonight — "

"Their place is too far," Elham said. "Someone will have to tell them, but my feet hurt just thinking about it."

"I'll do it," I said. "Tell me the address and I'll go."

Nura shook her head. "And then what? You tell them where to come to Adilah's funeral? Tell the Memory Keepers where Elham lives? That would put Elham, her family, and the rest of us in danger."

"If they don't already know where I live," Elham added miserably.

The other pallbearers mumbled something I could not hear, but their tones either rang as anxious or disapproving.

"Please give me her address," I said. "I'll tell Adilah's family so they can attend the funeral. I will tell no one else where you live, Elham, I promise."

"Promises don't carry a lot of weight with us right now," Nura said. "It's just words."

"Words are important to me," I replied.

It had been easy to intimidate the mean girls in high school, but that wouldn't work with a group of survivalists. They didn't deserve threats, either. They required honest answers. Just above a whisper, I admitted, "I am from Maine, but that is not my name. My name is Ovid Fairweather."

"The one the Memory Keepers are looking for," Thana said. "What did you do to them?"

"I cut one and I just killed another," I said. "I don't know if they know about the second one yet."

Thana turned to Elham and Nura. "Not quite so bookish as she looks. Go ahead. Tell Miss Fairweather how to find Adilah's house."

"And mine, too?" Elham asked in alarm.

"Of all the people she could be, Girl from Maine claims to be Ovid Fairweather. Under the circumstances, no one would claim that unless it were true. She's in more danger than you are. The marauders have a bounty on her head. We're more of a danger to her than she is to us."

"It's getting late and we all have a long walk ahead of us. Adilah's funeral will have to be tomorrow night."

"I can't be sure I'll be there, but I promise to tell her family," I said.

"Your promises just gained more weight with us, Ovid," Thana said. "Nice to meet you."

Dr. Rosa would have been proud of my progress in making friends. "Nice to meet you" was not a phrase I'd heard often.

As I trudged north through the broken city, it seemed I'd made another unexpected friend. The girl I'd freed from the Memory Keepers followed at a distance, mute as a shadow. Ghosts are both haunting and haunted.

35

WATCHDOGS

My trip back through the city was different from before. More Thirders wandered the streets. Some lay dead where they'd been shot. Others had been drawn out of their daytime hiding places, probably attracted to the cacophony of gunfire and explosions.

This was new. People made a lot of jokes about the virus attacking the brain early in the pandemic. Then, when it began to happen to people they knew and loved, most jokers went quiet. The addled were objects of compassion then. That phase did not last. As time wore on, we became more jaded. Survivors looked upon the infected with increasing annoyance. They'd follow people around until you fed them, eluded them, or locked them out. Shooting them en masse was a new low.

I had a general idea where I was going, but it was a part of the city I'd never visited. My destination was so far from the nearest food bank and the market, I wondered why Adilah had forced herself into such a long commute. There were plenty of abandoned homes that were more central. I assumed she and her family had been reluctant to leave their pre-pandemic home.

I took a circuitous route. Some streets were busier than others, and it wasn't just Thirders. A few people gathered outside to gossip about the attack at the market. Even though most people couldn't afford an internet connection, those who did spread the word quickly. As I passed people in the street, I overheard rumors.

"These Keepers're taking over the whole city," someone said.

Others began talking over each other, arguing that the marauders' numbers couldn't be so high that they could dominate all five boroughs.

It would take time for the Memory Keepers to take over the city, I thought, *but the fear they spawned seemed have swallowed all of New York in an instant.*

"The military invented the internet and still runs it, so they must know about the Memory Keepers by now. They aren't going to do anything about it, though. What's left of them would rather stay safe in their bunkers and bases."

"That's not fair. There's not much military left since so many got sick in the last two go-rounds of the variants. From what remains, they're guarding nuclear power plants, missile bases, and whatnot. They had to leave policing to the local militia and, man, the Watch got blown away."

"Shot some Turders right outside my door," said another.

"I thought we'd be beyond this by now, but every day it's all same shit, different pile."

A woman with a filthy bandanna over her face tried to console her friend. "Remember how it was at the beginning when we all pulled together?"

No, I thought. *I don't remember that we ever did that. Not really, not on the grand scale circumstances called for.*

As I passed some folks in front of their apartment buildings, they asked if I'd heard any news. I shook my head and strode on, pounding the pavement until my shins ached and my feet hurt.

All the way, the girl trailed after me. Somehow, that became more unnerving than being followed by beggars and catcalls. In different times, that girl would have been at home working on homework. Now she had no home, and I was more than a little afraid to return to mine. What hope was there for either of us?

When I finally reached Adilah's house, I slowed to a stop and stared. The address was correct, but the home wasn't what I expected. It was a large building, so big, that at first, I took it for a massive duplex or a small apartment building. A tall iron gate blocked the entry, and just beyond it, a teenage girl and a skeletal boy of perhaps twelve sat on the front step. Each wore dirty clothing, little more than rags. With their hair hanging in their eyes, they appeared very much like the Thirder following me. Tight leather collars encircled each of their throats. A ring in each collar connected the pair by a heavy chain that was threaded through the fence.

I turned to the girl I'd rescued. "Stay back."

My follower wasn't so far gone. Though she remained mute, I saw the light of curiosity in her eyes as she peered past me to the chained children.

"Stay back!" I pointed to the front step of a house across the street. "There. Wait there!"

She looked petulant, but she did as she was told. The girl sat on the wooden steps and stared at me as she rubbed her bare feet.

When I stepped within a few feet of the fence, the girl snarled and the boy howled. I think his was a cry of fear and pain. The girl flew into a rage at my approach. She leapt at me and banged her forehead against the fence. Her nose and forehead trickled with blood, but she cared nothing for her wounds. She glared at me like an animal that had been poked with a stick too many times.

Their dead-eyed stares made me shudder. I'd never seen a Thirder so far gone that they were that aggressive. Starvation and maltreatment had to be the cause.

My follower stood suddenly and called out, "*Sh! Sh! Sh!*"

That seemed to settle the girl's rage, and she stopped hurting herself. Suddenly inspired, I dug in my bag searching for a peace offering I could spare. I came up with a mealy apple and a small jar of nuts. I'd traded for both items earlier that week. I rolled the apple under the fence, and the girl snatched it up. She shoved the fruit in her mouth and scampered back from the fence.

I rolled the jar of nuts to the boy. He crawled for it eagerly, but seemed almost too weak to chew. As he faced me, I noticed his white lips were cracked and bleeding. He appeared dangerously dehydrated, and I instantly regretted my charity. I should have given him a little water first and less to eat. If he was as deprived as he seemed, too much food at once might hurt him.

The girl surprised me by taking the jar and offering him half the apple. As he struggled to gnaw at it, it was clear he was missing teeth.

Scurvy, I thought. I'd read about it in one of those romances where the woman is a pirate accidentally marrying a British nobleman she'd kidnapped. Despite the light fare, the author strove to make clear the signs and symptoms of the disease. It was an awful fate, but this boy's affliction was compounded by cruelty.

The girl unscrewed the jar and spilled some peanuts and cashews on the ground in front of him. As the children ate, they became less agitated. The girl looked up at me. There was no smile or nod of thanks, but she didn't look like she wanted to hurt me, either.

It was her eyes that fired up the spark of recognition. I realized who she must be, and my stomach turned at the realization. My first instinct was to deny what I knew in my heart, but I was quite sure. The infected girl had her mother's eyes.

Adilah's children! The ones she said survived the plague.

The virus had not killed them, but to say they had survived was inaccurate. The first variants took lives, but Zeta-3 was a maniac tossing wrenches into the gears of a precious factory. Feeling dizzy and nauseous, I grabbed hold of the fence to steady myself. *Oh, Adilah, the terrible secrets you kept to yourself. I wish you'd told me. Why didn't you tell me?*

No one knew how many Thirders roamed the city, or how many had perished from starvation or exposure. Carl seemed better off than many of the afflicted. I'd often thought of my friend as himself, but diluted, as if he might return to his old self one day. Then the virus really went to work, and he grew increasingly quiet. Carl had become a ghost of his former self, haunting the office tower and guarding my gardens.

The front door popped open. A tall man in his sixties stepped out. "I don't like strangers coming so close!"

"I'm not a stranger. I'm a friend of Adilah."

"So?" He brandished a small silver pistol.

"I'm here about her. Something's happened."

"Who are you?"

I tore my gaze from the children to take him in. He was white with bushy eyebrows knitted together in a permanent grimace. He wore no mask. His mouth was nothing more than a slash with an unlit pipe sticking out of it. It appeared that he did not smoke. Instead, he chewed.

Stalling for time, I asked, "Is this Adilah's residence or not?"

"It is. Get away from my watchdogs."

"They're *children!*"

He shrugged. "Used to be, aren't really now, are they?" After looking me up and down, he let the silver pistol hang loose at his side. However, when he saw my eyes track his weapon, he straightened and clasped it in both hands, as if he was posing for a movie poster.

"Like my revolver? It's an antique Webley I found in a gun collector's basement in the Bronx. I do love the feeling of it in my hands."

In the spy novels I'd proofread, his was the position of low ready. He didn't perceive me as a threat, but I had no doubt he'd shoot me anyway. Anyone who could do what he did to children —

The voice in my head had no mercy or doubt. *Kill him as soon as you can, Ovid!*

I pushed that thought away. I'd just erased an evil man with a hammer, but that didn't mean I should make a habit of it. "Are you Adilah's husband, then?"

"Yeah, what about it? Is this the day she's not coming back?"

I gave a shaky nod.

"I knew it would happen sooner or later," Bennington said. "And sooner is now, huh? Nothing's sure in this world except the bad news just keeps on chuggin'."

36

EPIPHANY ONE

The man regarded me as if his gaze were an X-ray. Finally, he nodded and lurched down the steps. Grunting as he bent to shoo the children back from the gate, I guessed his joints hurt. He didn't look like he'd be up for the long walks to the market or capable of carrying heavy loads of traded goods. No wonder Adilah had been the sole breadwinner of the family.

Despite his decrepitude, the children cowered as he neared. The boy crawled to his sister, and the girl hugged him tightly. She treated her little brother as if he were a fussy baby. I recognized their look: sensitive and smart enough to fear him.

Adilah's husband pulled a thin gold necklace over this head to retrieve the key for the gate. He unlocked it and waved me through. "You have my attention. Come in."

"What shall I call you?"

"Mr. Bennington. Get inside before someone sees you. We'll leave the watchdogs to their work." He nodded across the street. "You have a pet, too, I see."

As I looked back, my follower stood, staying put, but peering after me anxiously. The girl resumed her seat as I disappeared into the gloom of the entryway. I guessed that once I'd disappeared from sight, she'd soon become bored and distracted and wander away. When would she eat again? Where would she sleep? Would someone like the man I'd killed make her his prisoner again? And for what dark purpose?

As Bennington slammed the door behind him, darkness fell upon us. All the curtains were closed, and only one thin candle flame burned in the back room. My host became a gaunt silhouette in an ominous shadow puppet show.

"So? What's happened to my wife?"

"There's a new group trying to take over the city."

"The Memory Keepers, yeah. Tell me something I don't know."

"How did you know?"

"How did you not? Adilah's been talking about those rumors for months. Long time coming, finally here. There's a new sheriff in town, and they do *not* screw around."

She hadn't shared that information with me. She hadn't told me two of her children were enslaved as Thirder watchdogs at her gate, either.

"Do you have a child who was spared from the disease? Adilah told me — "

"Nah, that nonsense was Adilah's fantasy. The stories she told herself depressed me. She refused to move on and accept the world as it is. Her delusions and lies kept her going, though."

A fantasy world and comforting lies. No wonder I liked Adilah, I thought. *We were more alike than I had realized.*

"Pretending never did a thing for me," Bennington continued. "By design or by folly, seems everybody's living in a dreamworld of delusion, as if reality is going to work itself out in payroll."

"I prefer fiction because reality sucks."

"Your dreams of another reality make you weak in this one. Face facts."

Just statin' a fact.

"There's more idiots in the real world, but I acknowledge how things really are so I get to eat more and regularly."

Bennington gestured with his pistol down a hallway to a sitting room beside a large kitchen. Late afternoon light slipped through a barred window. The shadows striped us. I thought of caged tigers.

Adilah's husband sat heavily in a low, overstuffed chair. He did not invite me to sit on the stained couch beneath the window so I remained standing.

"Remove your mask and goggles," he said. "You look ridiculous and I like to see who I'm talking to."

"I don't — "

He waved the gun in my direction. "*Buh, buh, buh!* Shut up and get on with it."

Needing to get this encounter over with quickly and hurry home before dark, I stepped back to remove my protective gear. I felt naked. "I came to tell you the Memory Keepers shot your wife."

"I am not shocked. Bound to happen. Told her so myself. Did you know she was thinking of running away? She threatened to do so many times. With all her talk of taking the kids and getting away, she was one ornery woman."

"It happened at the market. The Memory Keepers attacked. When the militia showed up, the marauders had an ambush ready. It was a bloodbath. Adilah's body is with friends. They're going to hold the funeral tomorrow — "

"Never cared for funerals. When things are over, they're over. What have you got in that big pack?"

"Actually, I have something for you. Something owed. May I?"

Bennington motioned for me to proceed and rested his pistol on the arm of his chair.

"Adilah made a deal for you." I held out the two little pills.

"Stimulants?" He leaned forward and I dropped the caffeine pills into his upturned palm.

"You hiked all this way to give me these?"

"I owed them. Mainly I'm here to tell you where to find your wife's body."

"No sense me making that trip. I can say goodbye to her from here." His thin lips spread into a small cruel smile that revealed yellow teeth around the stem of his pipe. Stumbling over my words, I muttered something about paying his respects and cremating the body.

Even if I could sense their emotions, the hearts, minds, and motivations of others were a mystery, their choices unfathomable. In fiction, the narrative makes more sense than real life's twists. To avoid annoying readers, I worked with authors to bring verisimilitude to their stories. Even if the pulp was about hippie vampires battling robots on the International Space Station, we strove for some thread of internal cohesion to help suspend disbelief. Most readers met us halfway and understood they were on a roller coaster ride of the mind, getting a break from doing taxes and working themselves to death.

The real world was a drastic contrast and a conundrum. People frequently did stupid things. Villains had more audacity. Politicians would do or say anything and expect people to believe their lies (and we often did.) Reality had no writers to provide personal histories and helpful insights through omniscient narration. Fiction stuck closer to logic.

No wonder I preferred books to people. I also preferred everyone to Adilah's unfeeling widower.

37

EPIPHANY TWO

"These Memory Keepers ... I hear they're a cruel lot. Did they touch her first?" From his mouth, the question connoted more prurient interest than concern.

"I'm told she charged at them. She was among the first to fall. I didn't see it, but her friends assured me it was quick."

"Ah, Adilah. She put on a fierce front, didn't she? I knew that woman as no one did. She became a few different people after the kids got infected. She had one face when she toddled off to do her trading and, well...." He gestured vaguely.

I wondered how she was with the children. She was at the market for most of the day, and they weren't overfed, so that left the so-called watchdogs to his care. Or lack of care.

Bennington scratched his forehead with the pistol's muzzle. "So ... where do we go from here?"

I shrugged. "I just thought you should know."

"No, no. I mean where do you and I go from here?"

I stared. "What? I don't — "

"Adilah's ride is done. What about you? With my wife no longer trading, me and the kids are destitute." He bounced the little pills in his palm. "And I'm going to need more of these, of course."

"I don't have more for you."

"You found them before. Find more." He was one of those people who drew sudden intakes of breath between thoughts, rushing on to brook no interruption. "I'm going to need a new supplier, and lucky for us, here you are. You seemed concerned about my watchdogs. You should be."

"Don't call them that."

"Turders, then. They aren't my kids. They were Adilah's from a previous marriage. She insisted they stay, even after their brains got smoothed out. Nasty business. They're mostly useless except for the noise they make when someone comes around."

"They're starving."

"Most people would do the Turders a favor and kill them outright. Adilah listened to the propaganda. She thought a cure might be coming."

"It looks like you failed to feed those poor kids anything unless she was around, am I right?"

"That's kind of personal. Don't ask about the inner workings of a marriage." He looked me up and down. "Now, to business. I'm a widower in mourning. It wouldn't do for you to get too familiar too quickly. That would be unseemly. For now, you're a trader. What can you bring us?"

He flashed his yellow grin again. "You're worried about a funeral for a woman who has earned her rest and is past caring. Forget Adilah. As for these Memory Keepers, they're a group of rich kids determined to stay rich. Good on them. They found a way in the middle of an apocalypse, American dream and all that. Everything comes and goes. It doesn't do to dwell on the little problems of the day to day."

"The Memory Keepers killed your wife. That's not a small thing."

He smirked. "And you have feelings about how I should boo-hoo about it. You said yourself she charged at them. Look, you don't know my life. If Memory Keepers hadn't done it, I might have shot her myself. Things were tumultuous around here, but they are about to get much more calm."

I tried not to stare at the gun. He wasn't pointing the weapon at me, but the urge to get it away from him was almost overpowering.

"Don't look at me that way," Bennington said. "You don't know what it's like. The dumber the kids got, the angrier she got at me. The boy showed promise with the piano before he got sick. The girl was quite precocious at math. Now look at them. No concerts or astrophysics in their futures."

"I'm so sorry for your loss," I said.

"Sarcasm. You'll want to lose that if we're to get along. What's your name?"

"Girl from Maine."

"Ah, that makes sense. I've heard of you. Adilah said you're a strange one, kind of a Girl Scout. We discussed you at some length. Kind of amazing you've lived this long, what with your quirks and all." His chuckle sounded like a rock working its way down a tight drain.

"You shouldn't make fun of me, Mr. Bennington. It's not fun for me."

He laughed some more, and I wondered how Adilah could stand him. Dr. Rosa once told me that most of our decisions are made unconsciously. We jump to conclusions and rationalize what the logic must have been after the fact. We do things and call it intellect instead of instinct. We like what we like, and hate what we hate and don't necessarily know why. We act on biases we don't even know we have. Conscious thought tunes into one radio station, but our brains are busy with the whole radio wave spectrum. I couldn't say why I chose that moment to grab the gun, just that I did.

Clamping both hands on the barrel of the pistol and twisting it backward, I ripped the weapon from his grasp. Bennington made to stand, but he was weak. I had gravity and leverage on my side of the equation, so it took little effort to shove him back down. He winced and gritted his rotting teeth in pain as I dug the pistol's muzzle into his sternum. Then I pointed the gun at his crotch. "Move an inch and I assure you, Mr. Bennington, you will be extra, double-plus, oh-sweet-Jesus, sorry for your loss."

It was a quote from a spy thriller I'd edited for a freelance client. The action was so-so, but the dialogue was wry and witty. I like to think I delivered the line convincingly. Aiming the little pistol at Bennington's groin, I felt in control.

There is a moment of peace when everything comes together. This was not that moment. Bennington's steady gaze sucked away my confidence.

Ovid, if this guy were a villain in a novel, you'd think he was over the top. What does that tell you?

"You aren't really Adilah's husband, are you? You can't be!"

A slow, sickening smile started at the stem of his unlit pipe and spread across his smug face.

38

HEATING

Bennington slapped the gun from my grip with surprising force. It spun away, seemingly in slow motion. I watched it go with a lover's yearning. The weapon clunked harmlessly in the gloom of the front hall, far from my reach.

Though his legs had devolved to a shamble, his arms and hands remained surprisingly strong. He snagged my wrist and pulled me down to him, slapping me across the face — forehand, backhand, forehand, backhand.

I planted a foot on the seat of the chair and pushed off to escape his grip. Bennington let me go, timing it so, suddenly free, I reeled backward and landed on my back so hard that the wind was knocked out of me. Cheeks stinging and jaw hurting, I tried to breathe, tried to rise. He shoved me back down, and I hit the back of my head on the wooden floor.

When I looked up, I was staring down the barrel of the pistol again. He looked ready to use it.

"Congratulations," I said. "You must be a brave man. First, you abuse Adilah's children, and now you risk getting shot in the — "

"Don't be vulgar!"

"Shot in the pants."

Bennington chuckled wickedly as he looked down at himself. "I do love these pants."

"I'll be on my way. I liked Adilah. I'm sorry she had to deal with you."

"You barely knew her, but she started off in a situation something like you're in now. You're the new Adilah."

"It's a long walk home, and it'll be dark soon — "

"You will stay. Take off the canteen. Dump out that bag. No more surprises, *hm?* If I have to slap you around again, it'll be a pistol-whipping."

Staring into the mouth of the silver pistol, I slipped the canteen strap over my head. I glanced at his face, but I didn't dare meet his eyes for long lest it be taken for a challenge. Men and wild dogs can be that way. It wasn't the threat Bennington posed that bothered me most. It was his smug smile and those yellow teeth. He chewed on the stem of his pipe, grinding on it so it bobbed up and down.

I took things out of the bag one by one. Bennington leaned down and pressed the muzzle to my forehead, forcing me back. He snatched up my backpack and turned it upside down, unceremoniously dumping out my possessions.

Everything clattered to the hardwood floor. My pruning shears fell out of the paper bag first. Then came a package of masks with extra filters; water purification tabs; binoculars; a ball of heavy twine I used to support the cucumbers and tomato plants; a Swiss Army knife; packets of sugar and salt; vitamins; tampons; vinyl gloves; spare goggles and lens cleaner; empty plastic bags; a few rags and a handful of tissues; a few bottles of expired prescriptions; my stash of protein bars; flashlight; spare batteries; a map of the city; small first aid kit; notepad; pencil; a few packets of seeds; my phone; solar phone charger; a roll of toilet paper; a change of clothes; keys; and my copy of Elizabeth Smart's *By Grand Central Station I Sat Down and Wept.*

Bennington kicked the Swiss Army knife and pruning shears away. Satisfied he was safe, he picked up the thin paperback. "Long title. Any good?"

"It's supposed to be a work of genius."

"But what do you think?"

"It's a lyrical story about an adulterous affair, love, lust, and regret written in poetic prose."

"I could read that much on the back. I asked what *you* think, Girl from Maine."

"I'm not altogether sure what's going on in the text half the time, and the author refers to armpits as 'chalices' a couple of times. I'm having a hard time getting past that."

Bennington picked up my phone. He examined the device as if he'd discovered a long-lost treasure from an archaeological dig. He touched the screen, and it lit up. "Adilah didn't tell me you were a thief, too. Who'd you get this from?"

"It's mine."

His eyes narrowed. "Doubtful. Cell phones are rarely seen, not still working anyway. And, by all that's unholy, you have a working internet connection! *Whoo!* You've got yourself the full package on your distraction engine! You military?"

"I am not."

"Your haircut threw me off the scent. Cyber coyote?"

I shook my head.

"So you're rich."

"My father is fortunate, yes."

"He pays for it?"

I said nothing. Bennington tried to slap me across the face. I leaned back slightly so I caught the tips of his fingers. It stung, but not like before.

"How did he get rich?"

"He owns a farm in a county untouched by blight. Before the borders closed, he sent me the phone. I rarely use it. Mostly, he calls when he's drunk and feeling nostalgic."

"*Mm, mm, mm!* Daddy sounds like a bad boyfriend! But would he welcome you home?"

"It's all he talks about."

"You've got a rich daddy who wants you to come home, and you haven't escaped the city *yet*?"

"Obviously."

"Borders may be guarded, but they are permeable. Is it pride or stupidity that's kept you from doing the smart thing and sneaking home?"

"Pride or stupidity? Can't it be both?"

"Explain yourself."

"That's farther down my neural labyrinth than I'm prepared to share. I'm not your monkey. I don't dance."

"Aw, did Daddy hurt you or something?"

"Not *physically*."

I used to think I'd write an autobiography. It would be titled *All the Scars You Cannot See.*

Bennington chuckled as he slipped the phone into his pocket. "I look forward to seeing what the internet has to offer. I haven't seen that far shore in ages. Maybe I'll call up your rich daddy and ask if he wants to adopt me. Or do you think he'd pay a handsome ransom?"

"That wouldn't work out well for you."

"Why not?"

"I'd rather die." *Or kill.*

Bennington chewed on his pipe thoughtfully and proceeded to inspect the prescription bottles.

"They're all expired," I said.

"If they had no value, you wouldn't have carried them all this way. Sleeping pills, antidepressants, anti-anxiety..." He held up a bottle to show me the label. "Is this you?"

The prescriptions were mine, but he didn't need to know that. "Looted from empty houses."

"Probably still good enough, though," he said. "They can lose their punch, but I don't think they'll kill me just because they're old. Hey, it occurs to me that we haven't been properly introduced. My first name is Pierce. And you, Girl from Maine?"

"Just Girl from Maine," I said. "That's all."

"Hardly. What are you? Forty?"

"Thirty-eight."

"Well, we're all younger than we look these days, aren't we? Got a man somewhere?"

"A dozen. They know where I am, and they'll be expecting me back."

He sneered. "Yes, yes, sure, sure. Adilah said you were alone. If you had men around, you would have brought them with you."

Given what he did to the children, he must have been accustomed to inspiring fear. I tried not to tremble. Failing to detect the depth of my rage, he assumed I was scared.

Bennington sat in his chair again, but this time his aim did not waver. "What were we talking about before you got rude? Oh, yes. We'll start with supplies for me and the children. From what Adilah told me, you should prove a capable provider in troubled times."

"I can't afford to carry three of you. You'll have to trade for it."

"Since you seem to care, how about I trade the continued safety of those watchdogs out front?"

"Don't call them that."

"Watchdogs," he repeated. "In fairness, I should have put them down long ago. That's what you do with rabid dogs, even if they're puppies."

"They're sick children."

"Burdens is what they are. They can be trained to do simple tasks. Mostly I get them to dig trenches in the backyard. That's where the poop buckets go. When in need of a whiz, I usually pee out the back window, but the kids are useful for the rest as long as I don't turn my back on them."

"You are a disgusting person."

"Before the variant storms, I was a different man. You were probably different, too, before all this."

"Everything changes, nothing lasts."

"Methinks you haven't changed enough."

"A guy who uses 'methinks' without irony shouldn't lecture anyone about change."

"With that mouth, it must be more luck than skill that's kept you alive. Still and all, the children and I are in need. I hope you'll agree to fulfill our needs."

"I am not the new Adilah — "

"Why not? I'm still the one with the gun."

My cold rage shot up past simmering, about to boil over.

39

LION

"Now, maybe you can finally settle down and answer some questions," Bennington said. "You're in my home and I need to get to know you. What's your real name, Girl from Maine?"

"Nobody."

He sighed. "Not satisfactory, but since it's not that important, we'll come back to that. Right now, I'm most interested in all the blood on your clothes. What did you do to whom?"

"What had to be done."

"You sound so sure of yourself."

"This is what moral superiority sounds like."

"Arrogance in a stubborn person always leads to misadventure. Adilah had to learn that. You think you won't play fetch for me? I assure you, you'll work and even smile when I tell you to. Not that I care particularly, but maybe you'll come to believe that smile. Hate takes up too much energy, and sorrow drains the will. People find comfort in being led. Sheep crave the comfort of the flock. Having someone else in charge absolves them of responsibility."

Fresh apprehension slid over me like a heavy itchy blanket. I'd put up with a lot of mental and verbal abuse in my life. What if I did accept a new leash and a new lash? Surrender *was* easier.

Careful, Ovid. Do not backslide now.

Killing a man in grisly fashion had taught me it was easy to accept what I once thought unacceptable. Before the viral apocalypse, children dreamt of becoming rock stars, going to Mars, and saving the world. Then, they grew up and found themselves in dead-end jobs, wondering what happened. Somehow we stopped aspiring for more. When the day-to-day requires that we tolerate a nightmare, there's no room for dreaming.

"The moniker Girl from Maine is boring and linear. Since you won't tell me your real name, I think I'll call you Dancing Monkey — "

"No. I write my own script now."

"What are you babbling about? Your own ... script? What?"

I spat a string of burning curses at him. Bennington smiled and settled back in his chair, his flat stare unwavering. "Children have tantrums. Aren't you a little long in the tooth for these dramatics? You seem like a person in need of therapy."

"Tried it. I'm supposed to see a therapist twice a week, but she died early in the pandemic."

"You could just grow the hell up," he suggested.

"So I've been told, but you know what? Maturity is overrated. When you talk, I hear my parents. I hear 'Mask your pain and get pushed around some more.' When bad people do bad things, someone has to say something, to do something."

"But not you." He shook his head. "I am not your therapist. I'm a master of dogs, and you will heel, just like the rest."

I let out another string of curses. When he ran out of patience, he raised the pistol and I fell silent.

"Defiance," he said. "That's your problem. People are always going on about what the pandemic taught us, but it's all empty moralizing and bland observations. You know what the pandemic taught me? Everything changes. You're worried about the Memory Keepers. They're Taxmen, but better organized. Remember after the second wave, when the orphanages were full and riddled with plague? Remember the crowds outside of Central Park?"

I did. The smoke from the crematoriums took over the sky. We still had mask filters that smelled like pine forests then.

"They sold children into slavery because no one would adopt them," Bennington mused. "What was once reprehensible became a new standard. Better than starving and dying in a crowded orphanage, right?"

"False choice. The authorities had other options but — "

"It was *expedient*. Things change! Stop being a child and learn to go with it. Adapt! The death of others is the price of survival. Make someone else pay the bill. Everybody thinks they're so superior. You don't strike me as a great listener, but let me tell you something. You know my first inkling that everything we were fed was nonsense? When the vaccines couldn't stop the variants anymore, and federal aid didn't come, a lot of people woke up and rioted. For me, the wake-up call came when I was a teenager."

I let him talk uninterrupted, hoping to set him at ease enough to try for the gun again. Desperation does make one stupid.

"Eyes up here, Missy. Stop looking at my Webley. It's rude. Anyway, you know the saying 'I don't believe a word you say, but I would defend to the death your right to say it?' It sounded so noble, but it was silly. Listen to all the crap fools spout. Their delusions aren't worth my life. If something so fundamental as free speech was stupid, what else might be? You're old. It's past time you figured out that not everyone's life carries the same weight and worth."

I had to admit, he was right about that much.

Bennington chewed his pipe stem gleefully. "You think I should feel sad for poor little Adilah? She would have killed me if I'd given her the chance. I could have been kinder, I know, but needs do as needs must. Life is too short to dwell on the bad stuff."

"I have an eidetic memory for the bad stuff."

"You must have a long enemies list," Bennington replied. "Doesn't matter, though. Your little grudges accomplish nothing. Poisons the heart."

"The weight of the past is crushing."

The voices of my enemies swirled around me from all directions:

Born weird. A procrastinator with delusions of grandeur.

She's just not weird. She's crazy.

Always bawlin', like you got leaky faucets for eyes.

Ungrateful little bitch. And too fragile by half, whining and crying about every little thing!

You've always got your nose in a book. You should look up from time to time. We live in the real world.

Just statin' a fact, Ovid. Can't you take it?

Suppress, repress, oppress.

Stomach churning, my temperature rose from deadly cold to lethally hot. Dad was right: I was a procrastinator. Instead of threatening Bennington, I should have shot him as soon as I got hold of his gun.

"You look pale," Bennington observed. "Don't you throw up in here! I don't have any cleaning supplies or water to spare!"

Abuse, misuse, screws loose.

My gorge rose. I swallowed it back down. Coughing and sputtering, I hung my head and gasped for air.

Daddy issues, tearful tissues ...

I shot Bennington a hard look. "I'll find a way to purge the poison."

He wasn't paying attention. Of all the things I've ever hated, being underestimated is the worst.

"Tell me, Dancing Monkey, what valuable supplies can you get for the Memory Keepers?"

"*For* the Memory Keepers?"

His prideful smile suggested he was telling the truth. "Ta-da! Surprise! I am a Memory Keeper! We've been coming a long time, and we're finally here, filling shelves in warehouses all over the city and upstate. We are the regime that will bring the world back to What Was. The new order is a pyramid scheme, and you're at the bottom. You're going to be a tiny part of the big plan, a tooth in a gear.

When you're feeling sassy, keep in mind that you're a tooth that can be knocked out, just like the dear departed Adilah."

My jaw went slack.

"Where were we? Oh, yes, you were cowering and sniveling and about to tell me your new name." His wheedling tone mocked me. "Say it, Dancing Monkey. Say it and maybe I'll give you a treat! Say it and maybe I won't shoot you in the head. Say it: Dancing Monkey."

"My name is Ovid Enya Fairweather," I whispered as I got up off my knees.

Bennington roared with laughter.

His mistake.

40

HURT PEOPLE

Bennington had the pistol. I had hate. I did not scream. Instead, my silent rage built to a flash of kinetic energy. I rose from the floor and threw my canteen at him in one smooth motion. I followed the arc of the canteen, charging fast, my head low. The canteen hit him in the forehead. It was harmless, but it gave me a second more to close the small distance between us. I was an automaton, not even caring about the gun. I just needed him to finally shut up.

He began to rise, but my right shoulder caught him hard in the gut. We fell into the chair together. With the heel of my right palm, I drove his pipe down his throat.

Pierced Pierce.

In a novel, his name might have hinted at his fate. I pushed that foolish thought away and focused on surviving the next minute. Bennington's garbled cry sounded like a small wounded bird. Choking and bleeding, Bennington wheezed as he rained blows down on my back with the pistol.

Instead of trying to back up as I had before, I crawled over him, driving my right knee up into his face. The first strike caught him under the chin, and his mouth slapped shut with a wet smack. Dazed, he stopped hitting me, so I kneed him again and again. He turned his head so my strikes caught him just below his left temple. His grip on my clothes weakened. I leapt and tumbled to the floor behind the chair.

Before he could scramble away, I reached for his right hand to grab the Webley. He was still getting some air, and his grip remained too strong for me. The only other weapon I could reach was the canteen in his lap. I grabbed it and slipped the thick canvas strap over his head. He coughed and sputtered as I pulled the strap under his chin. No time for a proper noose, I twisted the strap tight.

Flailing, he tried to aim the revolver at my head. My fear returned, but lethal machines have no time to indulge anxiety. There was no future or past, only the moment. I spun the strap once more and grabbed the canteen. Bennington's head snapped back as I threw myself to the floor. Exhaustion enveloped me, but this killing wasn't about strength or luck. I had gravity and leverage on my side. The weight of my body did the rest.

Bennington's heels drummed the hardwood. The pistol clunked to the floor as he freed both hands to claw at the strap. Somehow, he managed to yank the pipe from his airway.

I would have prayed to God, but I was afraid of drawing divine attention to myself. In the middle of ending a man's life, it's best to assume any disapproving deity is busy elsewhere. I squeezed my eyes shut and clung to the strap.

I am a hurt person. Hurt people hurt people. Hurt, adjective. Hurt, verb.

The last of his energy ebbed. His struggles abruptly ceased.

I stayed huddled behind the chair for what seemed a long time, certainly long after Pierce Bennington was dead. "Hurt people hurt people. Hurt people hurt people."

What a difference the absence of a comma makes.

My fingers ached and my palms were red and raw. Eventually, sure I was safe, I let go and collapsed, panting until my breath steadied, and my heart rate slowed. Was it my canvas strap twisted around his throat that killed him? Or did he drown in his blood first? No matter. There are no medical examiners in the apocalypse, and no more militia to act as police, either.

I crawled to my feet. I didn't want to look, but I had to see. It was Bennington's eyes that bothered me most. They were wide and staring in surprise, the whites now pink from exploded capillaries.

"You shouldn't be so shocked," I told the corpse. "Everything changes. Death is the price of survival, right? Your words, my actions, our sins. Message received?"

I searched myself for a scintilla of regret. Instead of regret, I discovered something unfamiliar: victory.

So this is what winning feels like, I thought.

The Memory Keeper at the market had been a sneak attack, and I'd been more scared that time. This time, I'd erased a monster who'd held me at gunpoint.

I began to gather my things and put them back into my pack. "A lot of bad things have happened in the last couple of days," I explained to the corpse. "I've been thinking about how I can respond differently. I'm as surprised as you are. It all just kind of built up. I don't think I could have done this even a week ago. Big changes don't often happen all at once, but I feel like I'm crossing the bridge between contemplation and conviction, you know?"

Pierce Bennington stared into eternity with bloodshot eyes. Just as I'd read in some dreadful series about a funny and barely compe-tent hit man, the dead do indeed look drunk.

"I suppose I might thank you. You were the last straw that broke my resolve to ... to ... I don't know ... still be the old me. Being me was never any great shakes anyway."

With blood dribbling down his chin and staining his shirt, Pierce Bennington did not appear sympathetic to my concerns about my recent transformation.

Dizzy, I slipped to the floor to rest. For once, there seemed no hurry to do anything. "If this is what a psychotic break feels like, Pierce, it seems like a *really* good time to do it." I almost laughed, but I didn't want to be a sore winner. I'd always hated sore winners, espe-cially since I'd never had the opportunity to be one.

"Transformation isn't the right word, you know. I used to be in the brain tickle business, so I should be more precise. The right words in the right order, I always say." Shaking with nervous energy, I scrubbed my scalp with my knuckles so savagely it hurt.

Excavation, I thought. *The word I'm looking for is excavation.*

Growing up where I didn't fit, the anger was always there, but I didn't have the focus or the will to act on it until lately.

"You know, Pierce, I think the capacity to do this was always in me. That doesn't make me special. In fact, I think I just joined the human race."

That may have been true, but I hated that idea. When I got my job at Pilkington Press, Dad sent me a mug that read: Welcome to the rat race. The picture on the side showed a mouse at a desk in a cubicle with a harried look on its face.

The note that came with his gift read: Saw this and thought of you. When you're ready to come back to the farm, I'll be waiting with open arms.

To say I told you so, I thought.

I wondered what to do about the children. Reluctantly, I got to my feet. My right knee hurt, and I had to limp a little. I tiptoed to the front door and listened. The girl was crooning a sad and tuneless song, possibly to keep her little brother occupied. Peering through a narrow window at the front of the house, I spotted my follower across the street. Loyal as a well-trained golden retriever, she was curled up on the step where I'd ordered her to stay, possibly sleeping.

The sun was too low in the sky. I would have to spend the night and share the massive house with Bennington's corpse.

Finding a good supply of candles, I explored the gloomy house. Much of the home had been boarded up, probably to make it easier to heat through the winter. A large portrait over the fireplace told me this had not been Adilah's house originally. A happy family of six stared back at me. None appeared related to my friend or my victim.

"Not victim," I corrected myself. "Captor."

The voice in my head was still so silent, I almost missed it. If my father were present, he would have thought he was helping by reminding me, "Born weird."

I shouted through the house, "Shut up! Shut up! Shut up!"

I yelled so loud, my voice rang off the walls, as if sound could shine and light the way. I screamed at the past until I was hoarse. When I finally stopped, I heard the children's agitated howls from the front step, as if I were a wolf and they were my pack answering my call.

"Don't worry, kids. You've been through too much. I know what that's like. I'll feed you and I promise I'll never be mean."

If Dr. Rosa were at my shoulder, she would have whispered gently, "Is that compassion or is this penance for what you've done? It's true that hurt people hurt others, but weak people hurt others, too. Are you sure you want to leave this unexamined?"

After a beat, I answered the empty room, "Words were my thing. Now deeds are my thing. As for why? Who cares why?"

Of course, I cared, but I'd had more than enough therapy for one day.

41

ALONE

W hen hunted, rabbits run in circles. As darkness fell, that's how I felt, anxiously moving from room to room. Alone in the house with Bennington's corpse, my breaths became shallow and quick. The walls leaned closer as oxygen drained from the atmosphere. Tiptoeing around, I discovered that shadows have various qualities: short, shallow, and soft, or long, deep, and hard. That night, every shadow became a dark omen.

Without streetlights, Hell's Kitchen was a dangerous labyrinth. I could not navigate the streets home safely, not until dawn. If I dared to venture outside, my flashlight would act as a beacon. Muggers and Thirders targeted anyone going solo at night. The infected might stand in my way, creating a bottleneck, or follow me everywhere and attract more attention. With the Memory Keepers' bounty on my head, I did not need that.

We want her alive! For now, anyway.

I sat with my head in my hands as guilt washed over me. I did not feel I'd sinned in bludgeoning the monster at the market. Strangling Bennington didn't make me feel terrible, either. It was Adilah I'd wronged. I'd assumed too much about her. She had coped with tragedies and blackmail, and I'd had no idea. Worse, I'd cheated her.

Perhaps that's why I had really come all this way. My deception seemed a clever ruse at the time, but a couple of caffeine pills had set me on this path.

A deal's a deal, she'd said.

Author of my own misfortune, coming this far had been a stupid risk. I didn't want to believe a conscience was a disadvantage. However, I was only scraping by while sociopaths were establishing an empire. The Memory Keepers seemed unbound by rules, doubt, or fear.

Taking deeper breaths, which didn't really help at all, I got up and resumed my search of the house. Canned goods, batteries, and anything that would help me grow crops were all on my agenda. However, weapons and ammunition had become my highest priority. I couldn't stop the Memory Keepers hunting me by throwing rotten tomatoes and hurtful words.

The mansion was massive by any measure, but especially for New York. Even wealthy New Yorkers lived in smaller residences compared to any old Victorian home in Maine. Whoever had lived in this place must have been billionaires. It wasn't just the biggest house on the block. It must have been the largest private home for many miles.

Most of the rooms stood empty. All the bathroom fixtures lay shattered. What remained of the toilets jutted up from the floor like broken teeth. Furniture had been plundered. Hooks and outlines on the walls suggested the previous tenants had been art lovers. Maybe thieves took everything early on in the pandemic. Or perhaps Adilah had traded it all away after she'd made her home out of this sad relic of a palace.

It was easy to imagine this house fully decorated for Christmas, a home full of light. I imagined the smells I associated with the best times I'd had over Christmas holidays in Poeticule Bay: cinnamon, turkey, and freshly baked bread.

In What Was, the owners must have entertained lavishly. Standing in one of the great rooms, I pictured enormous feasts catered by servers wearing white gloves. Salons and guest poets in the summer, charity fundraisers in the fall. Elite, pretty, and happy people who assumed themselves immune to downfall. So used to continuous success, they never anticipated their dreams would end.

I stood where important movers and shakers would have rung in each new year with laughter and expensive champagne. How many times had the mayor mingled and glad-handed here, drink in hand, confident the city would stand forever?

The mother and father were, no doubt, sure of the bright futures that awaited their beloved children. Immune to disappointment, their family legacy had seemed secure.

The variant storms crushed those dreams as the math of transmissibility became irrefutable. Last we heard, the R-Naught had shot up to 19, more contagious than measles. Almost overnight, humans became mutation incubators and virus buses.

Dr. Rosa was in my head again. "Without a future, we obsess on the past. You're disturbing sleeping ghosts and torturing yourself with these imaginings. That happy family only lives on the mantle now. For your peace of mind, leave them in peace."

"I know you're trying to help, but please shut up, Dr. Rosa."

I wished to avoid returning to the den, but it was the quickest way to get to the dining area and kitchen. On the way, I glanced at Bennington's corpse. He'd looked surprised and drunk before. It must have been my mind playing tricks, but his face seemed to have sagged into a resentful glare.

Taking a wide arc, I stuck close to the wall, and proceeded to go through the kitchen cupboards. Every few minutes, I looked over my shoulder to make sure the body was still in the chair and not looming behind me with a butcher's knife.

One of my pet peeves was movies in which actors did not check behind themselves for murderers. Jump scares come easy when the victim fails to maintain situational awareness. It also made me itch when actors failed to keep their eyes on the road when speaking with someone in the passenger seat. I'd walked out of movies for these sins, and now I was trapped in a horror movie with no easy escape to the lobby.

Assessing the kitchen cupboards, it seemed Adilah, a woman I considered a relentless barterer, wasn't as successful as I'd thought. Nothing of value could be found in plain view. I found a box of salt and numerous spices. However, moisture had gotten to them so those powdered goods were clumped, not worth carrying all the way home.

I had better luck in the pantry where a stash of canned goods was tucked to the rear of a lazy Susan. Crawling halfway into the cabinet, I dug out several cans of salmon, beets, cranberry jelly, peas, and carrots. If they weren't spoiled, the canned soups with chunks of meat would be a nice change of diet.

One find excited me. It was a box of cornbread mix. I could hardly wait to make a pan of cornbread and binge on it while it was still warm. The recipe on the box called for eggs. I had none and was out of egg replacer, but flax seeds or cornstarch would save the bread from becoming too crumbly.

For a moment, I wasn't a killer. I was the urban farmer, the scrounger, and the cook. Killing people had changed me, but I didn't appreciate by how much. Not yet.

EPISODE FIVE

Until you make the unconscious conscious, it will direct your life
and you will call it fate.

~ Carl Jung

❦

"What is hell? I maintain that it is the suffering of being unable to
love."

~ Fyodor Dostoevsky

42

THE TRAP WE SHARE

Failing to find more supplies in the kitchen, I was sure there had to be more treasures stashed somewhere. Adilah was not lazy, so I had to be missing something. I climbed the stairs.

Bedrooms are personal spaces. Not wishing to stir the echoes of the dead, I'd avoided going upstairs. Tiptoeing from room to room, I explored seven bedrooms. Four still contained furnishings. Judging by the clothes hanging in the closets, Pierce and Adilah had slept separately. Her closet smelled faintly of cedar. The faint smell of tobacco still hung in Bennington's room.

I wondered about the timing of Adilah's entry to the mansion. When had she taken over this palace? Perhaps she kept the picture of the previous owners on the mantle as some kind of tribute or thanks.

Though it would be difficult to heat in winter, I couldn't imagine leaving such a fine and sprawling home willingly. It was a safe assumption that the original owners were dead. Sometime later, Adilah must have moved in with her children while they were still well. Bennington had not lied about that much. The kids' bedrooms were not mere bedrooms. They were shrines to the children now guarding the gate.

The girl's room was painted in soft pastels. Some clothes were still laid out on the bed. Gingerly, I picked up a nebulizer from the bedside table and sniffed. It still emitted a faint whiff of lavender.

When I closed my eyes, lavender's scent took me to my grandmother's house in Tiverton on Big Island off Nova Scotia. She was my father's mother. Grammy smelled of lavender. The aroma of fresh bread wafted over me as I entered her house. Grammy's dining room ceiling was ornate and made of tin. I salivated at the memory of her tea biscuits and egg tarts. What I wouldn't give to feast at her table again. The curse of the fall of civilization was that I was always thinking about food (how to get it or grow it) almost to the exclusion of everything else.

Coming up by boat from Maine took hours, so we did not visit my grandmother often. When I was nine, I wanted to run away to Canada to live with Grammy forever. When I closed my eyes, I was back at her dining room table informing her I did not like beets. Then I tried them and discovered I loved the taste.

Mom complained Grammy used too much salt in all her cooking. Long before the pandemic, my grandmother passed away peacefully in her sleep. At the funeral, my mother leaned close to me and gave a stage whisper so all could hear, "Grammy would have lived longer if she hadn't used all that salt."

"It's called taste and flavor, Mom," I replied. "You should try it with your cooking."

Some women in the pew behind us tittered. Mom gave me the silent treatment for the rest of the day. The event was somewhat redeemed because my mother's silence was not the punishment she imagined.

I wished I'd been born in my grandmother's time. She would have been appalled to learn that the word *shopping* had come to mean breaking, entering, and scavenging from the dead. Sometimes it meant stealing from fellow survivors, too.

The British tough guy who lived in my head spoke sharply. *Ovid! Stay frosty!*

My mind had slipped away, entranced by the past. When I came back to the present, I was disappointed to find that the ceiling was not made of tin. I sniffed at the nebulizer again, but the scent was too faint, and the moment of peace had passed.

Feeling like a grave robber, I moved on to the boy's room. It was painted in a light blue, probably a holdover from the days the bedroom had served as a nursery. There was a bed, a dresser, and a desk. I guessed the child spent a lot of time at the desk. The computer was gone, but a gaming chair stood before a large black screen, its glass shattered and useless. The boy who was now a watchdog had been a gamer.

Games were a thing of the past, too. I'd always felt harried. Trying to make rent, I took on too many freelance gigs. More manuscripts from the Pilkington Press's slush pile were always waiting. The life of an editor was like having never-ending homework. Still, in What Was, I had more free time and fewer cares.

Shutting the bedroom doors behind me, I stood in the dark hall. That's when the panic attack hit. The Memory Keepers were already after me, but if they caught an inkling of what I'd done to Bennington, what evils might they do before they killed me?

A sudden rise of nausea bubbled up as I dropped to my knees. I hung my head and struggled to breathe until the urge to vomit passed. Sweat dripped off the end of my nose. My back was so hot the fabric of my shirt sucked to my torso. I peeled off my wet shirt and put my back against the wall to cool myself. My spine ached where Pierce had hit me with the butt of his gun. After a long while, the pain dulled to an annoying throb. Eventually, I dozed.

Sometimes you know you're in a nightmare, but that knowledge does not ease the weight of terror. I sat in the audience of a magic show. It was Vegas and Penn Jillette was performing. His partner, Teller, was nowhere in sight. Drafted, Carl rose from the audience.

Somehow, he ended up in a milk carton, the prop not much bigger than his body. I could see his worried face through the circular hole illuminated by a tiny light.

Suddenly, it was me in the carton, trapped, claustrophobic, and hyperventilating. It was like getting buried alive.

Startled, I awoke on the floor, crying, breathing too fast, pulse-pounding. Worse, coming back to consciousness did not ease my claustrophobia. My skin felt too tight. I rushed to pull off my clothes as if they were on fire.

Naked, I paced and tried to rein in my thoughts. Humans are the only mammals who wallow in the existential abyss. Caskets are tight spaces, but thinking about death and dying too much makes the body a coffin for the mind.

Eventually, my heart rate slowed, and I got my breath back. I pulled a change of clothes from my pack. Unsure how long I'd slept, I changed in darkness.

Far off, I heard something. A beat ... no, *banging*, coming from inside the house.

My mind turned to *By Grand Central Station I Sat Down and Wept*. Elizabeth Smart observed that "At night, no one is safe from hallucinations." I tried to convince myself she was right.

I told myself I didn't really hear voices in my head, too.

"It's stress plus imagination," I told myself. "Working too hard to have an ally in a war of which I want no part."

The far-off banging continued.

A tree branch of a window, perhaps, or the wind against the iron gate? Or was it someone trying to get in ... or out?

"It surely *is not* Pierce Bennington coming back from the dead." I repeated that assertion several times, but with each try, I sounded less convincing, and the impossibility somehow seemed less remote.

The ruckus continued and its pace quickened. I pressed my palms over my ears to make a seal, to shut the world out. When I moved to New York, and before I found Dr. Rosa, the voice in my head had become bothersome and filled me with doubt. It was often my father's voice back then, ordering me to return home. I got pills to quell the chatter in my brain, but that prescription was long gone.

With Dr. Rosa's help, I told myself I would be okay without those pills. Several times she reassured me, "Let's not worry about it unless it gets in the way of living your life."

Unbidden, the inner voice chimed in. *I am here, Ovid. You'll never have to face the end of the world alone. I'll save your life.*

But no one is safe from their inner voice. Despite the assurances, I feared what it might tell me. Through gritted teeth, I said, "I need you to be quiet so I can listen for danger."

The banging somewhere below me became louder and more frantic.

A terrible thought triggered my pulse to race anew: *This isn't just nerves. I was nauseous. I'm sweaty! Oh, no!*

Suddenly sure I'd been infected by one of the variants, it was as if I'd swallowed ice cubes. Too cold, they stuck behind my chilled and pounding heart. The hair on the back of my neck stood up. I'd been so careful but I got infected! I was almost sure.

The voice in my head spoke again. *Listen up, lighten up, and loosen up, hypochondriac! Occam's straight razor excises the bad thoughts like brain tumor remover. Simpler explanations are better, remember?*

But panic had already taken hold. "I'm infected! It's evolved again, weaponized maybe. I'm going to end up wandering the streets, starving to death, and —"

It's not the virus. Slow down and think, Ovid!

My hands were cold and tingling. I shook them like a rag doll and tried to breathe through the panic.

"I've murdered two people in one day, and *now* I'm nervy? C'mon, get a grip! This could be just a panic attack, but it's really annoying that I can't decide if this is me going crazier. Or am I going sane and self-aware? Could be all of the above, I suppose. Life is complex."

The inner voice suddenly sounded like my mother.

That banging is reality come a-knockin'. You better go deal with it before it deals with you.

"She's all I need. Talk about making bad situations worse." *Mama! Drama! Trauma!*

Getting up and doing what I had to do was better than listening to her nag me from beyond the grave. Shaking and dripping with sweat, I rushed back to Adilah's room and took one of her blouses from the closet. White and billowy, it was at least four sizes too big for me, but it was dry and soft.

As I made my way back downstairs, the voice in my head was

again my own. If it was my pursuers breaking in, it was kill or be killed.

From everything I'd read, murder was supposed to get easier with repetition. I hoped that was true, but I also wanted to avoid bludgeoning or strangling anyone else. Once was an incident, twice might be coincidence, but thrice would be a pattern. I worried that after that, the act might become an addictive habit.

I had to admit something I didn't like about myself: Part of me had enjoyed taking Bennington's life. People hide the truth from themselves all the time, but I could not deny that fact. Maybe murder is an acquired taste. I didn't think I liked beets, either. Then I did.

43

QUESTIONS

Though the banging came from inside the house, its origin eluded me. The closer I got to the ragged beat, the slower I went, listening carefully for clues to its exact location. In the end, I decided the person had to be in the basement, and the noise was wood on metal.

I had not yet checked the basement because I couldn't find the stairs. I got it in my head there must be a secret door to a panic room.

Time to Nancy Drew this shit.

Listening for the noise downstairs, I finally discovered the way to the basement. Double doors were hidden behind an empty book-shelf, seven feet tall and five feet wide. I'd passed it several times as I explored the house. If not for the racket, I would have missed it alto-gether. I gasped as the massive shelf slid aside easily on wheels. The steel doors were secured with a padlock.

"This really is Nancy Drew."

Someone was downstairs, but there had to be treasures, too. No one would go to this much trouble to conceal the entrance were there not.

I fretted over the lock for a moment, but soon found the key to the rear of the highest shelf of the bookcase. In my excitement, I almost used the key immediately, but I wasn't alone. Caution was required.

Before daring to head downstairs, I doubled back to pick up Bennington's little handgun. It was some comfort, but it felt too light. I would have preferred something heavier and more substantial behind me, like an army or at least an angry platoon.

The banging continued as I used the key. Opening one of the doors a crack, I cut the darkness beyond with my flashlight beam. Unlike the rest of the house, the wide wooden staircase appeared rough and unfinished. I slipped in, pistol out and ready. Standing at the top of the stairs felt like an invitation to be pulled down or shot.

Fearing what might fly up at me out of the dark, I shone my flashlight and played the beam over a well-stocked workbench. A band saw stood near the bottom of the stairs. Hand tools hung on a pegboard. A few solar panels and generators the size of small filing cabinets stood against the nearest wall. As I ventured downstairs one step at a time and ready to run, I surveyed as much as my little beam could reveal. It was as well-organized as a hardware store and worth a fortune to survivalists.

This was only the first room of a vast basement. All this was obviously far beyond what Adilah could do trading on her own. I wondered why Bennington had bothered sending his slave to the market. With Memory Keeper muscle behind him, the dead bastard could have held an auction right here, set for life.

Halfway down, a riser let out a loud creak under my weight. The banging stopped abruptly. I froze as a mean memory ignited. As a toddler, I was afraid to go to sleep during a storm. Our old farmhouse windows rattled under the moaning wind.

My mother scolded, "Go to sleep! It's just the weather. Can't change the weather."

"But the noise — "

"It's the house settling, you big calf!"

For a chunk of my early childhood, I was convinced a stranger hid behind our furnace and occasionally banged on the pipes. Our basement was a gloomy and moldy place, a home to spiders and mice. My fear of spiders, mice, and strangers behind the furnace suddenly returned. My fears felt just as reasonable as when I was a child.

After a long pause, the banging of wood on metal started up again. My flashlight beam fell on the source of the scary noise: another set of double steel doors.

I crept forward. Every few feet, I checked behind me to make sure I wasn't falling into a trap. I didn't need the voice in my head to scream "Run away!" That's all I wanted to do.

Behind the door, an urgent male voice cursed. A woman spoke in a tone so calm she could settle a roiling sea. "It's going to be okay."

"You don't know that!"

"Then we'll make it true. Panic never helps."

"It's been more than two hours, maybe three. We haven't heard a thing since the scuffle," he said.

"We don't know what that was."

"If Adilah were alive, don't you think she'd be down here with the kids by now? He's finally killed her and left us to die, I know it."

"Henrik, we've talked about this. You've gotta be ready for when he slips up. Until then, settle your ass down. When it's muscle time, we'll muscle. Until then, we've gotta use our brains."

"I am using my brain. Adilah is dead!"

"Dude, you have got to find your chill. You're jumping to conclusions."

"Logical ones, yes! Or, what if he's gone or died? What are we going to do?"

"Someone will come to check — "

"And then they'll kill us."

"Don't jump to the end when things are just beginning," she said.

The banging resumed, even more frantic and staccato than before.

"Hello?" I called.

The banging stopped. I could hear him panting before he asked, "Who is that?"

"You first. How many are in there?"

"Two of us," the woman replied. "I am Regan Garnet, and my friend is Dr. Henrik Ebrahim."

"What kind of doctor?" I asked.

"Does it matter?" Henrik yelled. "Let us out!"

"It matters! If you're a doctor of philosophy, that's a lot less useful."

"Let me out! I must — "

"Wait! Wait!" Regan interrupted. "How many are you?"

"Never mind how many of us are out here," I said.

"Are you with Bennington?"

"Certainly not."

"Who are you then?"

"I'm a friend of Adilah's."

Henrik pounded on the door, with his fist this time, by the sound of it. "Where is Bennington?"

I leaned against the door and listened, trying to decide how much to share.

"Let us out!" the man pleaded. "It's late! Adilah's late! She always brings the children down here to sleep by now."

I had been too focused on the door. Looking around, I noticed the nest of soiled blankets on the floor. Bowls of water sat nearby, as one might leave out for neglected dogs shoved down in a dark basement each night.

It is easy for people to lie with their words, but emotions are harder to fake. The doctor was telling the truth, and there was no sense holding back any longer. "Bennington's dead."

"Is he still upstairs?" he asked.

"He better be. That's where I strangled him."

"Please hurry!" Henrik begged. "I must see the children!"

"The key to this lock is on a chain around Bennington's neck, or in his pocket, maybe," Regan told me.

I took a deep breath of stale air and let it hiss out slowly through my teeth. "Of course it is."

"It's a big skeleton key," she added.

A skeleton key from a dead man. That fit. I told them to wait as I went back up to the living room. He was still warm. In this heat, I wondered how long it would take him to stink and bloat. His keys hung on a thick gold chain tucked under his shirt.

Shuddering, I paused to stare at the dead man's neck. The red and white band left by my canteen's canvas strap had been so clear I could have read my name if it was embroidered on the strap. I could find no clasp. The necklace was a solid loop. His heavy head rolled to one side so easily I suspected I'd broken Bennington's neck.

"I swear to God, Pierce, if you hadn't laughed at me, I never could have ... well, maybe not never. You were what my dad would label 'a right bastard.'"

Not murder most foul, Ovid. Murder most fitting.

None of the keys were for a vehicle, just for door locks and padlocks. I'd have to walk all the way back home.

"I've got to get out of here," I told the corpse. "But first I've got to know, what were you up to with all the treasures in the basement?"

44

ANSWERS, PART I

As I unlocked the door, Henrik Ebrahim burst out of the basement room and rushed up the stairs.

Black, sharp-eyed, and thirty-something, Regan stooped to pick up the wooden broom Henrik had dropped. "I told him he would never have broken through these doors with this."

"If not for the noise, I wouldn't have found you. Lucky."

"Then you don't know lucky," she said flatly.

"Of course, sorry. I didn't mean to poop in your cereal bowl and call it breakfast."

She peered through my goggles for a moment before allowing a broad smile to brighten her lovely face. "Thank you for releasing us from prison. Bennington would let us out but only to hose ourselves down or to unload trucks."

"Unload what from trucks?"

Regan gestured to the dim storeroom behind her. The room was so large, dark, and deep that I could not see what the shelves held at the far end. Scanning the floor to ceiling metal shelves, the treasure trove appeared to be mostly canned goods. MREs, toilet paper, and facial tissue boxes were stacked all the way down one wall.

"It's like a grocery store!"

"More like a warehouse. If we dared to touch anything he didn't give us, Bennington would dole out punishment. It's tough being hungry while surrounded by food. Pretty hard to open cans without a can opener, too. The hardest part is trying to hide the evidence when we did take food."

"How would he know?"

"Bennington patrolled the shelves, tracked every item in his inventory, and watched us like a pissed-off hawk. Not that he needed an excuse to punish us. The first day I arrived, Henrik had been down here for months. Bennington pistol-whipped him in front of all of us, including the kids. He hadn't done anything. It was just a show of force. Big man with a gun in his hand, that Bennington. Another time, he locked Adilah outside in the cold rain overnight, chained to the fence alongside the kids. He'd deny us access to the garden hose to bathe ourselves sometimes. It's always about power with these assholes."

"I can't imagine how much you've both suffered."

"A little more than we could bear to stay sane. Henrik's been scratching at his scalp and pulling his hair out. Bennington's such a damn sadist — "

"*Was* a sadist. I killed him."

"That's a bit disappointing. I wanted to do it."

Regan leaned against the doorframe. She seemed exhausted. I asked her if she wanted to lie down.

"Once I'm upstairs. The good doctor says we're low on vitamin D. There are bottles of the stuff among the vitamins on several shelves right over there, but not for us."

I marched over to the shelves and began searching, peering at labels with my flashlight. The inventory was alphabetized. I retrieved bottles of B12 and D. Then I nabbed water from a stack of bottles covered in shrink wrap and handed it to her.

"So? Has our savior got a name?"

Out of habit, I hesitated for a beat. Then I realized how far past caution I really was. "My name is Ovid Fairweather."

She nodded her thanks and swallowed the pills. "Ovid, huh? That's a new one on me."

"I'm, uh ... different. Tell me, how often do the trucks come? Should we be running away right now?"

"Nah. Deliveries used to be every day, then it got down to once a week. Sometimes not even that. This place is just about full. That's probably why they were going to move us to a new location."

Regan pointed to some blankets on the floor. "Wish they stored king-sized beds here. I'm really looking forward to sleeping in a real bed."

"Shall we go find you one?"

Despite everything she'd been through, Regan held back. "Let's gather some food first. I've been chronically hungry for a long time. The prison diet is slimming, but it sucks ass. Besides, we better give Henrik a minute. Let him have some reunion time with his children."

"Uh, just to confirm, the doctor is the father of Adilah's children out front, right?"

"Husband, father, all-around good guy, yeah."

"Bennington told a different story. He had me fooled for a while."

"He once told me he competed in Olympic wrestling. After he forgot that lie, he said he was supposed to compete in cycling at the Moscow Olympics the year it got canceled. At first, he had us convinced he was the head of the Memory Keepers. Then one of the truck drivers showed up and started ordering him around. It was pretty clear who was in charge. Our jailer was nothing more than a slobbering lackey, one among many. His only job was to hold us and keep the supplies safe."

"One among many? The Memory Keepers have more warehouses like this?"

"I don't know how many. Bennington said there were stashes throughout the city. I think there are some bigger warehouses upstate. At least, that's what we got from the driver's conversation with Bennington. Food here, medical supplies and weapons there. The Memory Keepers are great hoarders. The driver told us we'd soon be moved to work in a warehouse storing construction materials."

"What are they planning?"

"Don't know. I doubt Bennington knew, either."

"I'm so sorry for all you've been through," I said.

She shrugged. "Yeah, I'm traumatized, but who isn't?"

I admired how cavalier she seemed. "Knowing that others suffer, too ... does that help you?"

"Of course not, but what would? If somebody's coughing themselves to death with the virus, and you've got a broken toe, that toe doesn't hurt any less."

"Sorry. I'm just ... my therapist tried to address my emotional abuse. The pandemic cut our sessions short before I had a major breakthrough."

"Pardon me for saying so, but that's Old World, First World thinking. We evolved from filthy monkey people, and countless generations suffered before us. Suffering's the norm, but at least we had Prozac."

"That's hard to come by," I said. "Trust me, I've looked. We gobbled all that up quick."

She jerked a thumb over her shoulder. "Sertraline and Citalopram, aisle 3 in the drug section, past the poppers."

"You know antidepressants and such?"

"Through Henrik, yeah. I want them, too. Who wouldn't, under the circumstances? They're all long expired, though. Maybe they kept the best stuff for themselves or stored somewhere else."

"Oh." Even with my mask and goggles, I couldn't hide my disappointment.

"Hard times make some turn to religion, some turn away. Bennington was the kind of below-average shit who eased his stress taking out his frustrations on others."

"And you?" I asked.

"I find no comfort in believing in God and no relief not believing. Time might ease the burden someday, but I don't know."

What could make this right? Nothing. What could ease her pain?

Nothing. I'd been told many times to get over and get past my regrets and resentments, but I never figured out how. Some trauma is built to last.

"Everybody's looking for something, Ovid. What are you looking for, besides antidepressants?"

"I don't know."

"Must be great to have such a short to-do list, huh? Nowhere to go and nothing to do?"

I thought about telling Regan about my father's farm in Poeticule Bay. Bennington had already mocked me for staying in New York when I had a safer place to be, so I kept that to myself.

"Personally," Regan said, "I'd like free transport to a well-stocked cabin in Iceland. Last I heard, life was pretty sweet there."

"I have a few phobias," I told her. "It doesn't come up much, but one of them is volcanic eruptions. Iceland isn't an option for me. Magma scares the shit outta me."

Regan chuckled. She stopped abruptly when she realized I was serious. I appreciated her courtesy.

45

ANSWERS, PART II

"How long have you been a prisoner here?"

"Three or four months, maybe."

"*Months?*"

"Feels like longer. It's much longer for Henrik. I tried to keep track of the days in the beginning. Keeping score got too depressing, so we stopped counting."

"I've known Adilah for over a year," I said. "I didn't even suspect — "

"You're here and she's not, so Adilah's dead, right?"

I nodded. "The Memory Keepers shot her. They took over the market and — "

She gestured for me to stop with a chopping motion of her hand. "I don't need to know the details. Henrik will want to know. I'll spare you from telling the story twice. It's stuffy down here. Let's get some air."

As Regan walked stiffly toward the stairs, I cast a long look back at the storage room. Rationed correctly, there were enough supplies to sustain a large group for a year or more.

"C'mon up!" Regan called. "You can drool over the treasure later."

Upstairs, we found Henrik hugging his children, Maurice and Parisah. My follower was still across the street, watching with interest. The doctor promised his kids that from that day forward, he'd keep them safe. The boy clung to his leg. The girl allowed herself to be embraced, but she stared at me with what I took to be a reproachful look.

She wasn't wrong. I had counted Adilah as a friend, but we weren't really. Proximity and familiarity do not equate to friendship. Adilah had not trusted me with her secret. With her husband and children held hostage, she must not have dared tell anyone.

The voice in my head rose unbidden. *Don't let yourself off the hook too easily, Ovid. You wouldn't have helped before Roger came after you. You wouldn't have wanted to get involved.*

With shame came the heat of embarrassment as I blushed and my scalp burned. My stomach churned and concerned I'd vomit, I tore off my mask to take deep breaths.

When I looked up, I saw the pain in Henrik's eyes. Worry lines etched his forehead. "Adilah is gone, yes?"

I nodded.

"Say it," he said.

"What?"

"Say it so I am certain of the finality. Gone can mean away or gone can be dead. Tell me."

"I'm sorry, your wife is dead. The Memory Keepers shot her this afternoon. That's what brought me here — "

The doctor cut me off. "Ladies, I'm going to take Maurice and Parisah out to the backyard for a while. I need to speak to them about how wonderful their mother was, how she sacrificed for us."

"Go around the house," I suggested. "Bennington's body is in the back room."

"Thank you for coming, for rescuing us." With tears in his eyes, Henrik turned and ushered the children away.

I found Regan standing in the doorway to the back room staring at her captor's corpse.

"I have more questions," I said. "The five Ws are who, what, where, when, and why. I guess I know most of that, but I'm wondering who you are."

"Told you, Regan Garnet."

"But how did you end up in the basement? Who are you to Adilah and Henrik?"

"Got scooped up off the street one day. I don't know who told the Memory Keepers about me, but apparently I have skills they can use. They gather up people they think are essential to whatever they've got going on. I would have been better off if I were useless."

"What skills?"

"I am a civil engineer. Until they got me, I was part of the team keeping the city's water treated and clean. When I was brought here, the crazy Memory Keeper who dresses like a clown said I was in the bank. Once they had a job for me, I'd get out to do the work."

"And Henrik?"

"He's an immunologist. They've got his whole team in a lab somewhere. They're working on producing a new vaccine. I got the new shot myself. We both have."

"For which strain?"

"All of them up to and including the Zeta-3 variant."

"So with the Thirders — "

"If everyone had been vaccinated with this one shot, there'd be no Thirders."

"I didn't know that was possible."

"Sure is. South Korea got the recipe and shared it with the world. All Henrik's team had to do was get the components together and do their thing."

"That's why Henrik could hug his children without any PPE? He's vaccinated?"

Regan nodded. "No fear of contracting it for him or me. Henrik says the Zeta strain got the Thirders' brains because the variant messes with glucose uptake in the brain. It makes holes, screws with brain density. There's no magic to reverse the damage already done to those poor kids. The Thirders aren't coming back."

"It's under control in other countries, though?"

"No time machines, Ovid. We're stuck with a population of people whose brains are not functioning at full capacity." She gave a grim chuckle. "You could say that was always true. Too much short-term thinking. If we had the science down early in the pandemic, everything would be normal. I'd still have a fab apartment with my sweeties in Queens. Imagine that. I sure do, all the time."

Healing was beyond the Thirders' reach, but I especially mourned for Carl. It was as if my friend had been among the last to die in a war, a short-timer who got killed off just when the ticket home was almost within reach.

Regan quickly disabused me of the idea that relief would come easily. "The problem isn't the formula anymore. It's the lack of infrastructure. Resources, leadership, and distribution are what's needed now."

"Why don't the Memory Keepers have Henrik working in a lab somewhere?"

"Leverage on his team. Henrik refused to work unless he produced the vaccine for everyone. The Memory Keepers want it all to themselves. He's too valuable to kill, so they squirreled him away here. I guess they keep more than just memories, huh? Selfish pricks."

"I suppose that's one way to get followers into their cult," I said. "Feed them and promise recruits freedom from disease. Then they'll do anything."

"Feed them and freedom. Yeah, I guess that strategy has worked before."

"Any idea how many Memory Keepers there are?"

She shook her head. "You taking a census?"

"They're looking for me."

"Why? What did you do?"

"I crossed them."

Regan grinned. "You, me, and the doc are in the same sinking boat."

She put a hand on my shoulder and gave it a warm squeeze. Ordinarily, I would have shrunk back, but Regan meant no harm. "We're gonna get out of this mess somehow. I'm never going to be a prisoner of these bastards ever again."

"I believe you."

"Then you're going to have to trust me for another hot minute, okay?"

"Yes?"

"Bennington's gun. The little silver pistol? I need it."

I didn't want to give up the weapon, but I found myself digging into my pants pocket. Despite all she'd suffered, she still seemed a kind person. We admire in others what we cannot find in ourselves.

As soon as her hand closed on the Webley, she whirled and strode to Bennington's corpse. She pointed the weapon at the dead man's head and pulled the trigger.

Click! Click! Click! Click! Click! Click!

"Empty? *Really?*" Regan let the pistol drop to the floor. She crouched before the body, put her head in her hands, and wept. "How could I have been so wrong?"

Gobsmacked, I stood in the doorway listening to her great shuddering sobs. "You were right about everything else," I said. "Bennington was a lackey. They knew he was unhinged, and you and the doctor were too valuable. The Memory Keepers didn't trust him with ammunition. You said it yourself: too valuable to kill."

If Bennington had been all he claimed, my pride would have killed me. I had not been as clever as I'd thought. Charging Bennington's gun, I'd been too furious to be intimidated. Strangling him, I'd been too stupid to wonder why he didn't pull the trigger. I'd merely been lucky.

Again, I searched my feelings for remorse. All I found was embarrassment. But it was for Regan that I wept. No one would miss Pierce Bennington. However, he had been right about one thing: Not everybody's life has equal weight and worth. From what little I knew of the Memory Keepers, that was one of their guiding principles. At least we could agree on that.

After a few minutes, Regan sat on the floor and ran her fingers through her hair. "What am I going to do now?"

"We are going to do something. I have to think on this some more, but I think I have a plan."

At the end of the world, *ambition* is a synonym for *dangerous* and *deadly*.

46

THE MAZE RUNNERS

S tiff and sore, I descended the stairs the next morning to find Bennington's corpse covered by a sheet. Henrik waved to me through the window, beckoning me to join him in the backyard. The doctor sat at a picnic table eating breakfast. Not far away, his children sat cross-legged in the grass sipping from juice boxes.

Despite the early hour, the air was still and thick with humidity that made me sweat. Too much moisture would render my mask useless, and I'd have to replace the filter again soon.

"I checked on your little friend across the street," the doctor said. "I gave her a can of strawberry-flavored calories with electrolytes and vitamins. She was skittish and seemed to be looking for you, but she accepted the gift."

I thanked him for his kindness.

"The girl has obviously been through a lot. I opened the can and put it on the steps and backed away. It was like trying to give an apple to a wild deer."

"Might be because you're a man. The Memory Keepers had her on a leash. I shudder to think why."

"What's the child's name?"

"No idea."

He shot me a quizzical look. "Sorry, I had assumed she was a relative. She seems to have imprinted on you, you know."

"When the fire at the market erupted and bullets whizzed by, I led her to safety. Not a responsibility I meant to take on, but here we are." Hoping he'd move on to another topic, I gave a dismissive wave. "Will Regan be joining us?"

"She's recovering from last night."

"Emotionally? Or did she eat too much too fast?"

"Could have been the whiskey. On the other hand, it might have been the rum. Pent-up emotions and drinking too much are probably related."

That worried me. "She needs to stay sharp. What if the Memory Keepers show up?"

"It's very early," Henrik assured me. "They never come early in the day. Probably too much liquor for them, too. They don't come often anymore. There's so little room left in the basement. Mostly, we've got canned and packaged food here. If I were them, I'd diversify the hoard so if one storehouse went up in flames or was robbed, I'd have other caches to fall back on."

"Do you have any clue as to how many Memory Keepers there are?"

He shook his head. "I gather they're busy expanding their empire, going public, if you will. As a precaution, I was thinking that by noon, we could move into the house across the street and keep watch. If they stay away, we could keep at least some of the supplies."

"Picnic!" Parisah burbled suddenly. "Thank you! Picnic! Picnic! Thank you! Picnic!"

"Yes, sweetie," Henrik said. "Thanks to Ovid, we can have lots of picnics."

Parisah favored me with a bright smile. Since she couldn't see my answering smile behind my mask, I bowed. She laughed and bowed her head until her long hair brushed the ground.

Her father's pale green eyes were wet. He knuckled the tears away. "Sorry, I don't hear them speak often."

After a few deep breaths, Henrik appeared calm. I must have

stared at him for a moment too long. He answered the question I had not uttered. "I'm okay, or at least I will be. I will grieve for Adilah in time and in private. Dissecting cadavers in medical school taught me to put my problems in boxes side by side. If you pile up the boxes, it's too much. By focusing on one problem at a time, I won't get overwhelmed."

"My therapist calls that compartmentalization. She said it's how we make our way from birth to death mostly smiling. It might be the most useful thing she suggested."

"Your therapist? Is she taking new appointments? I could use some counseling."

"Well, no, Dr. Rosa is gone, but I hear her in my head sometimes."

Henrik looked skeptical. "So she's still helping you?"

"Imaginary friends are still friends." I rushed to add, "But I don't take all her advice. For instance, she told me once that exercising self-control is a sign of strength, not weakness."

"You don't think that's true?"

"Sure it is, but at the time, I wasn't exercising self-control. I was being a wimp."

"After what you did to Bennington, seems those days are over."

"The struggle continues."

He gestured for me to be seated and handed over a bottle of water and an MRE. "Peach cobbler? It's pretty great."

Distracted by Maurice and Parisah, I gazed at them without moving.

Henrik cleared his throat. "They are far enough away, I'm sure it's safe to take off your mask and goggles. As for me," he pointed to an Adirondack chair eight feet away, "I'll sit in the chair."

"No, no! Please, I'll sit in the chair. You should be close to your kids."

My phone rang. The children sat up straight, shrieking in surprise and alarm.

"It's okay!" Henrik told them. "It's just an old thing." Nervous, he shot me a hard look. "Who's calling you here?"

Even though it was always the same person, I fished the phone out of my pocket and glanced at the screen out of habit. "No worries." I declined my father's call, set the phone to silent, and put it away. "Just my dad checking up on me."

"Shouldn't you answer him?"

"You're a father who loves his children no matter what," I said. "You wouldn't understand."

The doctor chose not to invade my privacy and let it go. I was grateful. What might seem a small courtesy to the giver can comprise a vast favor to the receiver.

I got comfortable in the chair before tearing open the MRE packet. As soon as I poured some water in, the contents began to sizzle and heat as I shook it. "Sitting on all this treasure, I'm amazed Bennington would begrudge the children. With all this surplus, why not feast every night?"

Henrik stopped chewing, his expression hangdog. "It's all meant for the Memory Keepers. They only value their own, and it's a pretty exclusive club. They've got little use for Thirders, and what uses they do have are pretty dark."

The peach cobbler thickened as I stirred it with a long spoon. "I saw them slaughter a bunch of Thirders yesterday. They just shot them for no reason. They kept a bunch, too. I don't know why."

"I do." Henrik looked pained. "They use the Zeta-3 infected like lab rats. I should say, they use them *instead* of lab rats."

47

CIDER HOUSE RULES

I stopped stirring the MRE and looked up in shock. "What? Why? Regan told me you already have a vaccine."

"For the past variants we already know, yes. They want to speed up experimentation with the new vaccines. They think we can put an end to new infections."

"Can you?"

"Not if we keep it just for the Memory Keepers, but they refuse to listen to reason."

Henrik looked over at his little boy and girl as they lay in the grass sunning themselves. Maurice had fallen asleep, his head on his sister's belly. "Imagine, to those marauders, my poor children are good for nothing but experimentation. Otherwise ... "

Worth less than a nickel, I thought.

"The Memory Keepers had the bright idea that if we skip straight to human trials, we could cut months out of the development process. It's easy to treat inconvenient people badly, and my children ... they aren't easy, you know?"

"They say history doesn't repeat but it rhymes."

"Whoever they are, they're wrong," Henrik said with sudden vehemence. "Experimentation on human subjects sounds like a straight-up echo of some of the worst experimentation that came out of World War II."

"But you refused to help them."

The immunologist dug into his pants pocket and pulled out a handkerchief to mop beads of sweat from his brow. "Anthony, a colleague of mine, is helping them instead. I was a hostage to make sure he kept cooperating."

"So your colleague is a collaborator. How could anyone work with those monsters?"

Henrik disagreed. "Things aren't so black and white as all that. Anthony only did it to save me and the kids."

"I don't understand."

"He convinced the MKs that I am needed for later in the process. Creating a vaccine requires many steps and resources. Anthony told them he may need my expertise for follow-up steps. He's running the clinical trials on the Zeta-3 infected, but his heart is pure. He convinced them they should spare my son and daughter to ensure my cooperation in case the research goes awry."

"You think this colleague of yours is a good man? Still?"

"Anthony Therrill saved me from myself," Henrik insisted. "One of the leaders of the group, the clown, threatened to kill my children in front of me. Anthony stepped in and said he could do what was necessary. I don't know if my friend knew or not, but I was bluffing. If not for him, it would be me experimenting on the Zeta-3s. I was about to cave to their demands, you see? My friend saved me from doing as they asked. I'm still a hypocrite, but I was not going to martyr myself or sacrifice my children. I put on a brief show of resistance, but I was going to collaborate."

When he looked up at me, there were tears in his eyes. "So, Ovid? What do you think of the prisoner you freed now? Not so noble, not such a victim after all, huh? What must God think of me?"

I took a moment to consider my answer. I'd killed two men the day before. After the first gory encounter, the girl I'd freed looked at me with gratitude. Though she was a Thirder, I was certain she saw me as her liberator. To her eyes, I'd committed no sin. To Regan and Henrik, I was a hero for strangling Bennington.

Careful, my inner voice warned. *Are you giving yourself the gift of forgiveness, or are you just rationalizing taking lives?*

Shut up, I thought.

Sorry, the voice replied. *I hadn't said anything in a while and thought I should chime in.*

Shut. Up!

"When someone puts you in an impossible position, the rules you thought applied don't necessarily work anymore."

"You don't have to tell me things have changed," Henrik said.

The doctor didn't deserve it, but some steel crept into my tone. "We haven't gone through a change. This is revolution and dissolution."

I ate peach cobbler, and when I spoke again, my approach was softer. "Henrik, my biggest struggle used to be dealing with social anxiety at office parties. Now I'm fighting crazy people. I'm still the same person, but the stakes are so much higher, and the obstacles are tougher now. If my life were a book, it would be titled *Book Editor Versus the Apocalypse* or *Neurotic Gardening at the End of the World.*"

The voice in my head piped up with a suggestion: *Nerdy Girl with a Hammer.*"

"Moral relativism," the doctor replied. "I don't know about your beliefs, Ovid, but my God has high standards. I worry for the day I must face judgment. I was lucky Anthony took my burden, but still, I was too weak. How will I ever enter Paradise?"

"Henrik? If I may, I am not religious now, but I'm used to the burden of guilt."

His eyes narrowed. "Let me guess, Catholic guilt or Jewish guilt?"

"Secular. I was inflicted with a metric tonne of guilt by my parents. All parents are gods to their children, at least until the kids wise up. I've long been troubled by the many ways I fell short of their expectations."

He shook his head. "It's not the same. You've got a therapist. I would have to take up my questions with an imam."

"Maybe, but if thoughts alone make us sinners, we're all guilty. Dr. Rosa taught me that a thought crime sets an impossible standard. Everyone has a voice in their head that suggests terrible things. You're setting too high a standard for yourself. Consider this: If a human can forgive another for their failings, surely God can and will, right? I forgive you, Henrik. Do you think I'm greater than God?"

"No offense, but surely not."

"Then if I, a mere human, can forgive you, why not — "

"I see what you're saying. Thank you. I appreciate the thought, but only God can grant grace."

"We're dealing with tough issues down here on Earth. He shouldn't be stingy with it."

Henrik gave a faint chuckle.

It was time to compartmentalize, open another box, and focus on the next task. "Doctor, there's a massive treasure in that basement. How would you like to take it all away from the Memory Keepers?"

"Grand," he said, "but unlikely and probably impossible."

"I know a guy with a truck who gets through checkpoints 'like shit through a goose,' as my mother would say. We can't save the whole world with those supplies alone, but I think we could save a good chunk of it. You want to go to Paradise when you're dead? How about we carve out a piece of Heaven on Earth while you're alive?"

Henrik did not look up from his meal. Too used to defeat, he couldn't even meet my eyes to refuse the offer.

I persisted. "I used to work with people who wrote autobiographies. Every life is a story. The pandemic ended too many stories prematurely. The rest of us still have a choice and a chance. Every morning we get up, we're still writing our stories. You know what mine's about? Redemption. I'm headed there. You want to get there, too?"

"Of course, but — "

"It'll be much easier if we go together."

48

MISERY

Despite eating my fill of at least 2,000 calories, I felt light and energetic as I hiked home. The Memory Keepers' hoard was the equivalent of a lottery win, but my mood was elevated by more than that. As Henrik took the children to explore the house across the street, Regan came out of the mansion to offer me a bar of soap. "The garden hose works if you want a quick shower."

Since it was her team that worked to keep the city's water flowing and filtered, Regan's offer seemed like a personal gift. Due to breakages in the lines and the lack of staff to maintain the system, water was not accessible everywhere in the city. The backyard tap gushed clear, cold water. The blast was shocking at first, but the day was so sultry that I shivered only briefly. With the possibilities the treasure made possible, I felt fresh and new. The cold water felt like a baptism.

The girl I'd saved from the Memory Keepers tried to follow me at first. Promising I'd soon return, I tried to convince her to stay with Henrik and Regan. She seemed to understand, but as soon as I waved goodbye, she made to come with me again.

In the end, I opened two cans of maple-flavored beans and set one at her feet. "You can have that," I said, "if you stay with my friends until I get back. Regan will give this one to you after I go, okay? These are good people, and you're safe with them. Deal?"

It was like the famous marshmallow experiment. If she could delay gratification, she'd get more of what she wanted. Some children, many dogs, and even cuttlefish passed the marshmallow test. Fortunately, my Thirder passed the test, too. She remained mute, but she nodded sagely, sat down on the step, and tipped the can back to eat the beans.

"They are trainable," I remarked absently.

Henrik's brows furrowed. "You're going to have to come up with a name for her. It won't do to call her your follower or girl or Thirder."

"How about Aldebaran?" I suggested.

Regan quirked an eyebrow at me. "She looks like a Susanne or Christine or maybe Linda. Something that isn't weird."

"In many apocalyptic stories, people give themselves unusual names. What better time to reinvent ourselves than at the fall of civilization?"

"But Aldebaran?" Henrik asked. "Why?"

"The word means *follower*. From Earth, it's one of the brightest stars in the sky."

"Nice," Regan said. "While you're gone, we'll try teaching it to her. Maybe I should come up with something flashier. Maybe I'm more of a Priscilla or a — "

"Katniss Everdeen," I suggested. "We need someone to lead a revolution. You'd be my pick."

She smiled in a way that left me unsure whether she was serious. "Not you, Ovid Fairweather?"

"I think I'm supposed to be a minor character, the one who does supportive things in the background and occasionally comments on how weird everything is and that we're all going to die."

"I'm not so sure about that," Regan said. "You sure kicked Bennington's ass."

"Since the day I was born, there's always been a big gap between what I want to do and what I must do."

Regan looked annoyed. "You think you're special? That's everybody."

Henrik stared off into the distance. "No one's leading a revolution anywhere, ladies. Let's just settle for survival, okay? Just surviving is hard enough."

"Same as it ever was," Regan said.

As I walked home, it was as if I was seeing the city in a new way. Oddly hopeful, I wondered if New York's glory might someday return. And could I play a part in that grand mission?

The goal was not easy to envision. The sidewalks were something of an archaeological phenomenon that told the story of the pandemic. At the bottom of the piles of debris lay garbage bags, broken and explored well by rats and birds. The waste management strike never ended, and citizens ran out of garbage bags eventually. Food waste that could have been composted was thrown into the street. When the toilets failed, human waste was dumped down drains. As municipal and bodily systems failed simultaneously, corpses joined the mounds of discarded things.

The variant storms killed those with comorbidities fastest. Then the viral tempest reached out for healthy adults. Finally, the children started coughing and struggling to breathe. Stressed beyond limit with ICUs beyond all capacity, the tide drowned them, too. Frontline workers left their professions in droves. No one sane could blame them. Doctors and nurses were soldiers sent to battle without weapons.

At our nadir, the so-called Red Tide took away many who survived the variants. Despair culled them. Hungry and hopeless, whole families took the flying cure. Parents with babes in arms leaped to their deaths rather than face another day.

Religious and political leaders condemned the wave of suicides, but I understood. If your house is on fire, you'll jump from any window rather than get burned. Those who couldn't take anymore felt like they were on fire. Watching loved ones die was the fire. Despair added to the heat. Loneliness burns. The certainty that things would never get better pushed a lot of people to step out into the air and let gravity do the rest.

No one needed to be persuaded to wear a mask back then. Fearful more disease would rip through the remaining population, we burned most of the bodies eventually. At the height of the crisis, the intense sun turned the city into an oven, and the foulest stench had settled over us. The smell of rot still lingered. Maybe the stench got better. Perhaps we just got used to it. It's amazing what people can adapt to if they can hold on and wait.

The butcher's bill added to the spiritual pain proved overwhelming. Feeling what others felt, empathy became a weight on my heart. However, wordless charity got me through the worst of it. To feed the living, I helped raid the houses of the dead. I couldn't speak to strangers then. Their stories hurt me. My solution was to pack boxes at the relief centers while pretending to be mute. By day, I handed out food. By night, I helped Carl construct the rooftop greenhouse.

New York isn't coming back, I thought, *but maybe we could pull the survivors back to a safer citadel.*

We needed a place where all the streets were cleared of trash and no stench lingered, a refuge where hope could be reborn. Isolation helped me during the days of the Red Tide, but solitude wasn't the solution anymore.

49

BAD WILL HUNTING

Adilah had walked too far every day. In my vision for the city, her home would be out in the Badlands. People could go wherever they wanted, but if we could make a central location clean, inviting, and functional, no one would want or need to venture beyond the ramparts of our one safe, shining citadel. It was a lovely fantasy, but I didn't really believe it could be any more than that.

As I hiked through more familiar neighborhoods, I worried more about Carl. If I didn't get to the grow-op every day, he became agitated. My friend would have to wait at least a day. After that, he'd have plenty of company.

So much had happened in a short time. I'd killed two men and witnessed the deaths of many more. Adilah was disappeared to wherever the dead go. The Memory Keepers were looking for me, I had new allies, and I'd named my first child.

It took me a while to emerge from my reverie. Something was different. The feeling that something was awry slowly crept over me. Then the realization struck: The streets were empty of the infected. I didn't spot even one Thirder wandering around.

Close to my home, gunfire erupted. I guessed it came from two or three blocks away. I rushed to take cover in an abandoned laundromat for a few minutes to make sure the gunmen weren't coming my way. I was too near-sighted to risk a scouting mission, but there was nothing wrong with my ears. Listening to the rattle of the weapons, it sounded like the same rifles firing over and over. The staccato reports came too steadily, incompatible with the back-and-forth of a gunfight.

Execution, I guessed. *They must be killing people who aren't running from them. Thirders, maybe.*

The gunmen weren't on the move, so I sprinted the last few blocks to my apartment complex. I was panting and sweat had soaked through my clothes again by the time I arrived.

Heather sat in her rocking chair as always, but her shotgun was missing from atop her pile of books. She was not reading. Instead, she glared at me through the glass. As I got past the inner door, I asked what was wrong.

"People came by looking for you."

"What people?"

"You know what people. You always had your secrets, but I never took you for a fool. There were four of them. I was reading and when I looked up, there they were, rifles pointed straight at me through the glass. That ain't bulletproof and neither am I! I had to let them in. The mean one up front had one arm in a sling. He seemed to know a lot about you. Seems your enemies know more about you than your friends." The old woman looked hurt.

"What did they want?"

"Wanted to know which apartment is yours and when you'd be back."

"What did you tell them?"

"The truth. Don't know where you live, somewhere in the complex."

"They didn't go looking?"

"There are 360 units in this building alone, and there are three connected buildings. Most are empty or the corpses are sealed in. Those places that aren't empty, the tenants might shoot through the door if you dared to knock. No, they didn't go looking for you." Her hands fluttered like frightened butterflies.

"Told those bastards I didn't know when you'd be back, neither. Hell, I didn't even know your real name, but *they* knew. He described you to me and said you sometimes go by Honey. What the hell kind of name is Ovid?"

"A silly one."

"That's all?"

"In Hebrew, my name means *worker*. It's also derived from a Latin word meaning *sheep*. Worker and sheep ... somehow, it seems I grew into my name. My parents named me after a Roman poet who wrote about abandoned women. That also feels like it fits."

Heather gave an impatient sigh and sat back in her chair as she rubbed her temples. When she looked at me again, her face was stone. "When I said to you 'that's all' I meant where's my damn apology? They took my shotgun, but not before they put the muzzle to my forehead to ask about you."

"This won't help, but he was probably bluffing — "

"These are the same people who killed Barry! Whatever's left of the militia ran away after what happened at the market! This town belongs to the Memory Keepers now. You must be crazy. Somebody saw you. They know what you did, comin' at one of their own with a hammer! They said you cracked open some poor soul's head as if you needed, and I quote, 'a cereal bowl made of bone'! What were you thinking?"

"At the time? Nothing much."

"You better start thinking. I can still feel the spot right between my eyes where the guy with the sling was gonna blast me apart! You got me deep in the syrup, and I hardly know you! Them comin' after you and here's me, wetting my drawers and rediscovering a childhood prayer! All because of you!"

"Sorry. Really, I'm sorry."

Heather regarded me sternly. "Not enough. You are going to supply me with all the glaucoma medicine I need for the rest of my life or at least what little is left of yours. I didn't survive the plague just to go out like that. Took years off my life! At my age, how many years do you honestly think I can spare? And get my damn shotgun back!"

"I understand you're upset, and I don't blame you."

"A hammer?" The old woman shivered. "You killed somebody with a *hammer*?"

My inner voice chimed in. *Don't tell her that was only one of your grisly murders yesterday.*

I admit that was probably good advice.

She shook her head in disbelief and whispered, "Jesus, you think you know a person."

"I don't think anyone knows anybody else, really. I'm sorry this happened to you, and I understand you're upset. That said, I need a favor."

50

THE VANISHING POINT

At eight that same evening, a knock came at my apartment door. At first, I froze. I was to welcome my first visitor since Carl made a hole in the floor to Dave Champion's apartment. Instinctively, I almost reached for my mask and goggles before rejecting the notion. I needed no protection from the Unicorn. Establishing trust would be key to the success of this meeting.

As the light from my apartment flooded the dim hallway, Virgil smiled. Except for a blue silk shirt, he was dressed head-to-toe in black leather. Freshly shaved and cleaner than any lowly survivor, his cologne smelled of mint and juniper.

"Hello," I said in a small voice.

He hefted a bottle of wine, showing me the label. "I hope you don't mind, but I brought a bottle of the cheap stuff. My good friend Barry has left the curses of this mortal realm behind. Heather tells me you've had quite a day as well. Downing the soda pop of wines helps me toast loved ones."

I stared at him long enough that he felt compelled to ask, "May I come in? It's customary with guests and vampires in order to cross the threshold."

"Sure, please pardon my near-crippling social anxiety."

He laughed in such a wholehearted way I guessed he didn't realize I was serious. Virgil took in my apartment. His gaze lingered over the hole in the floor, my treadmill, and my plants. "That's a lot of tomatoes," he said. "It smells green in here. Nice."

"You can't see right now because of the blackout curtains, but there's cannabis, parsley, basil, and ladies' fingers out on the balcony."

"Ladies' fingers? Sounds sexy."

"Most people call it okra, but ladies' fingers sounds more elegant, doesn't it? It's a pain, though. It likes these temperatures we've been having, but the plant prefers acidic soil and uh ... " I trailed off, suddenly cognizant that Virgil narrowly escaped a botany lecture he had not requested.

Instead of meeting me with a blank stare, he smiled. "A Chinese proverb states that life begins the day you start a garden."

"Very true for me," I said. "Hey, I'm curious about something. You drive through checkpoints. Why not use autonomous trucks?"

"Right into it without a howdy-do, huh? Coupla reasons. Autonomous vehicles are okay out in the country where there are fewer obstacles. In the city, there's a lot of detours. More importantly, the people who guard borders don't like them. With no driver, there's no one to bribe, blackmail, or shoot."

"It's really that bad out there?"

"It's that bad everywhere. I met two other Unicorns while I was in captivity at the CDC. When I got out of Atlanta, I persuaded them to come with me. Zate and Nella, good friends, good people."

"What happened to them?"

"I don't know the whole story. It was early days, before all the state borders slammed shut. We did some driving to help out the supply chain. Zate was a small-town kid — Oklahoma, I think — excited to move to the big city. He got shot within a week. Couldn't have been more than twenty-one, didn't know how to negotiate. The learning curve was too steep for him."

"How do you negotiate with hijackers?"

"You let them take a cut this time so they get a cut next time.

Smart hijackers don't kill the goose that lays the golden eggs. It's a great way to meet interesting people."

"And how do you deal with dumb hijackers?"

He raised his shirt just enough so I could see the butt of a pistol on his belt.

"What about your other friend?"

"Nella? She was older, smarter, and tougher. Lasted longer, but pirates or slavers or pirate slavers out of Rhode Island got her. So I heard anyway. I went looking along her route, but, *poof!* Disappeared without a trace. A lot of people do that these days. It's not like anyone's keeping track, whether it's gunshot wounds or the disease, dead is dead. Gone is gone."

"I heard a lot of gunfire earlier today."

"Might have been Keepers cleaning house. I hear they don't like people who don't cooperate. All rumors, of course. Who knows the truth?"

"I have a proposal — "

"Is it a wedding proposal? Maybe we better slow things down and do the social thing. Later, we'll talk too much business, huh?"

Virgil strode to my bookshelf. "Fastest way to get to know a person," he murmured. "Dostoevsky? Really? The Russians write too long and are so sad. But then I see there's some science fiction and a few mysteries. I've read *Murder on the Orient Express*, but so has every-body. I liked the movies based on Agatha Christie's work, especially Hercule Poirot."

"Christie didn't like the character of Poirot."

"Oh?"

"His eccentricities bothered her. I've always loved her, but I don't think she'd like me."

"Funny she didn't like her own detective. She wrote him. Why ache about it?"

"She didn't complain in public. Some authors control their char-acters, but making the players too relatable makes them boring. Other authors are at the mercy of the voices in their heads. I'm guessing she was more like Mrs. Marple, so she liked her old lady avatar more."

Virgil continued to peruse my bookshelf without comment. Nervous, I babbled on, "I would have liked to meet Agatha Christie. She disappeared once, you know. For eleven days, she pulled a vanishing act that made headlines around the world. The police thought she'd been murdered or committed suicide. She was finally found at a spa using the name of her husband's girlfriend."

"Stress plus depression, you think?"

"Maybe a bit of spite, too. She sued her cheating husband to get a divorce a couple of years later. I respect that about her. She was tired of getting pushed around, so she made the necessary changes. It's hard to make changes."

"You sound like the voice of experience."

"Oh, no, I didn't have much patience for sitting down to write. A single book would take years and years. I loved to do research, read plenty, and enjoyed working with authors. I earned a reputation for editing books quickly."

"Uh, cool, but that's not what I meant. You've got some spite in you, and you feel the need to make changes. Exhibit A!" He nodded at the hole in the floor. "Does your landlord know you've expanded your realm, my queen?"

"I keep thinking the landlord will show up to collect, but I haven't seen anyone from building management in a long time. I guess I can finally let go of worries about the rent. My super must be dead."

"Sad that you don't know. When people go missing, even enemies, it's good to know the whys and the wherefores. No wonder Mrs. Christie caused such a stir."

The Memory Keepers are looking for you. Get to the part where you charm the Unicorn!

51

THE QUEEN'S SPEECH

"Sorry, I don't have any chairs. I cleaned out the place as much as I could to make room for plants and books."

Virgil sank to the floor and sat cross-legged. "Then we'll picnic in the tomato forest. I've never seen tomatoes grown on horizontal vines before."

"It's efficient for the allotted space."

"I'm impressed."

"You'll be less impressed when I tell you I only have one glass for the wine. And it's a coffee mug."

Virgil let out a pleasant laugh. There are several kinds of laughter: mean, ironic, bitter, nervous, and evil, among others. His was a deep belly laugh. That's when I decided to like him.

After filling my mug to the brim, he held up the bottle for a toast. "To old friends we've lost along the way and to new friends tonight."

I didn't normally drink alcohol, but this was the sweetest I'd ever tasted. It didn't hurt to swallow, and the bubbles tickled my nose.

"As promised, like soda pop," Virgil said. "Now, before we move on to what I hope will be a very pleasant evening, I have to ask, am I in danger speaking with you? Are the Keepers going to bust through that door or up through the floor at any moment? I'm unaccustomed to danger, so it might be best if I run away now, right? Why did you call this meeting, Ovid Fairweather?"

I gasped. "Heather told you everything, didn't she?"

"She thought it fair I knew what I was getting into. She says you're what happens when an odd duck has sex with a strange cat."

"That's not very nice."

"Her point was that you're odd. Is that not true?"

"Can't say she's wrong, but not everything that is thought has to be said."

"How are you odd, m'dear?"

"Just ... different."

"Look, if you expect me to trust you, or even stay, I need to know more."

I took a deep breath and finally admitted what I'd only discussed with Dr. Rosa. "Besides a few assorted phobias, I have sensory processing sensitivity."

"What's that? Should I be wearing a full-body condom?"

"It's commonly known as being a highly sensitive person. It opens me up to stimuli too much so it can be overwhelming. I spend a lot of energy trying to keep it in check."

"Why's that?"

"Once I found out about SPS, my childhood made more sense. I was surrounded by insensitive people, which made things much worse. It's not pathological per se, just a character trait."

"Highly sensitive sounds like a superpower."

"I wish that were so. Other sensitives have better reactions, but for me, it's the opposite of a superpower. In practice, it just means I cry too easily when watching movies, commercials, or videos of puppies. Think of it as empathy that's turned up too high."

"That sounds kind of sweet."

"I discovered that if I can turn up the hate enough toward certain people enough, my empathy goes down and I'm protected."

"Isn't that everybody?"

"I was in elementary school when I made my first enemies list."

"Wow. So, a person can have too much empathy."

I shook my head. "If it's so much that emotions constantly hurt, yeah. I feel shame as a physical ache. Social interaction saps me so much, I get headaches and have to lie down. I have to be careful who I'm with and for how long, or they drain me like vampires. I had to learn to distance myself and compartmentalize or else other people's problems suck me down a sewer."

"Self-isolate?" He glanced around. "You mean like — "

"Yes, I know! The pandemic wasn't all bad for me personally. I don't mean to sound cold, but in some ways my life didn't change much with the lockdowns. On a purely emotional level, things got better. I'm ashamed to say it — "

"No, no, I understand. Anything else about how messed up you are? It's quite a list."

"I perseverate a lot. Like, a lot a lot."

"Meaning?"

"It's like dwelling on things that have hurt me in the past or will do me damage in the future."

"You obsess? Everybody does that, don't they?"

"I take it way beyond the amateur level. I'm a pro. You know how some people cope by giving themselves love? Self-love never worked for me. Others can say 'I love me' and mean it. When I say 'I love me,' I mean the opposite."

He laughed, but not unkindly. "Before you say it," I added, "just because a person has one phobia or eccentricity doesn't make them less likely to have others. I'm a trembling mass of insecurities, and I haven't cataloged them all yet." I hated how defensive I sounded, but I'd encountered ableist presumptions in the past.

"I wasn't going to invalidate your experience," Virgil assured me. "Remember? I'm one of those people who appreciated Hercule Poirot's eccentricities. You seem far more normal than the little Belgian detective."

"Give me time and I might freak you out."

He watched me with a soft gaze, saying nothing. I appreciated quiet moments when I was on my own, but in conversation, I felt I had to rush to fill the silence. "I can't say I'm not disappointed.

Heather told you about the Memory Keepers. I had a speech built up in my mind where I'd do the big reveal."

"Let me hear your speech."

"Okay, here goes. My name is not Honey. Some people call me Girl from Maine, but I am Ovid Fairweather, the one the Memory Keepers are searching for."

"There can't be more than one Ovid in all of New York State, probably the world," he replied. "What else?"

"That's really all I had planned."

"So, not such a big speech."

"Big for me."

He raised the bottle for another toast. "To my new friend, Ovid Fairweather. May she meet a better fate than my old friend, Barry Cupper."

"The other night, you thought the Memory Keepers were a myth."

"They have since asserted themselves," Virgil said. For the first time, he looked downcast. "If I'd heard more about them, maybe I could have warned Barry. From what I've heard since, the Watch was totally unprepared for that battle."

"I was there and saw the massacre happen."

Virgil took a deep breath, had another swig from the bottle, and gave me a serious look. "It seems the danger and brutality of these times keep going and going. I should be home, hiding in my basement, back to the wall with a gun pointed at the door. Still, your invitation intrigues me. Why am I here, Ovid?"

"The marauders are trying to control all trade in the city and take their pound of flesh. Once they have that, they'll go after the food bank network next."

"How do you know?"

"Megalomaniacs do that sort of thing. They don't want a piece of the pie. They want all of it. Once they have the power to dole out crumbs for favors, they'll have all of us under their boot. In your position, I'd worry I'm about to lose my job. You don't strike me as the sort of person willing to settle for crumbs, Virgil."

"So I'm here so you can give me bad news?"

"Oh, I don't just have threats to your survival. I'm also offering bribes and solutions."

Virgil tilted his head to one side and narrowed his eyes. "Pitch me, my queen!"

I rose, hurried to the kitchen, and returned with two MRE pouches. "Beef stroganoff or mac and cheese?"

Virgil's broad smile returned. "Definitely mac and cheese. Brings me back to my childhood."

After a few minutes of eating in comfortable silence, I asked Virgil if he enjoyed his meal. His mouth full, he rolled his eyes, and rubbed his stomach in an exaggerated pantomime of delight, as if he were a dapper silent film star come back to life.

"How would you like the opportunity to revisit those childhood memories and eat like a king for at least a year, maybe more?"

"What would you need from me to make that happen?"

"Secrecy, your truck, and your driving skills."

EPISODE SIX

Extinction is the rule. Survival is the exception.

~ Carl Sagan

∾

"The Shire must truly be a great realm, Master Gamgee, where gardeners are held in high honor."

~ J.R.R. Tolkien, *Lord of the Rings: The Two Towers*

52

BRIGHT LIGHTS, BIG DEAL

Virgil reached out to take my hand. Instinctively, I recoiled. My cheeks burned with embarrassment. "Sorry, I — "

"It's okay. You have not been touched in a long time, I'm sure. The virus can't infect me, and it hasn't gotten you, but we've had to deal with survivor guilt, stress, alienation, loneliness — "

My phone rang. To escape one conversation, I fell into another I didn't want to have. I held up one finger, signaling Virgil to wait, mouthing, "*Sorry!*"

"Ovid? Ovid? Are you there? Can you hear me?"

"Yes, Dad. I'm here."

"I called earlier. Where were you this morning? "

"Oh, you know, stuff and things, making my way."

"I worry about you. There's a big storm coming up the Eastern Seaboard. It'll hit you before it hits up here. We've been hearing about it over the ham radio. The hurricane has already torn up Cuba and Florida."

"Can we speak in a few days? I'm having a business meeting."

"A business meeting? What are you up to?"

Virgil was listening, so I gave him a wink, speaking more to him than to my father. "No need to worry. I've come upon a cache of supplies, and I'm engaging a kind gentleman who has a truck to take it to a safe location."

"That sounds like a great opportunity!"

"Yes, I — "

"To come home."

"What?"

"Your way of doing things doesn't have a great track record, Ovid, but I've got a bright idea."

"Oh?" My shoulders slumped. I could feel a migraine off in the distance. It was far off, but, like a storm, it was on its way and preparing to crush my skull.

"Did you hear what I said?" Dad asked.

Only then did I realize I'd blanked. "Sorry, you dropped out. Bad signal. Repeat that, please?"

"I said, here's what you're going to do."

At that sentence, muscles in my jaw spasmed. From experience, I knew my father's words had the power to increase the speed of a headache's arrival.

"Pack as much stuff as you can into that truck and sneak the driver and yourself up to Maine. Tell me where you'll cross into state borders along the way. I can send some people to meet you and get you past the guards. If you can pack enough into the truck, I can get you home, no problem. The guards and my people will take a thick cut, but everybody's gotta do what they do to get by. It's time you were done screwing around in the big city. This is fantastic! C'mon home, Ovid!"

"I'll certainly give that all due consideration."

"I'm not asking anymore," he added. "I'm telling. I've been generous and I've been patient, but you've gotta jump on this right away and I mean now. That hurricane coming up the coast may even help — "

"It's more complicated than that. There are other people involved."

"But now's your chance! For once in your life, just do what I tell you! Get the guy to drive, or steal his truck. Whatever it takes — "

"Dad — "

"Do as I say, or you can stop calling me Dad. Understood?"

"I'm with someone. I'll call you back .... " I almost called him Dad, but that suddenly felt like a giant concession.

"Ovid? Wait! Don't — "

I hung up on my father. It wasn't the first time, but in this instance, doing so felt quite good.

Virgil grinned. "Somebody's got Daddy issues."

I winced as I put away my phone. "That's kind of reductive. I also have Mommy issues. On the other hand, they both had issues with me before I could even talk. They liked me better when I was a baby and all I could do was cry. Maybe that's why they kept trying to make me do that as an adult."

"Families, huh? First, we love them, then we're stuck with them. We crave independence, so we eventually leave. That umbilical cord sure can stretch, though. I didn't feel I'd resolved the power struggle with my parents until they died. It's the only way I could get the last word."

"Unfortunately, my father is quite healthy."

Virgil burst out laughing, and I pretended I'd meant to joke.

"Now, where were we?" he asked.

"I was requesting to use your truck to load up a cache of supplies. You should know, it belongs to the Memory Keepers — "

"Oh, that? I guessed that, and of course, I'm in. I love mac and cheese too much to say no. I'm looking forward to getting fat. However, I was talking about you and me. Where were we?"

"We?"

"Poor Ovid, I think you must be desperately lonely."

Virgil leaned in, coming in for my first kiss in over a decade.

He thinks you're desperate, a damsel in distress. What are you going to do about that, Ovid?

I placed two knuckles on his sternum and pressed him back, gentle but firm.

"Got a vibe and I thought we might — "

"I don't do that."

"But you can't catch anything from me. Unicorn, remember?"

"Your truck and your cooperation are all I need. Nothing else. Sorry."

A man like Virgil would be unaccustomed to being refused anything. He seemed more stunned than annoyed.

You took one look at me and couldn't fathom me saying no, I thought.

I needed more friends to face the apocalypse. Lovers, however, could turn into an expensive luxury.

"You're very nice to help me, but like I've told a few people in the past, I don't have the bandwidth for intimacy. Don't feel bad. It's not you. I recognize you have a very symmetrical face and high cheekbones. Your shoulder to hip ratio is aesthetically pleasing. I know several of the women at the food bank who can't keep their eyes off you."

Virgil cleared his throat. "Well, first, I'm going to need the names of those ladies. Second — "

"I'm Ace," I explained. "Sex doesn't repulse me exactly, but I'm quite indifferent to it."

He stared at me blankly. "I ... uh ... I'm sorry, *what?*"

"Ace. Asexual."

"Whoa! That's sad!"

"Not for me," I said.

"Is this really about sharing air? I am not poisonous or venomous! *Heh.* Or is this a good-girls-don't situation? Maybe you just never found the right guy ... or girl."

I felt my energy draining rapidly, but my resolve was solid. "I know this is new to you, but I've had this conversation before. It's not about what you can bring to the table. This is about me and my choices."

"The old it's-not-you, it's-me thing?"

"I'm not comfortable with the kinds of expectations that come with romantic relationships. Even if it's just a one-night stand, it's problematic for me."

"So you've never had sex? Ever? How do you live? How do you know what you're missing out on?"

It was my turn to smile. "Oh, Virgil, if you saw a fat, middle-aged person walking down the street, would you assume they couldn't possibly have once been a great athlete? Maybe even an Olympian?"

"Uh ... so you're saying — "

"In my twenties, once I got out from under my parents' thumb, I committed to experiencing as much of life as my neuroses would allow."

"That didn't work out well, I take it?"

"It wasn't all bad. I discovered Monster Magnet. That song, *Queen of You,* really speaks to me. I could write a book over 100,000 words, but I feel like that song sums up my whole life in a few minutes. I also fell in love with dim sum. I found out spicy foods make me sweat, but I still crave bhut jolokia curries and chutney."

He seemed chagrined. "You and I will never repopulate the Earth at this rate."

Fairly sure he was joking, I plunged on. "I don't fool myself thinking I'm anybody's manic pixie dream girl, but I'm tall with long legs. For some men, that's enough to get me on their radar. For others, breathing and female are enough."

"I know a couple of guys who wouldn't care if you breathed."

"Exactly, but I'm not twenty-something anymore. I've got boundaries now."

"Pardon my curiosity, but what was your family's reaction? Or do they know?"

"Mom was dead and I was far from home before I started making choices for myself. I came out at twenty-eight. Dad called me, and I quote, 'a scaredy-cat.' He told me I should find a man, lay there and take it, grin and bear it, and give him grandchildren. He called me a pervert, too. Try to make sense of that! I mean, are *all* nuns perverts? Some sure, but all? Statistically, that seems unlikely."

"Oh, my! Ovid! I'm so sorry he was a dick about it. Truly, that was unkind. You have all my worthless sympathy and total lack of understanding."

"Thanks, I think."

Virgil straightened. "Well, to be totally honest, there go my plans for the evening. I'm an elder-sexual. I like older women, and you got that different colored eye thing going on that's kind of sexy so — "

"Two points there. First, I'm not that old, and second, even if I were — "

Virgil spoke over me. "Joking! Humor!"

My patience was beginning to feel like a flimsy thing. "Do you still want mac and cheese? Will you drive the truck for me and help me move the stuff?"

"Oh, Ovid, what must you think of me? Of course, I'm still in. No harm, no foul. I just need to know the route. How many blockages in the arteries of the city am I going to have to maneuver around?"

"Does your truck have a winch to move cars out of the way?"

He nodded. "Plus a snowplow blade."

"Then meet me downstairs with your truck at dawn. The way to the cache is clear. We probably have the Memory Keepers to thank for that. They must have cleared some routes to their regular destinations."

"Yes, but where are we going to hide the cache from the people out to capture and/or kill you?"

"Leave that to me. I'll show you the way."

"What are you going to do with the supplies?"

"I've been focused on saving myself for a long time. It's time I follow my parents' advice and expand my circle of friends. Will you be my friend, Virgil?"

He smiled broadly. "I'll do my best to serve you, my queen."

"No hard feelings?"

"None, but if you'll excuse me, I must run off and say hello to another friend."

"Are you headed off to pursue what we used to call a booty call?"

"Still call it that, and yes. This Unicorn has to get his horn waxed. It helps me focus. If I'm to be back at the crack to help save the world, I need to hustle." With the MRE already gobbled, he gave a cheery wave and took the wine bottle with him.

I lay down and waited for the migraine to hit. However, somewhere between hanging up on my father and turning down Virgil's advances, the migraine had changed course and wandered away.

"After tomorrow," I told myself, "no more scraping at the margins and barely making it."

Finally taking control in a way I never had, I would no longer live at someone else's whim. Ghost no more.

53

THE QUEEN'S GAMBIT

True to his word, early the following day, Virgil waited for me behind the wheel of his truck. He hopped out and opened the passenger door for me. "Ovid, I just want to apologize for last night. Like you said, your preferences are, uh, new to me."

I waved him off. "Don't mention it. I know, I'm a ... what was it? Odd duck mixed with a strange cat?"

"You'll have to forgive Heather, too. She's still upset."

"Someone put a gun to her head. I owe her some flowers."

"As long as she can smoke those flowers, she'll get into a forgiving mood eventually."

We headed north and it was pretty much a straight shot. Virgil knew the city, including which streets were clear or at least passable. He knew the dimensions of his vehicle well, too. We had to pull in the side mirrors to roll through narrow spots twice, but we did not have to use the winch at all.

As I directed him to park in front of the mansion, he let out a low whistle. "That's gotta be the biggest house around. Who lived here? The mayor?"

"I guessed hedge fund manager."

"Gotta give it to the virus," Virgil replied. "It hit the poor hardest and first. As time wore on, and the variants did what variants do, they became equal opportunity killers."

Henrik and Regan emerged from the house across the street and greeted me with big smiles.

By way of greeting, Henrik said, "The kids love the new house. They don't quite trust their new digs yet and got up in the night to pace. I pulled my bed into the same room so I could keep an eye on them, and they settled right down."

"What about Aldebaran?"

Regan assured me my follower had settled in, too. "As soon as we introduced her to Parisah and Maurice, they became inseparable."

For fear of hurting Henrik's feelings, she took me aside to whisper. "They don't play like normal kids, but if two move, the third follows. It's not always true. I guess it depends on their level of brain damage."

Virgil came around the truck, gave Henrik a nod, and waved to the children, but his gaze lingered on Regan. She didn't seem to mind.

It was Henrik who took control of loading the truck. "We prioritized food items, taking the freshest first. Must keep a wary eye on the best-before dates in the inventory. We moved the high-priority stuff to the front door for faster packing. The truck's bigger than I expected. We can fill it, easy."

"What about the Memory Keepers?" Virgil asked. "Shouldn't one of us act as a lookout?"

"They've hardly come here anymore and never once early in the day. The rich have the privilege of sleeping in and taking naps," Henrik said.

Virgil seemed troubled. "Meaning they're about due? Got any weapons in there?"

"Rifles, but no ammunition," Henrik answered.

Virgil nodded. "Seems they don't want to risk anybody mounting a revolution against their rule. The ammo must be stored elsewhere. Clever."

Regan agreed. "If I had weapons and ammo, I'd be going after them."

We loaded the truck as quickly as we could. Once they saw what we were doing, the children pitched in. Our line was so efficient that Regan stayed in the back of the truck organizing the load. "I love a puzzle. This is like playing Tetris," she enthused.

We soon gathered as much as we could fit on the truck. When we were done, Regan pulled me aside. "You are coming back, right?"

"What do you mean?"

"There's no room for all of us, so I assume you're going with Virgil to the new hideout. Can you trust him with all those supplies? Food, water, medical … it's like handing a stranger a lottery ticket. What if he pulls around the corner and hits you over the head?"

"The Memory Keepers killed a good friend of his."

"What about Henrik and the kids?" she asked.

"They can start bringing more up from the basement for the next load. The children still look frail, but they seem awfully eager to help."

Regan gave the children a long look. "When I was in school, I knew some guys who were into robotics. They were sure that would be the next big tech revolution. Butlers, maids, and home health care workers would all be luxurious wonders. Then a visiting professor gave a lecture noting that training people with developmental disabilities to take on those roles made more sense. Paying them a living wage was a much more practical and humane solution to elder care. She argued that we don't need more robots. We need more care and more people with purpose."

"You think Thirders could be our servant robots? Dangerous territory."

"No, of course, I don't mean that. Hanging out with these kids, though, I know they love attention, and they love to eat. Look, my dad trained dogs for a living. You know how you ease a dog's stress? Give him love and attention. You take him for walks and give him something to do, toys and stuff. Kids aren't dogs. That was Bennington's take, and we hated him for it. They aren't great conversationalists, but

their lives aren't over. Under all their problems, they need engage-
ment. Whatever you got planned, I don't want to see Henrik's kids left
out, you know? They've suffered enough."

I tried something I had not done, perhaps ever. I put my hands on
Regan's shoulders and looked her dead in the eyes. "Caring for the
afflicted is my vision. When a car is over on its side, people have to
work together to clear the road. You can't just push it over. You have
to rock it back and forth at first before you can set it right."

"So you're telling me what?"

"Over the last few days, a lot has happened to me. I've thought a
lot about how I might help change things. Then this cache of
supplies falls into my lap. We can make things better. I have to rock
some ideas back and forth a while, but I think we're on the right path.
My therapist would say change is a process, not an event. I'm getting
ready for the main event."

"You think or you know?"

"I'm building up to it, but my new motto is: Stay strong, protect
the weak."

"That's good."

"I had to think about it and kill someone before I could commit."

"Less good, but I understand. Just curious, what was your old
motto?"

"Oh ... uh, I think it was: I need coffee."

"So inspiring."

"I've been kind of focused on me, but hero's journey, right?"

She shot me a quizzical look.

"There are two kinds of readers for fiction. Some want heroes
who come out of the womb badass. Like James Bond, he doesn't
change much. Those kinds of fans don't want training sequences and
character development. They get frustrated if the protagonist doesn't
know everything they want immediately. For instance, they don't
want to see Luke Skywalker as a moody boy stuck on a farm. They
want him to jump straight to Jedi Master."

"They've got no patience for noobs? Okay, but sweetie, I just have
one question. What the hell are you talking about?"

"Me. I'm the other kind of protagonist. I'm the character who's scared and inexperienced but figuring it out. I've got an *arc*, see?"

"I guess. Whatever gets you through hell faster and to the other side before your pajamas catch fire. Me? I meditate and drink, sometimes at the same time, so it's not as boring, but you do you."

I felt safe with Regan, safe enough to open myself up to reading her. That smile plastered on her face was the nervous kind. Understandable. I'd saved her life, but I was still a homicidal stranger who talked a little crazy. I know how I appear to normal people.

"There's room for one more in the truck. Come with us," I offered. "Sit between me and Virgil. I think he wants to get to know you better. I have a friend on the other end who can help us unload."

Before I left, I gave Henrik and each child a tomato from my apartment garden. Aldebaran accepted my gift, but she grabbed my wrist. Maurice and Parisah saw her do it and rushed to do the same.

"Okay," I said nervously. "I'll be back soon. You can let go."

Aldebaran looked at me with huge puppy eyes, imploring me not to go.

"When I come back, I'll have more fresh fruit for you. I have to go get it. Then you're all going to come live with me in a tower in the sky. Okay? We're going to hide out together. With all this stuff, we can be self-sufficient for a long time. People like Pierce Bennington won't find us."

Gently as I could, I disentangled myself from their grip and climbed into the truck. I waved goodbye. Henrik and the trio waved back.

Aldebaran wept at my departure. I wondered if she knew something I did not.

54

BLOOD MERIDIAN

When Virgil asked for directions, I showed him the way street by street. "We're headed to my farm. You're going to love it for the food, but you'll want to stay for the view."

The route south through the city became congested as we got closer to our destination. We took several detours when the streets became impassable and twice had to use the winch to clear a path.

While I was in a rush to get the truck unloaded so we could go back for more that afternoon, I enjoyed the company. Regan and Virgil fell into a deep conversation about his time getting tested at the Center for Disease Control.

"I didn't volunteer," Virgil said. "I was volun*told*. Before I got there, I pictured a massive hospital with an army of docs. It's not nearly as big as you'd think."

"We were always fighting the wrong war," Regan commented.

"For my stay, I was mostly stuck in one room getting blood drawn. I didn't mind the needles. The worst part was sitting around, bored most of the time while more and more staff got sick, coughed, and dropped. The TV was just propaganda. It got wild watching all these doctors running around in a panic while the hair models on TV were telling everyone that everything was under control. It's fine, go shopping, then, oh, shit!"

Regan shared some of her life. She'd had a boyfriend and a young son before the virus crippled New York the second time. "My older brother's name was John. When I called to tell him my boyfriend and son had died, John told me it was a judgment put on me by God because I wasn't married. I had a kid outside of wedlock, so it was a divine curse. My brother was of the opinion that immorality weakens the immune system."

"Why?" I asked. "Because immorality and immune both start with *imm*?"

Virgil rolled his eyes. "Divinity in action, sure. That's what all those virologists should have been testing for."

"After that, my brother's name wasn't John anymore. His name was Dead-to-Me."

Virgil looked her in the eyes and said in all sincerity, "You want me to go beat the shit out of your brother?"

"No need," Regan said breezily. "A few weeks later, he died of the virus, too. If it hadn't killed him, the blight would have starved him to death. Alabama got hit harder than most states. Last I heard, it got so bad down there nobody's even burning or burying the bodies."

"I like the idea of a universe where pieces of crap like your brother get their just rewards," I said.

Virgil and Regan gave me a look that drained my confidence in the value of class participation. "Sorry, I wasn't supposed to say that out loud. Should have kept that to my inside voice. I meant no offense."

Regan smiled. "No apology needed. Nothing wrong with unvarnished truth."

"We don't live in a just universe where karma does its duty," Virgil said. "People who do what others won't are not punished. They're rewarded lavishly. If it makes you feel better, Regan, I'd still beat up your brother if he were alive."

"Raincheck," Regan said. "Somebody will come along who pisses me off. That train's always on time."

I directed Virgil to the loading dock at the rear of the Pilkington Press building. He looked at me skeptically. "Here? For real?"

"This is the place."

"You got the elevator working?"

"No, no elevator now."

"The power got cut to all the office towers," Virgil said. "How's this going to work?"

"I had some help from my father setting up my farm, and I've got a guy on the inside, too. I've climbed so many stairs, I lost twenty pounds and put on muscle the first couple of months. It's a lot of cardio, I know, but all those stairs are more discouraging than a moat."

Regan seemed impressed. "At the beginning of the third variant storm, the mayor's office discussed confining Thirders to abandoned office towers. Right about then, the power grid became iffy, and supply chains were breaking down. I was in on some of those talks, but the plan was impractical because no one could trust the elevators. Soon after that, the city preserved power by cutting off power to all those buildings."

"Ironic, since I'm in a huge apartment complex. The elevator doesn't work there, either."

Virgil shook his head in disbelief. "A high-rise without reliable elevators is a logistics nightmare, especially when you have a lot of stuff to move. I pictured a farm, maybe taking over a bunch of back-yards out in Queens or a bunch of playgrounds. You are literally in the last place I'd look."

"That was the beauty of it," I said. "It was difficult, though when I put in my gardens, the freight elevator still worked. I got the hardest part done — the construction — just under the wire. It's going to be a lot harder now, but we're going to have more bodies to help."

Virgil still looked skeptical. "You still want to unload the truck here? Why not at least take over a shorter office building?"

"Because it's still the last place the marauders would look. Office towers got passed over precisely because they are difficult. We won't have any problems because this is a castle. Let's unload to the first floor for now, then head back for another load. With all those food supplies, we won't have to worry about dehydration and not getting enough calories to do the heavy lifting."

Virgil grinned and struck a cheerful note, "We're about to get a buttload of free exercise!"

Regan still looked dubious. "I used to pay a trainer to do what you're about to do to me, Ovid."

Virgil's brow furrowed as he checked the truck's dashboard. "We have a problem. My battery is lower than it ought to be. Winching those cars out of the way must have killed the battery faster. Sorry, but the routes I travel for the food banks are always clear. To be safe, I'm going to have to recharge before we make it all the way back to the cache."

"Henrik will worry," Regan said.

"Let's unload, quick as we can, then get the truck to your charging station." I cursed myself for not stealing the battery chargers suitable for the truck.

"Wait here. I've gotta prepare my friend for your arrival," I told them. "He gets nervous around company."

I found Carl on his cot. He'd sweated through his sheets again. I could feel the heat radiating from his body without touching him. His face shone with a sheen of sweat. Opening one eye, he rasped, "Fairweather friend."

Making sure my mask and goggles were secure, I grabbed a water bottle from the shelf by his bed. "Sorry, I had to be away for a day. Looks like you're having an episode. That virus will not leave you alone, will it?"

I cracked the cap's seal and brought the bottle to his lips. He drank eagerly.

"Slow, slow. Don't choke."

After a moment, he drank some more, this time with a pill for the pain and fever. The medicine was over-the-counter and out of date, but not by that much.

Exhausted and panting from the effort to drink, Carl fell back onto his pillow.

"It's okay," I said. "This has happened before. It will pass soon." My words were soothing, but I did wonder how many times he could cook his fevered brain before he stopped recognizing me.

"I have good news. We've got new allies and food coming. You won't believe the supplies I found! Once we get more varied diets, I bet we'll both feel better. More protein is on the way! Some bad people are looking for me, but we can all hole up here and do some farming. How does that sound?"

Carl turned on his side to peer through my goggles. He was in no condition to help us unload the truck, so I told him to sleep. "Give the fever time to break. It always does. I'll check back in before I leave, and I'll be back soon with lots of presents. It's going to be Christmas in July!"

I waved from the doorway and hurried back to the loading dock. When I threw open the door, Regan was on her knees with both hands behind her head. Virgil stood behind her with a pistol to her head.

There were others, six in all, but three stood out above the rest. I recognized the woman with the bullhorn. Up close, she didn't look much older than twenty. A dusting of freckles and her red hair made me think of a Raggedy Ann doll, not an indiscriminate killer. She smiled and waved coyly. "I'm Anya. Pleased to finally make your acquaintance. We've heard a lot about you."

But it was the shirtless man that made my heart pound in fear. His bare torso was painted white, and his mouth was a careless red slash. His painted eyebrows were angled down in an exaggerated and permanent expression of fury. He carried a steel sword meant to be wielded with two hands. One side of the blade was serrated. The weapon was not artfully made, but even more threatening for its crudity.

"C-c-c-c-clown!" was all I could say.

The Memory Keepers burst into laughter, but none so hard or long as Roger, my former barista and mugger. He stood off to my right, training Heather's shotgun at my head.

Regan's face was stone. She'd been a prisoner for a long time. She refused to give her captors the satisfaction of witnessing her fear. Instead, she swore at them, showing nothing but anger.

Virgil leaned forward and tapped her behind the ear gently. "*Sh!* Bite your tongue. I'm a third of the Triumvirate of the Memory Keepers. I'd order you to kneel, but, of course, you already are."

Triumvirate. My unluckiest number had struck again. I bit my tongue hard seven times.

Keeping my eyes on the clown to make sure he stepped no closer, I said, "I thought you were one of the good guys, Virgil."

"Oh, Ovid, what must you think of me? I *am* one of the good guys, here to restore order. We remember What Was, and we're going to bring it back. Normal, or at least relatively normal, is on the menu!"

"Normal was never so great," Regan muttered.

"What? You against capitalism?"

"This isn't that," Regan replied.

Virgil gave a dramatic sigh. "We're bringing America back from the brink, and you resent us getting paid for such a large undertaking? *Tsk, tsk, tsk.*"

I hadn't realized how much the Unicorn loved the sound of his own voice. I envied him a little since I had several voices in my head and didn't enjoy any of them.

"And Ovid! Why the sour puss? I thought *you* were one of the good guys. You told me you wanted to save the world. Well? Here we are, ready to help in the grand task! We have so much to talk about. Come with us peacefully, please."

"If I refuse?"

"You're not volunteering," Virgil said. "You've been volun*told*." He tipped his head toward the clown with the sword and then toward Roger. "Remember how I said I knew a couple of guys who don't care if you're breathing? These are those guys."

55

THE POISON IS THE MEDICINE

oger handed Virgil the shotgun. My mugger chuckled as he stepped forward to handcuff me. "Been looking all over for you and here you are. We didn't get to finish our conversation. I'd hardly recognize you without your hair. Too bad you cut it all off. That was your best feature. You're nearly bald. For real, I don't think you have a good head shape to carry off that look."

"Hey!" Virgil said sharply. "She's innocent until proven useless. Cuff her, hands in front. It costs nothing to be kind."

"That's not how I do," Roger said, "and mean comes pretty cheap, too."

Anya cleared her throat meaningfully. "Hey, stupid! How are you going to get her in the back of the pickup with her hands behind her back?"

"Son?" Virgil cut in. "You'll go easy until I tell you to go hard."

Roger nodded and did as ordered, but his mouth was a thin line as the cuffs ratcheted into place around my wrists.

"How's the arm?" I asked.

"I'm only going to explain this to you once," Roger replied. "Shut up."

The clown let out an over-the-top demon's laugh that made me shudder. I could not look at him for fear of wetting my pants. Dr. Rosa and I never addressed my deep fear of clowns. Her only advice had been to avoid circuses, children's birthday parties, and parades.

He knew I was avoiding his gaze, so he stepped closer and placed the tip of his sword a few inches from my left eye. "Take off her goggles, plebe!"

Roger ripped my goggles up and off so fast it hurt. To my great dismay, he pulled down my mask, too.

I trembled as the clown brought the tip of his dirty, rusty sword ever closer. "Ovid Fairweather! First test: You familiar with the word pharmakon?"

I kept my eyes on the ground. He wore a pair of red Jordans. If he'd worn clown shoes instead of sneakers, I would have vomited all over him. Pharma was a clue. "Is, is it a-a t-toxicological or pharmaceutical term?"

He took a beat to recover before letting loose again with his demon laugh. It sounded forced this time. "All right, okay, I'll give you a quarter of a point for that, but here's the real deal: *We* are pharmakon. We're the stress that makes you better. We're the medicine that's also a poison. We're what New York needs. We've been taking over, but to do that, we gotta dose everybody, see? The medicine tastes bad, but we're putting everything right long term."

Despite his bizarre appearance, the clown was clearly used to being the smartest boy in the room.

Fiction Rule of Conflict #1: The hero is only as good as the villain, and nobody gets up in the morning thinking they're the bad guy.

"Thank you, Voice in My Head. Shut up."

"Oh, no, you did *not!*" the clown shouted. "*What* did you say to me?" The tip of the sword was all I could see now, an inch from my eye. "Say it again! Say it loud and proud!"

Virgil stepped in. "She's got issues, man. Be cool. Doesn't mean she's useless, just means she's a little crazy, like you."

"Like me? I don't think anybody's like me, but well, hell, if so, she's my new soulmate! Do you, Ovid Falafel Fairweather! Just understand right and wrong are fluid concepts and that I am thy lord and savior!"

The demon laugh came again, full-throated and only a few inches from my left ear.

I held my breath to avoid breathing his air.

"Well, hell, I said!"

I shuddered and hunched my shoulders, refusing to look at him.

Virgil lifted my chin so I had to look into his eyes. "You'll have to excuse my colleague. He's got a flair for the dramatic. Don't take anything he says personally. He's like this all the time."

"Your shtick is exhausting, Steven!" Anya called from the truck. "Give it a rest!"

The clown stomped off to confront her. "That's not my name anymore! Say my name! Say my name or I swear I will poop in your bed tonight!"

Anya replied in a bored, robotic tone, "Sid Serrated, The Killer Clown."

Virgil whispered to me, "Call him Sid. It calms and flatters him." Then he winked. "When I met Sid, he was a coder for a call center on Wall Street. His real name is Steven Herschenfeld. Don't ever call him that. He made the sword himself and will take any excuse to use it. He's crazy but he keeps the troops in line, so he's useful. It's important to us that everyone who joins our pantheon of heroes is useful, capiche?"

"The gardens are on the roof and take up the top three floors," I said. "Take what you want."

"We'll take an inventory of all you've got. It'll be part of your evaluation, but keep in mind our ultimate determination will also depend upon your attitude. Are you gonna be a good worker bee, or is Queen Anya going to have to eat you?"

"Just take everything and leave us alone, please."

"Did you not hear Sid Serrated, the Killer Clown? We're rebuilding and building an empire. You've got skills. Don't you want to get in on the ground floor?"

I shook my head. "Even in elementary school, my report card said I prefer to be alone."

"Don't play well with others, huh? I find that, given the correct motivation, anyone can change."

"You are murderers."

"And you're not?"

"Well, yeah, but I'm not proactive about it."

Virgil laughed. "Such fine distinctions you make! Let me tell you what I've learned. People try to do the right thing, but when times get tough, they do what's necessary to keep going, to keep living. Our words are far nobler than our deeds."

"As a book editor, I think words are important, too."

Anya rolled her eyes and tapped her wristwatch. "We're on the clock, Virg. Hurry up! Storm's coming!"

Virgil sighed. "Things change, Ovid. I think you have it in you to change with the times, especially these times." His eyes bored into me. "If you play your cards right, you could be a useful pawn in a much larger plan beyond your imagination."

"I don't know about that. I have a pretty good imagination."

Focused on Virgil, I hadn't noticed Anya step beside me. "I bet that defiance I hear sounded good in your head," she said. "To me, you sound dumb. Virgil is the one offering you a ride in the lifeboat. Me and Sid Serrated are the high judges you're going to need to convince."

"Convince of what?"

Anya chuckled. "That you can be that useful pawn in the big plan, stupid. Kneel or squeal! Jesus! Nobody listens! Bag her."

Roger slipped a black bag over my head, and the world went darker than usual.

56

JAM

I was led by the elbow and ordered to climb into the bed of a pickup truck.

"Oh, one more thing!" Anya called. "You and your friends stole from us. Punishment is required. Can't abide anyone thinking we're going soft, so say goodbye to Ovid!"

"Goodbye, Ovid!"

Regan!

"Tell Mom that you don't forgive her for getting you into this!" Anya demanded.

As the demonic clown giggled, I almost wet myself. "I'm sorry! Don't hurt her, she — "

"Tell Ovid how you really feel!"

Regan refused to grovel. Her tone was brave and defiant. "Go ahead and shoot. Is that the best you can do? Y'all are boring the shit outta me."

A single shot rang out. In my mind's eye, I saw the bullet drill through Regan's head, exploding her skull into a pink mist as her body slumped to the ground.

Sid laughed harder and it didn't seem at all performative. It was as if someone was tickling him.

I wept. I'd made a friend, and within a day, I'd been made responsible for her death.

My mind raced. If I could sit with Dr. Rosa one more time, I'd confess my failures. Then, in hopes of absolution, I'd add, "We all sank to the lowest common denominator. Our collective immune system failed. It's not just the virus that got us. Fear and anger are contagious. If existence is a test, we got an F. If God wanted better, He should have designed us differently. We can only rise above so much. Where intellect and high hopes fail, our lizard brains take over."

The voice in my head tried to soothe me. *A therapist can be a sounding board, a guide, a paid friend, or a cleric. Only you can forgive yourself.*

Fearing further retaliation, I forced myself to be quiet as someone clamored into the truck bed beside me. I was sure someone, possibly the killer clown, would hit me hard, and I'd never see it coming.

"It's me," Regan whispered, "alive and shit."

"Wow! Oh, *wow!*"

"Yup, they punked us. I really thought the nightmare was over. I didn't see my life flash before my eyes. Gotta say, that was disappointing. I thought I'd get a glimpse of my kid again before I went away."

I should have come up with some words of consolation, but what would have sufficed? Instead, all I could think to say was, "I've got tears and snot all over the inside of this bag."

"Me, too." Regan had a pretty laugh. I cried some more. We both stopped when we realized Anya and Virgil were sitting in the back of the truck with us.

"Lucky for you, we need a civil engineer," Anya told Regan. "You are going to be very useful in the big scheme of things. All we have to do is adjust your attitude and you'll be fine."

"You made me think you were going to execute me," Regan replied. "I'm not in a forgiving mood."

Anya giggled. "Deprivation can change that. Put somebody on minimal rations in a small locked room with no toilet, and I find they come around. Be good and you could be living on a high floor in one of the best hotels in New York."

"I'll pass on the torture," Regan replied. "I've already been locked in a basement for months. I'll take the luxury hotel room with a working toilet and three hots and a cot. A Jacuzzi would be nice, too."

"If you can fix it, you can have a hot tub," Virgil told her.

I could hear the approval in Anya's voice as she praised Regan, "Good! That's not cowardice. That's smart. You're skipping to the end and the inevitable. I appreciate quick learners."

"Where are we going?" I asked miserably.

"The Four Seasons," Virgil said. "Unlike you, we don't have the whole tower yet. Too many stairs to climb makes me tired."

The rumors about New York's elite hiding out at the Four Seasons had been true after all. Who knew how long they'd been plotting their takeover from within the city?

As the pickup wove through the city's heart, Virgil's phone rang. He said little and listened for a long time before hanging up. "I'm so glad we flushed you out, Ovid. I almost ended the charade last night, but it's good I held back. That was Sid. He's very impressed with your operation. I'm told the rooftop garden is wondrous."

"And I led you right to everything."

"Mom is a bit greedy, isn't she? We can use that," Anya commented. "Ovid Fairweather, poor little rich girl."

"How did I come to your attention in the first place?"

The bag was still over my head, so I didn't expect Roger to speak up from the rear of the truck bed. "Your comings and goings and offerings were of note. For the small price of a few bottles of jam, a little bird put me on to you at your apartment complex."

Jam from the Four Seasons, I thought.

"Peach this time," Heather had told me. "Sorry, no raspberries this year, even for the rich folks."

The old lady had betrayed me.

"Did you even steal her shotgun?"

"Roger put her through her paces," Virgil said. "We had to be sure she'd sell the story. Don't fret, she'll get it back. It's easy to buy forgiveness. Just a few more bottles of jam and a couple bags of your weed should do it. The desperate don't have the luxury of acting noble."

"At the end of the world, people are shit," Anya remarked, "but we can build on that foundation. A new world is coming. We're going to rebuild. Make that goal your daily focus and put it on your vision board. That's how you get to live, Ovid. Anyone who isn't on board is an anchor holding us back. If that's you, you will be eliminated from the competition, no consolation prizes."

Anya's words had the practiced cadence of someone who'd delivered the same speech many times. I would have bet she slept with her bullhorn. She didn't see herself as a marauder trying to control our lives. She was a new Napoleon. Maybe some villains are heroes who have lost their way.

But I didn't care about the Triumvirate of the Memory Keepers or their motivations. Careless and cruel, I'd seen them commit mass murder. No matter their goals, I hated them with a passion I usually reserved for family.

And Sid Serrated with his heinous hyena laugh? He'd been left alone with all that I'd created. What might the killer clown do to Carl? I despised anyone who laughed at me, but him most of all. His presence in my tower curdled my blood.

Dr. Rosa once challenged me to see my response to stress as nervous energy. We'd been discussing my terror of public speaking at the time, but perhaps the lesson was applicable to murdering an evil clown. However, I doubted sheer force of will could overcome my phobia. If deciding not to be afraid actually worked, surely I would have accomplished that already. Erasing Sid Serrated seemed the only way to ease my phobia.

The voice in my head spoke, but it was me and my voice whispering wise counsel: *Edit your life and delete the sources of your fears. Of the top three, Sid Serrated is the most unstable. If you can, kill the clown first.*

57

BOYS AND GIRLS TOGETHER

As we approached our destination, Anya yanked the black bag off my head and sat me up. Gesturing broadly, she proclaimed, "You are about to enter the inner sanctum of the Memory Keepers!"

Regan still had a bag over her head, but she was not intimidated. "Memory Keepers still sounds like a wedding album or a school binder to me."

"You'll see," Anya said. "Mom has a tower garden. We have a tower, too. It's our home."

"I thought you decided towers were impractical," I said.

"As our numbers and expertise grow, we'll take over the whole hotel eventually," Virgil said. "Right now, we only occupy the bottom three floors."

"But we're just getting started," Anya hastened to add. "Behold all we have wrought out of rot!"

"What did you do in What Was?" I asked her.

"Gee, Mom, not that it's any of your business, but I was a speech-writer ... well, an intern. I majored in Communications at Brown."

She must have been older than she looked. That didn't stop her from calling me Mom.

"I was hoping to become a speechwriter for the mayor of New York one day," Anya continued. "Now I'm a lot closer to being the mayor."

Virgil gave Anya a look. "Co-mayor in the Triumvirate."

"How progressive," Regan said. "A Unicorn, a psycho, and a killer clown walk into a bar and decide to take over the world. What could go wrong?"

"Our new hire is cute, but Ms. Garnet has a mouth on her. You better fix my hot tub before you get yours going."

Regan chuckled. After all she'd been through, my friend had somehow become numb to being kidnapped. Or maybe, pushed past the point of caring, she'd become resigned to her fate.

Two blocks out, we went through a checkpoint manned by two bored-looking guards with shotguns. I gasped when I saw the mob between the outer perimeter of razor wire and the inner fences. Thirders wandered about. Some of the Zeta-3 infected were naked or nearly so. The sun had broiled any exposed skin until they were red as steamed lobsters. Most trudged aimlessly in small groups, usually shoeless and, without exception, forlorn-looking. I'd never seen so many of them in one place.

The truck slowed to a snail's pace to press through the crowd. The driver honked the horn, startling some in his path out of the way. Others were attracted by the sound, but the driver kept nudging, pushing them out of the way rather than running them over. Some were mute and others mumbled. A few irate screamers made their presence known, too.

"Quite a sight, isn't it?" Virgil asked.

"Like herds of buffalo in the Old West," Anya said.

At least the buffalo could graze, I thought.

Anya chuckled. "The funny thing is if they get stirred up too much, they'll clump together more and more until they're just one mass. If they can walk or crawl, they'll follow each other. As if there's safety in numbers. Poor little foolish things"

"No safety for them," Virgil agreed. "Soon, we'll put them all out of their misery." He caught the shock on my face. "We must be cruel to be kind, Ovid. Nobody should live that way."

"They don't have to," I said. "You could help them."

"Who has the time or inclination?" Anya asked.

"That's a rhetorical question, right?" I asked.

Anya leaned forward and cuffed the back of my head. She called me Mom, but she reminded me too much of my mother. It bothered me that Carl might agree with her. He hadn't wanted to live with an infected brain, and I'd failed him in that regard. That didn't mean everyone would choose death over existence.

"What's happening?" Regan's voice was muffled, but she didn't sound at all panicky. I envied her remarkable equanimity.

"We're in a compound between two fences and surrounded by Thirders on the way to the hotel. I can see it."

A man yelled off to the left in a gravelly voice, "Unfair! Unfair!"

"That's what life is!" Anya shouted back. "Take it, baby, take it!"

"It's easy to accept that life is unfair when the inequality falls on someone else's head," Regan said.

"Shut up," Virgil ordered.

"Why are you the way you are?" I asked him. "You were nice to her all day. You were nice to me."

"Then your crew shows up, and suddenly you're a massive dick," Regan added. "And not in a good way."

"Sorry you feel that way," Virgil replied.

"I don't think he is at all sorry," I told Regan. "He puts the *lie* in replied."

"Someone's looking to get black bagged like her friend," Anya told me. "And here's me wanting to show off the benefits and features of being a Memory Keeper. Generosity is rarely rewarded."

"Like offering me the new vaccine you made by using innocent people as lab rats?"

"Jesus, Ovid! Way to skip to the end of our sales pitch!" Virgil looked amused. "You're interrupting the flow of our fine speeches and kind invitations."

His phone buzzed again, and he studied the screen for a moment.

"Sid's taken inventory. He's especially impressed with your rooftop garden and greenhouse, but he thinks your flowers are dumb."

"Yeah? Then he'd stupid. I spent a lot of nights up there. Some nights, those flowers kept me from jumping."

Virgil bobbed his head. "You win that argument, I guess."

What I didn't reveal was how many nights on the tower roof, especially on hot nights when I couldn't face hiking back to the apartment. When I visited my grandmother in Nova Scotia there was no light pollution. The whole of the Milky Way looked almost close enough to touch. New York no longer suffered light pollution, but I missed the glow of the city at night, and my vision was no longer good enough to see the stars. I was sure the cosmos must still put on a great show, but it was all a blur to me.

I'd blanked out again. For a moment, I'd retreated to my rooftop garden under a black sky, safe from people. Then I was cuffed in the back of the pickup again.

I couldn't have been gone long. Anya was still giggling and bantering with Virgil. "I'll text him to let him know she thinks he's dumb. He'll take that well!"

"Yeah, because he is so stable."

"Remember when we first ran across Sid? Wandering around, searching Albany for his parents?"

"And covered in other people's blood," Virgil replied. "He didn't have the clown with a sword show going yet, but I knew he had potential right away."

"How does somebody go from working IT on Wall Street to ... to *that*?" I asked.

"Like any good fish, evolving and crawling up on the beach for the first time," Anya said.

"The dude was diagnosed with Oppositional Defiant Disorder," Virgil said. "Luckily, he got born into a time when we could harness it."

"More than that," Anya said. "He adapted to his environment. It's not like he was going to survive if he remained Stephen Herschenfeld, King of the Coding Nerds. The killer clown is badass and useful.

Every government needs an arm in charge of enforcement, bullying, and spy ops."

"And what's your role in this new government, Anya?" I asked.

She smiled. "Propaganda and recruitment. Virgil has his eye on building future opportunities."

Virgil looked older to me suddenly. It was as if I was seeing the real Virgil Sine for the first time. He wasn't just a horny follower along for the ride. He was the leader of a lethal and ruthless cabal. The fact that he could hide his true self so effectively made him more dangerous than I could have imagined. He'd fooled me but I didn't blame myself for believing liars anymore.

Dr. Rosa taught me that, sensitive though I could be, anyone can be taken in by a pathological liar at least some of the time. "When you come up against conflict or even challenging social situations, you shut down. Because you're so sensitive, you're actually *more* likely to be deceived."

Whether it was my parents' emotional manipulations or transgressions by marauders, no one going at it part-time can beat monsters who make lying their full-time job.

58

THE BIG PICTURE

Self-righteousness is such a strong elixir that heroic legends tolerate little nuance. Batman's billions would have gone further helping unfortunates instead of investing in jet engines for his cars and beating up mentally ill villains each night. As Dr. Rosa told me, "You see the world through the lens of fiction. Real-life is much messier."

As Thirders milled in currents and eddies, the pickup slowed to a crawl. A contingent of the infected crowded around the truck. With filthy hands, they reached for us. Some muttered, "Please, please, please," without indicating the object of their desire. It could have been food or water.

"Clear the way, Gerald!" Anya ordered.

The driver threw something in front of the truck: a flashbang. The bright white flash and loud report of the grenade's explosion sent the Thirders scurrying this way and that. Several let out high keening wails that made me wish I were deaf.

"Popping smoke!" Virgil announced. He tossed another grenade a few feet past the truck's tailgate, and a green cloud rose behind us.

Disoriented, the closest to the infected retreated. That left three young men, clinging to the rear bumper and undeterred.

Casually, as if the Thirders were paper targets, Virgil drew a pistol and shot two in the head. Anya shot the last in the shoulder. The man screeched as he dropped away. She laughed at his pain.

"You didn't have to do that!" I protested.

"Why not?" Anya said. "They're gross and they're dross."

"Then why have you got them rounded up here?"

As the truck lurched forward, Virgil squatted to look me in the eye. "Because they aren't totally useless. Usefulness, remember? It's our watchword."

"Vaccine testing? Do you need all these people for your experiments?"

Anya tapped me on the shoulder. "Hey, *Mom*! You do realize these aren't people anymore, right? The virus made them a subspecies, and we're playing our part. This is Nature in action, and we can't be weak. It's no time to be passive."

"You see monsters when you look at them. That's what we see when we look at you," Regan said.

Anya didn't value my opinion, but when Regan spoke, I thought I caught a flash of self-doubt in our captor's eyes. Then she did what most people do when challenged. Anya doubled down.

"Look at what happened to the Neanderthals," she said. "They weren't just a dead end on the evolutionary tree of life. They were smart and strong. The Neanderthals may have even had music, but they didn't just die out. Some were assimilated into our genome, and just like now, disease and climate change played a part. Mainly? *Heh.* They were competition for food. Humans *killed* them. It wasn't genocide then, and it isn't genocide now. Self-defense *is* evolution."

"They teach you any ethics at Brown?" Regan asked.

"That was an Intro Philosophy elective. I signed up for Spanish, instead."

"The Thirders serve another function," Virgil told me. "I tell you this because I'm your sponsor, Ovid. I want you to succeed. Tonight you'll be on trial. The prize is admission to our intrepid little tribe of survivors. The final test will come when you come back out here and shoot a few Thirders in the head. If you want to survive and earn your place in our community, you're going to have to show commitment."

"Commit murder to commit to the Memory Keepers? Why not just let me go?"

"Because we're eliminating competition for resources," Anya replied.

"You aren't a tribe or a superior species. You're just another gang," I said.

"This is going to be a short trial." Anya's raucous cackle gave me clarity. I had to come up with a plan. To succeed, I would have to sink to their level, possibly lower.

Let go of quaint ideas of good and evil, Ovid, my inner voice whispered. *Be practical and ready to do what needs to be done. Be the hammer not the nail.*

For a long time, I'd thought that voice was my conscience speaking. Given my new insights, I'd simply heard what I wanted to hear. That voice had long assured me I was a blameless victim. I had believed that. But underneath that veneer, something more dangerous lurked. I was the girl they called the Ghost in high school. It was me who'd threatened to burn her bullies to death in their beds. The girl who dreamed of obliterating a classmate's face in a water fountain for a casual act of disrespect still lived in me. She'd been waiting a long time to come out, but now her talents were needed.

Hurt people hurt people, I reminded myself. *Hurt, adjective. Hurt, verb.*

Flawed and weird and broken, who else was more qualified to break the Memory Keepers? Anya's laughter was my trigger. Their ruthlessness would fuel my own.

For a moment, I was back on Dr. Rosa's ugly couch. She sat before me, sipping her tea and musing, "Every victim carries a secret power. Many are pushed down so hard they never get back up. The successful victims, though? You push those special few down hard enough, they'll spring back up twice as hard. I think you have that power within you."

That had been the last time I'd visited Dr. Rosa. The next I heard from her, she was coughing into her phone, informing me that she had a fever and would have to reschedule the appointment for our next therapy session. I never heard from her again.

But fiction has a power and flexibility that reality lacks. Dr. Rosa was dead, but I could keep her alive. In my head, she was still on my side and encouraging. "The tide will turn when your wrath is bigger than your fear. Fear can lead to paralysis. Remember: Anger is not wrong. It's an emotion you can use for good or for bad. Choose then express it."

As we made our way past the remaining Thirders toward the gate at the front of the Four Seasons Hotel, Virgil wiped his victims' gore off the truck with a rag. Shielded from brutal reality by the bag over her head, I was glad Regan did not witness Anya and Virgil's crimes. However, it meant I had to carry those heavy memories alone.

I'd warned Bennington I had an eidetic memory for the bad stuff. Dad badgered me, trying to make me let go of lifelong grudges. Everyone said I should leave my regrets and resentments behind, but no one showed me how. Dr. Rosa offered therapy, not personality transplants.

My inner voice came to my rescue: *Your worst flaw is your greatest power, Ovid. Unleash the beast.*

In my defense and in the defense of another, I'd killed twice. However, that was rage harnessed in the heat of battle. Witnessing my enemies' crimes, fury was in order. Only wrath might restore order.

Therapy helped me go far. I would ride trauma the rest of the way. My resolve hardened when I realized the person I'd been all along.

59

YOUR TURN TO CURTSY

When we arrived at the hotel, Anya pulled the black bag from Regan's head with a gentleness that surprised me. "There you go, Ms. Garnet. Based on your credentials and capabilities, you are a keeper, so you're Memory Keeper material. Welcome to the fold."

"You must really want that hot tub," Regan said.

"I really do," Anya replied. "The apocalypse is so damn dirty and stressful, don't you find? Water management is your thing, so now you're our thing."

Blinking in the bright afternoon sunshine, Regan gasped when she spotted the horde pacing behind the fence. "Man, that looks like it could be a hundred Thirders! And they're all so damn skinny! Looks like — "

"Animals on the edge of extinction?" Anya suggested.

"I was going to say a refugee camp. Are you feeding them *anything*?" Regan asked.

"Not much. We don't want to waste resources. They're just walking test tubes."

"But — "

"And I don't care for the term Thirders," Anya said sharply. "They have all sorts of names. Call them Turders, dummies, or if you're feeling fancy, smooth brains. I like the term guinea pigs, or just pigs."

"Nice."

"You've got technical skills we definitely need, Ms. Garnet, so I'm prepared to endure a small amount of back sass. You'll be skipping any trial because you're already drafted to the cause. All I can do is make your stay with our tribe pleasant or very much the opposite. Your choice, my hot tub."

"You gonna give a speech again? So far, that's been the most unpleasant part. Keep in mind, I was stuck in a sadist's dark basement for months, so — "

Anya didn't hit Regan. She slapped me across the back of the head instead. I cringed, but held my tongue.

"I'm trying to play nice with you, but if you can't be civil and be obedient, I won't beat you. I'll slap Mom around. Is that okay with you, Ms. Garnet?"

Anya didn't give her a second to answer. She punched me in the back of the neck. Unable to contain the pain, a low moan escaped my lips.

"All I need from you is a yes or a no, Ms. Garnet. Will you cooperate, yes or no?"

"Yes."

"See how easy life can be? Now, both of you, off the truck! There's bad weather coming, and we have business to attend to elsewhere."

For a moment, Regan and I were shoulder to shoulder. The last thing she whispered to me before Anya hustled her away was, "Remember your new motto and do not deviate."

Stay strong. Protect the weak.

"Thanks, Regan. See you soon."

"Maybe, maybe not," Virgil told me. "I'm taking a chance on you. I hope you get with the program. I think you could be a very productive member of our community."

"I thought I was a pawn."

He shrugged. "Some may rise to a higher rank. Many have fallen. Let me tell you something: I appreciate you for who you are, but Sid and Anya want to fill the organization with badasses. I'll give you a for instance. Anya and I had another enforcer before Sid came along. Former Marine, seemed like a good fit at first. His trouble was he was only tough on the outside, soft on the inside. We differed on what to do about the Thirders. He tried to appeal to our humanitarian instincts, but Anya's heart is a small target. When the Marine wouldn't see things our way, we went recruiting at the local clown college."

I stared at Virgil for a beat. "Joke?"

"I had hoped so, yeah. Anyway, Sid became our new enforcer when he opened up the Marine to look inside. That was the killer clown's personal assessment of the Marine's situation, by the way: tough on the outside, soft on the inside. You've already got my vote, so show the other two you're down to clown, if you know what I mean."

"I do not."

"Are you soft on the inside, Ovid? "

"What do the proceedings entail?"

"*Mm*, first, don't answer a question with a question. Second, you could say kangaroos are involved."

"You, Anya, and Sid are the only judges?"

"Of course. We'll determine whether you're useful enough to join the Memory Keepers. I've seen your organizational skills and your home garden. The reports from the office tower are impressive. You will have my vote, but it's got to be unanimous. Show peaceful cooperation and a commitment to serve. Don't mess around or Sid Serrated will open you up to see what's inside. That's kind of his thing, so play nice."

"Will I have a lawyer or a representative to do the talking for me?"

"As the old adage goes, you'll have a fool for a client."

"Public speaking? I don't know if I can do this."

He touched my cheek, stroking it softly. The sweet odor of gun oil was still on his hands. "You've survived this long on your own, so I know you have it in you. I respect that. Rise to the occasion, Ovid. If not, seriously, it'll be Sid's serrated sword for you."

"I hate it when people overdo alliteration," I said.

Virgil laughed as he walked away.

"Hey!" I called after him. "If the Memory Keepers had a motto, what would it be?"

"Easy. Survival of the fittest, but we define 'fittest' as the sociopaths with firepower. Can I get an amen?"

"Amen!" Roger declared before hustling me off to a maintenance closet full of cleaning supplies.

My mugger became my prison guard as I waited to stand trial. The door slammed behind me. I immediately turned and rapped on it. "Can I get some water?"

"No resources go to outsiders until after your trial."

Aching and sore from where Anya struck me, I lowered myself to the floor and leaned my back against the door. "Can I ask you a question, Roger?"

"You can ask."

"I have the impression the triumvirate doesn't care that I cut you and killed a Memory Keeper."

"That's not a question."

"But that doesn't factor into whether I become a member of the club?"

Roger took a long time to answer. "Loyalty goes up, not down. As long as you can do more for the Memory Keepers than the people you killed, you matter."

"How does that make you feel?"

"I'd rather be slingin' lattes, but the triumvirate calls this a meritocracy, so here we are."

"Barbarism, not meritocracy. But that's not what I asked. How do you feel?"

"Devalued. I'd love to slap you silly, but you got gardens going, and you know how to trade and survive. If you cooperate, there's a chance I'll end up working for you. I like to eat, so I'll make my peace with their judgment."

"And if the triumvirate rules against me?"

"If you're stupid enough to let that happen, I'll race against the clown for the chance to cut you up."

"Good talk, Roger. Thank you."

60

MY TURN TO BOW

"I have a question for you," Roger said. "Learned anything yet?"

"One thing. It might be helping me deal with my coulrophobia."

"Your what?"

"Fear of clowns. It seems to be easing a little with more exposure."

"You should be afraid of him. Sid Serrated is Death. He's insatiable."

"The trick is to see Sid as a little boy playing dress-up. He's basing his whole life on movies about the end of the world. If I could see through the cosplay, I would almost pity him. I stress *almost* but I'm trying to look at this as exposure therapy. I wonder if Sid even knows he's playing a part anymore? They say method actors can lose themselves — "

Roger kicked the door to bring me out of my reverie. "Can you shut up?"

"Sorry, I talk to myself mainly, and in the last few days, I've spoken to more strangers than I have in over a year. It's — "

"Ovid, cooperate or die. It's pretty simple."

"Alternatively, you could let me out, and we could escape together."

"Jesus, how desperate are you?"

"It's a big city, or we could head north — "

Roger kicked the door again, hard. "You expect me to risk my life for you? *Ha!*"

"You're already risking your life. You've already admitted that if I killed you, your leaders don't even care. What are you bringing to the table? Lattes?"

"I know my way around an espresso machine if we can get one working again. And I already had my trial and became a scout. My continued membership was iffy, but I think I proved my worth at the market."

"Blowing up the trucks that belonged to the Watch?"

"Yeah."

"So they scared you and they use you."

"How different is that from the way it ever was?"

"I knew a lot about death before the pandemic. My mother died screaming in pain, but at least she was on clean sheets in a hospital surrounded by people trying to help her. Then I learned more about it through my work. Authors often wrote about murder as an intimate act. In fiction, writing sex scenes and fight scenes have a lot in common. It's about the mechanics between one character and another. Good fight scenes capture the breath, the smell, the feelings — "

Roger smacked the door again. "What are you gassing about?"

"What I've learned: Murder is a lonely business. You can't think of the victim as a person, only a thing. Anya dehumanizes the Thirders. It's easier to torture and slaughter them if they're pigs instead of sick people. Murder is lonely because it's an act of separation. The killer refuses to conform and sets herself apart from society."

"Yeah? We got a new society going with new rules — "

"Is this really how you want to live?"

"Is there an intermission coming? Because this is a *long* movie."

"I'm tired, Roger. At this trial, I'm supposed to fit in, but I'm tired of trying to fit in. I'm always the one on the outside of the joke, banned from the inner circle. All my life, people have judged me harshly even though I never went out of my way to bother anybody unless they came at me first. I've apologized so much people thought I was Canadian, and still nobody's happy enough to leave me alone. All I ever wanted was to be left alone."

"I'm not your priest, Ovid."

"I'm telling you I won't make it through this trial. I don't fit, so let me out and help me and my friends escape. Help us and I'll do what Virgil, Anya, and Sid won't do. I'll think of you as a human being again."

Roger just laughed.

"Since the moment you came after me in that alley, I've been dreaming up ways of murdering you in inventive ways, heinous ways. I've seen and done a lot since our encounter in that alley. It's getting easier to kill you by the minute."

"You realize you're my prisoner, right?"

"We're both prisoners."

"You think you're so smart, but I'm not the one on the wrong side of a locked door."

"We all need something. How would you like to live and have dignity instead of playing Heavy #4? Aren't you tired of being an extra in someone else's movie? Don't you want to step into the light and be the star of the show? You have that choice."

"The woman I remember from work never yakked this much."

"Okay, fine. I'll make this easy for you. Help me or I will kill you."

His laughter didn't sound nervous. "You really don't know what's going on, do you? You took Virgil at his word? I've been around these people longer than you. They talk to each other as if I'm not even here, like I'm wallpaper. I hear things."

"And?"

"Virgil will break your spirit, but that won't be a challenge. He doesn't respect you, chick! Of all of them, Virgil's the one who thinks long-term. Anya and the clown focus on what's in front of them each day. They're short-term thinkers who can't think of anything but taking the city. Virgil's got his eyes on another prize. He wants your rich daddy's farm."

"Oh."

"Once the Memory Keepers are done with New York, he'll expand the mission to Vermont, Massachusetts, Connecticut — "

"Poeticule Bay, Maine."

"Before he's done with you, you'll be leading us home."

"Message received," I said miserably.

The door remained locked, and I sat in the dark. Before the virus, people bought lottery tickets hoping to win a ton of cash so they could finally feel safe. In What Was, we aspired to insulate ourselves from collection calls, the stigma of failure, and the constant grating background static of worry.

Money wasn't necessarily my goal, but I did desire independence. I'd always dreamt of possessing power. That's what people do when they don't have any.

61

NO WAY TO TREAT A LADY

T he courtroom had once served as a ballroom. Wedding receptions, business meetings, and prom parties had once been the norm. Now it was a big room with tables and chairs piled down one side atop a parquet dance floor. A single long table and three chairs stood at the front with a white linen tablecloth draped over it. It was stained with a spray of what I assumed was blood.

I complained to Roger that my handcuffs were too tight. He stood behind me, enjoying my discomfort. "Yeah? My arm still hurts where you cut me and still doesn't work quite right. Took a lot of stitches."

Virgil, Anya, and Sid strode in. Virgil and Anya had changed into formal wear. The killer clown was still shirtless and carried his sword by a strap on his back. His one concession to the gravitas of the occasion was a stovepipe hat. I tried to focus on the hat rather than his face. Making Sid ridiculous was all I could do to tamp down my urge to run.

"This court is now in session!" the clown announced grandly. "Since God has abandoned us, we are the new gods and we are *judgy!*"

"Let's hurry this up," Anya said. "Storm's coming and we've got somewhere to be. The trucks are almost fully charged up."

"Ovid Fairweather!" Virgil began as if he was surprised to see me. "Your usefulness is on trial right now, not you. Try not to take these proceedings too personally."

Anya cackled. "But if I were you, I would!"

"I'm sure I will," I said.

Sid smacked the broad blade on the table as if it were a gavel. "Silence! The court has not heard evidence yet."

Virgil nodded. "Very well. Let's hear the evidence." Before I could speak, he held up one index finger to his lips. "Not from you, Ovid. Sid? Please enlighten us."

The clown stood and came around the table to pace before it, dragging the tip of his sword across the floor, scratching it with each step. "I have evaluated this woman's holdings. She had an impressive hoard, but it was the build that got my attention. The greenhouse and solar panel set up at the office tower suggests she has resources we could exploit — "

"Courtesy of her rich daddy," Virgil commented.

Sid continued, "The water collection and distribution system tells me she's got urban farming skills. On the other hand, so what? We can copy that without her input. What I found interesting, and stupid, was her choices of crops. There were the standard plants you'd expect, cannabis among my favorite." At this, the clown smiled at me and winked. "I favor Jamaican Haze, but I'll take what weed I can get. Helps me sleep. On the other hand, of all the urban farmers we've interviewed, how come nobody thinks to grow poppies? How can we get some opium goin'?"

Anya rapped her knuckles on the table. "Sid? Time crunch!"

"Right. Okay, so, Stupid here had flowers down on the second floor and on the roof. Decorative flowers are a silly choice, obviously, so I brought us bouquets for our table. I may be a clown, but Sid the Killer Clown appreciates beauty."

Only gods and narcissists speak of themselves in the third person, I thought. *He's trying to embarrass me and it's working.*

Sid snapped his fingers, and a man and a woman brought in the marigolds and devil's helmet the Memory Keepers had confiscated. I tried to put up a brave front, but I felt violated.

"Searched her apartment, too. More of the same. Lucky for this membership candidate, I enjoy tomatoes. Good for the prostate, right? Unlucky for this candidate ... " He nodded offstage and another woman took her cue, scurrying out with two baskets, one of tomatoes, the other was full of nugs from my cannabis crop. The woman carried something else under her arm I was too near-sighted to see.

Sid's back was to me as he showed something to Virgil and Anya. They leaned forward, their heads together, nodding.

The clown whirled suddenly and tossed a thick stack of paper bound in rubber bands at my feet. It was my prized manuscript, the book that had allowed me to survive: *Grow Anything, Anytime, Anywhere* by Nora Jean Stone.

"So we've got her manual," Anya said. "What do we need her for?"

Roger stepped forward and cleared his throat. "May I speak? I just want to say this woman is also bad for morale. She killed two of ours."

Sid glowered at Roger. "The monkey's trying to talk. Who said you could interrupt these hallowed proceedings, Rogerino?"

"And who told you we care about your morale?" Anya demanded.

Sid turned to Virgil. "Did you create a Human Resources Department for the Memory Keepers? I didn't get that memo."

"No such department, no memo," Virgil replied flatly.

"Does this jabbering gibbon not understand how old school we are?" the clown asked. He stalked forward and slipped the battered sword under Roger's chin. "Do you not get our guiding principle? Were you not informed?"

"I, uh — "

"I wasn't done."

Eyes wide, Roger trembled and nodded, not daring to meet the clown's eyes.

"Speak now! What is the guiding principle of the Memory Keepers?"

"It's, um, a ... keep the memories alive and bring back What Was?"

"Wrong! That's the mission, not how we're going to get there." The tip of Sid's sword touched Roger's throat. "What do you think, members of the triumvirate? Is the gibbon wrong, or is he dead wrong?"

To avoid feeding my phobia, I set my gaze on the white tablecloth. The fabric's bloodstain held me back from achieving a state anyone could reasonably call Zen.

"The correct answer to Sid's question is: Might makes right," Virgil told Roger.

"Do you know what that means?" Anya asked.

Rogers' voice climbed and quavered, "Just like any job I ever had, you don't give a shit about me. I just do what you tell me and get it done right to justify my day's food ration."

"And how often do you have to make good?" Sid pressed.

"Every day, all day."

Sid chuckled and withdrew his blade from his underling's Adam's apple. "Correctamundo, Rogerino! Now where was I?"

"You were telling us that Mom is useless." Anya's gaze fixed on me. She smiled so sweetly, I abandoned my plans to kill Roger first.

"Before we come to any conclusions, we need to hear from the candidate," Virgil suggested.

Anya seemed irritated. "What is it about this woman that makes you so weak in the knees, Virg?"

"I'm not weak anywhere. I'm only one vote of three, but I think she could be useful."

"Why?"

He grinned. "Because she's so damn broken. You're so keen to surround us with lions —

"Power rests with the few who are prepared to do anything," Anya said. I sensed she was quoting from one of her own speeches.

"You don't see the wisdom in adding a few sheep to our numbers?" Virgil asked. "She does have skills — "

"The gibbon there does have a point, you know. You can't call her a sheep. She killed two of ours," Anya said.

"One of them was stupid, and the other was stupider," Virgil replied. "Bennington could barely be trusted to babysit two prime assets. Bear wandered into the battlefield with a lab rat to gawk at the corpses."

Staring at the floor, Roger dared to murmur, "The man had a name."

Virgil looked to the others. "Did he? I don't recall."

"His name was Robert Paulson," Roger said.

Anya's eyes widened. "Really? Bear's name was — "

"He was a monster with a rope around a girl's neck!" I exclaimed.

"The dude was in a dark place," Roger conceded.

"I met him there," I said.

"And murdered him," Roger replied evenly.

When I found words, my voice had steel in it. "Darkness had already claimed him. I just pushed him deeper into the dark so he can't come back and hurt others."

I shuddered at the memory and for a moment I was back at the burning market. I could still feel the weight of the hammer in my hand and the heat of his blood hitting my cheek.

"Read the room and shut your yap," Anya told me. "Bear was a Memory Keeper cowboy, always ready to capture, corral, or cull Zeta-3s."

"The big lug was also good for carrying heavy things," Virgil said. "That so stipulated, I've spent time on this little butterfly. Spent time *with* her. She's — "

"The facts remain, we've got her instruction manual. What do we need Mom for?" Anya asked.

Sid nodded to her approvingly.

In the beat of silence that followed, I cleared my throat. "Sorry, I read books, not rooms. Is it my turn to speak?"

EPISODE SEVEN

"Your strength is just an accident arising from the weakness of others."

~ Joseph Conrad, *Heart of Darkness*

"Revenge, the sweetest morsel to the mouth that ever was cooked in hell."

~ Walter Scott, *The Heart of Mid-Lothian*

62

CONTROL

Virgil gestured to let me know I had the floor. "I can do a few things well. I can sew, garden, harvest, trade, cook, and edit a full-length novel very well in half the time it takes other editors."

Anya and Sid burst out laughing, and it took them a while to settle down. "Where do you think you are, Mom?" Anya asked. "Or when? Have you got a time machine? No editing gigs in the apocalypse!"

"I was attempting to be whimsical. Turns out I'm hilarious. That was unexpected."

Anya and Sid laughed some more, but Virgil was dead serious. "Ovid, you can cook, right?"

"Yes."

"I was not a vegan before the supply chains failed. I am not a huge fan of eating my veggies, and I'm sick to death of chickpeas and egg replacement powders."

"I'd kill for a real burger," Sid winked. "A nice steak would be even better. Vegans graze. We hunt."

"Add onions and mushrooms, mashed potatoes, and Yorkshire pudding and you've got yourself a feast," Anya said. "Remember those big warm rolls they'd serve you in a fancy restaurant, slathered in a thick pat of melting butter? *Ooh!* I know! Barbeque that steak to medium-rare perfection and give me Key lime pie for dessert — "

Obviously annoyed, Virgil cut her off. "You know the rules. Don't talk like that unless our bellies are full. It's torture. You're making me drool."

Virgil turned back to me. "We have canned meat, but at some point whatever's in cans is going to be too dangerous to eat, same reason the food banks are failing. We've got a supply of MREs. That's an okay treat until they give me the runs. Can you make a delicious meal out of your crops?"

I nodded. "My parents and I didn't get along, but the kitchen was the one area they gave me confidence."

Anya eyed me suspiciously. "You're not like a raw food chef, are you? We had this bullshitter in here last month, standing right where you are now. He claimed he could cook. Turns out a raw food chef is a guy who can cut vegetables and put them on a plate. I was like, dude, *anybody* can do that!"

Sid Serrated's smile was a rictus grin, suggesting more madness than joy. "After he demonstrated his culinary skills, I sliced him up, diced, and julienned him."

Virgil turned to his fellow judges. "Given our forced dietary choices, we're all slim and healthy, but I gotta tell you, I'm sick of bland and healthy. Her farming skills can bring us fresh food. Maybe we don't really need her for that, but if she could make our meals more palatable, I want to give her a shot at impressing us."

"Yeah, I'm losing weight as if I'm on chemo," Anya remarked. "What do you say, Mom? Wanna give us a nice home-cooked meal so Sid doesn't have to decapitate you?"

"Sounds fair to me," I said.

Apparently, I should have just nodded or kowtowed, because the word fairness was a landmine. "Fairness?" Virgil's voice rose for the first time with surprising vehemence. "Ha! The last scintilla of What Was stands before us: A privileged girl in the body of a woman who can't get along with her rich daddy! She doesn't know how she fits in the new way of things! She didn't know before everything went to shit, either!"

"Quaint," Anya said. "*We're* supposed to be the last of the privileged ones."

The real Virgil revealed himself. His eyes were nailheads pinning me in place. "In this brave new world, you will learn that you are neither brave nor new. You don't have what it takes to be a Keeper, but I want you to succeed, to stay with us, and to serve us."

Sid stared at Virgil, incredulous. "I know you love a challenge, man, but I don't! If she's not up to the game and that's how you feel, why cut her any slack? We've got her farming manual. We can get cookbooks anywhere — "

"With no butter for the asparagus, all I taste is green chewiness."

Anya tapped her watch. "Let's wrap this up. Fine, let's suppose for a moment that Mom isn't dead weight. How are you going to keep her in line, Virg?"

"Easy." He waved to a guard at the back of the room. "I'm confident we'll get Ovid's cooperation. We have her smooth brain."

Roger threw Carl to the floor in front of me. Wide-eyed, sweating, and disoriented, the whites of my friend's eyes were visible all around his pupils. He goggled up at me. "Ovid? The worms. The worms!"

Anya giggled.

Sid looked down at Carl, disgusted. "What's the point of bringing this thing in here?"

"Control," Virgil said. "You know how I like to be in the driver's seat."

"Don't hurt him, please!" I begged. "Just leave him alone. I'll cooperate!"

"Will you? Because your smooth brain's comfort and safety totally depends on you, Mom. Kneel or squeal!" Anya relished her position of power as much I loathed my helplessness.

Virgil wasn't done eviscerating my life, however. "I have the best reason to keep her around."

Anya scoffed. "What? That farm up north? It's so far away, I don't understand why you're even bringing it up. Maine may as well be on the moon. Why is it in the equation?"

Virgil answered her question, but he stared at me as he spoke, burying me with every word. "Let's rub her nose in our success. I want precious, crazy, nutty Ovid Fairweather to see our rise. I need her to understand how far off course she was stealing from us. She wanted to turn us down. Soon, she will see and understand."

I understood *him* then. The night before Virgil had assumed he could have me. He was one of those guys who desperately wanted what they couldn't have. I didn't kid myself that I was some grand prize, but denying him had only fueled his rage and desire. He wasn't trying to save me, only protecting his ego.

"She's a perfect example of what we're doing for all of New York: creative destruction," Virgil continued. "I need her to feel every inch of how wrong and broken she is. When we succeed, she can apologize to us and mean it. Just like this city, I will break her to make her."

Faced with a devastating loss of dignity and his utter contempt, I tried something out of character. I attempted a joke. "So, you want me to feel like I'm in high school? It's nerds versus jocks all over again?"

They didn't laugh, but they didn't kill me, either.

63

THE GHOST

I awoke to the roar of thunder overhead. Roger soon freed me from the closet, but did not let me go. He held the sawed-off shotgun on me as he tossed me the key to my handcuffs. I unlocked them and rubbed my sore wrists, waiting for the tingling in my fingers to ease. "You going to return that gun to Heather?"

"Sure, next time I see her."

"So, no?"

"She was of limited use as a scout. That's done, so Virgil probably won't be sending her any more jams and jellies. Don't worry about the old lady. Worry about you. The triumvirate has taken the crew on a big supply mission. Meanwhile, your job is to impress them with a big feast when they get back tomorrow night. You're cooking for the big three. I'm supposed to help you in the kitchen. You do a good job, you'll prove yourself useful."

"One good meal and they'll forget all my grisly sins? That must make you feel terrible. I mean, I could have killed you in that alley, and you'd just be another forgotten tool left out in the rain. As long as I can do wonders with nutritional yeast, all your work for the Memory Keepers is an afterthought, huh?"

Roger shrugged. "Now I'm really struggling with what to root for.

I want to kill you for stabbing me, but I'm really excited about what you can do in the kitchen with nutritional yeast."

"Really?"

"No." He gestured with the gun, ushering me down a dim candlelit hallway to the hotel's restaurant.

I had to see what ingredients I would be working with first. The kitchen had power, gas stoves that worked, fridges, a walk-in freezer, plenty of ingredients to play with, and hot water. I washed my hands and forearms thoroughly. If Roger hadn't been watching, I would have stripped down and given myself a hot sponge bath from the big stainless steel sink.

Three silver goblets, fine china, and silverware were set aside for the triumvirate. I wondered if any of them had any allergies that would incapacitate them instantly. That was too much to hope for, but I could dream.

Roger sat back and watched as I took an inventory of my ingredients. "What do you think? Borscht or bisque?"

"They're looking to be impressed, so I'd do both," Roger replied. "In fact, I'd try a bunch of recipes and go with what's best. I'm always hungry, and they got me on strict rations, so I'll be glad to act as your taste tester."

"Why are they away until tomorrow night?"

"Told you, supply run. All of them."

"Must be special."

Roger sighed wistfully. "I'm hoping they come back with tons of canned food that's nowhere near its expiration date. Won't need you around if they do."

I spotted the basket of nugs on a far counter. "First, I think we're going to need you to test out my cannabis. How do fudge brownies plus a buzz sound?"

His eyes lit up. "Sounds great! Do it."

"Stop waving the gun around first. You can put it down."

"And give you another chance to stab me?"

"You've got Carl. I won't do anything that endangers him. Besides, are you really that scared of me?"

He stared at me with unbreakable eye contact as he removed two shotgun shells from the breech. He pocketed the ammunition and set the weapon on the counter. "You run, your boy dies and you watch. Then you die."

"I get it. If you're supposed to help me, grab a couple of those big pots and put them on the stove."

"Hell, no. Anything else?"

"Fine, where'd the bad guys go?"

"The triumvirate's working on a big score scavenging a container ship that ran aground a while back. It's down the coast. We've had our eye on it, but it's hard to get to and harder to unload. With that big storm rolling in, they're worried the boat might up and float away."

"Pirates pirating. What's onboard?"

"So far? IKEA furniture. If that's all they find, they'll be in a bad mood when they get back."

"I better cook."

"Like it's meth and your life depends on it."

Much of what we'd stolen from Adilah's house had been moved into the storage room beside the kitchen. I got to work.

"Roger? If you really want those weed brownies, get out a colander and a stiff sheet of paper. I'll show you how to get the seeds out and not waste any of the buds."

Roger must have been eager to eat because he did as I asked. Cannabis isn't addictive, but chocolate is. He did not wait for the first edible to take effect before he devoured the second and third pot brownie.

I chopped vegetables to make a broth. I was washing the cauliflower for my second cauldron of bisque, and he was five brownies in when the buzz hit him all at once. He complained of dizziness, but complimented me on the potency of my crop.

"I thought it would be the easiest to grow, but I had a steep learning curve," I said. "My first couple of attempts ended up a mildewed mess."

As Nora Jean Stone had taught, I delved into the common problems of growing cannabis, from spider mites and temperature control to sterilizing tools with hydrogen peroxide. My lecture lowered my anxiety. The dullness in his eyes assured me that Roger was no longer paying me much attention.

I'd prepared a lot of food, and he was quite high before I dared to make my move. The shotgun was empty. I could have tried bludgeoning him with it, but the weapon was too short and light for that. He watched me carefully when I stepped close to the knives, so the obvious weapons were beyond my reach. A heavy cast-iron skillet proved the best choice.

With one big swing to the back of Roger's head, he went down hard. I expected the skillet would give a hollow *clang*. Instead, it was a dull *clung*. Satisfying, nonetheless.

I'd been furious about being underestimated before, but now I saw it as my superpower. They'd left me with a pliable one-armed guard. Their mistake.

64

AND THE DARKNESS

I fished the shells out of Roger's pocket. There were only two cartridges. I rushed to load the shotgun. Then, very still, I strained to hear footsteps coming my way. The hotel was as silent as a tomb.

Roger hadn't lost consciousness completely, but he was senseless long enough for me to put his hands behind his back and use his handcuffs to subdue him. I tried dragging him to the walk-in freezer. Heavy and hard to budge, his shirt rode up and his bare skin acted like a screeching brake on the bare tile. However, after I poured cooking oil on the floor, I zipped him into the walk-in freezer easily.

"I'll get back to you as quick as I can," I told him.

He moaned in pain. "You bitch! What are you going to do?"

"Well, you're drenched in cooking oil. I *could* light you on fire and dance around the flames singing happy songs."

His eyes bugged out, and he shook his head wildly. "Please don't."

"Roger, you're on my enemies list. Before I do anything drastic, I need you to ponder a question. If the killer clown knew I had you at my mercy, could you count on *his* mercy?"

As I gagged him, he mumbled mean curses.

I leaned down to whisper in his ear. "I understand. You need some time to work out how they'd punish you for such a terrible failure. You're useless and I'm up here, cooking and doing the survival of the fittest thing. Think on that."

After commandeering two room service carts, I slipped out a rear door. As I made my way to the fence line, the carts rattled on the uneven pavement, but the tureens did not spill a drop of soup. I searched for a gap in the fence behind the hotel. There was a gate of sorts, if you can call a spot where two fences meet a gate. Two heavy chains joined by a heavy padlock offered too narrow a gap to squeeze through. The fence was topped with rolls of razor wire. No way out.

Abandoning the carts, I slipped down one side of the hotel, alert for sentries. The container ship must have been quite a prize because I could detect no movement on my side of the fence. Close to the front gate I'd come through that afternoon, I squinted hard. I could just make out a single figure with a rifle on an elevated platform with a powerful searchlight. His or her back was to me. The way the guard directed the light at the far fence, it was apparent the Thirders were not their concern. The guard probed the far perimeter, alert for uninfected interlopers out to steal the Memory Keepers' hoard.

Upon my return to the rear of the hotel, I found a few Thirders milling about. The smell of cooked food attracted them. As I called for Carl in a stage whisper, some more wandered over. Soon others arrived, following those first to appear. Hungry, they all sniffed the air. I did not see Carl.

I threw a few chocolate bars deep into the compound beyond the fence. More of the infected noticed, picked up the rations, and devoured them. Some might not have stopped to remove the paper wrapping first. Soon they were crowding along the fence. My goggles were gone, but I made sure my mask was secure as I used the ladle to reach through the tiny gap above the lock and chain.

An older woman, her right eye was blind and cataract-white, asked plaintively, "Food?"

"Soup," I said.

"Soup is food," she said.

"It is. Have some."

She took several long slurps from the ladle and then, at my urging, made room for the people behind her.

Not all the Thirders were cooperative about moving along, but the infected who stood behind them were starving. None were shy about pushing forward to get their ration of a full ladle of hot bisque or borscht. It wasn't much, but the meager meal was undoubtedly the first hot sustenance they'd had in a long time.

Attracted by the commotion, even more of the infected made their way to me. Most were cooperative in waiting their turn. When a few of the Thirders clung to the fence and refused to move, I tossed energy bars over their heads. They rushed to get their share.

A figure appeared out of the darkness, and I recognized him before truly seeing him. It was Carl, sweaty but looking better than he had earlier. Despite being taken from the comfort of his cot, his fugue with the virus had passed, at least for the moment. I gave him some soup, passed him a painkiller, and offered his favorite ration: a strawberry oatmeal energy bar.

"Carl, I need you to listen to me."

His steady gaze connoted nothing. For all I knew, my friend may as well have been staring at a foreign language film sans subtitles.

"If you can hear me in there, please hide! There are only a hundred or so of you, so you can't hide among the others. Go to the far end of the fence and find a way out. Dig under it or climb over it, I don't care. Just get away! Whatever you need to do, get out of here and take people with you. I'm about to take a big risk. Can't risk you, too. Understand?"

He stared, blank and inscrutable.

"Go on! Get out of here! Go! If I live, I'll find you, but you have to go, or they'll use you against me! Please, Carl, find a way out of here!"

Finally, Carl spoke. "Thank you, Ovid. I'm worried about the worms and the plants."

I was about to give up and retreat to deal with Roger, but more Thirders appeared. They looked so neglected, miserable, and sunburnt, I couldn't bring myself to abandon them. I kept feeding the infected until the tureens and the water bottles were empty.

To my horror, I discovered the Memory Keepers had even more leverage over me. Aldebaran, Maurice, and Parisah appeared behind the fence. My follower looked particularly forlorn. When I offered Aldebaran one of my few remaining chocolate bars, she held my wrist. She didn't want to let go. For a change, I did not recoil at another's touch.

"I have a plan to get us out of this, but in case I don't make it, better for you if you aren't here. The Memory Keepers know I know you, and that means it's not safe for you here. Take Carl ... take everybody and find a way out, okay? It's a lot of fencing. There's got to be a weak point out there somewhere."

Aldebaran's grip, gentle yet firm, told me she would not attempt to leave without me. I begged all of them to flee or hide with Carl. Henrik's children only stared back.

Finally, I returned to the kitchen to fetch more food. Even condemned killers on death row get their last wishes for a meal fulfilled. It was the least I could do for the infected innocent.

65

HEAT

Aldebaran's cries followed me into the hotel. My promises that I'd see her again sounded hollow. The Memory Keepers were not to return until the next evening. That left me too much time to stew. Their return felt like a doctor's appointment I couldn't dodge.

Standing in the middle of the Four Seasons restaurant kitchen, my mind was still outside with the Thirders. Rechecking the pantry's inventory, I could hardly focus on the clipboard. It seemed all the odds had been stacked against Zeta-3 infected. If slow starvation and the elements failed to kill them, the Memory Keepers would hasten their end.

When I was eight, I asked my parents if I could have my own dog. My father's dog, Tippy, had been a golden retriever. For some reason, I'd become fixated on wire-haired terriers. "You love dogs and books more than you love people," Mom said. "So go read about dogs."

"I have. I want a wire-haired terrier, and I want to call him Scotty and — "

"We can't afford it," Dad said. Then they put in a pool. I learned three things that summer. First, they could so afford a dog. Second, I learned to swim. Third, whether you're a fat kid in a bathing suit, or if you were all bones and angles like me, some parents feel it's within their right to destroy their child's self-esteem.

Ours was not a familial relationship. My parents owned me. I was their pet just as the Thirders had become the Memory Keepers' property. No amount of knocking on wood or biting my tongue for luck would change that. "It's all up to me. Alone."

I slid to the floor as the panic attack hit. It started with weeping, then hyperventilating. As my breath grew shorter and shorter, I didn't have the strength to go look for a paper bag to breathe into. My legs felt like water balloons. Desperate to slow my breathing and escape the crushing weight pressing down on me, I pulled my mask over my mouth and nose. Yanking my shirt up so I was rebreathing the same air, the dizziness eased. My breaths grew deeper and slower just as the stress headache arrived. My forehead burned hot against the cool tile.

Where was that voice in my head always telling me what to do? Usually, it would pop in with something annoying and/or true by now. The voice had fallen silent. When I searched for those thoughts, the echo was just my voice, asking questions and getting no answers.

As I waited out the headache, I tried to think of pleasant things: *Nerds versus jocks. I made it through high school, I can do this!*

I'd read all of Kurt Vonnegut's works except for *Galapagos*. As a reader who was a completionist, survival was imperative. But my obsessions, even my idolatry of sweet Kurt Vonnegut, were insufficient. What else?

Marigolds are so beautiful. The flowers symbolize power and joy, but they also represent despair and love lost. The editor in me appreciated the dualism and the oxymoronic conflict of the metaphor. It spoke to me personally, mirroring what I could have been and epitomizing what I felt.

Nora Jean Stone's manuscript had informed me that marigolds attract spider mites and snails, thus protecting other plants. Marigolds cured my spider mite problem with the cannabis crop. However, I'd cultivated marigolds for a more sinister purpose, as well.

Their seeds work as a powerful hallucinogen. Take too many and they kill.

"*That's* how I'm going to get through this."

I'd begun growing marigolds in greater quantities when my prescription medicines started to run low. My compulsive exercise routine was supposed to yield helpful mood-boosting endorphins. No matter how hard I pounded my treadmill, I suspected there would come a time when my sadness would be too much to bear. If I went mad or got infected, I had a painless escape plan. I could grant Carl's fondest wish, overdose beside him, and together we could slip away into the dark.

The voice in my head remained mute, so I gave myself a firm pep talk. "Stop feeling sorry for yourself, Ovid. Think of the people depending on you. Yoo-hoo? If not you, who?"

Solitude can be crushing, but it also absolves one of many responsibilities. Carl was trapped out in the Memory Keepers' compound along with Aldebaran, Maurice, and Parisah. Killing myself would be the same as murdering them all. Henrik and Regan were probably being held somewhere nearby, and they needed my help. The only way to aid my friends was to kill my enemies.

"Murder can be quite empowering."

My fear turned to anger. I could march into the walk-in freezer and do away with Roger. It would boost my self-esteem to cross him off my enemies list. For Barry Cupper, Adilah, and the victims of the explosions at the market, that seemed reasonable. But was it smart?

Pondering vengeance enabled me to sit up. I sat on the kitchen floor in the dark for a long time, picturing how the next few minutes, the next day, and the next night might play out. I imagined a flow chart, trying this option and that. Most of my projections ended in disaster for me or for the Thirders. Usually, we all met our demise by Sid Serrated's sword, gutting us and laughing as he did so.

Headache ebbing, I climbed to my feet and took a few deep breaths. This new Ovid, with no strange voice in her head to guide her, felt like a cosmonaut stepping out of her spacecraft on an alien planet, testing the air to see if it would suffocate her.

"No," I told myself aloud. *"Don't* start talking about yourself in the third person. It's as obnoxious as Époisse de Bourgogne."

Époisse de Bourgogne was the smelliest cheese in the world, so deadly to the olfactory senses that export from France had been banned. As a book editor, I had retained so many useless facts like that. As a killer making her way in the viral apocalypse, I didn't have to know so much. However, in my new profession, the future was very uncertain.

"Ovid chastises herself for being a whiny twit who can't let go of one damn thing," I said.

Then, "Stop it!"

To speak in the third person was just another way to avoid being me. The extra voices in my head had always been about stepping outside myself. For what I was about to do, I had to take full responsibility. At that realization, I considered myself twenty-eight percent less mousy than I'd been before the world ended. Progress.

No matter my steps toward self-actualization, Dr. Rosa would have preferred I stick with talk therapy. With the moral superiority afforded those who never had to fight clowns with swords, she'd undoubtedly counsel, "Don't try this at home, kids!"

"Leave the murdering to me!" I announced as I ripped open the door to the walk-in freezer. Fresh energy surged through my body as I stalked in, planted one foot on my prisoner's back, and pinned him to the floor.

To Roger's terror, I added, "What happens in the next few minutes is all on me."

66

COLD

R oger lay on the cold floor, shivering and screaming. I hadn't tied his gag tight enough. He'd maneuvered it down to his chin, but no matter. No one was around to hear Roger's cries for help. He fell silent when I set the bottle of cooking oil on the floor beside him.

"You look cold, Roger. I could solve that problem for you. Options, options, whatever shall I do? I *could* give you a blanket, let you out of here, and warm you up with some hot soup. Or — "

I pulled out the lighter.

His eyes widened as his teeth chattered and his body shook. He pulled uselessly at his handcuffs, contorting his body until I kicked him in the side. "*Sh!*"

I bent down and flicked the lighter again.

"You wouldn't!"

"All through my childhood, people tormented me, even my family ... *especially* my family. My parents treated strangers better. Later, I tortured myself. I'm finding this new phase of my life, with all its potential for violence, quite liberating. See what you've done, Roger? See what you and the Memory Keepers have made? It's as if I'm ascending to my final form, isn't it?"

"You're crazy!"

"Old news everybody knows."

As I brought the flame closer to his face, Roger pleaded in a low whisper, "D-d-don't!"

Nervous energy radiated off him, as strong and clear as a radio signal. Desperation and feelings of helplessness had long been my home. From my vast expertise with fear, I recognized its purity in Roger's eyes. His pride would determine how the rest would play out.

"I have to hasten your growth, so let me explain something. If this were fiction, my character would be at a crossroads. At Pilkington Press, I edited many stories about heroes and heroines doing the right thing no matter what. The anti-hero stories were more compelling. I could do the evil thing, light you on fire, slam the door, and rationalize. Eliminating you and disappearing into the night would lower my personal risk and satisfy my lust for vengeance. Revenge is the only lust that can sustain throughout a lifetime."

"What do you want?"

"Shut up, I'm on a roll. Some say an argument shouldn't be about winning. It should be about coming to a greater understanding. For our negotiation to succeed, we have to talk about what you want first. You want your life back. Living or dying at the whim of an unhinged clown is no way to make your way. I've seen how they treat you. You'll have no longevity with the Memory Keepers. Sorry about braining you with a frying pan, but you know ... reason and reasons."

His cheeks were wet, but his throat was dry. Roger rasped, "What do you want? Just tell me."

"Cooperation, of course. Things won't get set right if we keep running from your bosses. We're all in the same boat as long as the triumvirate is in control."

"Same boat? Doesn't feel like it from where I am."

"The boat is sinking, Roger. Everyone is waiting for someone else to start bailing. The triumvirate's solution is to throw people overboard to save themselves. The boat will be lighter, but you know the problem: more dead people. They'd throw you off the boat in an instant and you know it. They'll run that big sword through you before they'd kill me. You do see that, right?"

Roger closed his eyes. He might have been praying.

"I know how it feels not to be valued. I've felt the pain you're feeling now. There is a way out for both of us that doesn't end with you getting impaled by a rusty sword."

Roger opened his eyes. I sensed curiosity somewhere beneath all his sweaty fear.

"So?" I probed. "Have you worked through what those maniacs would do if they knew I'd escaped?"

He nodded.

"I'm going to get you out from under the Memory Keepers," I said. "But we're going to have to trust each other."

"So you *won't* kill me for coming after you?"

"Roger, if you promise you're with me on this, I swear I will not seek revenge on you for attacking me in that alley. I have a history of not quite killing you, but make no mistake — "

I placed the shotgun behind his ear, "Betray me, and my third try will be the charm. You owe me a life."

"I get it." He was still eyeing the lighter, so I put it away.

"Good. Can you get me keys to the gates? Or a bolt cutter? Maybe a wire cutter would do."

"Keys. I can get you keys."

"You mean you can get *us* keys."

"All right."

From editing thrillers, I knew the first thing a professional burglar should do is plan a secondary escape route. If my plans went awry, I'd be on the run. Beyond the outer gate, I had no idea where I would go, but as my father would say, "Let's burn that bridge when we get to it."

I removed his handcuffs and helped him stand. He walked stiffly to a chair by the kitchen counter and plopped himself down, shivering. I found a heavy moving blanket and draped it over his shoulders. "The woman, Anya, she calls me Mom — "

"A lot of moms are dead. Take it as a compliment."

"She doesn't mean it that way."

"No, but you could decide to not be offended."

"People have told me that, but I don't know how. You ever notice when someone says 'no offense but,' it's because they're about to say something that will keep you up all night and haunt you forever?"

"You a drama queen, Ovid? Seems so."

"Lately, I'm giving more drama than I take. I finally understand why people enjoy dishing it out."

His hands shook. "It does get the blood pumping."

I heated water for two bowls of instant chicken noodle soup. He didn't say anything for a long time. I watched him carefully, looking for some clue he would betray me. He didn't lunge for the shotgun, so that was a start. I had a test in mind. "Get me the keys, and I'll make you a hot chocolate."

"Like Mom used to make?"

I shrugged. "Sure."

Roger reached into his jeans' front pocket and tossed a ring of keys onto a cutting board.

"Those were in your pocket this whole time?"

He managed a grin. "Diggin' into my friggin' thigh, yeah. Hurt like a bitch. What have you got planned for the bosses?"

"Something dramatic. I just came pants shittingly close to torturing and killing you, but I need to insert another action beat here to drive up the rising action toward the narrative crescendo."

"*Whut?*"

"Never mind, that's a note for me, not you."

"I repeat, *whut?*"

"My whole life has been a slow burn, but I'm accelerating the pace of my plot. Respect my process, Rogerino."

67

THE DARK HALF

T here were five keys. Two were for the inner compound gates on the street out front. One was for the padlock on the fence behind the hotel's loading dock. Another unlocked the padlock on the gate at the outer perimeter. The last was for Roger's old Ford F-150 parked two streets over. It was out of gas, and all the tires were flat.

"That's where they trapped me," he said, "in my truck. Well, stolen truck. I tried to get to Jersey, but the border guards turned me around. When I came back to the city, Virgil found me sleeping in the driver's seat. First, he blocked me in with his truck. Then he shot out all four tires while he conducted my intake interview. I joined the Memory Keepers, but I never had a real choice."

"Intake interview? *Hmph.* Makes the organization sound so corporate."

"They joked about it, but I wish we had an HR department. Plenty of complaints if they did. For instance, I shit my pants as soon as he started throwing bullets into my ride. Friggin' psycho. Virgil seems the most rational, but really, he's the one who scares everybody the most, including Sid and Anya. That dude is hot and smooth on the outside. Inside? His blood is ice, and his bones are made of nails. You've only seen his shiny side."

"For your interview, what did he ask you about?"

"He gathered intelligence. He's good at it, and by that I mean he freaked me out, kinda like you just did."

"And Virgil hired you on the spot?"

"Yeah, lucky me. The pay was just a few cans of Spam at first. They treat us all like idiot shit, and everybody hates Anya and the clown. It's Virgil that's scariest because he can turn it on and off, easy one minute, iron the next. I'm not alone in how I feel about them, but if we don't look enthused about everything, they hurt us."

"Hurt you how?"

"I've seen Virgil keelhaul offenders as an example to the rest of us."

"Keelhaul? Isn't that a nautical torture?"

"What they call keelhauling around here involves tying a rope around your waist and making you jump off the front of the truck. Virgil goes slow at first, then he floors it until the victim is dragged behind the truck. There's an empty stretch of road in front of Macy's. Nobody's ever come out of that as anything more than a skid mark."

I winced. Practiced at concealing his true self, Virgil had managed to be mostly charming when he'd visited my apartment. Ironically, the man who didn't need to wear a mask had worn one all along. He'd been very convincing. Sociopaths are often clever that way.

"They're monsters," Roger said, "but the nasty shit they do ensures loyalty."

"They've gone too far! Even the worst dictators get overthrown."

"Eventually, maybe."

"Haven't they gone too far for you? What they've done to the Thirders was terrible, but it hadn't occurred to me they'd torture and kill their own army."

"The Memory Keepers aren't an army, Ovid. Looks that way from the outside, but we're just another bunch of survivors jumbled together loosely by fear. Sid says the triumvirate can rule by love or by fear, but fear lasts."

"Until someone finally stands up."

Roger let that pass. "Anyway, Virg made me a scout for new recruits."

"And you found me."

He bobbed his head. "I spotted you trading at the market and again at the food bank off Central Memorial Park. I remembered you from before 'cuz of your hair. Looked like you were getting on all right. I followed you a few times. You lost me past the market. It's a big city, but with so few people on the street, it's impossible to not get spotted. I was under strict orders to find your farm but avoid spooking you. You're so cagey I couldn't do both those things at the same time. Virgil was sure your farm had to be close to your apartment."

"Spy craft, subterfuge, paranoia, and terrible inconvenience paid off," I said. "I have cheap genre thrillers and a terrible childhood to thank."

"I suppose, though we did forget about you for a while when other stuff came up. It is true, Virgil insisted no one would try to make a greenhouse out of a high rise."

"I know, but I didn't *try* to do that. I *did* do that. Your bosses put the word out, and Heather gave me away, I take it?"

"Don't be too hard on the old lady."

"You were really hard on her, I hear." I pointed at the stolen shotgun with my chin. "If not, you wouldn't have that."

"That performance was for show," Roger replied. "I had other members with me. Had to look tough in front of them and get results."

Members, as if the Memory Keepers were a cozy club.

"I'm going to demand results, too, Roger."

He took a long breath and let it hiss through his teeth. "We're all just trying to live, you know? Most of us don't know how anymore."

"Wait here," I ordered.

Snatching up the keys, I took the shotgun with me out of the rear door, back to the padlock and chain. The wind was whipping up and thunder rolled overhead. I worried for Carl and the children, but it was too dark for me to see where they'd wandered off to. The Thirders had dispersed, and I was glad of it. I had no food or water and didn't want to tease them.

Hurriedly, I tried two keys before I found the correct one. It slid into the padlock easily and popped the shackle. I left it unlocked, but kept the shackle in a link of the chain. To make a quick escape, all I had to do was lift the padlock free.

Roger had passed my first test: The keys were real. He passed my second test when I found him where I'd left him. He could have made a run for it and alerted the guard at the front gate.

"Still cold?" I asked.

"All the way through, yeah."

"I'll make that hot chocolate."

"Got any marshmallows?"

I shook my head.

"Still, a hot chocolate would be nice. My parents used to take me ice skating at William Vale every Christmas Eve morning and every New Year's Day," he said. "Family tradition, twenty-three stories up. I wasn't much of a skater, but it's a great view of the city from that rink. We always had hot chocolate when we got home."

"Uh-huh."

"My dad was an accountant. Mom was an OR nurse. She worked front line on the ICU wards when the operating rooms shut down and died way back in the very first wave. Dad killed himself, but I don't think he meant to. Maybe it started as a binge, but it ended with alcohol poisoning. Couldn't blame him since he felt like nothing without her. My earliest memory is of my parents slow dancing in the kitchen. No music. Just dancing."

Not knowing what to say, I said, "I see."

"You're wondering why I'm telling you history, huh, Ovid?"

From my experience editing spy thrillers with hostage scenarios, captives should share personal stories and use first names a lot. The tactic was to make the prisoner appear more human to his captor. It was a ploy to gain trust until the schemer could attack or break free. I still had the shotgun on my side of the counter, and he was appealing to my humanity. That worried me. I was taking a chance on him, but I couldn't afford to make my heart a large target.

Same as it ever was, I thought.

"I tell you because, before the pandemic, I mean ... the Memory Keepers ... " Roger trailed off, drew the blanket around him tightly, and stared down into his empty bowl. His voice broke when he began again. "I tell you because I want you to know I wasn't always like this."

"I was," I admitted, "Took me some time to figure it out, but I was always like this."

I used to ask the tough voice in my head, "What are you? Why are you?"

Now I knew.

68

THE DRAWING OF THE THREE

The Memory Keepers returned from their scavenging mission early. While their small army of marauders wandered off to their rooms to feed on assorted rations, I'd prepared a banquet for the triumvirate alone. The tablecloth was of fine white linen. Three lovely vases of devil's helmet stood tall, their beautiful purple flowers lent color to the table. I placed one goblet at each place setting. The plates had shiny silver covers to match.

Anya, Sid, and Virgil arrived at the same time. "The container ship was a bust, Mom," Anya said. "So you better be good."

"It was full of furniture," Virgil complained. "I can't think of anything we need less. We've got a city full of furniture. Worse, it was the kind you put together!"

He gestured grandly, as if he could see all of New York at his feet and all of her survivors on their knees. "Here we are, the three richest people on Earth, the new mayors of the greatest city on the planet! We're beyond desks and bed frames you have to screw together yourself. Ridiculous!"

Anya ignored him, focusing on the table I'd set. She eyed the sweating pitcher filled with ice and a red liquid. "What's this? Blood?"

Sid grinned. "Thirder blood?"

"I dug into the stocks for canned pineapple and found frozen strawberries at the back of the freezer. Put together with a nice bubbly white from the hotel's wine collection and you've got a sweet cocktail to begin dinner. Moscato sangria. You'll love it."

"Excellent." Virgil's eyes were bright with anticipation.

Swallowing my pride, I enthused, "Thank you for this opportunity. I haven't had all the ingredients to really let loose in the kitchen in years."

Virgil applauded my efforts, but he clapped alone. "Good, good! This is a nice change, huh, guys? All day I anticipated finding some useful treasures. Each container we cracked was a disappointment. No more of that!"

The other two crossed their arms and said nothing.

From Roger, I knew better than to believe him anymore. However, Virgil persisted with his chipper tone. "I know what you're feeling, but all in all, it wasn't really such a bad day. It was several hours of somebody shitting in your hat, but let's put that behind us. I'm starved." He lifted the plate cover to peer at his appetizer and sniff the food before covering it again.

"Vegan crab cakes," I explained.

Sid snorted and slammed the flat blade of his massive sword on the table. "Not a crab and not a cake. Bad start. For real, what's to eat?"

I'd gone over my presentation with Roger and rehearsed the spiel all day while I prepared their feast. "After the Asian fusion salad and carrot soup, you'll enjoy a roast cauliflower for the main course. I have a bottle of red ready, and the matcha tea will go nicely with peanut butter bars for dessert. I didn't know if any of you had allergies to nuts, so as an alternative, there's a sweet potato pudding with pumpkin spice."

"Ha! Somebody wants in our treehouse club! Mom wants in and she wants it bad!" Anya cackled.

The clown wrinkled his nose in disapproval. "Man, I miss a juicy steak. Remember grilling a nice steak? That's the only way I want onions and mushrooms — on top of the meat. I miss the smell of barbecue wafting through the air over freshly mown grass. That's the aroma of summer."

Virgil gave Sid a hard look. "Man, we talked about this. Stop it."

The clown was unmoved by Virgil's plea. "I love the smell of cooked meat. All I'm saying is, makes me feel the ache for a New York striploin in my eye teeth. I foresee a time in the near future when cannibalism will be on the menu."

"Whoa, there! No talking about eating people!" Virgil objected. "Turn down that noise! You'll scare the fish!"

I rushed to add, "I found maple syrup from Quebec. It will go well with the side dish of acorn squash. The secret to loving vegetables is in the spices and — "

Sid stared at me. "I find blood from a rare steak adds a lot to a baked potato. It would be good even if the steak were a hunk of Rogerino there. Don't you agree?"

Certain that no answer would satisfy him, I said nothing. The clown had sweated off so much of his pasty white makeup that I could see through his facade. To maintain my fragile calm, I focused on the skinny computer programmer he'd once been. I still couldn't bring myself to meet his gaze.

"Oh, Rogerino!" Sid called in a sing-song voice.

Roger stepped forward. He still held Heather's shotgun, but I had the shells and his ring of keys in my pocket.

"Did you watch the prisoner prepare our meal?"

"Yes, sir."

"No hanky panky? No spit in soup?"

"No, sir."

Anya gave Roger a nod, and he stepped in front of me to handcuff me. With his back to the triumvirate, he murmured, "Stay cool."

That done, Anya beckoned me. "Approach the bench."

Steam rose from their plates as all three uncovered their appetizers. At Anya's signal, Roger produced a fork and shoved it into my hands.

"I'm hungry, so show them, Ovid," Virgil commanded. "Eat!"

"W-what?"

Sid slammed his sword's pommel on the tabletop as if it were a gavel. "You think we're morons? It looks good but show us how it tastes. Shove it into the lowest hole in your head. Take some from every plate."

When I hesitated, the killer clown raised his sword high. "What do you say, Virg? She's your recruit. Do you want to keelhaul her, or do I get to use the pointy end of old Betsy here and pop her head like a balloon?"

69

DEAD MAN'S FOLLY

I did as I was told and stabbed two crab cakes from each plate. I'd already sampled everything in the kitchen. In truth, it was delicious. Despite its long disuse, I hadn't lost the only talent my parents encouraged in me.

With each bite I chewed, Anya seemed disappointed she hadn't caught me poisoning them. She ordered me to test the sangria. When I reached out a trembling hand for her silver goblet, she slapped it away. Roger appeared by my side with a tall water glass.

I drank the sangria and then some wine. Sid and Anya watched carefully, waiting for any symptom of poisoning to strike. Virgil seemed relaxed, confident I was utterly cowed.

After a few minutes, Virgil crowed, "Told you! My find is a treasure! You guys think my little Ovid has it in her to do us dirty? C'mon! She knows the penalty! What'd I tell you? Ovid Fairweather is a sheep!"

"She's killed before," Anya said.

Virgil ignored her and made a show of eating every crab cake on his plate.

To me, he spoke with his mouth full. "They're just mad because they lost the bet. Little butterfly, you make me want to be a badder man!"

You are, I thought. *The question is, am I more clever?*

Sid and Anya still refused to partake of the meal.

He jeered, "She used to edit books! Now she's a farmer and a cook. She knows her place in the world. I'll give you a hint. It's at the bottom."

My jaw tightened. Before I could stop myself, I blurted, "You sound like my father."

"Wise man, your dad. Family understands family best."

"That's not my experience."

"Well, welcome to our family, Ovid. You're a Memory Keeper now. We have warriors and our warriors must be ruthless and brave. I prefer my personal chef to be a coward."

I gritted my teeth to stop myself from screaming. *I am not owned!*

Virgil giggled as he reached to grab Sid and Anya's appetizers and dump them on his plate. "You lose, suckers! Told you!"

Smug and self-satisfied, he gobbled it all. He licked his fingers and guzzled two glasses of sangria before pouring himself a goblet of wine.

"Well, little butterfly? Bring on the next course! Proceed to dazzle us. Bring it all out at once! I want it all!"

"Reckless," Anya said. "That's always been your problem, Virg. The plague didn't get you, so you think you're untouchable."

"She's not wrong," Sid agreed. "Also, not for nothing, you're being kind of an asshole about winning the bet."

"Our new chef and chief food taster didn't drop dead, so you lose, I eat, you watch. I *love* to say I told you so!"

"That's why nobody likes you," Anya replied.

"Everybody who's smart likes me. Don't be a sore loser. When I'm done, if there's any left, you can enjoy my crumbs."

With mounting resentment, Anya and Sid watched Virgil eat his fill.

Working in the kitchen all day over the stove, I'd already gotten too warm. However, it wasn't the heat of the summer day that made me sweat. I'd begun to worry I'd gotten it all wrong. With Sid and Anya refusing to eat, two-thirds of my plan had already failed.

Tiring of being patient is not what patience is, I reminded myself.

Virgil was halfway through the roast cauliflower before he stopped chewing and looked up at me, his eyes wide with wonder. His face darkened as he drew his pistol and pointed it at my head. "W-what did ... what did you do?"

All eyes turned to me. Virgil looked stricken. Anya frowned. A maniacal grin spread across Sid Serrated's face as the truth dawned.

I pulled my mask down to my chin so he could see my face. "My name is Ovid Fairweather, and I am not a sheep."

Sweating heavily, Virgil's pistol grew heavier in his hand as he struggled to focus. He wasn't dying fast enough to save me from getting shot. Fortunately, his curiosity gave me the opportunity to stall. He demanded to know what I'd done.

Pointing to the three vases of purple flowers decorating their table, I managed a smile. "Devil's helmet has several names. Agatha Christie would call those poisonous plants wolfsbane. They're more popularly known as aconite, but I prefer their most dramatic alias: queen of poisons."

Anya reached for Virgil's plate and flipped it to the floor. Too late for that, and not on point, either.

Staring down the pistol barrel, I explained, "There are many toxins, but only a few ways to poison someone effectively given my resources. I would have preferred the skin of your hand absorbing the poison. If I was miles away when it happened, even better. Technically, devil's helmet might do that, but it probably wouldn't be fatal. I could poison the food or the drink, taste it, and survive as long as I took an antidote first. However, I have no antidote, Virgil."

The pistol clattered to the tabletop as he clutched his chest and fell back in his chair.

"You were right," I admitted. "I was a coward. Being brave is a new thing for me. That's why I grew marigolds and aconite. The marigolds alone would kill me with a big enough dose, but I had to be sure I'd get more than a bad trip. In case I got sick with the plague or anything else, I wanted to be sure I'd overdose and go all the way. There were two dangerous plants in my office tower, and you brought them both here to mock me. Thank you, Sid."

"You're welcome," the clown replied.

Virgil tried to speak, but all he could do was grunt in pain and pant. His breath grew shallower with each frantic respiration.

"It was your stupid silver goblet," I explained. "I coated the insides of each one. *Just* a book editor? You might have lived if you'd read more Agatha Christie."

Virgil slid to the floor with a thud. He died astonished.

70

THE STAND

F urious, Anya stood. "God, Mom, you *do* go on, doncha?"

Sid touched her arm and pointed to the fresh corpse on the floor. "It may not be exactly kosher, but I gotta say, winning the bet and all, that was pretty satisfying. I thought that guy would never leave!"

Anya gave a perfunctory nod. "Yeah, feels as good as pickin' a scab."

The clown turned back to me and gave a slow clap. At first, I thought he was mocking me, but when I dared to look him in the eye, his appreciation and gratitude seemed genuine.

"We did not like Virgil," Anya admitted. "Damn Unicorn, always thinking he was so special."

"As if he built the Memory Keepers on his own," Sid said.

"And we were afterthoughts." Anya looked me up and down. "Still, Mom tried to kill us, too, and that is not cool."

"And Rogerino? *Yoo-hoo!*" the clown called. "Don't think we've forgotten you! You were supposed to make sure she didn't spit or shit in the soup. I conjure that what Madame Fairweather did was far worse, but you let her off the leash in the first place."

I glanced Roger's way. Trembling, he muttered, "That wasn't the deal."

"You made a lethal deal with your prisoner *before* you came to me. You think I would be okay with that? Really? Have you met me? She almost had you on her side, didn't she? Took too long to come to me, man! You thought about it long and hard. Shoulda come to me right away."

Anya's gaze fixed on me. "Roger should have shot you on the spot. Listen up! Keelhauling was Virg's thing. Making julienne fries out of people is Sid's kink. You know what I like to do to sneaks and traitors? I boil a big pot of water and fill it up with sugar. That way, when I pour it over you, the hot water doesn't just slide off. The sticky mess makes the scalding go on and on. How's that sound, Mom?"

"Less than ideal. I want to live forever, or at least until the sun explodes ... though that desire for longevity is more of a hate-watch situation than anything."

Turning back to Virgil's corpse, Sid laughed and pointed, "*You* said she wasn't funny. She *is* funny!"

When I tried to be funny, I usually failed. When I spoke honestly, I was hilarious.

Sid started clapping again, slow at first, then faster and faster as if he were delirious. Anya gave a long-suffering sigh. "I don't find her near as amusing as you do, Sid. I'm hungry and tired. Can we get on with setting a good example for the crew?"

"Slow down!" Sid yelled. "This is the most fun I've had since the last time I had fun! You are such a pooper of parties and panties!"

Anya's answer was a withering sneer.

"Fine." The clown picked up Virgil's pistol from the table. "Rogerino? Kill Mom so we can eat. Or we could have a hot sugar water party for you, too. What do you say?"

"How about let's not and say we did?" I suggested.

Anya began climbing over the table. "This is bullshit. I hated the damn Unicorn, too, but we can't show weakness or we'll lose people."

As she drew a revolver from her waistband, she sunk one knee into her roast cauliflower. "Oh, that's it! These are my favorite pants. Mom's gonna burn!"

In moments of indecision, the person who moves first and aggressively tends to win. At least, that's what I'd learned from a series of novels about a goofy assassin. Fiction authors make up almost everything. I hoped my strategy wasn't some figment of some moron typing away in his blanket fort.

I leaped behind Roger and slipped my handcuffed wrists over his head. The short chain caught him under the Adam's apple as I pulled him back toward the exit.

"Anya!" Sid called. "Mom is using poor Rogerino as a human shield. That would work if we gave a shit about him, wouldn't it?"

I whispered in Roger's ear, "Raise the shotgun."

"What?"

I tightened the chain across his throat. "*Point it!*"

Roger did as he was told. The weapon was empty, but I assumed they didn't know that. Anya retreated behind the table. Sid just stood there laughing.

"I'm sorry, Ovid," Roger said. "He knows."

"What?"

"I made a mistake," Roger admitted. "I was more scared of Sid than you so — "

I pulled the handcuffs chain tighter across his throat. "Being terrorized by the clown was the crux of our deal!"

Giggling like a drunk child, Sid fired two shots into the floor next to us. "The bet was rigged, Ovid! The bet was rigged!"

Anya's infuriated gasp sounded a lot like my own. Judging by her reaction, Sid had kept Anya in the dark. She cursed him, loudly and imaginatively.

The clown didn't look at all concerned. "Triumvirates and tribunals. Not a fan! But being king to your queen, I can get behind a good old-fashioned dictatorship! The value of our votes just went up recently, didja hear?"

Anya was not so easily appeased. "Virgil was one of us! Even if — "

"In my defense, bloodless coups are tough to pull off," Sid said. "Are you on board to be queen, or what?"

"What's done is done," she said. "I guess I choose what as long as I get to give Mom a public execution."

I almost got to the door when Sid took aim in earnest. It was a long shot for a pistol so we almost made it out safely. "Come back for your sentencing, Ovid, you naughty minx!"

He fired twice and took shards of wood out of the door frame and the door. As I yanked Roger into the corridor, a round burned through his shoulder, and we collapsed to the floor together.

Roger howled in pain. "Same shoulder as you cut," he said. "That's gotta be a sign. I deserved it. Sorry."

"You owe me another life," I said.

Hurling curses, Anya came for me. "Kneel and squeal, Mom!"

I scrambled for the shotgun and dug into my pocket for the cartridges. The handcuffs plus my hurry to load the weapon seemed to slow me down considerably. Trembling fingers can only work so fast, and despite my recent experiences, I was not used to people pointing guns at me.

I closed the breach just as Anya emerged from the courtroom. On my knees, I had no time to raise the weapon and aim. The butt of the stock bucked against my right hip as I pulled the first trigger.

The shot went wide, barely spraying her with pellets. The second shot tore through her side, spinning her to the floor face down. Anya writhed in agony.

Her blood pumped across the floor, as if reaching for me. Roger lay in a pool of blood of his own, but his injury didn't seem mortal. She was already turning white as the stench of fecal matter rose from her wound. Abdominal wounds, according to the author who wrote the goofy assassin novels, are among the worst pains a human can suffer.

Good!

Anya managed to roll over. She still held the revolver, but seemed to have forgotten it was in her hand. "Mom?"

"I'm not your mother," I said. "My mom thought I was bad, but you? *Huh.*"

Sid appeared in the doorway. He looked down at Anya and gave a carefree shrug. "Oh, well, looks like I'm gonna be a sexy bachelor monarch. I'm too young to commit to a long-term relationship anyway."

The clown raised his pistol and pulled the trigger. I squeezed my eyes shut, only to hear a loud, empty *click*!

Laughing, he held the pistol's magazine high. "People don't like mind games, but I *love* 'em! Monopoly takes too long, and since money doesn't mean anything anymore, I get no thrill from blackjack and poker. But the look on your face! *Ha!* That's a trip!"

Roger tried to rise, propping himself up on his good arm. Sid gave him a vicious kick to the head and he fell back. "Got no time for traitors."

He pointed the empty pistol at me. "That's a lesson you learned too late, eh, Ovid? Don't worry, I won't burn you. That's Anya's thing. Truth be told, she was kinda sick in the head."

He bent over her, staring into Anya's hazy eyes. "Bye, girl! I always hated your long tirades on that damn bullhorn, but that won't be a problem anymore, will it? You're going over the rainbow bridge! Tonight you dine in Valhalla! Bye-bye, you crazy bitch! Bye-bye!"

I got to my feet, lunged forward, and swung the shotgun at his head. He was younger and much faster. I missed and put a dent in the wall.

He knocked the gun out of my hands and tossed it down the hall.

"Go," Roger told me. "Run!"

"No, no, don't run away. That would be rude, and it is my turn." Sid pulled his serrated sword from the sling across his back and gave a wicked grin.

I ran.

Sid shouted, "I'm gonna go slow and take my time! This is going to be fun, but not for both of us!"

71

REVIVAL

S id Serrated, the killer clown and new king of the Memory Keepers, did not sprint after me. As I headed toward my planned escape route, he walked. That should have been a clue that Roger had given everything away. When I got to the kitchen, my route to the unlocked gate was blocked. Perhaps a couple of dozen Memory Keepers waited for me.

They chanted my name, "Ovid Fairweather! Ovid Fairweather!" They formed a wall with their bodies. Once I became his prisoner, Sid would make an example of me, and I doubted anyone present would dare to defy him ever again.

Sliding on the kitchen tile, I struggled to maintain my balance and failed. Falling to one knee, I grabbed the edge of a counter, righted myself, backpedaled, and sprinted back the way I'd come. My left knee burned so badly, my sprint became an urgent limp.

Brandishing his ugly sword, Sid blocked my way. I changed directions and headed through the hotel lobby. I burst through the front door into torrential rain. Another group of Memory Keepers stretched across the street to my right. They chanted, too, "Ovid Fairweather! Ovid Fairweather! Ovid Fairweather!"

Veering left, I bore down. I ran through the pain and splashed through puddles to get to the front gate and the Thirders' compound. The Zeta-3 infected must have been attracted by the loud chanting. As soon as they spotted me, they pressed forward, their faces to the gate. Their dirty fingers poked through the wire. The same half-blind woman who'd informed me the night before that soup was food reached for me through the small gap where the gate stood chained.

I dared a glance behind me to see Sid stride out of the hotel. The Memory Keepers who had been waiting for me in the kitchen marched out in a loose group, joining the chant of my name.

Sid didn't come straight for me. Instead, he moved to stand in front of his little army. Then, as he advanced, they followed behind in a phalanx that took up the width of the street.

Wet and trembling, I fumbled for the ring of keys and rushed to pop the padlock as more Thirders pressed forward. The weight of their numbers jostled the gate and made it harder for me to try the keys in the lock. The first key was the wrong one.

"Where do you think you're going?" Sid called. "You don't think we can catch you? You're just putting off the inevitable. To be fair, I'd do the same if I were you!"

I almost dropped the key ring. My hands shook as I tried again. When I realized I was attempting to use the same key twice, I cursed.

Take a breath, I told myself. *Haste makes me into paste.*

The next key slid into the lock and turned. The gate burst as the Thirders pushed in. They reached for me and pulled at my clothes, searching for food and water. They all wanted some kind of mercy, but mercy had been in short supply for a long time.

Sid was only ten paces away when the Thirders pulled me out into their compound. I slipped and fell on the same knee I'd just injured, but it hurt much worse this time. No more running in the rain for me. No mask. No goggles. Handcuffed. No escape plan. With the madman coming at me with a sword, I'd never felt so naked, vulnerable, and alone.

Someone grabbed my shoulders and yanked me to my feet. Twisting away, I was certain it was Sid about to saw off my limbs. When I turned to discover who had helped me up, I froze.

Carl!

The Memory Keepers were all chanting my name, but my friend still seemed unsure it was me. He frowned. "Ovid?"

Time stopped for a moment. I hadn't stood so close to him without goggles and a mask in ages. "Yes, it's me. Hi, my friend."

"The garden needs more weeding," he said.

"Yes, I guess it does."

"Get back, ya diseased smooth brains!" Sid shouted. Wading into the crowd, rain droplets flew from the battered steel as he swung his sword in a wide arc. Frightened, the infected rushed to get out of his way.

Carl patted my shoulder, smiled, turned, and ran at the clown king. Sid laughed as he thrust his blade through my friend's stomach. I screamed as the tip poked out of Carl's back between his spine and left kidney.

Witnessing the horror, I shivered as though the rusty blade was ripping and tearing through my organs, too. Hot tears blurred my vision and the world slowed. Sid cackled and crowed as Carl sank to his knees. Even the Memory Keepers seemed shocked. They abruptly stopped chanting my name, and after the echoes died, it got so quiet, like all sound had been muted by a thick blanket of snow. Cold gripped me as if it was my guts spilling blood on the pavement.

The Memory Keepers had once been ordinary Americans. Judging by their stunned silence, at least some of them weren't numb to such violence. I could feel doubt winding through the mob, tightening around their hearts. I hoped that with my sacrifice, someone stronger than me might awaken. Sedition could take root in the ranks. That seed had already been germinating before I arrived.

Days before, my damnable inner voice would try to distance me from reality. That male voice, filled with equal parts certainty and nonsense, would have said, "Sid Serrated, killer clown and king, is vicious with the viscera!"

I'd let that voice go and did not miss it. The only voice I heard was my own. *When is enough going to be enough?*

I did not fool myself into believing that I had the strength or skill to take Sid down. It would have to be enough that I showed his followers that he could be defied. Someday, someone might remember their dignity and find courage. Bad men tend to meet mean ends. Maybe the next rebel would have more luck.

"I always told myself I'd die with Carl." Thunder crashed and lightning flashed as I limped forward to face the Memory Keeper's mad king.

72

ELEVATION

I was not alone after all. Aldebaran and Parisah pulled me back and pinned my arms while little Maurice clung to my injured leg. Aldebaran reached up to my jaw with a grubby hand and forced me to turn my head to look at her. She shook her head as she stared into my eyes.

Full of mirthful scorn just a moment before, Sid began to curse. Carl was not dead yet. As the clown attempted to withdraw his nasty blade, Carl grabbed his arm and pulled the clown king closer.

The Thirders, too, had had enough. The infected surged past me and attacked the swordsman who'd been deprived of his weapon. Driven by starvation, humiliation, and abuse, they were no longer a crowd of victims. They became a mob. Exhausted of being pushed around, they pushed back.

It was not exactly a coordinated attack. They were more sick than skilled, but before they were done, the killer clown was bruised and battered. His scalp bled from where they'd pulled out hanks of hair. His white makeup became sparse, replaced with crimson where he'd been struck, scratched, and bitten.

Somehow, Sid shoved one of his bigger assailants off him, got to his feet, and stumbled back through the gate. He wept and cursed, knuckling tears from his eyes. In the short melee, the clown had lost two front teeth. When he spoke, it was with a lisp. "Tonight, we *featht*! We're going to roast the librarian on a *thpit*!"

"Book editor!" I said. "I wasn't a librarian! I was an editor!"

A beanpole of a Memory Keeper stepped forward to scream at me, "Nobody cares!"

In my fury, I was not eloquent. Searching for a pithy reply, I sputtered, "D-don't ask for me-my h-help when you can't figure out the difference between *a*ffect and *e*ffect!"

Rough launch, stuck the landing. Someone to the rear of the phalanx tittered.

I didn't feel brave, but I wanted to appear so. Encouraged by that lone reaction, I tried another joke. "Without me around, you're going to have a lot of dangling participles!"

That was weak but there was so much tension in the crowd begging for release that the gambit worked. When the woman tittered again, the effect was contagious. Others joined in. Maybe they were laughing with me or at the clown. Either way, it was the first time I could recall laughter sounding pleasant.

Furious, Sid cried. "Kill her dog*th*! If you don't you'll dine on *th*mooth brain tartare tonight!"

I broke free of my protectors to crouch beside Carl. His breathing was shallow, and his skin was cold, but he seemed to have moved beyond pain. My defender smiled up at me.

"The worms need the soil, and we need the worms." Carl's smile died and then so did he. I had denied him the merciful death I'd promised, but his fondest wish was finally granted.

"No more pain," I muttered. "No more pain. Goodbye, my foul-weather friend."

"Well," Sid jeered. "I*th*n't that *th*weet?"

I laid my friend down carefully, took a deep breath, and stood. As I did so, I drew the bloodied sword from Carl's body. "Sid ... no, you're Steven. Steven Herschenfeld, you talk too much. For a guy who calls himself a clown, this is the first time you've actually made me laugh. I wouldn't ordinarily mock someone's speech impediment, but wow, you're a funny piece of shit now. And you have gone too far!"

Talking to him like an angry and disappointed mom wasn't going to do the job. I applied a rule I'd learned from years of reading and editing fiction: Show, don't tell. I raised the sword high, ready to bury the blade in the clown's head. "You deserve this. Um ... the pointy end, I mean."

"Agreed," someone behind him added. A single shot rang out.

The clown fell face down in the dirt, blood gushing from an ugly chest wound. Bug-eyed, he looked to me, trying to talk, but out of air. Blood bubbled up from his gaping mouth.

Roger took a few unsteady steps to stand over the clown. With Anya's revolver, he fired two more shots into the body to make sure the king was dead.

Swaying, pale, and shaky, Roger turned to me and offered the key to my handcuffs. "I owe you."

I tucked the bloody blade under my arm, hurriedly unlocked the cuffs, and dropped them atop the dead clown. I wasn't sure how relieved I should be yet, but Roger eased my fears. He held out Anya's weapon. "Hope I didn't steal your thunder. You killed two of the big three, so don't feel bad."

I took the pistol from him as the Memory Keepers murmured in a mix of confusion and concern. "Anya's dead?"

"She might still be at it, I don't know. Beyond help and well on her way, for sure. I've seen Anya burn friends with her sugar water trick, so I got no friggin' sympathy." He winced as he pressed his good hand to his shoulder wound. "One more thing I've got to do toward paying my debt."

Somehow, he mustered enough energy to turn to the assembled and shout, "All hail the new queen of the Memory Keepers!"

My acceptance as their new leader was not immediate. A woman pushed forward. I recognized her as the one who'd brought out a basket of my marigolds. "Why should we?" she demanded. "We should follow her just because she can cook? I don't think so!"

"Follow her because she won't make you eat raw Thirder meat. She can feed us, but that's not the most important thing. She remembers something we've forgotten."

I assumed Roger meant that I knew enough details about urban farming to remake the city into a peaceful, agrarian society. I was wrong.

"She's still human," he said. "She's got empathy. That's the memory we didn't keep."

The sole objector hung her head and melted back into the ranks.

Roger dropped to the pavement. I knelt beside him and cradled his head. "You've lost a lot of blood."

"You care?"

"I feel it. When I look at your shoulder, it feels like mine is ruined."

"That's nice. Sorry I betrayed you," he said. "Sid was ... well, Sid was Sid. I got too scared."

"Sid is Steve now. We'll have no more performances inspired by the Joker. Um, you should know I planned to kill you long before you betrayed my trust."

"You swore you wouldn't get revenge."

"I wasn't going to do it for me. I was going to kill you for the people at the market. Your victims."

"Oh, yeah, that. Life is friggin' complicated, huh?"

"I'm not afraid of you right now, so pulling the serrated part of the blade across your throat wouldn't be self-defense. I might murder you when you're feeling better."

"You're forgiving."

"No, I'm not. Don't get comfortable. You want life? Earn it."

"Okay," he said. "In the meantime, I'm wet and cold, getting colder."

I looked to the Memory Keepers. "Hey! Gawkers! Are there any medics here? He needs medical attention."

A man and woman rushed forward to assess his wounds. I stood, Sid's crimson blade in one hand, Anya's revolver in the other, and my army of Thirders at my back.

"Roger, if you give up and die, you lose your chance at an atonement and redemption story. I command you to live!"

Neither Roger's endorsement, my weapons, nor my infected friends made me queen. I believe the tide turned when I called for a medic for the man who'd betrayed me. Virgil, Anya, and Sid made the ordinary New Yorkers into monsters by terrorizing them and treating them as disposable, worth less than a nickel. With no solutions offered, despair inevitably sets in. I understood those feelings. That is how I found compassion for the assembled.

The woman at the back of the phalanx was the rudder that turned the crowd my way. It was she who'd laughed at my joke minutes before. Her voice was high, but the cadence she struck with the syllables of my name was compelling. She chanted, "Ovid Fair-weather! Ovid Fair-weather! Ovid Fair-weather!"

This time, the chant was not ominous. Others contributed their voices until, slowly, all the Memory Keepers joined in. Even a few of the Thirders, those who could still vocalize well enough, added to my choir. The rest of the infected hummed.

Long before I understood what it meant, I'd been a Memory Keeper. I had kept my terrors, failings, and regrets alive for too long. To turn things around, the world needed Memory Makers.

Dr. Rosa's words came back to me, "Without a future, we obsess on the past."

The first thing we had to bring back was the fact that wars end. Enemies today can become allies tomorrow.

I addressed the crowd. "We've all been stuck in What Was. Let's start thinking about What Will Be. I'll never ask you to die for me. I want you to live for all of us."

The storm did not break at the crescendo of my speech. No sudden sunbeam shot through the clouds to spotlight me and signal my inevitable ascendance. Such cheap symbolism would have been too on the nose, and we had too much work ahead of us.

If Dr. Rosa were present, she'd counsel, "Remember, it's a process."

Trying to understand the world through fiction, I'd assumed my narrative would fall inevitably into the category of dark dystopian memoir. In the end, I pulled back on the murder throttle, aiming for the more niche genre of hopepunk. If we can't hold on to our humanity, why bother hanging on at all?

73

CARRIE

D r. Henrik Ebrahim was soon reunited with his children. We held proper funerals for Adilah, Barry Cupper, and all the other victims of the triumvirate. Except for me, none of the Memory Keepers attended. The wounds were too deep for the community to accept the group's change in direction so quickly.

One of the first missions I assigned my followers was to find Cheryl. Carl's widow ran from the searchers at first. Convinced I was bent on revenge for the raid on my grow-op, she had to be subdued and handcuffed. She didn't begin to relax until I offered her a place in the hotel and meal rations.

Cheryl joined the kitchen staff and turned into a capable cook for the whole crew. She never spoke of Carl, and I respect her ability to do something with which I struggle: she's putting the past behind her.

Henrik, too, was skeptical of my newfound status as queen of the Memory Keepers. He called my strategy "Making peace with pirates."

"But there aren't any pirates anymore," I argued. "It's not because they were all hanged. Some of them reformed and went on to become regular citizens. Don't forget, many Memory Keepers were just like you. One way or another, they were coerced."

As Henrik predicted, my transition into leadership was not entirely smooth. Not everyone was on board. I sent away anyone who had killed people at the market. We needed a place of banishment, so Staten Island became our Australia.

Whether it was guilt or fear that I'd poison him, Roger volunteered to lead the exiled. His right arm will hang uselessly in a sling for the rest of his life. However, he can lead the rogues we've come to call the New Australians. Their task is to work the land and provide a percentage of their crops to the city's food banks. The amount they supply will depend on their yield.

Committed to crushing the threat of famine, I will use them for good instead of holding mass executions. Show trials, torture, and casual murder were too much of the previous regime's brand. The Memory Keepers need a makeover, and I am their new, gentler face. Ironically, many of them call me Mom, but they don't sound like Anya when they say it.

Regan's mechanical expertise has been instrumental in hooking up the old photocopiers at Pilkington Press. Powering them up and tinkering a bit, she got the machines working again. To change people's minds about the organization, we have to save lives. Finally published for the masses, Nora Jean Stone's *Grow Anything, Anytime, Anywhere* is a hit despite its incredible heft. Maybe I should write a vegan cookbook to go along with it so readers can get more enjoyment from their gardens' yields.

Something Roger said gave me the idea. "We're all just trying to live and most of us don't know how anymore."

As Pilkington's industrial copiers *ka-chunked, ka-chunked, ka-chunked* away, Regan asked, "You really think a book can save us?"

"Originally, I cut the chapters on forest foraging. I put them back in, so — "

Ever the wise counsel, she stopped me. "You don't sound certain. We need you to sound confident."

"I never got to be valedictorian. A kid I hated named Chris Haig won that honor. I can still paraphrase the speech I wrote and never got to deliver, though."

Regan nodded for me to proceed.

"Does anybody read anymore? I'm not sure, but if we can get books into the hands of readers, maybe there's hope. With organized thoughts and symbols scratched into dead trees, the written word can serve as a hedge against cynicism. That's how books work for me. They can be instructive and entertaining. Books have kept me relatively sane."

"No wonder you didn't get valedictorian," Regan said.

"You're not wrong," I admitted. "I can see the headline now: Four Dead as Valedictorian Melts Down at High School Graduation. I think they're all dead, but I still fantasize about murdering people with my mind."

I confessed to Regan that I'd threatened the 3Cs. Every kid in my high school suspected me of arson for any fire within three counties after that incident. Dr. Rosa would have put on her concerned face. However, when I told Regan about the girls who tried to bully me, she gave an unconcerned shrug. "Everybody wanted to murder people in high school. A reasonable response, weird if you didn't want to. I'd only worry if you actually did."

It was hard to find friends who can deliver that high level of committed validation. Her take was so fresh, Regan became my right-hand woman at that moment.

"If you turn into Anya, or start putting on too much white makeup and rouge, I'll pull your plug," she assured me. "Otherwise, I'm with you."

In the spirit of creating goodwill and a new society, we made hundreds of copies of Nora Jean's opus. To beat the blight and survive, we must transform New York into a peaceful agrarian haven. The Memory Keepers are quickly turning into a farmers' army, becoming expert in constructing greenhouses, water cisterns, irrigation systems, and solar arrays. The only sword we aren't beating into a plowshare is the one on my back.

Just as Carl helped me, under supervision and care, many of the Thirders were able to assist with the gardening. Those who cannot help are still fed, sheltered, and protected. One of my first decrees was that no matter their ability, everyone is to be treated kindly.

"We all have something to heal," I told my Memory Keepers. "I have more deficits than many of you, so listen when I tell you the infected should not be underestimated. They're sick, but they're often sensitive. They are not pets, slaves, or commodities. Don't even think of them as patients. Before anything else, they're still people. Respect neurodiversity in all its many forms, and please do tolerate the odd bit of emotional disregulation."

Someone stuck up a hand. "What the hell is emotional disregulation?"

"Panic," I explained. "If you don't lose it from time to time, you aren't blowing off enough stress. Have a good cry. Crazy if you don't."

Whether they understood I was talking about the Thirders or myself, the majority complied with my edicts. Those few who failed me were shunned and exiled immediately. I didn't even have to swing Sid's sword around to make my point.

Eager to remind doubters who and how many evildoers I'd killed, Regan made sure everyone took me seriously. She hyped me up, telling and retelling the story of how I rescued her. In her version, I kicked Bennington to death using Tae Kwon Do. She also told everyone his pistol was loaded. "Don't wanna see Mama when she's mean, do you?"

Despite my newfound security, I remained as paranoid and hypervigilant as ever. Unaccustomed to the role in which I'd been cast, I feigned confidence. When someone seemed reluctant to perform a task like lugging garden soil up twenty flights of stairs, I gave my best steely glare. "My mother trained me in the dark arts. Didn't you hear? I'm a Death's Head Moth."

For all his faults, I learned something from Sid: People look for leadership. I don't really want them to fear me, but they don't all have to like me. As long as I deliver on my promises of a better future, the Memory Keepers will acquiesce.

Regan gives great lectures on how to build compost toilets and solar stills. With her help, my public speaking skills have improved, too. The information in Nora Jean's book has lent credence to our claim that I am out to make allies. At every stop, people see the value in what I'm offering. They ask what we want in return for Nora Jean's book.

I tell them, "We have doctors working on new preventative measures and treatments. The Memory Keepers are scrounging for all the medical resources needed. This fall we'll have more vaccines. You only owe me what you owe yourself. Join us and we can all help each other."

We have all endured enough pain. Like Regan says, "Pain and strife are part of life, but suffering should be optional."

74

NEEDFUL THINGS

Three weeks after the coup, I took my first trip away from my tower farm. Regan drove me to Upstate New York to visit the Memory Keepers' caches. To prepare for the future, we needed to take inventory of all they'd stolen, scavenged, and stored. Aldebaran came, too. Her role was to carry my pack and watch for danger, a job she seemed to relish. Paid in food, she no longer looked sickly. As long as she could see me, she seemed content, perhaps even happy.

Virgil, Anya, and Sid may have been evil, but they'd been great scavengers. Their impressive collections of supplies were stored in huge mansions along the Hudson. As with Adilah's house, the old manses were stocked with everything the elite survivor could need. Besides food, we found more solar panels, construction materials, farm equipment, fuel, spools of cables, generators, batteries, hand tools, weapons, and ammunition.

At Staatsburgh, in a mansion that looked much like the White House, the triumvirate had stashed enough supplies to stock several pharmacies and a hospital. "A lot of the drugs are out of date," Regan observed, "but the equipment looks fine. So far, I've counted twelve rooms that are packed floor to ceiling with diapers."

The Kykuit mansion in Pocantico Hills harbored the greatest treasure. All four stories of the old Rockefeller residence were packed with bags of heirloom seeds. Sealed safely in plastic storage containers, the stores were free of fungus and blight. Peppers, eggplant, squash, turnip, pumpkin, sorghum, spelt, barley, and a vast variety of beans had been sitting there all along, waiting for the future to arrive.

"This is amazing. The MKs must have raided all of FEMA's seed vaults!" Regan said.

Gobsmacked, it took me a few moments before I could reply. "They just *hoarded* all this?"

"Saving it for a rainy day, maybe? Building up value?"

Silent tears rolled down my cheeks as I stood before the treasure.

"You okay, O?" Regan asked.

"Just feelings ... hope, mostly. This is the real beginning of our resurrection."

"What? We're necromancers now? Cool."

"We're all going to be farmers. With these stores, we can make calories come cheap again. That's how we're going to turn things around. It'll be a lot of work upfront, but when the food comes easier, we can reboot civilization."

Regan smirked. "By the bible of Nora Jean Stone, we're going full Amish? I look sexy in black, but I do not care for bonnets."

I smiled. "Pilkington Press didn't even want to publish her book, you know. The acquisitions editor said it was too ambitious, too long by half, and too vast in scope. It was the only manuscript from the slush pile I really fought for."

"Saint Nora Jean, wherever you may be now, many blessings upon your house!" Regan dipped her head and crossed herself.

"Industrial farming with tons of fertilizer used to be necessary when we were out to feed the masses. If there's an upside to the pandemic, it's that the population is small enough we can make homesteading and community gardens work."

"Way to see the bright side, O!"

I shrugged. "Helpless in the face of reality, peering into the ghastly abyss, we must confront the suck."

"True. We used to throw out almost half our food," Regan said. "We won't be doing that anymore. When reality gets to be too much, and the booze finally runs out, I'm going to figure out how to make dandelion wine. I sing when I'm drunk. Do you sing?"

"Badly."

"How bad?"

"Dogs howl in pain. Birds drop dead from the sky."

"Good. You'll make me sound better. Also, your jokes are improving. Keep trying."

"Thank you. It's because I'm letting go and getting better at accepting risks."

Friendship used to menace me, but simply by smiling, Regan boosted my confidence. "Planting these crops will mean more long-term stability and leisure. More leisure means more babies fed and more babies getting made. Eventually, we'll have time for art and science again. People think hard work alone built empires, but having more downtime to sit, to think, and to dream is the key. Give people time to do more than attend to basic survival needs and who knows how much we can achieve?"

The triumvirate had held the keys to the future, but incredibly, Virgil, Sid, and Anya had had neither the interest nor the expertise to turn the lock and end the famine. They could have won hearts and minds by feeding people rather than dominating them. That sounded stupid, but as Regan pointed out, choosing violence had a long history among dictators. The triumvirate had been conquerors. As queen, my sole strategy was peace through service.

"We'll make friends and allies by feeding and protecting people," I told Regan.

"Solid," she agreed. "The fact that is a radical idea is why things got so messy in the first place."

Most caches only had one guard, and none were as bad as Bennington. They all seemed relieved that Virgil, Anya, and Sid were no longer in charge. I was particularly pleased to meet one man at the Van Cortlandt Manor. Living alone in the former museum, Garrett Hack was a boyish thirty-year-old. Though he'd been recruited for his medical skills, the triumvirate had underutilized him.

"It's been a long, lonely watch," he admitted. "Trucks rarely make it up here anymore. This stuff was set aside for a rainy day or a bad winter. Most days, I play sax and listen to old jazz records. With the isolation and all ... I go a little stir-crazy."

"How does that manifest?" I asked.

"Sometimes I stay in bed and try to sleep my life away. When I can't sleep anymore, I break into the stores and eat candy until I'm sick."

Depression and seeking comfort, I thought. *We're social, emotional, and anxious primates. Who could blame him?*

"And other times?"

"Once in a while, I pretend I'm a dragon guarding a hoard of gold."

With the toe of her boot, Regan poked gingerly at a leaning tower of porn magazines. "What does pretending to be a dragon entail?"

He blushed. "Running around in circles naked, roaring, and screaming, mostly. You're the first people I've seen in months. The few locals still alive around here tend to keep their distance. They give me no trouble."

"Because of all the naked roaring and screaming?"

"Don't forget the running in circles, but yeah."

Regan broke into a bright smile. "*You,* I like."

I liked him, too, not least because he will allow me to see the stars again. In What Was, Garrett was an optometrist. Eager to get back to the city, he'll give me my first eye exam in years. He assures me he can set me up with new glasses.

"That's a relief to me, too," Regan teased. "Queen O looks badass walking around with that sword on her back, but between that squint and her brown pantsuit of the apocalypse, it's a dead giveaway she's kind of lame and feeble. Help the queen see, Naked Dragon Eye Guy!"

"Naked Dragon Eye Guy, *hm*?" Garrett muttered. "I'm concerned that nickname might stick."

They laughed together and I joined them. Used to assuming the worst, I no longer felt homicidal impulses the second I heard any laughter. Even if someone laughed at my expense, I didn't lay awake nights plotting their grotesque deaths. *Usually.*

Dr. Rosa would be so proud. Underneath the facade, I still bit my tongue for luck. When insomnia took hold, I continued to review my every mistake. I still wished I'd filled my high school's water fountain with that dismissive fathead's teeth.

I was somewhere between sleeping and waking the morning Dr. Rosa came to me one last time. The hotel stood dead quiet. My therapist's ghost whispered, "Fair weather or foul, Ovid?"

"Still healing, Doctor. I still have too good a memory to sleep deeply and sweetly. Sometimes I panic when I go to scratch my nose and realize I'm not wearing a mask anymore. I gotta be me, but the violent fantasies do come less frequently and with smaller amplitude. I think I'm getting better because I've got so much to do, this time with more friends than enemies."

Dr. Rosa smiled at me. "Remember what I told you at the beginning of our first session together? Change isn't a state you achieve. Nobody gets to coast. Change is an ongoing, active verb. The drug addict and the dieter are back at square one every morning. Sometimes the struggle is every hour."

"I remember, Doctor. 'The tightrope walker doesn't look down or they fall. The race car driver doesn't look at the wall, or they'll unconsciously steer into it.' I have to make my unconscious behaviors conscious."

"Right! And if you chart progress, it doesn't go up at a forty-five-degree angle. We climb, we slide back, recover, gain, and lose ground. So? Where are you on a scale of one to ten? Rate your anxiety, pain, and health. Go!"

"Doesn't matter. What matters is which direction I'm pointed."

"Good," my dead therapist agreed. "What's next and how are you going to get there?"

"Rebuilding requires me to be a social animal. Under their old leadership, the Memory Keepers got one thing right. Being a better person is an individual choice, but building a better life is a team sport. I can't do it all alone. I never did. Learning to be okay with that is the next step."

"I'm glad for you."

"You know I miss you, Doctor. You helped me through the toughest times after you were dead and before I wasn't alone anymore."

"You know there's something important you still have to do, right? You pride yourself on your memory, but you've blocked something I told you in our first session. Trauma is an injury, not an illness. You can heal from your father's barbs just as you'd heal from a cut."

I nodded.

"You get stuck in your flashbacks, Ovid."

"Too much back and forth can annoy the impatient reader, I agree. The device can slide from informing and enriching the narrative to impeding the story. But how can I fix that?"

"You know how. You have always known the way out of the deep, dark forest but lacked the will to do so."

"Less metaphor and scolding, please, Doctor. Read me the directions."

"You may owe, but you are not owned, remember? Instead of allowing your consciousness to be swamped by your tragic history, focus on your reactions in the present."

"You mean I should stop feeling sorry for myself."

"To get past the past — "

"I know, I know!"

"So go do it, then. Use your words."

I was talking to myself again, but my fantasy ghost wasn't wrong. To plunge into the future, I had to close one more dark chapter.

75

CELL

Excusing myself from Garrett and Regan, I took a stroll by the river. Ever loyal, Aldebaran trailed after me, watching my every move. The girl seemed to pick up on the turns of my mood. When I sat on a bench beside the water, my bodyguard lay her head in my lap. As I stroked her hair, I wondered which of us benefited more from the calming gesture.

"Pardon me, Aldebaran. Before we move on, I have to do one last bit of ... editing."

My heart skipped a beat as my father answered his phone on the third ring. "Well, well, well! Haven't heard from you in a dog's age! Thought you were dead! Finally come a cropper and crawling back where you belong?"

"Don't start. I have some news. I've made some friends — "

"That *is* news. What else?"

"Well, for one thing, I think I'm pretty much over my clown phobia."

"Uh-huh. So useful at the end of the world," he observed. "Are there even any clowns left?"

"One less than before. Anyway, I ran into some doctors in the city, and I'm vaccinated now. They're working on something new, too. They think we're coming out the other end of this thing, for real this time. Someday soon, there'll be no more masks, goggles, and terror."

He gave a scornful snort. "After all this, you believe that?"

"I've made some other changes. I've been helping some Thirders — "

"Why would you want to do that?"

"They're people, Dad. If you treat them right, they can even make good allies," I said. "They don't say much — "

"I have no idea what you're talking about!"

"Never mind. I wanted to tell you that you were right about something. I do only remember the bad stuff. We did have some good times."

"I know that," he shot back. "Thanksgiving dinners, lobsters on Christmas Eve, you and your mother making fresh bread."

"You have helped me, and I have thanked you many times."

"Sure! I paid for that university where you learned you were better than me. When everything went bad, and you lost your job, I set you up so you wouldn't starve — "

"I was always better than you, Dad."

At that, he gave an honest laugh, and I thought the conversation might go well.

"I have been selfish in not recognizing your strengths. That's why I had to call you, to offer you the vaccine. You and everyone back home."

"I'm not leaving the Bay for love nor money. Bring it with you when you come."

"We're going to make the new vaccine available to everyone. I've got a group organized to get it done."

"A group?"

"I'm leading over a hundred people, more each day."

"And here I thought you'd never be rich."

"I always had a rich inner life, Dad."

He chuckled. "I meant rich in the only way that counts. If you can get that much together, you've got the resources to get yourself home.

Try getting your ass up the coast, maybe get a boat somehow. How about that?"

"Why? So you can criticize my looks, and we can argue in person without the comfort of limiting our exposure to each other to a few minutes of an angry phone call?"

"When did you get so mean?"

"Learned from the best, but look, I didn't call to have a fight. I'm trying ... I don't want to be mad at you anymore."

"Born mad."

Born weird, worth less than a nickel.

Despite my best efforts, we'd fallen into the same pattern again. His demand for me to come home didn't feel like love. For a moment, I blanked out, unable to hear him. Was it habit that had us stuck in this loop? Or the bond of familial duty? In the Fairweather family, obligations were heavy, but we always seemed to come up light on love.

Aldebaran tugged on my sleeve and that broke the spell. I must have been away for only a few seconds. I looked down to find the phone beside me on the bench. My father was still speaking.

Maturity begins when we stop trying to escape ourselves and deal with the world as it is. Taking a deep breath, I plunged back in. With the cell to my ear, I heard Dad admit grudgingly, "Sounds like you're doing well for yourself."

"I don't care about doing well. I care about doing good. When the meds are ready, I'll find a way to get them shipped up to Poeticule Bay."

"So my little girl's a boss now? New for you, huh? How does that feel?"

"I was always a boss, Dad. I just didn't know it."

"You think so?"

"Just statin' a fact," I said. "Message received?"

"Well, smell your fire! Still, we need a real plan, boss girl."

"We?"

"When can I expect you? I'll have someone make up a calendar and mark the date."

"I am home. I'm not coming back."

"What? Why?"

"You know why."

"Jesus! This again? God, how you wallow and whine! So much self-pity! You're always beating me over the head with your victimhood."

And you exalt in self-righteousness, I thought.

He wasn't all wrong, but I was making big changes. I didn't retreat into dissociation this time. I stayed in the present and did not back down. Getting chased by a maniac with a sword put my other challenges into perspective.

"You should be relieved," I told him. "I won't be bothering you anymore. You've made it clear my quirks embarrass you. There were other girls in town you wished were your daughter. Jane, the girl who stayed in Poeticule Bay and took care of her mother? You often said you wished she was your daughter, not in addition, but as a replacement."

"I don't remember that."

"I do, and actually, I get it. I'm different. I never meant to be difficult, but I was. I'm sure dealing with my eccentricities was frustrating. All I can say is, I'm letting you off the hook, and I sincerely wish you well."

"Look at you, all high and mighty, as if you're firing an employee. I'm your father!"

"When you complain about me later, and we both know you will, try to remember I don't care about who's right and who's wrong anymore. Just tell people I chose kindness."

He sputtered, "K-kindness? *This* is kindness?"

"The kindness is for me this time. Love requires vulnerability. I can't do that with you."

I shut off the phone and pocketed it. Filling my lungs deeply, I drank the air, fresh and green. A few tears welled in my eyes but quickly ebbed. I'd been so braced for conflict, the depth of my relief surprised me when I finally let go.

Aldebaran looked up at me, her brow furrowed.

"It's okay," I said. "If he didn't still care, he'd be indifferent. Strange how we can love and hate the same person simultaneously. He was trying. That's the hell of it. We wasted so much energy going at each other. People don't come with instruction manuals. I wish Nora Jean Stone had written as much about life as she did about plants."

Her eyes were so kind, I felt safe.

"Quick story, a confession, really. All my life, I felt alone because I was weird, but we're all weird. None of us is alone, either. I've been trying to measure myself against normal, but there is no normal. There's only what we're used to, and that's not necessarily normal! *Heh.* See, the trick is, we're all fictions. All we think we see is a fuzzy approximation, like me looking at something far away without glasses. Dad thinks Poeticule Bay is God's Country. Not true for me, but for him, that's nonfiction. We each see the world in our own way. That can be a power. But distorted through the lens of the mind's eye and sorted by the sieve of our memories, that can be a curse. Through a glass darkly and all that."

Aldebaran sat up very straight. I sensed her impatience.

"I'll get to it! I'd swear you to secrecy, but ... right. Look, my truth is I never believed in me. I was singled out, That Fairweather Girl, the odd one with the eyes, one green, one brown. Add in OCD, all my quirks and phobias, the funny voices in my head, and well ... I know I can be off-putting."

The girl nodded, whether in agreement or to encourage me, I wasn't sure.

"*Ahem!* Anyway, I was always a voracious reader. That was my escape, but I did write something, too. With Mrs. Garilyn's encouragement, I started researching and writing my book in the high school library. Later, I came to New York with big dreams for that book, even got a job inside publishing while I waited to be discovered. That didn't happen. I hated my bosses at Pilkington Press and wasn't making enough money, so I cheated. I used a pen name and pretended I'd pulled a stranger's offering from the slush pile. She's a part of me, but I can't be her. I'll strive to be more *like* her. My nom de plume is so real, I guess she became one of those subselves Dr. Rosa told me about. I never liked Ovid Fairweather, but Nora Jean Stone is smart and kind and lives in San Francisco. She's good and safe. People like her. She will live forever."

My follower reached out and squeezed my hand. Her hand was so small in mine. I squeezed back gently.

"I've been too cynical, haven't I? Anything can happen. People have seen me as a witch, a ghost, an arsonist, a mad cow, a twitchy bitch, a bad daughter, easy prey, a pushover ... and here I sit, suddenly a queen. And a mother."

Aldebaran nodded sagely, smiled, and put her head in my lap again.

"Thank you for listening. I got in my own way a lot, but I'm pointed in the right direction now. I always cared about people who needed help, you know. That's the job, but when I help somebody, it doesn't feel like a job. It just feels good. Feeling good is my new addiction. It beats the shit out of self-loathing."

Aldebaran and I stayed on that bench for a long time. We watched the burning orange sunset in the mirror of the dark river. Sensing the day's end, the birds began to settle. She closed her eyes and I did, too.

"This is what I've longed for," I whispered. "The quiet space between heartbeats."

She settled in, using my leg as a pillow. Together, we experienced the joy of having nothing to do and nowhere to go. The muscles in my jaw relaxed. As my tension eased, my shoulders dropped. We weren't in survival mode anymore. No one was meant to stay in survival mode all the time.

The Hudson runs in two directions: north and south. My mind flows forward and back, anticipating future pain and weighing my many regrets. In the stillness of the fleeting present, stroking the child's head or laughing with Regan, I found peace. Only by accepting the moment's fragility could I deepen my tranquility. "There is no perfection, Aldebaran, but this time with you right now? It comes close."

At last, my mind was quiet.

In the distance, Regan called my name. "Ovid? Ovid? It's getting dark! Are you guys okay?"

Hearing the worry in her tone, Aldebaran rose quickly. I stood slowly, assuring the girl that everything was as it should be. "You're a highly sensitive person, too, aren't you? Regan's okay and so are we. Let's head back."

The girl scampered ahead but kept looking to make sure she knew where I was. I followed slowly, enjoying the forest's hush and looking forward to a hot meal.

I came to a footbridge and paused in the middle. My reflection in the water was mostly a silhouette against the weak pink of the fading sky. My hair was growing back. There would be more gray this time. I looked older. Growing up is overrated, but there I was, finally an adult in middle age.

The phone made a satisfying *plunk* as I dropped it in. My father was lost. It made no sense to follow him. I was indebted, but I did not owe anyone my mental health. As I walked away from the past and toward my people, I felt younger.

Tomorrow might be a great day, I thought, *full of all the potential we create together.*

THANKS FOR READING ENDEMIC

That was fun, wasn't it? Books (and their authors' souls) live and die by reviews. If you dig what I do, please leave a happy review to spread the word and share your joy with other readers.

BONUS

If you caught the *Fight Club* and *As Good As It Gets* references, you are awarded an extra 100 hit points and automatically rise to the rank of Dragon Mage. Treat yourself to something nice. Thanks for playing.

MORE DYSTOPIAN & APOCALYPTIC BOOKS BY ROBERT CHAZZ CHUTE

This Plague of Days
What will you do to protect your family in the zombie apocalypse? Young Jaimie Spencer is an unlikely hero amid the ashes and ruins of our world. On the spectrum and selectively mute, he's more obsessed with his dictionary than with the fate of humanity. However, before this epic story is over, Good will do battle with Evil and Jaimie is our champion.

Robert's most successful series to date, *This Plague of Days* won Honorable Mention in their Self-published Ebook Awards from *Writers' Digest*. All three seasons of this trilogy are available as an omnibus or individually as ebooks and paperbacks.

∾

AFTER Life
Zombies will soon invade the United States. Which side will you join, the infected or the damned?

Artificial Facilitation Therapy for Enhanced Response (AFTER) was a biomimetic stem cell nanotechnology with numerous health and wellness applications. Then a military contractor weaponized it using brain parasites. When the zombie apocalypse arrives, we soon discover that genetically engineered zombies are hard to kill.

Officer Daniel Harmon is tasked with stopping the epidemic. Dr. Chloe Robinson needs to get her creation back under control. We can't always get what we want.

The *AFTER Life* trilogy is available in ebook and in paperback.

∾

Citizen Second Class

Set a decade later in the same universe as *Endemic*, Kismet is a young woman who must travel to Atlanta to find work to feed what's left of her family. The city has become a fortress for rich religious zealots who care nothing for the poor. Just below the surface, a revolution simmers as disaster looms. Join the fight.

∾

Amid Mortal Words

A dangerous stranger met on a train leaves behind a powerful book. With mere words, this book could destroy the world or save it. This power is now in the hands of one man relying on a mysterious woman to guide him toward the Apocalypse or away from our destruction. It's a roller coaster ride filled with twists and turns toward a surprising conclusion that will keep you up all night reading.

∾

Robot Planet

The robots are unfailingly polite until the moment they kill you. This future isn't merely a forbidding dystopia. It's cyberpunk scary. In this series of four novellas, three very different people join forces to combat the rise of the Next Intelligence. The odds are against us. Start your next adventure by grabbing *Robot Planet, The Complete Series*, available in paperback or ebook.

~

Haunting Lessons (with Holly Pop)
This is not a ghost story. It only starts out that way. Tamara Smith is a young woman from the Midwest who experiences an unspeakable tragedy. Soon she sees apparitions. That's only the beginning of her adventures. Running away to New York, she soon discovers a secret world of dark magic doing combat with alien forces from another dimension.

If she is to save the world from the coming invasion, Tam must train to become a leader among the Choir Invisible. She fights for us all. *Death Lessons, Fierce Lessons,* and *Dream's Dark Flight* are also part of this series of gripping adventures.

~

All Empires Fall
How will the world end? In this short story collection, Robert shares several tales of the apocalypse. It comes in flood and fire. It stabs at us out of the darkness of space.

Robert Chazz Chute has lots of dark ideas for you to consider and revel in as you stay up through the night, turning pages to each ending of our world.

~

Our Zombie Hours

Strap in for five adventures from the front line of the zombie apocalypse. As society collapses, humans often prove themselves more dangerous than the infected. Enjoy these fresh stories that explore survival, heroism, and betrayal in a world gone mad. A fun night of horror awaits.

ALL BOOKS BY ROBERT CHAZZ CHUTE

Find links to all books by Robert Chazz Chute at

AllThatChazz.com

~ DYSTOPIAN AND APOCALYPTIC FICTION ~

This Plague of Days, Season 1

This Plague of Days, Season 2

This Plague of Days, Season 3

This Plague of Days, Omnibus Edition

THE AFTER Life TRILOGY

Inferno

Purgatory

Paradise

AFTER Life (Box Set)

Endemic

Citizen Second Class

Amid Mortal Words

Robot Planet, The Complete Series

Haunting Lessons, Book 1 of *The Dimension War*

Death Lessons, Book 2 of *The Dimension War*

Fierce Lessons, Book 3 of *The Dimension War*

Dream's Dark Flight, Book 4 of *The Dimension War*

~ TIME TRAVEL ~

Wallflower

~ CRIME THRILLERS ~

The Night Man

Brooklyn in the Mean Time

Bigger Than Jesus, Book 1 of The Hit Man Series

Higher Than Jesus, Book 2 of The Hit Man Series

Hollywood Jesus, Book 3 of The Hit Man Series
Resurrection, A Hit Man Novel

~ COLLECTIONS ~

Murders Among Dead Trees
Sometime Soon, Somewhere Close
Self-help for Stoners
All Empires Fall
Our Zombie Hours

~ NONFICTION ~
Do the Thing: The Last Stress-busting Book You'll Ever Need

ACKNOWLEDGMENTS

My work would not be possible without incredible assistance from She Who Must Be Obeyed. Janice, you make all this possible.

A special thank you to Gari Strawn of strawnediting.com for her expertise, continued support, and friendship. You make the process more fun and less stressful, Gari!

Thanks and extra shout outs to Russ for his proofreading and his wisdom, to Peter Hawkins (my emotional support animal), and to my fan group who are so helpful, fun, and supportive.

ABOUT THE AUTHOR

Robert Chazz Chute is a former crime and science journalist. A winner of eight writing awards, he pens fiction full-time from Other London.

For updates, links to his books, and Patreon support of his fiction podcasts, please visit Robert at AllThatChazz.com.

www.ingramcontent.com/pod-product-compliance
Lightning Source LLC
Chambersburg PA
CBHW050918030726
47503CB00007BB/2347